VOYAGE

TO THE

NORTH STAR

Also by Peter Nichols

Sea Change: Alone Across the Atlantic in a Wooden Boat

VOYAGE
TO THE
NORTH STAR

A NOVEL

PETER NICHOLS

CARROLL & GRAF PUBLISHERS, INC.
NEW YORK

For Annie

First Carroll & Graf edition 1999

Carroll & Graf Publishers, Inc.
19 West 21st Street
New York, NY 10010-6805

Library of Congress Cataloging-in-Publication Data is available.
ISBN: 0-7867-0664-3

Manufactured in the United States of America

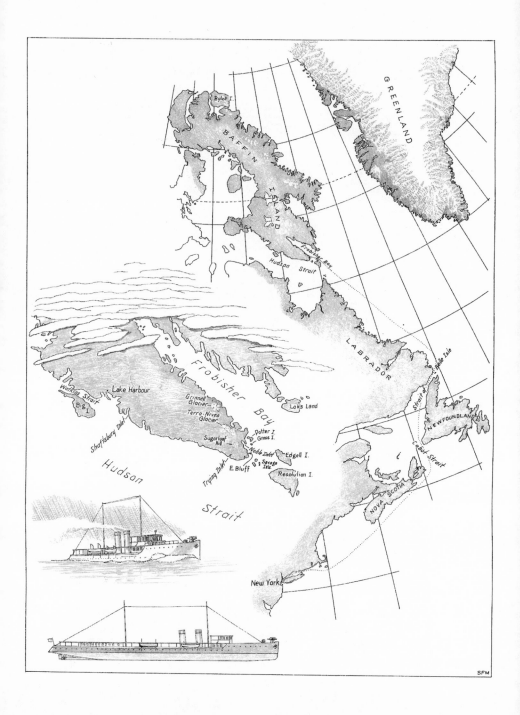

GREENLAND

BAFFIN ISLAND

Bylot I.

Frobisher Bay

Hudson Strait

LABRADOR

Watkins Strait

Lake Harbour

Big I.

Grinnell Glacier

Terra-Nivea Glacier

Shaftsbury Inlet

Sugarloaf Hill

Frobisher Bay

Loks Land

Potter I.
Gross I.

Noble Inlet

Trying Inlet

E. Bluff

Savage Isle

Edgell I.

Resolution I.

Hudson

Strait

Strait of Belle Isle

NEWFOUNDLAND

Cabot Strait

NOVA SCOTIA

New York

SFM

It is vain to dream of a wildness distant from ourselves. There is none such. It is the bog in our brain and bowel, the primitive vigor of Nature in us, that inspires that dream.
                    —Henry David Thoreau, *Journal,* August 30, 1856

. . . the ship, a fragment detached from the earth, went on lonely and swift like a small planet. Round her the abysses of sky and sea met in an unattainable frontier. . . . She had her own future; she was alive with the lives of those beings who trod her decks; like that earth which had given her up to the sea, she had an intolerable load of regrets and hopes.
                    —Joseph Conrad, *The Nigger of the Narcissus*

PROLOGUE

ON HIS FIRST AND only Kenya safari in 1932, Carl Schenck was attacked by his white hunter after he machine-gunned the heads off three loping giraffes from the open cab of a safari truck. The white hunter had been annoying him with his pukka bwana talk and lengthy pipe-lighting pauses and the condescension with which he treated Schenck and his wife, and Schenck became gripped by the desire to do the most unpukka thing he could imagine. On the fourth morning he got into the front truck with the Colt tommy gun he had brought from home and squeezed off at midneck height through the giraffe herd and got the reaction he wanted from the white hunter. He was back in Nairobi after only four days in the bush, bruised but unrepentant, and he cabled his bank in New York to stop payment on the white hunter's check.

Schenck and his wife, Mamie, then proceeded by rail to Mombasa where they boarded the Royal Mail Ship *Staffordshire* on its run from Rangoon to London. By this time, Schenck was unable to restrain himself in the company of Britishers. He spoke his own inventive pukka bwana talk to them. In the face of their stoic reserve, he became loud and garrulous. When they dressed for dinner, he put on his safari clothing, although he was barred by an embarrassed steward from the *Staffordshire*'s first-class dining room. And during their early days aboard ship, when he could still find passengers to play

1

with him, he cheated blatantly at bridge, accusing dismayed fellow players of the same. He pretended to drink too much. He tipped hugely and with vulgar ostentation. In Port Said, he threw wads of dollar bills from C deck onto the quayside and created a riot among the Egyptian stevedores. Mamie enjoyed the high jinks as much as her husband and, finally shunned and whispered about throughout the ship, talking loud pukka nonsense to each other, they enjoyed their cruise.

However, by the time the ship reached Marseilles they had become bored, so they disembarked and went to Monte Carlo where they lost grandly at the casino. The next day Schenck bought two varnished mahogany Riva motorboats he spotted in the harbor and had them shipped to New York. Then he and Mamie boarded the *Conte di Lombardia* in Genoa and sailed for home. The Italians loved him.

It had been great fun, but not what Schenck had hoped for. As a young man in Minneapolis he had watched the newsreel footage of Teddy Roosevelt's fabulous 1909 African safari that bagged and brought home 4900 mammals, 4000 birds, 500 fish, and 2000 reptiles. Five hundred Swahili porters had borne TR and his dull boy Kermit and their weapons and tents and bathtubs through the Kenyan bush. The safari had cost $75,000 and had been financed by Andrew Carnegie and the Smithsonian Institution. Roosevelt's rifle was said to be the finest ever made, a Royal grade Holland & Holland double-barreled 500/450 Nitro Express. Roosevelt's favorite safari dinners were elephant-trunk soup, oryx tongue, and ostrich liver. He loved heart, particularly giraffe and ostrich. He toasted slices of elephant heart over his campfire. The young Carl Schenck bought TR's book of his bully adventure, *African Game Trails,* which the New York *Herald Tribune* called Book of the Year in 1910. He pored over the photographs of TR looking like an American maharaja in his pith helmet, sitting atop felled elephant and wildebeest and Cape buffalo. It made a deep and lasting impression on Schenck. He wanted to dine on elephant-trunk soup and giraffe heart. He wanted to shoot brindled gnu with a Holland & Holland rifle. As he grew older and rich enough to rearrange the world around him to his liking, Schenck fashioned himself somewhat on Roosevelt. He welcomed the opportunity to wear small rimless glasses when, in his twenties, his eyes began to fail. He believed his own teeth-baring grin resembled the former president's, and in time it came to. He grinned forcefully and acted boldly. He charged up San Juan Hill every day.

Back in New York in April 1932, Schenck was dissatisfied. He still wanted to go on a safari and kill prodigious animals. He wanted those heads and hides and snouts and antlers to put in his houses, and he wanted to rout the beasts out of the bush and shoot them himself. He had all the clothes and the guns now. Surely, he reasoned, he could go somewhere and shoot without a pukka Englishman running the show.

It came to him that there was no reason he could not organize a safari himself. He could hire his own people, go where he wanted, and shoot whatever he saw. To hell with the Bennett Safari Company.

It might not be in Africa, he realized. The English had the place sewn up. He looked about for somewhere else.

CHAPTER 1

THE BOAT FOR THE chipping crew didn't leave South Street until five in the afternoon. And then it took over an hour to get down the bays to Sandy Hook, where the crew had been sitting on planks hung over the side of a Dutch freighter, pounding at the hull since six that morning. That made twelve hours. The crew was supposed to work ten hours before the boat came and got them, and the men were paid by the day, not the hour. But the contractor, Brant, always left his crews out late. He knew that a man's self-respect in hard times was a funny thing. Given the opportunity to sit and do nothing or do simple work, most men would still work those last late hours. Particularly on a chipping crew, where the sullen pounding of a hammer against a hull was exactly what the job called for. Men might grumble, but in New York in 1932 few would quit any job at all.

There were six men on the crew, and they worked in two groups sitting on two planks. Kruger and Mills were Reds, they said. They had worked in the logging camps in Washington and in the mines in California, and they had ridden the rails east to help old Bill Foster bring down the banks and kick out the bourgeoisie. They usually started the day hungover and spent most of every morning and late afternoon cursing Brant, who was a member of the bourgeoisie, blaming him for their sore backs and empty pockets. Brant, of course, was not on the freighter. He was back up in Manhattan, probably having a

5

long lunch with one of those women who stayed the same shape when you took her clothes off. Kruger and Mills always worked together on one plank, either with Jim, the kid who had run away from college to experience life, or with Giuliano, the wop carpenter who was waiting for a call to work on a house in Brooklyn Heights. Both seemed able to endure Kruger and Mills for hours on end.

On the other plank, on the other side of the hull, with either Jim or Giuliano, sat Moyle, a stringy elderly man who rarely said a word and pounded as hard as the kid or the wop and with greater concentration than any of them; and Will Boden, a man just under forty, with a hollow poker face and the body of a longshoreman on the skids: thin from months with only barely enough to eat, but with unusual development in his upper body from long days of brutal work. There were many men along the New York waterfront now who looked like this. Boden didn't talk much either.

The work was monotonous. The men pounded at lumps, welts, blisters of rust that broke away from the hull in flakes and fell into the water below with a soft showering noise. Every now and then a man shinnied up the falls and dropped the plank a few feet. When they reached the waterline, they moved the plank forward a few feet and worked back up the hull. The freighter was small, 180 feet long, but sitting on a plank with a square foot of corroded hull filling a man's whole field of vision, making progress by inches, there would appear no end to the job. But all the men on the chipping crew took grim comfort from their slow insect crawl around the hull because when the chipping was finished, the freighter's crewmembers—who refused to pound at rust—would begin to paint the hull and they would all be looking for work again.

In the late mornings, Giuliano would sing the songs he had heard Caruso sing on the radio, and Kruger and Mills would talk about women they had known in Seattle and San Francisco or tell Jim about the yard dicks and the two-stepping gandy dancers who made it hard on a man trying to ride the cars down south, but in the afternoons all the men would fall silent. Then the pounding became rhythmic as they unconsciously hammered in concert, squinting against the flying chips, mesmerized by the pounding.

Boden looked away from the hull often. He watched the traffic going in and out of New York. He found he could no longer tell, looking at a ship, where it was from or where bound. Most were steamers, going anywhere you could guess, always by way of the canal if Pacific bound. No ships headed out for the great capes anymore. A week earlier he had seen the four-master *Theoline* come down the bay under lowers, spanker, and staysails, and watched her turn south and fade into the uncertain glim. Rockland-built, now out of Boston, she was carrying whatever she could find that had not gone where it was going by steamer or rail or truck. She was the only working sailing ship, apart from fishing smacks and schooners, he had seen in two weeks on his plank. When you saw a sailing ship these days, she was as likely a Gloucesterman hogged and strained from a short hard life on the Grand Banks, on her way now to a rotting dotage hauling lighter cargoes and palmetto bugs between warmer ports. Or she was bound to a breaker's yard and you were among the last to see her lift to the swell in the way that had filled the hearts of the people who had first known her.

In another field of vision, he watched the spiders that were blown offshore out to the freighter. He saw them borne through the air like dandelion seeds, landing on the hull and crawling along the rusty steel, trying, he supposed, to make some sense of the vast, rough vertical plane on which they found themselves, their world suddenly turned strange on them. He banged his hammer near them when they got close enough, to get them headed up onto the deck where he knew they would find good places to live and bugs to eat. Kruger and Mills, he had observed, hammered them flat and kept score.

At six, when the boat finally arrived to pick them up, Kruger and Mills jumped off their plank as it passed beneath them on its way to the ship's ladder, only Mills missed and fell into the water. Hartz, the boatman, swore at them, saying they could start a seam. Giuliano hauled their planks and hammers up onto the deck. Boden, Moyle, and Jim all shinnied up the falls to the deck and stored their gear together in a deck box and stepped down the ladder into the boat, where Kruger and Mills were howling at Mills's mistake.

It took longer for the boat to get back to South Street because the tide was ebbing down the bays, with a breeze on top of it. Hartz hugged the Brooklyn shore going past Bay Ridge and Red Hook and up Buttermilk Channel behind Governor's Island, where the current was weaker. Boden sat low in the stern out of the breeze and watched the tugs and ships moving up and down the rivers, and the sky going pink over Bedloe and Ellis islands.

The boat pulled alongside Pier 11 on the East River at the foot of Wall Street a little after 7:30, and the chipping crew climbed up the ramshackle ladder to the top of the pier and crossed South Street and went their own ways.

Boden stopped in at Morahan's saloon near the corner of Fulton Street for a glass of beer and a handful of peanuts in their shells. After twelve years of Prohibition, New York was still a wide-open town. Morahan's had never bothered to water down its beer or appearance, and it had never been raided; cops drank there, and the young men and the slender girls from the magistrate's office in City Hall up Beekman and across Park Row, and longshoremen and fishermen off the schooners, and men like Boden who lived in the neighborhood, and the women friends of these men. Boden ritually drank a glass of beer there every day after work. They drew it cold up copper pipes out of the basement and he drank it slowly and relaxed.

Outside again, walking up South Street, he looked up at the Brooklyn Bridge and saw Moyle walking across the promenade on top, going over to Brooklyn. It was some distance away and in the fading light the walkers on the bridge were small dark shapes partly obscured by the latticework of steel. But he saw it was Moyle. Caved-in, pushing forward.

THE NEXT EVENING, AS they came up the Buttermilk, Boden said, "Moyle, you live over here in Brooklyn, don't you?"

"Yeah."

"Cap," he said to Hartz, giving the boatman the courtesy of the title of command, "how about pulling in here on the

Brooklyn side to let Moyle off? Save him going over the bridge."

"I just go to the pier," said Hartz.

"That's where I'll get off," said Moyle.

"Moyle lives in Brooklyn," said Boden. "You can come alongside anywhere here and let him off. Save him the walk."

"Yeah, and pretty soon I'm playing taxi and taking everybody everywhere. I take them from the pier down to the boat and back. I got to get home too."

"No one wants to go anywhere else. We're all going into the pier. It's not going to take you any time."

"Say, maybe you could drop us off at the New York Yacht Club," said Kruger.

Boden turned and looked at Kruger.

Moyle threw the stained fag-end of his cigarette into the water. "I'll walk."

Boden turned back to Hartz. "All I'm asking is for you to pull over here fifty feet and let him out anywhere. You can do that without going out of your way."

"If it's so goddamn close, let him jump overboard and swim."

Boden looked away at the docks sliding past close to starboard. Then he stood up and moved to the side of Hartz's seat and sat on the edge of it, his thigh next to the boatman's shoulder. Hartz tensed. He tried to pull away but he was up against the side of the boat. He had to turn his head and look up and slightly backward to see Boden's face.

"What do you want?"

"I'd like you to come alongside over here and let Mr. Moyle off. Right there." Boden pointed to a dock. Hartz, who was younger and heavier than Boden, twisted his head around again and looked up into Boden's hard-lined face. He looked ahead once more, then pulled the throttle back.

"Why not? Take everyone where they want to go. Why the hell not? I got anything better to do?" He spun the wheel and the boat veered toward the Brooklyn shore.

Hartz put her alongside the wooden pilings of the ramshackle pier Boden had indicated, the prop in slow ahead to hold the boat stationary in the strong ebb. Moyle hopped ashore. Boden followed him.

"Much obliged to you," Boden said to Hartz.

Hartz slammed the throttle forward, swearing inaudibly against the noise of the engine, and the boat jumped out into the river.

"What'd you do that for?" said Moyle. He was angry.

"I saw you walking over the bridge last night."

"So what?"

"I figured he could let you off this side."

"You figured yourself fired is what you did. Maybe me too."

"It wasn't out of his way."

"Fuck him. Fuck you too." Moyle turned his bent back away and stomped down the pier.

Boden walked up to the bridge and back across the river to Manhattan. He liked walking across the Brooklyn Bridge.

THE NEXT MORNING, BRANT was at the pier at six when the men arrived to go down to the freighter.

"You're fired," he said to Boden. Hartz was smirking. The rest of the men stepped into the boat. "I don't have trouble-makers working for me. Any man wants to make trouble, he can get out of the boat now." The men in the boat were silent. "Okay. Get 'em out of here."

Hartz backed the boat neatly off the pier, spinning it around in reverse between the piers before moving out into the river current.

"You got anything to say?" Brant looked at Boden.

"I want the money that's coming to me."

Brant pulled two tens and four singles out of a fat billfold and handed Boden the money. He ran a hand along the brim of his hat and walked toward South Street.

Boden walked fast across town to the Chelsea piers and joined a shape-up at Cunard-White Star. The crowd was a big one and some of the men wore homburgs and suits and looked as if they had lost their way to work in an office and found themselves in a strange place and were frightened.

A man started shouting, "There's no unemployment in the Soviet Union, comrades!" Four men came away from the straw boss's hut beside the terminal and surrounded him. For a moment he continued shouting, "And there wouldn't be any here either if the workers—" An elbow rammed into his mouth, a baseball bat hit the back of his knees, he went down. The four men knelt around his head for seven or eight seconds, quick jerks convulsing their backs and shoulders, then they rose and dragged the limp Red away.

Minutes passed. At seven-twenty the boss and his foreman, well-fed men in clean suits, came out of the hut and they made the call. The regulars and the straw boss's favorites filled the crews, and at seven-thirty Boden turned away. It was too late to try another pier.

He walked back to the east side. The fishing schooners had all unloaded and were quiet again, their crews asleep below, or rolled in a sail on deck. He walked through the Fulton market and looked at the fish, fat and firm and clean-smelling in boxes of ice, iridescent markings still strong. The place smelled clean and of the sea. He watched people selecting fish. A restaurant buyer in kitchen livery followed by three boys carrying boxes full of bright shellfish. A man in a threadbare suit carried away a small, carefully chosen fish in a paper bag.

He walked up Pearl to the Blossom Restaurant on the Bowery, where he ordered a pork tenderloin and coffee for fifteen cents. You could eat for less, but the cheaper food would turn your muscle to fat, and he wanted to keep strong. He found a copy of the *Herald Tribune* near the door, and read the paper through while he ate.

THE NEXT DAY HE joined a crew breaking up a Hooverville in the old Armour packing plant on West Thirtieth Street. The pay was two dollars for the day, a whole day guaranteed.

They went in at six in the morning, fifteen men on the crew and three cops, two more cops and a wagon on the street. On the plant's large open second floor they found eighty bodies huddled in cardboard boxes. Some of the men slept in cubicles made of packing boxes in which they had set up small stoves and arranged old chairs and their cardboard suitcases, and boards with their pants draped neatly over them, and even shelves filled with books, so that these rough boxes in the empty meatpacking plant had become, to the men who made them, a form of home.

A few of the men had dogs with them, and as the crew and the cops came up the stairs, the dogs began to bark savagely, or mournfully, as if they knew what was coming. The cops blew their whistles and the bodies on the floor began to sit up in their blankets, and waited to see what would happen.

"Okay," shouted one of the cops, and he banged his stick against a pipe, "Up an' at 'em! Get what you're takin' and get outta here. Let's go!"

The dogs continued barking. Men rose slowly to their feet in their blankets like spectral figures. Some got up and walked straight to the stairs, others began cramming belongings into suitcases. A number of men pushed baby carriages filled with blankets, books, kerosene lanterns, paper packages. Men pulled their shanty cubicles apart and went away carrying bundles of splintered boards.

A man started shouting angrily at the cops. "Just where should I go? You want to tell me that? Where in ever-loving hell should I go?"

"I just got orders here, bub," answered a cop in an amiable, conversational tone, but as loud as a tenor at the Met, louder than the man shouting at him. "You can't stay because it's against the fire laws, see? Now don't gimme no trouble and make me break your head and drag you outta here."

They found a man dead in a cardboard box and three others still breathing but unable to move. Boden and a wordless young man in a pinstripe suit were detailed to carry the body down to the street.

"But keep him in the box," the crew boss instructed them.

The skin on the face appearing at the edge of the box was blue-blotched with decay like a Stilton cheese. The corpse stank of defecation and something else, rich and sweetish. Boden took the lower end of the box and most of the weight going down the stairs. The young man kept his head turned to the wall all the way down. Outside, the cop on the street told them to put the stiff in the wagon. When they'd finished, the young man in the pinstripe suit walked away up Tenth Avenue.

The cop put a hand on Boden's shoulder and pointed a fat

finger up the side of the packing plant. "We got a bird building a nest." On the top of the building's fire escape, cardboard was flattened against the railings, enclosing the top landing. "Go on up and throw that stuff down."

As Boden neared the top of the three long flights of the fire escape, which vibrated and rang as he climbed, the head of an elderly man poked out of the huddle of cardboard and looked at him.

"Please go away!" said the man, already looking hopeless, knowing that Boden would not.

As he drew level with the top landing, Boden saw the man had strung a clothesline to the building and hung dark socks and a pair of long boxer shorts on it.

"For the love of Mike, leave me alone!" The man had an accent Boden recognized as Swedish. "I'm not hurting anyone up here!"

"It's got nothing to do with me," said Boden. "It's the cops. They say it's on account of the fire laws."

"Fire laws! They're not worried about no goddamn fire! The second a man finds a place to flop they got to run him out! It's got nothing to do with no goddamn fires!"

Boden didn't argue with him because the man, who appeared to be about seventy years old, with a face that made Boden think of a college professor, was already taking in his laundry. He untied the string and wound it into a small ball and took that too. A minute later he was dressed in a suit and descending the fire escape with a cardboard suitcase. He had said nothing more. Boden watched him reach the street and walk away without looking up.

"Now throw all that mess down," the cop called up to him.

Boden began pulling the cardboard shelter apart and throwing its pieces down to the street. The flattened boxes sailed down through the air in swooping arcs, scattering widely around the patrolman who stood with his face upturned, watching like a kid lost in the play of birds.

Inside the plant, the crew gathered up all the boxes and clothing, books and bundles the evicted men had left behind and went through everything themselves, taking what they wanted. They brought all the rest outside and heaped it in the

vacant lot beside the building. Later in the afternoon a fire
crew arrived and set fire to the bundle, and the men of the
wrecking crew stood around the fire and stared into it. A couple of them threw potatoes into the ashes and ate them afterward. At the end of the day, Boden got his two dollars, and the
crew boss offered him more work.

The next day the crew cleared another jungle at West Thirty-
eighth between Tenth and Eleventh Avenues. For the rest of the
week they broke up Hoovervilles that were growing inside
warehouses and old ferry terminals on the East River piers.
Some of the men they evicted joined the crew, which by the end
of the week numbered more than thirty. They were as black-
faced as coal miners from days spent removing other men and
their debris from abandoned buildings and from standing
around fires. At night the men drifted away and reappeared
wherever the boss told them to meet in the mornings, many as
filthy as they had looked the night before.

The crew boss said there was talk that a bunch of crews
might be put together to break up Tin Mountain City, the great
four-acre camp of huts and junked automobiles down along
the Red Hook waterfront that was home to 8000 men. They
would all get extra pay for that. The boss said it would be like
something out of the Bible, like kicking out the Canaanites, to
go down there and break up Tin Mountain City.

"Yeah, but where would all those people go?" said one of
the men on the crew.

"They'd go somewhere else," said the boss, "and then we'd
throw 'em outta there too!"

At the end of the day on Friday the boss told the crew where
to meet on Monday morning. The men wanted to work the
next day, but they were city employees now, the boss told
them, so they had the weekend off.

BODEN RENTED A ROOM for nine dollars a week at
Meyer's Hotel at 115 South Street, across the street from the
docks where the fishing schooners tied up. When he approached the hotel that evening, a man came away from the
shadows at the side of the building and moved toward him. He
turned and saw Moyle.

"You feel like a beer?" said Moyle.

They walked around the corner to Morahan's and ordered two beers with shooters.

They drank in silence. Boden waited. They had almost finished the beer when Moyle said, "I know a guy looking for a navigator. Couple weeks' work. You interested?"

"Yeah, I'd be interested. How do you know I can navigate?"

"I know who you are. I read about you in the papers." Moyle coughed suddenly, horked, and spat a green gob into the sawdust on the floor. He took a sip of beer.

"So what's the job?"

"Going offshore with a bunch of nobs. Guy I know works for one of them, was asking me if I knew someone."

He handed Boden a smudged, folded sheet of paper. Boden unfolded it and read "American Yaht Club Rye Shred saterday" written in pencil in a cramped scrawl on the center of the sheet.

"You go out there to that yacht club at Rye, tomorrow morning at eleven. You see a man called Shred. Don't bring nothing with you then, you're just going to talk."

"All right. Thanks. I appreciate it." Boden looked at the older man. Moyle was wearing a grimy singlet and the same oil-stained dark blue trousers he had worn every day they were chipping rust on the freighter. "You still on that rust bucket?"

"This week I been cleaning airplanes." He told Boden he had been hosing down and polishing the small commuter seaplanes that sat in the water beside the docks of the Downtown Skyport at the foot of Wall Street. "They like small guys like me who can climb around without denting them. They're made of nothing. You?"

Boden told him of his work on the clearing crews.

Moyle finished his beer. He got off his stool. "I got to be going." He fished in his pocket for some change.

"Let me get it," said Boden. "Thanks for the tip. Hey, let's have another beer sometime."

"Yeah, maybe," said Moyle, and he left.

Boden had another one right then.

CHAPTER 2

THE NEXT MORNING BODEN put on his suit and took the Second Avenue El uptown and walked west. Inside Grand Central he bought the *Herald* and read it while waiting for the train. On the front page was a picture of scandal-enmeshed Mayor Jimmy Walker and his pals Knute Rockne and Cornelius Vanderbilt at a Yankees game. Inside the paper he read that everybody everywhere was listening to "Wrap Up Your Troubles in Your Dreams, and Dream Your Troubles Away" by the sensational tenor Morton Downey.

He read as the train rattled north beneath Manhattan, but after it surfaced at 125th Street, he found himself looking out the window, occasionally seeing his face reflected in the glass across the wasteland of tenements. An unrecognizable version of the boy from New Jersey who rode east on these tracks to the good boarding school in Rhode Island. A boy with a future, sharp in his school uniform.

On Sundays in that last year before he ran away he took the train up to Boston with Newt Crowther and saw the ships and the characters on T Wharf—the T-Wharfers, they called themselves. Old Bern Shake in the sail loft. The dory men offloading the Gloucester schooners full of—the way they put it that so struck the boy—"twenty thousand of cod," just in off the Grand Banks. Then back to school and algebraic primers. He was never good at that, until much later when, to his surprise, he discovered in himself an instinctive feel for the use of a

16

sextant, and the sensible arrangement of degrees and minutes of latitude and longitude, and the mystery shrouding numbers fell away and he could use them with skill. English was his subject at school, not to punctuate or compose, but to read. He read Homer, Conrad, Thoreau, and Melville, believed them, and took them deep to heart. Before them was *A Sea Chest to China,* about Tim the Cabin Boy, who sailed to China entrusted with his family's fortune and filled his chest with silks and then lost the chest to an Asiatic confidence man and could not go home for shame, but found work on a sealer in the South Seas and sailed back to China, a young man now filled out with muscle, and sold his pelts and brought home to Salem a fortune in Oriental goods.

Sixteen-year-old Will Boden ran away to sea, signing on as Fireman No. 6, shoveling coal on a freighter bound for Havana. A bottom bunk, two-by-six, right over a boiler, one of fifteen in the firemen's fo'c'sle. Willy the new boy threw up all the way to Hatteras and planned to jump ship in Miami, but then, as the ship sailed into the warm Gulf Stream, it all got better and he exulted in being at sea, far from school. In Havana there was the first drink of rum, then the second, and a quick, terrifying ejaculation shortly after climbing aboard a broad-beamed Cuban woman at the place he went to with Joe the Canuck. He was paid off in New York, forty bucks in his pocket, with a letter stating that he had served well and could be recommended to any fo'c'sle. You couldn't go back to school after that.

But he went home to Montclair and there was the last almighty row with his father. Later in his room his mother gave him a hundred dollars for an emergency or if he needed to come home, and told him not to tell his father.

He went back to Boston and got a berth on Captain Ben Pine's schooner and shipped out to dory-trawl on the Grand Banks. That meant pulling for six hours sometimes in twenty-degree weather, with snow maybe too, often losing sight of the ship. Most of the older men were down a finger or two on each hand, but they could still haul a dory. And he thought nothing on earth could be this miserable and he would quit as soon as he got back ashore. But at the same time he saw it all as if in a book, a boy's book, and he thought, All my life I'll be able to say I hauled a dory on the Grand Banks.

THE OLD RIDE TO the boarding school was barely begun before he got off the train at Rye and walked downhill to the water.

The noise led him to the American Yacht Club. He knew at once what was making it. Every morning they came roaring down the East River from Long Island Sound. They came in packs at thirty miles an hour and more, and hard-boiled New Yorkers at the river's edge stopped to watch them pass. The Commuter Flyers, sixty, eighty, ninety feet long, but only ten to fifteen of beam, built by Luders, the Purdy Brothers, Herreshoff, and Consolidated, driven by V-12 engines developed for the air power of the Great War. They came downriver from Hell Gate with the hair-raising drone of a squadron of bombers. High fantail spume rose at their sterns, wakes curled and ran like breaking surf, and damaged boats and piers along all the shoreline of two states, between Oyster Bay and Greenwich and the city. Lawsuits were raised against the craft. Their owners, Olympians of commerce, fought off plaintiffs, or ignored them, but they continued to instruct their captains to drive at full speed because it was for that alone the flyers had been built.

The noise of those engines—throttles opened for the gauging of power and smoothness of carburetion, and continuing longer than necessary simply for the joy men took in making such a sound—led Boden down a hill to a large white wooden building on a neck of land. Fourteen long, narrow flyers lay at the club docks, rafted two and three abreast, others idled and grumbled in the water a short distance offshore, circling slowly. Boden recognized many of them, boats he had seen thundering away from Pier 11 at the foot of Wall Street. As he entered the club driveway, one of these, *Scaramouche,* accelerated away from the shore with exactly the obliterating noise of a heavy aircraft moving down an airfield and taking to the air. As the boat raced farther out into the Sound, the noise expanded, blasting ashore with the percussive impact of a long rolling thunderclap, drowning out all other sounds, until it fell

in on itself and rumbled back out across the water like a passing storm cloud.

In the driveway, men and women stepped down from black
Cadillac Phaetons, Dusenbergs, and brand new Chrysler
Straight Eight Coupes. Boden in his heavyweight dark suit
made his way through the round, well-fed, white-ducked and
navy-blazered crowd. He asked a young man at the door where
he could find Mr. Shred, and the young man looked blankly at
him. Then the eyes flicked down over Boden's suit and the
young man directed him to the "Engine Room" bar.

The long dark entrance hall held the club's history. Framed
photographs of its founding fathers in high-buttoned suits and
sea captain's hats, and their great playthings: J. P. Morgan's
185-foot *Corsair*, and *Corsairs II* and *III*; William Randolph
Hearst's *Vamoose*, 112 feet, designed by the "Wizard of Bristol," N. G. Herreshoff; Charles R. Flint's *Arrow*, 135 feet long,
12 and a half of beam, clocked at 45.06 mph on the Hudson in
spring 1902; Gordon Hammersley's 70-foot *Cigarette*, 50 mph
attained with the aid of five Wood/Liberty V-12s; Peter Rouss's
battleship-looking *Winchesters III* and *IV*, full-sized ships built
for a short commute, later owned by Guggenheim, Astor, Vanderbilt. And more.

Boden paused before these photographs, absently reading
their inscriptions. He was a few minutes early and he wondered about Mr. Shred. The name was familiar to him; but not
with the smack of such company.

More photographs covered the walls of the Engine Room
bar, along with half models of famous hulls, and historic propellers ruined in glorious service. The bar was also crowded
with men, younger versions of their photographed elders, exuberant and confident in their sense of membership.

Boden spoke to an elderly bartender who inclined his head
toward a figure seated at a table at the back of the room, away
from the windows: a small, stout man, no blazer and white
ducks, but a blue suit too tight, a brown derby on his head.

"Mr. Shred?"

"Yup. Cap'n Boden? Sit down. What'll you have to drink?"
He waved at the bartender.

"Nothing, thank you, sir."

"Don't go sirring me. Have a drink." Shred looked at the bartender, who now stood nearby, and pointed to his glass.

"I'll have a cup of coffee," said Boden.

The bartender moved away.

A man of fifty or more, hard to tell because of creasing and wear, with the thick hands of a working man, Shred lifted his glass and drank the last quarter inch of whiskey. He squeezed his eyelids shut, popped them wide open, showing yellowed, bloodshot circles around the small dark pupils, before relaxing the lids to half-closed and aiming his eyes at Boden.

"This is a charter, Captain. And the thing here is to bring the party home safe. I know you know how to do this. Mr. Moyle give me the rundown on you. I don't mean to say nothing about that other business, but the thing here is to do the same thing again, if it comes to that. That's the trick here. You don't worry about the boat. There's plenty more where that come from. You just bring the party home."

"Am I skipper?"

"Navigator. Owner and his party'll drive, maybe you'll spell them. They'll tell you where they want to go and you tell 'em whichaway."

The bartender returned with Shred's whiskey and a cup of coffee. Shred sipped from the new glass.

"You from up in Fairhaven?" Boden asked him.

"Yessir. Shreds of Fairhaven." The name of the family of shipbuilders known to sailors and merchants since colonial times. Once of the big yard on the Acushnet River, builders of whaleships, of three- and four-masters that took forty-niners around the Horn to San Francisco; who weathered the shift from wood to steel and sail to engine poorly and by the early 1900s had lost their yards and land and become rowboat builders, caulkers, and clam-diggers. "That's me. Clement Shred. Still on the water." He sipped again. "More like squeezed to the water's edge."

"Who's the charter? And where to?" Boden asked him, and outside, immediately beside the building, a single V-12 opened up and it was no longer possible to say or hear anything. The men in the bar crowded to the window.

Shred picked up his glass and drank it down, blinked eye-poppingly again, and jerked his head toward the door. He stood up, short, thick, bowlegged. Boden followed him out of the bar.

They walked around the clubhouse to the slipway, where a large group of men crowded around a single long, naked V-12 engine bolted to an oak strongback, displayed like an exhibit at an agricultural fair, gleaming with enamel paint, bright steel, and brass. It was racing with a fluid power, its cooling water coming to it through a hose leading along the ground into the sea. Sound blew out of it like a storm wind, buffeting those who tried to get close. Men grinned painfully and looked at each other and held their hands to their ears, hunching their shoulders up. Farther away, across the clubhouse lawn, ladies made appalled faces at one another and moved away as if from a spraying hose.

One man stood still and upright beside the engine, his hand on the throttle, smiling with all his teeth bared, showing his joy at the shattering sound, and at the discomfort it provided.

Boden and Shred stopped at the edge of the group around the engine. Shred put his hands over his ears. Boden wanted to move away but did not and soon covered his own ears. He watched the man beside the engine, who played with the throttle now, pushing the engine until it screamed, and men bowed their heads and yelled inaudibly, and the man at the engine laughed at them all. He was perhaps fifty, short, square-shaped—the same age and size as Clement Shred, but the two were different species. This one was smartly dressed in a striped blazer and white flannels. He wore small round rimless glasses, and with his bared-teeth grin and build he reminded Boden of Teddy Roosevelt—that and the authority with which he controlled the scene around him as certainly as he controlled the engine. It was his engine, his show. Boden knew that this man was his charter and wondered where he would go with him.

Finally the man eased back the throttle until the engine was idling, and he walked away from it. He came straight toward Shred and Boden.

"What do you think, Mr. Shred?" he yelled.

"She'll get you where you want to go, I reckon," answered

Shred. He nodded at Boden. "This is the man I told you
about."

"Good! Captain . . . ?"

"Boden, sir," said Shred.

"Captain Boden! Schenck," the man said, grabbing Boden's
hand and shaking it vigorously. He looked around. "Eddie!
Charlie! Lou!"

Nearby, three men broke away from a group of the older
club commodores and walked toward them. Boden thought he
had seen one of them somewhere before, looking younger.

"Captain, I'd like you to meet my partner, Mr. Eddie Rickenbacker, whose exploits in the sky I'm sure you've read
about."

The flying ace, member of the Hat-in-the-Ring squadron,
who had shot down twenty-six German fighters in the Great
War and won the Congressional Medal of Honor, was now in
his early forties, still handsome, grinning with the ease of long
practice. He was dressed as if for golf, in an argyle sweater,
baggy knee breeches, and a wide tweed cap, an outfit that min-
imized the paunch he had put on in more than a decade of
undiminished celebrity.

Schenck introduced the other two men. "Charlie Chapman,
editor of *Motor Boating* magazine. Lou Rootenberg, my public
relations man. Says he's not a kike, but I don't believe him. Put
a towel over that face and what do you get?"

Rootenberg, who was bald, dark, trimly mustachioed, and
actually resembled an Argentine bandleader who was currently
big in New Haven, laughed gamely.

"Gentlemen, this is Captain Boden," said Schenck. "Now
what do you say we go for a spin!"

He turned and walked quickly across the lawn. The other
five men followed him down to the club's dock, where they
boarded a black-hulled 60-footer. The name *Tally Ho!* was
painted in gold leaf on a mahogany plaque mounted amidships.

Schenck climbed immediately to the open bridge, enclosed
by a windscreen, and pushed his thumb down on a control
panel button. A rumble came from inside the boat, followed by
a roar from the stern. He pushed his thumb at another button

and a second engine fired. The other men stepped up to the bridge, except for Shred, who was uncomfortable at joining the owner's party, and wandered aft along the narrow deck. Schenck gunned the throttles and looked at Boden.

"You know engines, Captain?"

"Enough to have stopped a few from quitting on me."

"Well, these are Liberty V-12s. You know the Liberty engine?"

"No, sir."

"Aircraft engine. Four hundred horsepower, designed in six days in a hotel room down in Washington D.C. for flyers like Mr. Rickenbacker. But no sooner did they build twenty thousand of them than *wham!* the war was over and the engines were surplus. I bought three hundred of them for fifteen hundred bucks apiece. Eddie and I are going to build a few boats to stick them in, like the one you're going for a ride in now."

Schenck looked past Boden. "Let's go, Joey!" he called to the paid hand, a compact, tightly muscled man in a snug white T-shirt, white pants, and tennis shoes, who was standing on the dock, head raised, his eyes locked on his employer.

Like a gun dog released by a command, Joey uncleated the stern line and threw it aboard. He ran lightly along the dock, throwing off spring and bow lines as Schenck gunned the engines, turning the screws against each other, kicking the stern out.

"Eddie! Charlie! Get a load of this guy! Up front, watch this!"

As the bow came in, Joey pushed against it and held it off the dock, and when it was clear he flipped himself over the rail like an acrobat, somersaulting and landing upright on the foredeck.

Schenck laughed, and turned to his friends. "We got a bonus system going here—the better he jumps, the better I pay!"

The boat continued moving backward away from the dock in a wide arcing turn, until Schenck spun the wheel and eased both throttles forward. The boat trembled and its stern bit lower into the water. The bow continued to swing away from the shore, but now moved ahead. Schenck pushed the throttles forward again, and the boat picked up speed. Shred, who had been standing on the deck, tottered backward, off balance, until he grabbed the rail.

"Take a seat forward, Mr. Shred!" called Schenck, and Shred, looking like a beetle in his too-tight dark suit, obediently pulled himself forward along the rail and stepped down into the open forward cockpit—an exposed, upholstered hole in the deck at the very front of the boat. Here he took a seat, facing forward, looking to Boden on the bridge thirty feet aft like a man gone completely mad and waiting for a train in the most mistaken of places. "You might want to remove your hat," Schenck yelled forward, grinning at the other men on the bridge. Shred took off his derby, put it in his lap, and waited.

Tally Ho! moved out into the open Sound. Schenck scanned the water in all directions. Boden noticed that Joey had moved to the stern and appeared to be bracing himself in the corner of the rail.

Schenck pushed both throttles forward again.

The long thin boat accelerated smoothly but with a growing purpose. On the bridge, the men shifted their feet, placing one behind the other, and held onto the varnished rail.

"Revs are out of sync!" Rickenbacker yelled. Schenck played with the throttles, while still moving them forward, until the oscillating hum of the twin engines lengthened into a deep synchronous drone. The two men looked at each other and Rickenbacker nodded. Schenck continued his steady push on the throttles.

"Thirty!" he yelled.

As the boat's speed across the flat water increased, the bow rose significantly. Small wavelets smacked into its flat underside sections in irregular bursts that grew closer together until they became a single thrumming beat beneath the cataract wash of water passing along the sides of the hull.

"Forty-five!" yelled Schenck, but his voice blew away in ribbons.

The noise of the engines elongated into a deep, steady, sonorous hum that passed up through the deck into the bodies of the men and combined with the noise of the water and the gale-force wind that blew off the windshield and roared over the bridge, until the men could no longer hear anything but the single giant organ chord of the boat's run.

Schenck steered south from Rye and the boat quickly crossed three miles of open, unobstructed water. Other boats moved at a distance. Matinecock Point and the tree-covered rise of Long Island appeared ahead. Schenck turned the boat twenty degrees to starboard, pulling away from the shore as it trended southwest toward Glen Cove. *Tally Ho!* bore across the wide funnel mouth of Hempstead Harbor and began to close on a line of craft ahead. Sailing yachts ghosted or wallowed in the wakes of overtaking motor craft; commuters and runabouts sped in and out of the harbor; fishing boats drifted.

"Fifty!" Schenck yelled, but nobody heard him. Everybody on the bridge was looking at the boats coming up fast across the bow. Eddie Rickenbacker started laughing and shaking his head, looking at Chapman and Rootenberg. Boden involuntarily grabbed the windshield and pulled himself alongside Schenck to within reach of the helm. He pointed ahead and made a lowering motion with his hand. Schenck turned and looked briefly at Boden, then looked ahead and laughed, his fist remaining closed over the throttles.

In the bow, Shred turned and looked aft.

Schenck turned the wheel slightly, pointing *Tally Ho!* ahead of the bow of a slow-moving schooner, at an apparent hole in the line of traffic. Boden shouted in his ear, but Schenck did not catch it.

"Wake!" Boden shouted again.

Schenck did not care what the *Tally Ho!*'s wake might do to the schooner or the fishing boats and he waved dismissively at them as they drew closer, but Boden pointed ahead with a rigid arm and shouted again, *"The wake there!"* He meant the curling two-foot wave on the far side of the schooner, left by a speedboat that had crossed their course minutes before and was long lost from view. Schenck's mouth opened wider in a unheard laugh.

Shred had seen the wake too and had stood and was still standing up in the bow cockpit pointing forward and looking back at the bridge when *Tally Ho!* hit the curling wave and became entirely airborne. It took off with only the slightest impact, and a soft splash unheard above the noise of the boat, which dropped a note as it left the water and sailed through the air, a long two seconds of relative calm disturbed only by the sustained roar of the aircraft engines. Then the boat came down and the little damage that was done happened immediately. Three steam-bent oak frames amidships—where all the weight of *Tally Ho!* was concentrated as it belly-flopped back onto the surface—merely cracked. No seam was started in its planking: the workmanship would be remarked on afterward.

It was Clement Shred who got the worst of it. Right forward, he too became airborne, flicked upward into the air as if off a springboard. Then he came down again, but a crucial moment later than the boat's rise and fall and rebound, so that all the jarring shudder of the bow's impact on returning to the water was transferred upward as Shred's feet returned to the cockpit floor. Bones in his left leg shattered immediately and he pitched forward into the teak coaming and broke his nose before crumpling to the cockpit floor.

Schenck could see Shred on the cockpit floor, and his initial concern that the man was going to be tossed overboard was assuaged. He maintained his grip on the throttles, whooped with the thrill of it all, and *Tally Ho!* charged on across Hempstead Harbor, not slowing until Boden had gone forward and Shred's condition had become known. Boden, Chapman, and Joey carried him below into the saloon and Schenck turned the boat and headed back to Rye, making all speed and blowing *Tally Ho!*'s electric horn.

"YOU BEEN TO FLORIDA, Captain?" Schenck asked him.

They stood watching the ambulance crew take Shred off the boat onto the dock, where they put the stretcher down again and adjusted Shred's legs. Boden said yes without thinking and without looking at Schenck. He was waiting for Shred to be gone before he walked away up the hill to the train station.

"Ever been down there by train? You know the one I mean? The Havana Special. The crack express. Runs from Penn Station to Miami in forty-eight hours. That sound fast to you?"

"I've only been to Florida by ship."

"Good! So you know your way down there. You know Cape Hatteras and all those places, right? Sure you do. Let me tell you what I'm going to do. I'm taking *Tally Ho!* down to Florida. I'm going to race this boat down there and I'm going to beat that train. I'm going to race the Havana Special. You think we can do it?"

"I really don't know." Boden was on the point of turning away. He began to.

Schenck placed himself directly in front of Boden, close, and Boden could not look away from him. "Well, I'm going to do it. This boat is a prototype of the line Eddie and I are building. Eddie Rickenbacker's a real flyer, a guy who went up a hundred times and made it, not a one-shot deal like you-bet-he's-lucky Lindbergh. No one was shooting at Lindbergh on his jaunt to Paris! Eddie's got a name people respect. I got a boatyard on City Island full of wood and engines. I'm going to drive this thing down to Florida and beat that Havana Special crack express train, and we're going to sell a thousand of these boats. I want a navigator, someone who knows the waters out there and what the tide's doing. Shred told me you're a real sailor, you go by the sun and stars. You want to come along? It's going to be a hell of a ride. I just gave you a taste of it."

Schenck's face was a foot from Boden's, inches lower, but charged with energy, defiance, his hands on his hips. He was ready to take Boden into his grand design, or swat him aside and find someone else.

And Boden, who was sure this man was a wrecker, an uncontrollable jinx at sea, thought about what his train ride back to the city would be like if he said no.

"Don't feel sorry for Mr. Shred. He's in my employ. He'll make as much money lying on his can for a month as he would've standing on both feet—more, he'll get more. I did him a favor. I'll pay you twenty-five dollars a day, all the food you can eat, and you'll be bringing the boat back up here from Florida with Joey. We'll leave in about a week, according to the weather. I'll put you on salary right now, and take you off when you get back here with the boat. That's at least four weeks' work. If we beat the train, I'll give you a bonus of two hundred dollars. I want your answer right now."

The man was still directly in front of Boden's face. Again he thought of TR and his pugnacious, forward-leaning speechifying. He felt the force of this man, his determination, like strong weather blowing him where it wanted to go, and he realized he was ready to be borne along with it.

"Why me?"

"Two things. One, the way Shred talked about you. Mr. Shred I think knows his stuff. I can get all kinds of sailor boys who know their way around Long Island Sound. I want a seaman. I want someone who's been through the wringer out there. Two, you're available. So are you in or not?"

"I'm in."

"Good. You took the train out?"

"Yes."

"I'll give you a ride to the station."

"That's okay, I'll walk."

"I'll give you a ride," said Schenck. "C'mon, we're going to have a drink with Eddie and Charlie first." He turned and walked across the grass toward the clubhouse bar. Boden waited a moment, then followed.

SCHENCK DROVE A LE BARON–MARMON V-16. "Same as Bugatti's V-16 airplane engine. Only better. This thing'll do seventy-five miles an hour. What do you think of that?"

"The station's that way."

"I'm taking you to Greenwich." Schenck handed Boden a hundred-dollar bill. "I want you to come back out on Monday and move aboard. That okay?"

"That'll be fine, sir."

"Good. The boat'll be at my dock. You come back out to Greenwich station Monday morning and call the house. Somebody'll come and get you. You and Joey'll bunk in together on the boat. He'll take care of the boat. I'm not asking you to do any spit-and-polish. You get what you need for charts and take care of that end of it. We'll talk later on about the route and where we can get gas and all that. You can use the Chevrolet at the house. You need more money you let me know. You'll see me every day."

They drove north on the Post Road. Schenck drove fast.

"Fifty miles an hour. That's how fast we were going in *Tally Ho!* What did it feel like to you?"

"Too fast."

Schenck laughed. He turned his head toward Boden, looking steadily away from the road, grinning at him, until Boden felt he wanted to slap the man's face away from him. "When we were getting close to those other boats—" Schenck looked back at the road again. "—before we hit that wake. You moved, remember? You came over and stood right next to me. You were getting ready to push me aside and take over. I could feel it. Weren't you?"

"I was pointing out the wake."

"If you saw me making a wrong move, heading at another boat, say. You're standing right next to me, like today. What would you do?"

He looked away from the road again, leaning back in his seat, his head turned sideways, smiling at Boden, and Boden knew then that Schenck would not look back at the road.

"What would you do?"

Boden looked at him. Schenck's smile was relaxed. One arm lay across the steering wheel, the other was draped across the back of the seat between them. Boden looked ahead through the windshield and saw the oncoming traffic and how the Marmon V-16 was beginning to waver on the road. He looked away then, sideways out his passenger window, at the passing trees, and through them he caught glimpses of the water on the Sound. He kept his eyes on the water.

"I'd have to think about that for a while," he said, and he heard Schenck bark a laugh, and felt the car respond to a touch at the wheel.

"I like that!" Schenck yelled, still laughing.

He turned the car off the Post Road and headed for the water. They pulled into the wide gravel driveway of another yacht club, past a number of parked cars, and stopped before the large white clubhouse. Schenck left the car running.

"I'll be right back."

He walked around the house onto the lawn overlooking the Sound.

He returned a minute later with a young woman. She got into the back behind Boden. Schenck let out the clutch and the car moved off.

"This is my daughter, Harriet. A sailor herself. She's been in a race." His voice had changed.

Boden turned around to say hello and saw her making a face at her father's remark.

"This is Captain Boden. He's coming to Florida with me on *Tally Ho!*"

"Hello," she said. She had short dark hair, a round pale face, large dark eyes. She reached toward him and they shook hands.

"What were you sailing?" Boden asked the girl.

"A snipe," she said.

They dropped Boden at Greenwich station.

SCHENCK DID NOT TALK until he had turned off the Post Road and was once more driving toward the water.

"I'm going to have someone look at that boat. I'll get Henry over there to check the sails."

"It's not the boat, Daddy," said Harriet. She was still in the back.

Schenck looked at his daughter through the mirror. "Butch, if you sit in the boat and steer, you ought to do better than that, unless there's something wrong with the boat. Eleven out of thirteen is no good."

Harriet said nothing.

A minute later Schenck said, "Did you try?"

"Yes I tried, Daddy."

"You need lessons again."

"I do not need any more lessons. I know how to sail, I'm just not as good as other people at it."

"That's what lessons are for, to make you as good as other people. It's the beginning of the summer, you need to get back into it. You'll do better."

"I don't care about winning. I sail for fun, but it's not fun anymore when it's like this."

"You'll have more fun when you do better. Believe me. Do it for me, Butch. You can do better than eleven out of thirteen. I'm going to have Henry look at that boat. Sails can be made a hundred different ways, and the wires can be tightened or loosened. Don't worry, you'll do better."

CHAPTER 3

EDDIE RICKENBACKER, WHO HATED boats and the sea and was bored by the screaming monotony of their passage, left *Tally Ho!* in the dead of night at its first fuel stop at Cape May, New Jersey. He made his way by taxicab to Baltimore and flew from there on United Airlines to Miami, where Lou Rootenberg kept him out of sight but happy until twelve minutes past five on the second afternoon after the boat had left New York, when it closed within inches of the dock of the Biscayne Biltmore, at the southern tip of Miami Beach. Rickenbacker stepped aboard and the *Tally Ho!* pulled away and tore on across Biscayne Bay to the Port of Miami's Dodge Island Railroad Bridge, where Schenck brought it alongside the small bridge-tender's dock on which Lou Rootenberg had gathered the gentlemen of the press, all of whom were looking at their watches. It was five twenty-three.

Eddie Rickenbacker stepped ashore saying, "I hope this is Paris!" and the reporters laughed. Flashbulbs popped and crackled. Carl Schenck then talked about the forty-seven-hour, twenty-three-minute trip, the five fuel stops, and the matchless power and performance of his prototype commuter flyer, the *Tally Ho!*, which showed no more sign of its epic dash than the twinkling of its coat of salt crystals in the late tropical afternoon sunlight. Twenty-one minutes later, at five forty-four, the Havana Special thundered across the Dodge Island Bridge overhead and everybody cheered.

* * *

A LITTLE AFTER TEN the next morning, the boat set off again, with Rickenbacker once more aboard, along with Charles Chapman of *Motor Boating* magazine, a reporter and a photographer from the *Miami Herald*, and Captain Spike Smith, the great Florida fishing guide, who had bonefished and hunted alligator with Teddy Roosevelt and Al Capone, had made and lost a pile running boats from the Bahamas during the early days of Prohibition, and was now in his seventies, dying slowly of syphilis, his skin like walnut shell and eyes watering behind thick smoked-lens glasses as he sat in a wicker chair in the aft cockpit. Lou Rootenberg read from the morning papers, shouting above the cruising speed drone of the engines, of the *Tally Ho!*'s record-setting run, while Schenck drove the boat far up the Miami River.

They sped through the city and beyond, past the wooden cracker shacks at its Everglade outskirts, until they reached a group of low, newly built agricultural-looking structures rising out of the swampy marsh at the end of a network of channels dredged from the river's bank. Across the entire front of the largest building, a prairie-sized barn, gleamed the words: OCEAN DAIRY PRODUCTS COMPANY. A group of men in khakis was waiting for them on the wooden dock on the riverbank. They took the lines Joey and Boden threw to them and secured the boat to pilings. Schenck and his party stepped onto the dock.

"Captain Boden," said Schenck, "come with us. I want you to get a load of this."

Schenck led the group along a boardwalk that ran beside the channels toward the barn. Boden took Spike Smith's arm, as the old man seemed to be tacking into the light breeze and veering too close to the boardwalk's edge, and they trailed behind the group. Ashore, no longer moving upriver at speed, it was hot and steamy. The easterly wind that blew coolly off the ocean at Miami Beach was faint here, and blowing across miles of hot mud and dank vegetation. The reporter and the photographer had left their suit jackets aboard the *Tally Ho!* and waved their hats in their faces.

"Okay, Mr. Schenck," said the reporter, "what's the racket here?"

"What's it look like to you?" Schenck answered.

"Jeez, I dunno. A farm, maybe?"

"That's right. It's a dairy farm."

"I don't see any cows," said the photographer.

It was the remark Schenck had hoped for. "I'll show you cows!"

Close to the barn, the dredged channels led to a series of pools. Steel gates rose out of the murky water where the channels met the pools, closing the pools off into watery corrals in which, they all now saw, swam a number of large gray elephantine creatures.

"Jesus, what the hell is this?" said the reporter, who had only recently arrived in Florida from Oklahoma, and had mostly written about the swells on Miami Beach.

The khaki-trousered employees of the Ocean Dairy Products Company had begun pulling handfuls of cut grass and weeds from burlap sacks and were throwing the cuttings into the water.

"Manatees," said the photographer.

"Sea cows!" said Spike Smith, the first words anybody had heard him say that morning.

"That's right," said Schenck. "The manatee, gentlemen, is the cow of the sea, with a milk as rich as any produced by Mother Nature."

"Christ, they're ugly!" said the reporter.

"I fucked plenty worse in Nassau," said Spike Smith.

"Carl," said Chapman, "what exactly do you mean by this Mother Nature's rich milk business? What have you got going here?"

"We're going to milk these manatees and can the stuff and sell it cheap. This country is hungry and what it needs is cheap milk."

"You think people are going to drink fish milk, Mr. Schenck?" asked the reporter.

"It's not a fish. The manatee is a warm-blooded mammal—"

"Sonny, look in the water there," said Spike Smith. He gripped the reporter's shoulder with a brown scaly hand and pulled him close to the boardwalk edge. "This ain't no fuckin'

fish. It's something like a big nigger woman living in the water.
See? There's no difference, except she's in the water."

"Can I quote you, Mr. Smith? And I don't see any tits."

"You can do what you like. You don't know shit."

The photographer raised his camera and took a picture of a
manatee.

"Carl, are you serious?" asked Chapman.

"Yes, I'm serious. So's Eddie. He's in on this."

"I'm in if it works," said Rickenbacker, looking down at the
manatees, who were circling and nibbling tentatively with their
large blubbery mouths at the grass floating on the water. "But
I'm not putting any in my coffee."

"How do you milk them, Mr. Schenck?" asked the reporter.

"We hook 'em up to machines, like the ones they use for
cows."

"And that works?"

"We're making it work. I grew up on a farm," said Schenck.
"I made my fortune inventing farm machinery. This is going to
work."

"Jesus Christ," said Eddie Rickenbacker, still looking down
into the water.

"That must take some doing, Carl," said Chapman. "They
look like walruses to me and I don't know how the hell you'd
milk a walrus."

"Look at that!" said Spike Smith, gazing down into the water. "Like a big old Nassau gal rolling around in the hay!"

"You milk the women in Nassau, Spike?" shouted Schenck.

"Sea cow's the best fuckin' milk in the world!"

"I can't say I envy you the acquisition of your frame of
reference, Mr. Smith, but I am impressed by its breadth," said
Chapman. "To me, though, they look quite like the walrus
Newbold McKenzie brought back from Baffin Bay aboard the
Arundel. A sweet little critter, but I didn't find her attractive."

"It was actually a Harp Seal," said Boden. "Mr. McKenzie
found her as a pup abandoned on a floe off Labrador on the
way home."

"Whatever it was, he sure loved that thing."

"They were both in love. McKenzie tried letting her go a
number of times and she wouldn't swim away from the ship.

He pushed her overboard at sea well off Monhegan Island and she followed the *Arundel* all the way back up the Sheepscot to Wiscasset. He let her stay after that."

"How do you know all this, Captain Boden? You knew McKenzie, evidently?"

"Yes, sir. I was first mate aboard the *Arundel* on her overwinter trip of '20–'21."

"Were you really? I came aboard the *Arundel* in Wiscasset in the fall of '21. That's when I saw the seal. Were you aboard then?"

"No, sir. I'd left the ship by then."

"Well, I remember that seal. Followed McKenzie around like a dog. Barked at him! What'd he do with it?"

"I heard she was clubbed to death by a Newfie sealer in St. John's when McKenzie went north in '22."

Carl Schenck had listened to this. "So, Charlie, who's this seal-loving McKenzie?"

"J. Newbold McKenzie," said Chapman. "What they call an old arctic hand. He went up to the Arctic in, what, 1914, Boden? Got stranded and spent three years stuck on the Greenland coast. Liked it so much he came back and had the *Arundel* designed to his specifications by Starling Burgess. Had her designed so she wouldn't break up in the ice but get squeezed upward out of it instead."

"That's exactly right," said Boden. "And it worked wonderfully."

"He had her built by Hodgdon in East Boothbay. Boy, she was quite a vessel—still is I guess. Has McKenzie still got her, do you know, Boden?"

"Yes. He still takes her up north every couple of years. She's a good ship, all right."

"Oh, she was good. Very plain, but, my God, he had her built. Quite a fellow, McKenzie. Has some strong views. He fell out pretty badly with the National Geographic folks over Peary. He went north with Peary in 1909, and he didn't take to him. Thought he was a grandstander. He never believed Peary made it to the North Pole. Didn't believe Cook either. He thought they were all liars, and that National Geographic was fudging for Peary. Oh, there was ink flying about that!"

"Anybody who'd go to the North Pole is nuts," said Eddie Rickenbacker, who had grabbed a clump of grass and was throwing handfuls down to the manatees.

"So, what's this fellow do up there in the Arctic?" asked Schenck. "What's up there to go look at again and again?"

"You better ask Boden here," said Chapman. "He's been there."

"Mr. McKenzie collects information. He charts the land, and the ice, where it flows to and from, and he studies the natives and the animals up there."

"What animals?"

"Seal, walrus, all sorts of birds, guillemots—"

"Walruses with tusks? You shoot them?"

"We shot for food, occasionally. Seal and walrus. We ate eider duck sometimes."

"And I'm sure you saw polar bears, didn't you, Boden?" asked Chapman.

"Polar bears?" said Schenck, moving close, planting himself in front of Boden. "You saw polar bears? How big?"

"Why, they're enormous, Carl," said Chapman. "My God, I saw McKenzie's photographs of them. You've never seen anything like it. They're in a class all by themselves."

"Man-eaters?"

"They eat seal and walrus," said Boden. "But they'll eat a man if they can."

"You saw these bears?"

"A few."

And the notion gripped Schenck's mind, fully formed. "Are they prodigious?"

"That's the very word, Carl," said Charlie Chapman. "Prodigious."

"You going to go milk some bears, Mr. Schenck?" said the reporter from the *Miami Herald*.

"Count me out," said Eddie Rickenbacker. He was on his knees at the edge of the boardwalk. One hand was extended, holding grass over the quivering, winsome snout of a round-eyed manatee. His other hand was reaching down to the animal as if to caress it.

"That's a mermaid you got there, fella," said Spike Smith to Eddie Rickenbacker.

CHAPTER 4

BODEN AND JOEY SPENT four days driving the *Tally Ho!* back north.

Schenck had instructed them to go inside, up the Intracoastal Waterway, rather than offshore, their route south against the train. Boden told him the boat would be safer offshore, the trip faster and more certain, but Schenck suffered the landsman's delusion that a boat was safer nearer shore, amid the clutter of other shipping traffic, debris, and the unyielding land itself, than out in the wide deep sea. And he wanted it that way.

So they sped north up Florida, then through the Georgian and Carolinan low country, across Pamlico and Albemarle Sounds. Up the Dismal Swamp Canal. Up the Chesapeake.

Joey wanted to steer, and steered all day. Boden made offers to relieve him until he realized Joey was not going to let go of the wheel, so he settled himself in cool spots around the boat, shifting during the day as the sun wore west across their wake, watching the swamp country and the small towns passing by. Through these long days droning north, Boden found himself remembering the Arctic, and what a glory it had seemed to him.

They reached Smith Island in the Chesapeake Bay on a Saturday night, and the next morning Joey wanted to attend church. Boden went with him. They took seats in the rear of the congregation. Near the end of the service, the churchgoers stood up to testify.

"They pulled me off the dock in Somersfield with my head stove like a egg—I seen the pictures my boy Earl taken. Them doctors at the hospital all give me over for dead, but the good Lord's will had its way with me and I'm still on the water today."

"Amen!"

"Hallelujah!"

At night they tied to fuel-and-bait docks in remote places on the Tolomato, the Neuse, the Piankatank Rivers, and Joey fried himself an icebox steak and pored over the hard-boiled accounts and stark photographs of the slayings and kidnappings featured in the April issue of *True Crime Magazine*.

Boden took long walks away from the boat. He liked the southern houses with their wide porches that he saw from the waterway and on his evening walks, and he thought about how it might be to live in a place like New Harmony or Smith Island or Deltaville and run a shrimpboat or a skipjack or a Jenkins Creeker. He found small places where he could eat shrimp and crab and drink beer and listen to the talk of local watermen.

"Jimmy ain't a-crawlin' yet."

"Not a-hardly."

"Arthur Hurlbut found sooks over to Merther's Bend."

"Oh my, yes! The white sign is on 'em sure!"

The lives and speech of the people in such places had remained unchanged for generations. The boundaries of their world were close and well-known to them, the existence within those boundaries so spare and established in adversity that even the nation's depression had had little apparent effect. Boden found himself envying them.

WHEN THEY REACHED GREENWICH in the late afternoon of the fourth day, Schenck was not at home. His man Arthur, a distinguished-looking colored gentleman, tall, slim, gray-haired, with the air of an aesthete pained by contact with the humdrum, asked Boden to wait for his return. He and Joey hosed down the *Tally Ho!*, and wiped the boat dry with new squares of chamois leather.

For supper Boden and Joey were served pork chops in the kitchen by Hermione, the Schencks' elderly Irish cook. At six, Hermione turned on the radio next to the table where they ate.

"Good evening," came the sonorous voice. "This is Gabriel Heater. We have bad news tonight."

Hermione paused by the sink, a dishtowel in her hand, and stared attentively into the ether.

"The body of Charles Lindbergh's twenty-month-old son, Charles Jr., was found today in woods only five miles from the aviator's home in Hopewell, New Jersey. The child had been bludgeoned to death."

"Oh, Jesus," said Hermione.

Joey stopped eating, and hung on every dreadful word.

"In the seventy-three days since the kidnappers took the young child and left their ransom note, the most intensive man-hunt in history failed to locate the boy, until today. Police still have no suspect."

"That poor woman!" said Hermione.

They finished supper listening to reports from New Jersey, and when there were no more, Joey retired to the *Tally Ho!*'s fo'c'sle with several new magazines that had arrived for him in the mail.

Hermione told Boden he was welcome to stay in the kitchen and listen to Edgar Bergen and Charlie McCarthy, who were coming on after the news broadcast. He thanked her, but went outside to read her copy of the morning's *Herald* on the kitchen patio at the side of the house, which overlooked the dock and the water from a small rise of ground. A day too early for the discovery of the Lindbergh baby, the paper was in a buoyant mood. "Babe" Didrikson, the United States's track and field hopeful for the upcoming Olympics in Los Angeles, was featured in a photo spread showing her playing golf, football, basketball, and throwing a slick right to the chin of her boxing trainer.

" 'Is there anything at all you don't play?' we asked. 'Yeah,' said the Texas Babe, 'Dolls.' "

Petey Rodda blasted Primo Carnera's win in his title fight

against Jack Sharkey. "Da Preem" took out Sailor Jack in the sixth with a punch that had yet to be seen, but no one was looking, with gangsters like Owney Madden and Big Frenchy DeMange in Carnera's corner. Sharkey was backed by Detroit's Purple Gang, which was the only way anyone could explain the pairing of Sharkey with "Phainting" Phil Scott, and the whole Heavyweight Championship now stank worse than a bucket of dead worms.

Boden looked up and saw a dinghy approaching the dock, making no more disturbance on the breeze-ruffled water than a loon. It was silhouetted against the twilight-colored Sound, but the June evening carried enough light for him to make out the warm mahogany of the hull and see that it was Schenck's daughter in the boat, the dark-haired girl they had picked up in the car. She sat in the stern, her arm on the tiller. He forgot about the newspaper as he watched the girl bring the boat up to the dock.

The breeze was blowing offshore; this meant she had to sail the boat right up to the dock, maintaining some speed until the last moment, when the helm would be abruptly pushed down to bring the boat sliding alongside instead of crashing its nose into the dock's pilings. It was a maneuver requiring confidence, timing, and some boldness, and Boden waited to see how she would do it. He was in shadow on the patio, and though the dock was only a hundred feet from where he sat, he did not think she would see him.

She was too timid, he saw: afraid of hitting the dock, she turned too soon and was blown off. Then the breeze caught the mainsail and the boom swung over her head in a messy jibe. The snipe drifted away from the shore as the girl rearranged herself, brought the boat around, and began tacking upwind again. This time she made for a point to one side of the dock, came about, and headed in to the pilings at a shallow angle—a glancing blow if she misjudged and hit the dock. But this angle put the snipe nearly broadside to the wind, its fastest point of sail. To slow down she let go the mainsheet and spilled wind from the sail, again too soon. The boat lost its upwind drive and sagged off the dock, and again she drifted away.

Boden had decided he would stay in the shadow of the patio

and say nothing and leave her alone; he could only fluster or embarrass the girl if he tried to help. But then he stood up and walked down to the dock. He stopped at the water's edge as Harriet drifted away and gathered herself and the boat for another run.

"Hello there," said Boden. The evening was quiet and his voice carried well over the water.

Harriet glanced at him and looked away. "Hello."

From the dock he could see her face redden and her movements grow clumsier. He was making it worse for her. He wondered if she remembered him.

"Your first run was fine. You turned a little early."

"I know." She was angry at herself. Maybe annoyed at him too.

"Shall I go away and leave you alone?" he called.

He saw her smile. "Well . . . I don't mind." She got the sails trimmed and the snipe began to lift to windward. "I always think I'm going to hit the dock," she called out over the water.

"How about if I stop you?" said Boden. "Come on in like you did before, which looked fine. Wait a little longer than your instinct tells you before you come about. I'll fend off if you're going to hit. How about that?"

"Okay."

"Be bold!"

"All right! I'll be bold!"

Boden saw her grin and he felt unaccountably happy. She came on, tacking smartly now, back and forth, making straight for where he stood on the edge of the dock. As she neared, her grin widened with nerves and self-consciousness. She tacked onto the final slant and came at him. Then he could see her about to push the helm down.

"Hold on . . . Hold on."

Harriet opened her mouth in surprise, and then made a face for a crash.

"Wait . . . Now. And the sheet."

She pushed the helm and released the mainsheet. The snipe's beautiful manners brought an immediate response. It cut a tight arc, the bow passing within a foot of Boden's sneaker before curving away, and the hull came gliding alongside the dock. He took hold of the shroud as it came by, and the boat stopped.

"Can't do better than that."

"Thank you," said Harriet. A flush was filling her pale face. "You did it."

He handed her docklines, which she tied to the bow and stern.

"I just always think I'm going to hit the dock."

"So go ahead and hit it. Put a few dings in the bow. It's a boat, not a highboy."

Now she looked up at him, still smiling. She was wearing khaki pants and a tennis sweater, and her pale face was flushed to a rose color against her black hair. She's so young, he thought.

Harriet looked down at her boat. "I'll try to remember that."

"Captain Boden," said a voice behind him.

They turned and saw Schenck walking across the grass from the patio.

"What do you think? Will she make a sailor?"

Harriet lowered the mainsail and began to tidy up her boat.

"She's a good sailor now, sir. Made a nice job of coming in."

"With some instruction from you. That's what I've been telling her. She needs lessons."

"She's doing fine without that."

"She can do better. She can learn to make that thing go faster, for one thing. Captain, let's you and I go inside and have a talk."

Schenck walked away toward the house.

"Well, so long," said Boden. "Bang that boat up some."

Harriet looked up at him with a small tight smile. "Goodbye. Thank you."

He walked away.

SCHENCK'S STUDY REMINDED BODEN of the Engine Room bar at the yacht club in Rye. The walls were covered with framed photographs of boats, of Schenck among groups of men standing in front of boats at docks and in shipyards, half models of hulls, bent propellers, steering wheels. Boden noticed too the photographs behind the mahogany desk, in which a younger Carl Schenck appeared in scenes of rural farm country with groups of awkwardly grinning young men, and several in which Schenck stood beside different automobiles.

"Have a seat, Captain. Whiskey?"

"Yes, sir. Thank you." Was Schenck really going to ask him to give the girl sailing lessons?

Schenck brought the drinks from the long bar, handed one to Boden, and sat down. They faced each other on leather couches.

"How long did it take you to get up to the Arctic in that boat?"

"About a month, with stops in Maine, Nova Scotia, and Newfoundland."

"That was a sailboat, right?"

"Yes, sir."

"How far was that?"

"About two thousand sea miles. That was to Baffin Island."

"We just did fourteen hundred miles in forty-eight hours— less!"

"There were no icebergs. You couldn't go to the Arctic in the *Tally Ho!*"

"Why not?"

Boden wondered how to say it plainly without sounding ridiculous. "Because of the icebergs. And the weather. It wouldn't be what we had going to Florida."

Schenck threw back his head and laughed, hard, baring his square yellow teeth, and Boden understood suddenly that his reluctant fascination with Schenck came from the man's deliberate heedlessness, in all things, to obstacles that would be so apparent to others.

"I want to go up there, wherever there are icebergs and polar bears and walruses, and shoot. Maybe for a week or two. I want to get up there and back fast."

"Fly up. There are planes that'll—"

"I want to go in a boat. Be comfortable once we get up there. Move around. Like a safari, you see? Why couldn't *Tally Ho!* take us up? We'd keep a lookout for ice. Go around it."

"There's no getting away from the ice up there, at any time of year. You'll encounter it, and need to push through water that contains large pieces of it. You need a vessel with a hull thickness built to withstand that."

"A bigger boat?"

"Size isn't the answer. It would have to be something like a sealer, or a whaler, a vessel built to go there."

"How big do they come?"

"Eighty, a hundred, hundred and twenty feet maybe."

"Take a party of ten, say?"

"They don't take parties. They go up with a crew—"

Schenck waved his hand impatiently. "Yes, yes, I understand. But if I give an owner more money than he could dream of making catching his seals or whales, he'll take me, and my party. Easy money for him! No hard work, coast around while we shoot and do a bit of sight-seeing. Easy money! Or I'll buy a boat."

Schenck stood up, returned to the bar, and refilled his glass. He came back and sat down on the edge of his couch, directly in front of Boden. "That's the plan, then. I want you to find me a good ship, something comfortable, that Mrs. Schenck can travel in, and we'll go in August."

"August is too late. It starts to ice up in August."

"August is the middle of the summer, I don't care where you are. I'm from Minnesota, I know what cold is and when it starts. August'll be fine. Are you in or out?"

"I'll think about it."

Schenck looked at Boden and laughed. "I like you. You know why? Because I get the feeling you don't like me. And you don't hide it. I like that. That makes me feel I can trust you. I don't care if you don't like me, but it's important for me that I like you."

Schenck jumped to his feet. "Now listen. I'm going to make this trip, and I want to get ready now. I'll want my own captain, not some greasy fisherman, but a man I can trust." Schenck stepped forward and thrust a check at Boden. "Here's your two hundred bonus for the Florida trip. And another two hundred to start you off looking for my ship."

Boden put his unfinished drink on the table before him and stood up. He looked at Schenck.

Schenck held the check out, watching him as a man watches a feral creature to see if it will take the food held out to it. It was this trait in him that enraged Boden. Schenck was not insensitive, but acutely aware of his effect on others. He seemed to know at all times how to push those around him to the edge of their tolerance for him, and then provoke their humiliation as they confronted their reasons for accepting him. His avidity and pleasure at watching them do this was naked. At the same time, he presented them, as he did now to Boden, with something they wanted, that only he could give them. The opportunity to make a passage to the Arctic, the chance of such a command, swept through him like an electric charge, and fought against the bile of his distaste.

"Are you in or out?"

"I'll see what I can find." Boden took the check from him and put it in his pocket. "But August is too late."

"You let me worry about August," said Schenck. "Take the Chevrolet, go wherever the ships are, report to me by telephone every day. Every day!"

"It won't be easy to get a ship—"

"You'll find it. You find me the right ship, tell me where it is, and I'll secure it. And take Mr. Shred with you. He'll help you."

"I don't need help."

"Maybe you don't, but he might know where some boats are that you don't. I want him in on this. Take him with you. You'll cheer him up. He might cheer you up, Captain Boden."

CHAPTER 5

THE YEAR HE TURNED fifty, Clement Shred became aware of a discontent with his life.

Repairing moldering boats—when that work had not gone to another Shred, one of endless brothers and cousins begat and strewn in biblical numbers through the Massachusetts town of Fairhaven and up and down the eastern bank of the Acushnet River—or digging through unyielding sand and mud for clams and quahogs, began to seem insufficient work. Scarce, that is. And then, when such work was available, it still seemed insufficient.

At home, his wife Hezzie's dull complaints started him asking himself if she had always complained so, and he had paid no heed, or if her complaining was on the rise. Whichever it was, he began to find it nettlesome. He spent more time away from home, moving up and down the river, growing more aware of the lack in his life.

In early summer he told his wife he was going across the river to look for a new situation, and when he found it he would return for her. Hezzie was flummoxed dumb for a short time, then found her voice and started in on him, but Clement Shred was fixed on the notion. He rowed his skiff across to New Bedford. He spent a day there before he realized it was too close to home: he could look across the Acushnet and see Shreds on the far bank. He could almost hear Hezzie. He broadened his idea of range and turned and rowed south and west, looking for something in the water trade.

He spent the night on the beach inside Point Judith. He had brought bread, a tin of jam, a board-stiff slab of New Bedford bacalhao, and a stoppered bottle of beer with him, and he ate his supper sitting beside his boat on the beach, his suit jacket across a thwart, his pants riding up around his chest, suspenders slack, brown derby pushed back on his head, gazing across the water at the winking Race Point light on Fisher's Island.

He felt a sense of wonder and freedom he had never known before. He had never in his life been any distance from Fairhaven. He had never been to Boston; seldom gone across the river to the teeming confusion of New Bedford. It was travel, he reckoned, that was now affecting him so. Putting ashore when necessary for food, and pulling at an easy stroke, he supposed he could travel on in this way for some time. Why, he thought, a man could go on like this indefinitely, stopping only to work at any odd thing long enough to make the cash to move on. The notion opened up before him and made him dizzy, and sitting there on the beach, he barked a short, amazed laugh.

Several long sunburning days later, Shred found himself in narrowing waters, the shores of New York closing in on both sides. The water traffic around him had grown worrisome thick with black-belching steamers, tugs and barges, and ferry boats; the houses alongshore had become considerable and grand, and the look of the coastal towns less likely by the stroke as places where a man of his particular skills might find a living. He knew working boats and fishing craft, and he had seen none such since far astern in Connecticut. It was all yachts, thick as a run of fish, he saw around him now, small and stupendous large, dainty things of marvelous light construction that made him wonder how they fared in a seaway, how much they cost, and what sort of life they led, the folk who owned these picture-pretty but useless toys.

He had never thought to come this far, but he had found no work astern. He knew what lay ahead: the East River, the Hell Gate, and New York City itself, a millrace of sluicing currents and clever characters, a place he feared to go in his skiff. He could get no farther south without going this way, through the city's river heart, and he thought about turning around and trending east again along the Long Island shore, a place about which he knew little, except that it was all New York too when he thought about it, and that gave him pause.

He sat in the skiff, oars raised, irresolute, until he noticed that the tide was drawing him faster than he could row away from it into the turbulent bottleneck ahead. He dipped oars and pulled hard for the northern shore. Over his shoulder, he made out a shipyard: ways, docks, men caulking seam, painting, and laying on varnish, a familiar, comforting sight. He adjusted his stroke.

He put the skiff alongside dock pilings in a space between two large craft, shipped his oars, tied her painter off, and sat breathing heavily, his derby pushed back on his head. Unresolved, and too tired to ponder on much at all, he let his thoughts follow his eyes, which now began to look over the boat, a great fancy yacht, immediately astern of where he bobbed. Mighty narrow of beam. She'd have to roll something awful in a beam sea. Well, you couldn't take her to sea; all that glass, and rails as fine as birdcage wire to keep the nobs aboard. And the work to keep her up! He smiled and shook his head at the thought of it.

This one, he saw right off, had hit something in the hollow of her fine bow, low down just above the water. A gash in her paintwork, already sanded down and primed. And as he looked and wondered what was wrong, a man appeared on a fendered yard float, hauling himself along the hull to this spot on the bow. Up on deck another man tied the float off, and the man on the float, a well-creased, bent-foward, string-bean old fellow, knelt down and began to paint over the primed spot with a badger brush.

Shred watched with growing dismay. Was this a decree from a rich owner, paint her and the hell with it? For show, was it? Or did they not see, down here in New York, what he saw so clearly, that made a foolery of this paint repair? It was none of his affair, but finally his curiosity moved him to speak.

"Afternoon," he called to the man on the float. The old

geezer looked over at him, his eyes noting briefly the skiff, nodded, and looked back at his brush stroke.

Shred looked up to the man on deck. "Going to haul her or leave her as is?"

"We can fair in the paint pretty well. She'll be fine."

For nearly a minute, Shred watched the man painting, and then he could not stop himself.

"No amount of paint going to patch that up. She'll open right up the moment she hits her first wave."

"Huh?" said the man on deck.

And the man painting on the float stopped and looked at Shred, and spoke. "What's wrong with her?"

"Well, sir. Whatever she hit done its job, what no amount of paint going to hold together. She's already stove."

They stared at him.

"Seems to me, anyway."

The man on the float looked back at the wet paint on the hull. He began tapping the spot with the handle of his paint-brush.

"No, sir, not there. Farther aft. You see her?"

"You show me," said the old skinny fellow.

Shred slipped his painter free and drifted down onto the float. He leaned across the paintpot and rapped a thick knuckle against the planking about a foot the other side of the painted spot.

"Hear that? She's stove right here."

"I don't see anything," said the man on deck.

Shred pulled back his hand, made a fist, and punched. With a slight dry sound, the planking beneath his fist separated in a diagonal crack and was pushed inward. He pulled his fist away and the thin plank sprang back, almost concealing the break.

"Jesus, you punched a hole in the boat!" said the man on deck.

"No, sir!" said Shred, worried now. "I only pushed her in where she was already stove."

"He's right," said the painter to the man on deck. "I see it now. Go tell them we got to haul her."

The man on deck disappeared. The man on the float

coughed deeply and spat a green gob into the water and watched it float away. "Where you from?" he asked Shred.

"Fairhaven, back east over to Massachusetts. The name's Shred."

"Moyle," said the older man on the float, "from Brooklyn. Though I been to Massachusetts."

To Shred, it sounded as if Mr. Moyle did not like Massachusetts. He decided to push on and find a spot for the night. "Is there a beach near here?" he asked.

"Around that point," said Moyle, nodding. He could see that Shred was traveling. "There's a street comes down to the water there, Markle Street. You go up there to the Black Rose Restaurant if you're looking to eat somewhere. It's cheap."

"I'll try it. Thank you, sir. And what town is this?"

"City Island."

"City Island," repeated Shred, struck by the paradoxical-sounding name. "An island, then?"

Moyle grunted.

The beach was a tumble of dark stones covered with a stinking, oily wrack. It seemed the only bet on this metropolitan island and he did not want to pull out into the Sound again before dark. He hauled his skiff above the tide line, slipping on the slimy stones. He ate a fair bass for seven cents at the Black Rose and returned to his skiff, sleeping inside it rather than on the rocks, his stomach grazing the center thwart as he lay on his back and looked at the stars, dimmed here in the bright aura of City Island so that they seemed, as he felt them to be, farther away than usual.

He was preparing to leave when Moyle found him in the morning. They returned to the yard in Shred's skiff and he met the owner of the stove boat. This man—a short man about Shred's size—also the owner of the whole shipyard and docks along the shore here, got right up in his face and questioned him closely about how he had seen the plank was broken, for which he had no clever answer except he'd just seen her right off. The owner then asked him where he was from, and what he had done there, and Shred told him some about the Shreds of Fairhaven, shipbuilders since centuries past. He didn't know why the man was asking him about himself, and he was

wary—the man seemed every inch a New Yorker, and a nob
without doubt—but once he realized the owner understood he
hadn't caused the damage himself by punching the boat, he
talked freely. The man had a concentrated way about him
which Shred supposed was probably a type of heated-up New
York friendliness. He finished by asking Shred if he was busy,
or if he had time to look over his own shipbuilding operation.
Shred said he didn't mind.

Later that morning, the man offered him a job. It was unclear to Shred what the job was; there looked to be shipwrights
and foremen aplenty at the St. Clair Boatworks, the name of
the man's concern, right there on City Island where he had
pulled up in his skiff. The nearest he could later recall of the
nature of this job was his new boss's saying he thought he
could find a place for a man of Shred's talents in his operation.
The boss then wrote him a check for more money than he had
ever seen on one piece of paper, told him to settle himself there
on City Island and report back to him in a week.

He sent for Hezzie, who let their house in Fairhaven to her
niece, and they moved into a tall, narrow place on Markle
Street, close to where he had eaten his supper that first night on
City Island.

Hezzie complained about the house, about the going up and
down stairs, but she got used to having her hair done by Phyllis
at the beauty parlor, and bought herself new clothes with some
of the money that began to come in regular every week for
Clement Shred. She soon looked altered and strange, like
someone else, Shred thought, when he came upon her at home,
a large woman with her thin hair cut short, gone a glossy
darker color, and made wavy; lipstick on her wide, floured
face, a new dress, stockings and shoes, and reading the magazines all the time now.

He found his new boss a hard man to report to. He couldn't
find him much of the time. The men in the office at St. Clair
never knew where he was, and Shred felt foolish going in there
and asking after him. At first he had stood about in the yard
fretting that there might be some work he should be doing if
only he knew what it was. At the end of the day, when the
whistle blew and the shipwrights came out of the sheds to go

home, Shred followed them, feeling shameful and useless. On his way home his eyes always found the sign on the bell tower of the Methodist Church: *Time is the Seed Plot for Eternity.* He was unsure of its meaning, but it admonished and disturbed him.

He began to avoid the yard. He did not want to stay at home and have Hezzie see him so adrift, so he began to walk around the shores of City Island. He noticed other men on the island's tidewrack perimeter: somehow they did not appear to be local burghers out for a stroll or to skip a stone, but seemed to have washed ashore like castaways. They fished and ate cans of soup heated over driftwood fires. Some of them lived in small shacks built of packing boxes and odd salvaged pieces of boat erected above the high tide line. He had not seen this before, not back in Connecticut or Rhode Island or Massachusetts. Once he talked with one of these idling, hiding-out men, a tailor by trade from a place called White Plains, who told him that President Hoover was a criminal and that a revolution was coming, and when it came the tailor was going to fight.

He found three or four wide-open saloons selling bootleg beer and whiskey, and in the afternoons he often took a drink or two before going home. There were always fellows in a saloon to talk to, men who had worked out profound philosophies covering any trouble you could mention. A saloon, he found, was a more natural place for a man to be than wandering about out of doors in the middle of the day. He came to spend more of his time in Ivorson's gin mill on Harbor Street. He made friends there, among them men who knew no more about watercraft than he knew about airplanes, yet they found much to talk about. He had money enough. He put on weight. It was the strangest time of his life.

But the boss would find him when he wanted him, a note run to his home a day ahead of time, and send him off on some errand, or task, though it never seemed to Shred what he would have called work. He was driven in an automobile all the way to Long Island to fetch a windlass, which was brought back to the St. Clair yard on a truck that followed his automobile. He was driven to a great wharf in Brooklyn to look over a cargo of Russian plywood called Venesta Board, made of veneers of alder and birch, great sheets of it eight feet by sixteen. He reported back to Conklin, the boss shipwright at the yard.

"Look all right, did it?" Conklin asked him.

"What I could see of it. Great flat sheets. Looked fair and true." In all his life, Shred had never handled or worked a scrap of plywood. He had no feel for great boards made of thin shavings of wood stuck together with glue.

"Atkin over at Hungtington uses it," said Conklin, who seemed doubtful. "Well, anyway, we'll try her."

Later, Shred saw a stack of Venesta Board the size of a house sitting in the yard and wondered uneasily what part he had played in its arrival, and what would be built of it.

The boss liked to have him aboard his new boats when he took them on sea trials. He would ask Shred's thoughts about this piece of gear or that, the boat's trim and ride. Shred would say what he thought, most often simply that it seemed all right to him, which always pleased the boss. He learned to have a care over what he said did not look right, for the boss then would go to any trouble to put it right, according to Shred's lights.

Two years passed. Shred grew stout, pushing at his suit buttons until he had to buy two new ones. Hezzie grew even larger, and slowed with ankles, knees, and every part of her legs, hips, and back giving her grief, so that Shred, who passed Ambrosiano's Pianos on his way to and from Ivorson's, and had seen Luigi Ambrosiano's men moving the great instruments in and out of the store, thought Hezzie resembled one of the thicker-legged baby grands in size and difficulty.

He remained in touch with Moyle, the thin old geezer on the paint float the day he had first come to City Island, although Moyle lived a distance away in Brooklyn and had never worked full time at St. Clair. Moyle seemed to want no steady work, leaving a job if it threatened to harden into a full-time arrangement, moving from painting crew to dock or barge, wherever there was casual work. During the winter of '31-'32, Shred ran into Moyle several times on his travels for the St. Clair Boatworks. After that, sometimes on weekends, he would travel into Brooklyn by tram and train and he and Moyle would drink together at Horgan's in Red Hook.

After a first silent beer, while the two men adjusted to their convivial state, Shred might say he found it more peaceable in Brooklyn with all its clamorous goings-on than with her indoors at home. Moyle might grunt, commiserating in his way. Moyle had had a wife at one time, he mentioned one day, and left it at that. In time he learned that Moyle had been a navy man, and then a sailor before the mast, had rounded the Horn between New York and San Francisco fourteen times, had sailed to Australia and westabout around the world three times on an English grain ship. He had gone wherever sailing ships could go until there was no use for them anymore and they were all stoppered up in port for their short rot to oblivion.

Shred told Moyle of the schooners they used to build in Fairhaven, how he'd been a planker boss in '17 and '18 with a crew of thirty men under him, and about old Ray Budd and his Stanley 55 plane which Ray used so you would think that one plane was an entire joinershop. Moyle had known men like that, but you wouldn't see their likes now, or again. No call, he said, and Shred knew he was right. Brooklyn and all of New York, wherever he went, was full now with men like the castaways on City Island, the refuse of some country very close by, like America but gone awful wrong, who had woken up and found themselves in a place like home but lost, looking for any work, living in shanties and Hoovervilles. There was precious little work of quality for a skilled man anymore. Not in a shipyard. Ships were all steel lungers now, filthy things put together fast for a price, no skill gone into them, no grace. Moyle told him of what men did along the waterfront and for how little money. That was their work now, if they could get it.

Excepting the yacht-building yards, said Shred, thinking of the filigree-fine bits and pieces that went into the fancy craft built at St. Clair, whittled down to a nicety by the shipwrights kept on there. Shred said he was beggared if he knew why the boss kept him on, paying him a good wage, when he had not done a day's work for the man since he arrived on City Island, but spent his time riding about in the boss's cars and boats like some politician.

"He reckons you've got the nose," Moyle told him.

"Nose?" said Shred, looking at himself in Horgan's mirror.

"A nose for what's good in a craft. The way some has for horseflesh, or money. Maybe you do, maybe you don't, but he reckons you have it. So you're his lucky mascot."

Shred grew uneasier as time went by. He thought dimly that at some point ahead, it would have to change. He didn't know how or when, but he didn't see things going on forever as they were.

A LARGE WOMAN WITH a face like a side of raw veal, on which features had been crudely drawn with bright crayons, opened the door to Boden.

Mrs. Shred, he supposed. She invited him inside, offering coffee, but Shred appeared from behind her, hopping through the doorway with a cane, one leg in a cast.

"We'll push off," he said.

"When will you be back?" said Hezzie, with an unhappy note.

"I'll let you know by telegram." He seemed to know the Chevrolet and was at its door, backing himself in, pushing at the pavement with his cane. "Let's go," he said to Boden.

"You got a grip you want to bring? We'll be on the road for a spell."

"No, sir. Reckon I'll try to keep out of the rain."

Shred directed Boden through the streets. As they crossed the bridge off City Island, he asked, "You got any notion where to look for this ship?"

"I don't think we'll find anything south of Boston. I was thinking of trying Gloucester. What do you think?"

"Gloucester! Oh my! Cold country up there. Find some sealer, would that be it?"

"There, or farther down east."

"Oh, sure. How long a trip would that be, here to Gloucester?"

"I don't know. It's about a day by train. Maybe a day and part of a night in this."

They reached the Boston Post Road and Boden turned north.

"Go by way of Fairhaven, do we?"

"Can if you want."

Shred imagined himself rolling into Fairhaven in a Chevrolet, on the lookout for a ship.

"Let's make for there, then. We can put in to Fairhaven for the night."

"Okay."

They fell silent, neither saying much until they crossed over the Connecticut River. Shred turned with difficulty in his seat to look upriver, and told Boden how he had rowed upstream on the flood looking for a place to settle and taken one look at paintsmart Essex, where he had felt like a piece of sorry flotsam blown ashore by mischance, and had rowed downriver on the ebb. They were quiet again until New London.

Then Clement Shred said, "Would you mind telling me how you lost your ship, Captain? I never did get it clear from the newspapers."

Boden didn't answer immediately.

"Maybe not, then."

"No, it's okay. It was a Gulf Stream storm. My crew was green—"

"Kids, wasn't it? Wasn't one of 'em a politician's son?"

"Yes. Young people. I was taking them south for the winter. They pay and they learn the ropes. It's about the only way to make a sailing ship pay these days. Well, we got knocked down. She wouldn't come up. She was filling. I thought she was going. Boston-bound freighter hove up by some fluke, offered to take the kids off by breeches buoy. It seemed the thing to do at the time. So we all got off."

"But she didn't go."

"No." Boden smiled. "A garbage scow got a line on her and towed her into Baltimore. Claimed salvage."

"You couldn't get her back?"

"I abandoned her at sea and she didn't sink, so the insurance wouldn't pay. I didn't have the money to buy her back. So that was it."

"That's a rough deal."

"Yep."

"Is that what you'd been doing with her? Cruises for young folk?"

"Yeah. For about five years. Went up into the Arctic twice,

but she wasn't the best ship for those waters. Then tried the
Caribbean in winter."

"But you made a go of it, then?"

"I was getting by."

"Mmm. You got family at home, Captain?"

"I got a wife. Not at home, though. We don't live together
anymore."

"Oh." Shred felt he was on thin water, and said no more.

LATE IN THE AFTERNOON they drove across the Acushnet
and came into Fairhaven.

"Oh my!" said Shred several times, before they were off the
bridge. He stared out the car window. "Lots has changed."

"How long have you been away?"

"Two years. Oh my, look along here. All shut up. Didn't
used to be a filling station there." He was up close to the windscreen.

"You know somewhere we can stay?"

"Yessir. We can put up at the Josh motel. If it's still there.
Right along here, maybe a mile."

"You don't want to stay with anybody you know?"

"Nossir. We'll put up at the motel. There it is. God, it looks
all shrunk."

They checked into a cabin at the Joshua Slocum Motel,
named for Fairhaven's onetime resident, the first man to sail
alone around the world. Boden put his grip on one of the beds,
and Shred went back to the office and got the manager working the phone. In five minutes, men began to turn up at their
cabin.

"Well, lookit you, Clement! Gawd, you got all fat! What've
you been eating down there in New York? What happened to
your leg?"

"Holy shit, Clement! You been livin' too well down there in
New York!"

More men came by. They gawked at their prodigal relative
and sniggered.

Shred sent one of them off to find liquor. He introduced
them to Boden, respectfully titling him *Captain*: Ray Shred,
Joel Shred, Shoal Shred, Jared, Little Raymond, Elder Lucas,

Paulie, all Shreds, cousins, nephews, brothers, and more turning up. And a red-haired undertaker named Lareau, and Vinnie da Rosa, who owned the diner along the road.

Shred told them about his job in New York. He was a project foreman for the St. Clair Boatworks, he said, and his duties had taken him far and wide.

"My Gawd, Clement, you're no longer working with your hands. You're tellin' others how to do it. You've come far, boy!"

The other Shreds told their successful cousin and brother what a thin time of it they were having in Fairhaven. No work anywhere, no boats wanted built, no one ready to pay a man to caulk a skiff. They were all clamming, and growing cabbages, and repairing their houses with shingles and tar paper torn off houses abandoned by others less fortunate.

Shred was sympathetic. No doubt he would be in as sorry a place if he had not struck out when he did. His own good fortune, he admitted with wonderful humility, was simply a question of being in the right place at the right time.

He now outlined their mission, to find a boat suitable for an arctic voyage. To a man, every Shred lifted his eyebrows, swayed back, and stared at another and then at his relative, returned from New York, and back around the tight cabin.

"Get a big fishin' boat. Gawd, there's enough around!" said four Shreds at once.

Boden explained that any regular fishing boat, no matter how large or stout, had the wrong shape for arctic work. Their holds were deep, and the sides of their hulls dropped vertical and straight from the deck to the turn of the bilge, far below the waterline. If beset in ice, or pushed into it, this flat wall rising from the waterline was easily crushed. Hulls built for the arctic had to be the shape of an egg split lengthwise, the cut edge being the deck, the hull bottom round, curving inward at all points going down, so that when ice pressed in against it, such a hull would lift up on top of the ice. The men listened respectfully.

"Like a sealer, right? That what you're lookin' for, Captain?" one of the men asked Boden.

"That's right."

The Shreds gazed around the room for certain confirmation. "Not around here, Clement."

Most of them wanted to eat at Vinnie da Rosa's diner, but Shred insisted on the Grill, a dark, nearly empty place with a mournful atmosphere. He was on expenses, he said.

"Well, all right, Clement! You're the man driving the Chevrolet!"

"I'm not buying for you fellas. But I eat first class when I'm traveling for Mr. Schenck. No offense, Vinnie. You want to join us, that's where Captain Boden and me are eatin' supper."

Boden liked the sound of the diner, but he left it to Shred, who had a strong notion of how he wanted to spend every minute in Fairhaven. It was his town. And Boden didn't feel the need to be alone. He preferred Shred's company to the mute and enigmatic Joey, and after the liquor bottle had gone around the motel cabin a few times, he was happy with the company of all Shreds.

IN THE MORNING, AS they drove north out of Fairhaven, Shred was once more looking through the car windows like a stranger. He had taken one of the car's lap robes from the backseat and laid it across his legs.

"It's all changed. Completely, somehow." He sounded surprised.

"You've changed, Clement," said Boden. "You left, and it'll never be the same again."

"I guess that must be it."

He watched Fairhaven falling away.

CHAPTER 6

NOTHING IN HIS LIFE gave Carl Schenck as much satisfaction as seeing the old money—the smug, tight members of the club to which he would never be admitted—fallen. To see them down there, suddenly below him, looking up at him, hating him but needing him, resentful but helpless. It never palled, and after the Crash, he found no end of ways in which he could contrive this favorite view.

He had made his own pile so simply, almost accidentally. Wealth had not been on his mind when he had done the thing that brought it to him. He had only been concerned with a mechanical problem. *Made it moving shit!* he liked to tell people, loudly. With scrap tubing, discarded tractor gears, and, in the very beginning, crankcase sludge, Carl Schenck had made a hydraulic lifting device in the lean-to machine shop he had fixed up behind the family milking barn, and bolted it under a truck bed. Tons of cowshit could be loaded onto the truck, taken a distance, and then Schenck's device raised one end of the truck bed and the shit slid out. Whole operation done by himself, one man, in an hour. He had begun by hiring himself and his truck out to perform this service, but what other farmers really wanted, he found, was their own dumping truck. He started making them.

This occurred at about the same time that Albert Kahn designed for Henry Ford a new plant in Highland Park, Michigan, around the idea of the moving assembly line. The plant turned out six thousand automobiles a day, and people's thinking about numbers changed. In a poll taken by a Detroit newspaper, Henry Ford was voted the greatest man in History, after Napoleon Bonaparte and Jesus Christ.

In the fall of 1915, Schenck Hydraulic Hoist and Body began supplying his patented dumping truck mechanism to auto builders, who attached it to trucks on moving assembly lines, and Schenck never got close to shit again. By the following spring he had become, on paper, a millionaire. This led him to the view that the automobile appeared the thing to which the greatest numbers were attached in every direction. With his new money he bought his way into the Prest-O-Lite company, whose reliable carbide headlamps were becoming the favored choice of Ford, Leland, the Dodge brothers, and one hundred and five other automobile manufacturers. Schenck's own thinking about numbers was changing too.

A few years later, he moved his family east, where the big money lived. In New York he got to know a smart crowd of bankers, brokers, politicians, baseball players, and movie stars, and out in Greenwich he lived like a squire. Being a farm boy from the Midwest, his discovery of the watery playgrounds of the east coast was a revelation. He found a second great passion—after the sweet view from money—in boats. Schenck loved boats because they were bigger and more beautiful than cars, and they made him look good. He fell in love with boats the way other people with newfound money fall in love with art. Then he came to love the places where boats were found in the greatest numbers: Newport, Palm Beach, and all the golden pockets along the shores of Long Island Sound. He bought boats, took them to these places and played in them, and eventually he began to make them after his own ideas of what they should be.

In 1931, while on a cruise to Newport, he stepped ashore, walked up Bellevue Avenue, looked around, and bought a cottage, Aquitaine Castle, from a Biddle straitened by a cascade of margin calls. It was a solid stone place designed by Richard Hunt, with turrets and elevations borrowed from Louis XVI's hunting lodge, that Hunt had seen in the forests of Poitou-Charentes. The dining room had been redone by Stanford

White and was more famous for that than for its marvelous friezes. In early June of 1932, six weeks after coming home from Africa, Schenck and his wife and daughter and his man Arthur went aboard the *Tally Ho!* at Greenwich, cruised up the Sound, stopping for the night at Fisher's Island, and the next day thundered on to Newport, where they settled into the cottage for the summer.

Harriet started tennis lessons on the grass courts of the Newport Casino. Every afternoon she was coached by a young man named Edward, who hailed from Middletown and had a Rhode Island accent. "Edwud," he said his name was. But he was sweet. He would have come to the courts of Aquitaine, but she wanted to mix with the other people at the club, and soon she was playing doubles with her Bellevue Avenue neighbors Cindy McCann, who enjoyed a Woolworth connection, and Alison Dick, whose father made elevators. In no time she met the whole crowd. Boating was the thing in Newport, and Harriet discovered that here too she owned a snipe. And when she took Cindy and Alison sailing and they raced other kids around Goat Island, she unexpectedly found herself popular— not, for once, because she had money, which had previously brought her difficult friendships tinged with envy and resentment, for Cindy and Alison and all the other kids she met in Newport had scads of money too. Apparently, her new friends liked her simply because they had fun with her.

Tally Ho!, because of its dreadful airplane noise and speed and beauty, was much talked about, and Harriet's father let her arrange a day when she could take her girlfriends on a cruise up Narragansett Bay. Mamie suggested she join them with some of her friends, but Schenck said no deal, it was Harriet's charter, no grown-ups allowed. A lunch was brought aboard in hampers, accompanied by Arthur. Joey and two other crewmen took the boat roaring up the bay to a small deserted island, not at full speed, but none of Harriet's friends knew that, and there they anchored and Arthur served them lunch. While they ate, Joey performed flips on the foredeck that had them screaming. He did not acknowledge his fresh, young, slightly perspiring audience, or make eye contact with the young ladies. He appeared to perform for himself, and his tight-lipped face and averted eyes made it all the funnier. The girls became hysterical. *Monte*, one of the Rivas Schenck had bought in Monte Carlo, followed *Tally Ho!* up the bay and took the girls ashore after lunch for a swim. They had the little island to themselves, and they all agreed it was just like Robinson Crusoe. Despite their bathing hats and jersey costumes, all the young ladies returned home with fetching sunburns on their arms and legs and faces.

IN THE MIDDLE OF June, in a manner of announcing themselves, the Schencks held a ball at Aquitaine. It was far too early, they gave rashly insufficient notice, and the date conflicted with other engagements everybody else had already made. But the newcomers and their noisy boat and what they might have done to poor Dickie Biddle's Aquitaine proved too tempting. Excuses were made, commitments were broken, and in the end absolutely everybody came.

The cottage was not the largest or grandest in Newport, but like the best of them, it contained many fabulous and singular features. Mamie had already made some alterations with the help of Gratian James, who had started out at McKim, Mead, and White, and gone off on his own to great success. The Schencks' guests that June evening remarked on the new silver grilles on top of the translucent alabaster panels lining the vestibule entrance. They went so well with Hunt's original silver staircase that had been modeled after that in the Petit Trianon at Versailles. It had been polished until it gleamed like new coinage. Roman Doric doorpieces were a feature throughout. The library—described by Samuel Johnson (who had perused some of its volumes on his tour of Scotland with his biographer Boswell in 1773) as one of the finest in the land—had been purchased by Hunt entire, complete with armchairs, carpets, lamps, paneling, and plasterwork, from Newhailes House in Scotland, sold by an impoverished Earl of Galloway. Mamie took the ladies upstairs to show them around. Many of them, Bellevue neighbors, had of course been through the house before, but the silver bathtubs surrounded by a dark blue Italian marble shot through with fossilized sea creatures—a James touch—were new to them, as were the frescoes on the ceilings above the tubs. Portraits of the Schencks' newly acquired ancestors hung everywhere on the walls.

Mamie shone as she greeted her guests, standing not far from her portrait in the central foyer. The painting itself was of considerable note, being one of the last commissioned portraits done by John Singer Sargent. It had been painted while the Schencks and Sargent were staying at the Charles Deerings at Brickell Point, Miami, in 1921. Sargent had come to Florida to paint John D. Rockefeller. It had cost Schenck $10,000, donated to charity in Sargent's name. It was an unusually informal composition, showing Mamie turning slightly, looking up, smiling a little to herself, Sargent having caught her, as it were, in the middle of some amused thought, and she looked, quite credibly, beautiful. She had changed since the date of the portrait, thickened out to the shape of a sea buoy, her face fallen below her jawline, but her guests could see that her beauty had been real and the artist true. It was a Sargent, after all.

What was more, and afterward talked about for days by the ladies who had observed the host and hostess when they were together that night: whenever he turned to her, or introduced her, or listened to her, it was apparent to anyone that Carl Schenck was still in love with his wife. When he looked at Mamie he obviously saw the woman in the portrait. It was irresistibly charming to see, and quickly deflected all the silly things the ladies of Newport might have said about them, or about Mamie's French gown. Mamie's giddy enthusiasm as she showed them around the house was infectious, and Schenck's loud, vulgar manner could be seen as something boyish and really quite sweet. As a couple, it was agreed, they went well with the house.

Harriet pulled Cindy and Alison and her other new friends away from their parents as they arrived and took them through the house and outside again, where two canopies had been erected on the lawn sloping from the house to the sea. Under one a small orchestra was playing jazz, and under the other Harriet's friends were served cocktails and Coca-Cola. They ogled the musicians and then walked down to the dock to see who was arriving by boat, and then they ran up to the house and went inside to explore. Harriet herself had not been everywhere in the house yet, so they managed to become lost in an upstairs wing and separated into small groups and screamed and whooped like children to find each other again. Finally they discovered a staircase that led down to a pantry, and they spilled out a door onto the lawn and hiked up their dresses and raced shrieking down to the water. The summer equinox was a week away and it stayed light until late, though the green lawn darkened imperceptibly and the girls' bright white dresses slowly faded into ivory silks and linens. It was one of those summer evenings that went on forever and ever.

A number of guests came by water. A succession of craft, gleaming in coats of enamel and varnish, rumbled alongside the Aquitaine dock, deposited their passengers, and moved off to anchor fore-and-aft in neat parallel rows in the rocky cove that embraced the Aquitaine property. Larger craft remained offshore in the cove, their passengers descending ships' "ladders"—what might ashore be called rather solid staircases—into smaller tenders, which ferried them to the dock. Dockhands held lines and fenders, and footmen accompanied alighting guests up the crushed seashell path to the refreshment canopy or to the house.

At seven o'clock, a boat hove in sight beyond the cove. It loomed in the humid air between the flat sea and the sky like an apparition, nothing close by to give it scale. It approached so slowly as to barely make headway, but it grew, and swelled, and acquired definition. As it reached the arms of the cove and passed between them, turning slowly to show its whole broadside, its true size became apparent, and people on other boats, on the dock, up the lawn, under the canopies, and in the house, turned to watch.

"Carl, what on earth is that ship doing here?" said Mamie, who had followed her husband out onto the patio. "Is it the navy, do you think?"

"No, it's Dudley Carroll, cupcake. He's come for supper."

They stared, silent for a minute, and then Schenck said, "And that's *Lodestar*," and he walked quickly down the path to the dock.

He had seen *Lodestar* only once, in 1929, on an air trip to Florida. She was then owned by Vincent Astor. He had flown over her as she was traveling south in the waterway above Palm Beach. A tantalizing glimpse. And yet she had often frequented the waters on which he too traveled, and he had always failed to meet her by a series of unlikely near misses. He knew her much better by reputation: designed by Cox and Stevens, built by the Bath Iron Works in Maine in 1915, she was 225 feet long, powered by two Bath-built steam turbines that developed 7000 horsepower—sufficient (as the cryptic engineers at Rolls Royce might have put it) for a destroyer. Her first owner, John Parks LeClair, had used her to travel between his offices in Manhattan and his 52-acre estate in Oyster Bay, and it was said that before he could stroll up her portside deck and down her starboard, his short commute would be over. She was famous for the damage repeatedly caused by her wake. Vincent Astor had kept her only two years before deciding she was inconveniently large for the docks at his estates north and south. Dudley Carroll had taken her back to Bath for a refit, and afterward largely cruised her in Maine waters. She was only in Newport now, Schenck had heard, because it was still early in the season and too chilly in Maine for Mrs. Carroll.

Schenck reached the dock and hopped into *Monte*. Joey was immediately behind him, quick as a gundog, throwing off lines and starting the low rumbling gasoline engines.

"Take me out to her, Joey."

The Riva came alongside the long black hull as *Lodestar*'s foredeck crew was letting go her anchors. Her ladder—a generously scaled affair of teak, deeply varnished except for the bare grated treads, with a handrail of large-diameter white silk rope—was lowered from davits by more liveried crewmembers, and Schenck climbed up to the deck.

"Glad you could make it, Carroll!"

The two men had met on several occasions at the American Yacht Club in Rye, and in the city at Fraunces Tavern, but they were only casual acquaintances. They had talked only of boats. Dudley Carroll, third-generation banker, associated mainly with his own crowd: men with whom he had played as a child, schooled, and done business, and their wives and children and mistresses. Schenck was in fact surprised to see him responding to his invitation. But he had heard that Dudley Carroll had taken a bit of a fall; he had even heard that Carroll was ruined, but he didn't believe it. However, the air was thick nowadays with tales like that of Samuel Insull: for thirty-five years the strongest name in American business, political kingmaker, supplier of electricity to half a continent, one day controlling a light and power empire worth three billion dollars, the next day in receivership, and very soon afterward, a fugitive in Greece. (Why Greece? everybody said. Did he have family there?) After that, no man appeared immune in the wake of the Crash. It was entirely possible that Dudley Carroll too might be feeling the pinch. It was under such circumstances that men's behavior changed, and they did things they had never done before, because they had never had reason. So Schenck wondered that Dudley Carroll had come to supper in *Lodestar*.

"Mrs. Carroll wanted to go to a party," said Carroll, a large man, overweight, thick gray hair cut to short bristles. He was badly sunburned, or plagued by rosacea, and appeared to be wearing a creased dickey of a size too small under his dinner jacket, something he might have borrowed from a slimmer servant, for a gray undershirt could be seen at its edges beneath his jacket lapels. His bare, purple-mottled, water-filled ankles were visible beneath his trouser cuffs, above the tennis shoes worn without socks or laces. "Have a drink. Let me show you the old tub."

He took Schenck below to the owner's quarters, adequately furnished, with gold toilet fixtures, but the cabins for six beneath the aft saloon were not roomy. The engine room, housing the gleaming and refurbished steam turbines, the fireroom, and the coal bunkers, took up the greater part of the yacht's midship length. Schenck admired the ship-sized pipes, and the commercial scale of the machinery belowdecks, although Carroll did not seem to know or care much about this. Forward of the main saloon and dining room was the galley, beneath it the captain's cabin and head. In the fo'c'sle the crew's quarters, with accommodation for fifteen. There was not room for a large complement of crew and guests, but the ship had, after all, been built simply as a commuter.

Up on the bridge, forward of the two funnels, Carroll introduced his skipper, Captain Percival, an Englishman in his forties who wore a beard that was luxuriant in its moustaches, pointed at the chin, and closely clipped toward the ears, after the fashion of the British Navy. He put those old enough to remember in mind of Edward VII, the longtime Prince of Wales and nine-year king, and of his cousin, the late Czar Nicholas of Russia. He made an imposing figure in his navy double-breasted jacket, with brass buttons and white hat, and spoke with an accent that many of *Lodestar*'s American passengers took to be finely bred. He ignored Schenck until Carroll introduced them, and then nodded his head and said, "Afternoon," crisply, without appearing to move his mouth beyond shaping a small opening, and then gave himself over to the observation of his crew's activities on the foredeck.

The two men walked aft to join Mrs. Carroll, who sat with another lady in large wicker chairs on *Lodestar*'s canvas-covered fantail aft deck. One of the ship's gasoline launches was already pulling away from the ladder, carrying three men in dinner jackets toward the dock.

"Duddy, are you ready?" said Mrs. Dudley Carroll. "Gray and the boys have gone ashore. They wouldn't wait. Cynthia and I are famished."

HARRIET HAD BEEN SUMMONED away from her friends by her mother, who asked her to remain with her in the main hall to greet their guests. Sometimes her mother left her alone for minutes at a time as she took guests into the drawing room, or out onto the patio. Harriet said hello and good evening to one person after another for more than an hour, until the sounds of those words lost their meanings and she heard herself uttering polite gibberish. She became so aware of her smile that she lost the ordinary reflex of it and felt her face creasing into insincere grimaces. She grew terribly thirsty, but she couldn't stand there sipping a drink while she said hello and good evening and smiled with all her strength.

"Hello, good evening," she said, and it was Gar Chamberlain Jr. in front of her.

"Hello, Harriet," he said.

Gar was twenty-one, a year older than Harriet, tall, with nearly black hair that usually fell into his blue eyes. With his height, he gave a first impression of slimness, and she had always thought of Gar as skinny. And handsome. But she had not seen him for almost a year, and now she noticed a soft slackness in his body, a puffiness in his face. He was still handsome, but no longer beautiful.

Two years earlier they had spent much of the summer together. Gar had taken her out in her snipe to improve her sailing skills.

"Now don't hold on to the tiller like that," he had said the first time, picking up her hand and shaking it gently. "Relax, don't grip. Look at the tiller. See? It's got a life of its own. You don't yank it. You've got to feel it, and then respond." His touch had sent a charge through her body.

She had looked down at the slender, arcing, varnished length of wood, three feet long but no more than an inch wide. It trembled as the snipe moved to windward.

Gar had pulled her hand down into his lap. "See?" he said. "Same thing here."

But she had surprised him. She had opened his buttons and pulled her underpants aside and climbed on top of him, and the snipe's mainsail swung wide and flopped and shuddered in the breeze while she maneuvered herself above Gar. What she had really found funny, and sweet for a while, was that Gar thought it had been his idea. They went out in their snipes a lot that summer, and to country club dances in Gar's Chrysler coupe. Then she got into trouble, but her mother took her into New York and had it taken care of. Her father never knew about it. She did not tell her mother who the boy was. She certainly had not told Gar. At the end of the summer, to his great confusion, she dropped him without a word.

He had come up, he was saying now, with the Emmetts, as guests of the Carrolls, on board *Lodestar*. He was grinning at her, but a little nervously, she thought.

Gar said good evening to her mother, and then moved on, with Gray Emmett and his son, Critchell, into the crowd in the drawing room.

Later, when the arrivals slowed and her mother let her go, Cindy McCann said, "Who are those two boys you were talking to? They came off that gigantic boat! Let's get them to take us aboard!"

They found the boys drinking gin slings in the refreshment tent. Critchell was as tall as Gar, though skinnier, and both boys were sunburned and looked dashing in their dinner jackets, their hair slicked back.

Cindy said, "We want to go aboard that boat. Will you take us?"

"Sure," said Critchell, grinning.

But at that moment a man dressed as a huntsman, in shiny boots, red tails, and a top hat, appeared on the patio above the tents and blew a long horn.

"Oh, it's suppertime," said Harriet.

AFTER DINNER, SCHENCK TOOK some of the men into the smoking room—a dark, ancient-seeming cloistered space, hung with paintings of hunting themes by Sir Henry Raeburn, and lit this evening entirely by candles stuck into odd, round, dented iron candelabra that had formerly been cannonballs fired during the siege of Paris in 1871.

Schenck poured brandy and lit his guests' Monte Cristos, and the dense smoke drifted across the candlelight and sank into the vespertine paneling while the men discussed the parlous state of business. Schenck could not complain, he said. No matter how dismal the country's economy, ever-increasing numbers of people seemed inclined to buy cars with headlamps provided by the Prest-O-Lite company. His contracts with Ford and other manufacturers were secure. He had scientists and inventors working around the clock to stymie or stay ahead of developments produced by his would-be competitors, and he had firm friends at the patent office down in Washington.

Gray Emmett, his silver-haired patrician looks marred by fat lips that distended grossly around his cigar, remarked that he had pulled out of the market in January '29. His money was in Switzerland, and in the Bank of England, although he had gone in with Bernie Baruch and Joe Kennedy on a piece of the Brooklyn Manhattan Transit Corporation. Herb Swope, a boardmember of BMT, had told Baruch that the city's transit system would be unified in the next year and BMT was set to make a killing. He looked at his cigar and then rolled it between wet lips.

Bayard Vogler, one of Schenck's Newport neighbors, whose manufacturing concerns appeared so far unscathed, said that he had recently bought, for cash, four estates in Maine, New Jersey, Rhinebeck on the Hudson, and on Fisher's Island. The prices had simply been too good. He had put a skeleton staff in each, with orders to do no more than maintain, and when, in a few years, people were buying large houses again, he would sell quite handsomely.

As they smoked, Dudley Carroll remained silent. He had removed his battered tennis shoes and stuck out his bare purple feet toward the fireplace as if a fire had been burning there. Presently, he appeared to fall asleep.

By turns, the men finished their Havanas, put down their glasses, and left the room, until at last only Schenck and Dudley Carroll remained. Then Carroll opened his eyes and Schenck, who had been waiting to hear it, learned why he had come.

IT WAS DARK WHEN they reached the dock. Gar found a slender Whitehall with long oars across its thwarts.

"I guess we can use this."

He stepped onto the center thwart and held the boat steady alongside the dock as the others stepped in. Cindy and Critchell sat bunched together in the narrow stern and Harriet settled into the bow. Critchell placed his arm tentatively over Cindy's shoulder, and she slumped against him.

Gar dropped the oars into the oarlocks and pushed off. He spun the boat around, pulling at one oar and pushing with the other, and then leaned back, pulling hard on both oars, feathering between strokes as if rowing a shell, and the boat slid fast and quietly away from the shore. *Lodestar* filled the small cove like a liner, its bright lights and their striated reflections across the water bringing down a wall of darkness at the edge of that great pool of light, obscuring everything around it except the dazzling mansion above the lawn.

In the bow, moving backward toward the ship, Harriet

looked at Gar's back as he rowed, his head occasionally turning sideways toward her to see where he was going, and at Cindy and Critchell snuggling in the stern fourteen feet away. Then she leaned back on her elbows and looked up into the indigo sky, and she saw the Big Dipper. The cooking pot, as she always thought of it. Her eyes moved along the imaginary line running off through space from the two stars at the end of the pot, and she found the North Star. It was low down in the sky, but blinking brightly.

Gar brought the Whitehall alongside the ship's ladder and held it steady as Cindy, Critchell, and Harriet stepped onto the ladder platform, aided by one of *Lodestar*'s uniformed crew.

The boys took them on a tour, circuiting once the long, narrow deck. They pointed out the enormous windlass and the size of the anchor chain, and the horizontal dumbwaiter that carried snacks or whole meals one hundred and sixty feet from the galley forward to the bar on the aft deck. As they strolled around the boat, the crew remained discreetly out of sight, and the elegant young people had the impression of having the great ship all to themselves.

"I want to see the bedrooms," said Cindy. "Can we go downstairs?"

"Sure," said Critchell. His protuberant Adam's apple bobbed.

The boys took them down to the owner's suite.

"I thought it would be bigger," said Cindy. "It's small."

"Well, the boat's only twenty-one feet wide, and half its length, about a hundred feet of it, is taken up with the engines," Gar said.

"Where's your cabin?" Cindy asked Critchell.

Critchell grinned at Gar. "I'll show you."

Cindy and Critchell moved down the paneled hallway.

"I'm hot," said Harriet. "I want to go back up on deck, if you don't mind."

"I'll come up with you," said Gar.

They stood by the rail looking out over the cove and smoked cigarettes. The music of the orchestra and voices and laughter came across the water.

"So. How long are you cruising?" asked Harriet.

"Well, I came up with Critch, but I've been talking with Captain Percival, and I might stay aboard for a while."

"Wouldn't you get bored?"

"No, I'd stay on as a deckhand."

It was a moment before Harriet thought she understood. "Do you mean you'd go to work for Mr. Carroll as crew?"

"Yes, that's right," said Gar, smiling at her.

"Would that be fun for you?"

"I think so. But it does mean I'll be one of the boys in white, fetching and carrying and snapping to it."

"I don't understand, Gar. Why would you want to do that?"

"Well, you probably heard. I had to drop out of Yale. My old man's broke. I've got to get a job, so I thought I'd try this."

"For the summer, you mean."

"No. I'd like to be a captain someday. Do what Captain Percival does, skippper one of these babies."

"How would you make any money?"

"I'll make twenty-five dollars a week to start. I get a bunk and all the grub I can eat." He looked at her uncomprehending face and he laughed.

"That's not funny. I believed you."

"I'm serious!" he said, but he was still laughing.

"You're not at all."

"I am! Really."

"But Gar, what does a captain make? You've got some money, but still—"

"No, I don't have any money, Harriet. I told you, my old man is broke. Jumping out the window broke. He lost more than all of it. My old man's got about seven million dollars less than the guys on the streets selling apples."

"What do you mean?"

"I mean, he had that much on margin. He lost everything he's worth and that much more."

"But . . . What are you living on?"

"On Critch right now. My mother feeds me when I'm at home. I don't know where she's getting it, but she's got grocery money."

"What about your house? And . . ."

"The house is for sale, and everything in it. The servants are gone mostly. The mighty have fallen." Gar pulled on his cigarette and blew a smoke ring out over the water.

She could not believe it. Gar looked so handsome and wealthy, which was simply all that he was. Now he was telling her that he had lost the most crucial part of himself, the only part that might be of interest to anyone else. He would be nothing without money. It was as if he had told her he was dying while he still looked so well.

"Gar, I'm sorry. I don't know what to say."

"It's okay."

"But . . . there are other things you could do. Why don't you go into business?"

"Business isn't too good right now, Harriet. I don't know anything about it anyway. I never understood what my father did and all I can figure out now is that he didn't either. I like boats, though. I understand them and how they work, and I like being on them. So I'm going to try to stay aboard *Lodestar* for now. I'll go where she goes."

Harriet was shocked. Of course this was happening everywhere, but not to anybody she knew well, or had grown up with. Girls she had gone to school with had suddenly become poor after the Crash, but she had known Gar since she was small and had moved east from Minnesota. Her newly poor girlfriends had moved, some had found jobs, others were looking, but it seemed less terrible for girls. They could always get married. They could do things that men could not. She couldn't imagine being interested in a man who worked on a boat. She felt terribly sorry for Gar.

"Gar, is there anything I can do for you?"

"You could let me kiss you."

She felt so sad for him that she didn't mind at all.

"All right."

Gar threw his cigarette into the water and put an arm around Harriet's waist and pulled her close. "My last chance to consort with a lady," he said, grinning as if it were all such a joke. Then he bent his head and kissed her lips. He put his other arm around her. Harriet felt nothing. And then her body awoke to a memory, and she felt herself sink into Gar, and he felt it too, and pulled her closer. She pushed him away.

"Just a kiss, Gar."

"Okay," he said, and laughed. "What do you think those other two are up to?"

"Let's get them. I'd like to go back ashore."

"Yes, ma'am."

CHAPTER 7

THEY FOUND NO SUITABLE vessel in Fairhaven, or in New Bedford or Boston, and they headed north and east.

They drove through the pretty old villages, Revere, Swampscott, and Salem, an easterly blowing a short chop onshore, and the sun unable to hide the paint-peeling boarded-up sag and quiet of hard times.

Another day and night in Gloucester, where the local fisherman and his schooner had found fame on the Grand Banks to match the Basques and the Portuguese. But now the banker's mark was on the town, and fishing boats were everywhere for sale. Prices ranged from good to giveaway, but there were no takers, and men stood along the broken waterfront, adrift but held together in groups by common talk and ruin. The huge cheerful billboards of folks having a ball with Beech-Nut gum, Mom ladling out Campbell's Soup to her delighted family, and the Ipana toothpaste girl dazzlingly munching her leg of lamb looked misplaced in Gloucester, like unseemly memories of peacetime in a war zone. Boden and Shred saw no sealers. They asked around in the bars and shipyards and were always told the same place to go: farther north.

"Up in Bath, maybe."

"There might be a few of that kind in Portsmouth, making ready to go north right now."

"Lunenburg. See them Charbonneau fellas."

They drove north through Portland, Rockland, and Bath, and sent wires to St. John and Halifax.

North of Portland, Boden and Shred saw no more sullen huddles of defeated men standing on the docks or smoking outside bars and diners. Mainers ashore and afloat seemed better off than people farther south. Houses possessed all their shingles. Lobsterboats and skiffs had been painted over the winter. Watermen went about their business; their outfits were smaller, their lives more austere. They had built their own boats and pots and small houses; their docks stood up; they ran their jalopies into the ground, and every yard floated one or two rusting wrecks sinking into the weeds, a kitchen garden of spare parts. They had little truck with banks, and those who did had not overreached themselves. In Maine, things had not gone too bad. The State of Maine, they all called it, making it sound like another country, and so it seemed.

Fellow on a lobsterboat in Rockland said Belfast, for sure. He'd seen her there: a Norwegian boat, peculiar-looking, don't you know, maybe what they were after. Moored off the cannery, up the Passagassawaukeag.

"Oh, sure," they said in Belfast. "She was in here. Norwegian. Funny koinda boat. Funny name too. Isby-somethin'."

"Come again?"

"I-S-B-J-O-R-N," a man spelled.

"Where'd she go?"

"Dunno."

They had been a week on the road. They were still driving north at eight o'clock on a Sunday night, and they heard *Amos 'n' Andy* on the Chevrolet's radio. Boden had called Schenck with their empty-handed news, daily to begin with, as instructed. He telephoned in the evenings, not always finding Mr. Schenck at home and then leaving a message with Arthur. He had skipped a day north of Gloucester, when he had been dispirited, thinking they would never find a boat, and realizing that Schenck would forget all about it soon enough and none of it mattered anyway because they were on a fool's errand, and the next day Schenck had reiterated firmly that he wanted to hear from him every day. He wanted to know exactly where they were and where they were headed, and the tone in his voice said he was not forgetting anything. Boden's spirits rose. He started daydreaming again about the Arctic. The evening he telephoned from Belfast, Schenck said he was going up to Newport the next day and gave Boden the Newport phone number and told him to keep calling. Every day.

They drove east through Maine. They spent a night at Stonington, on Deer Isle. Small white houses amid as many house-sized clumps of granite on grassy hills that looked out to the islands of the Deer Isle Thorofare; heaps of rock and fir trees all the way to Isle au Haut. They stayed in the Lookout Hotel, a spare white house between two brethren rocks on a hill. Boden telephoned Newport and left his news with Arthur: where they were; no boat here; they saw nothing for it but to take the ferry to Nova Scotia and look in Halifax.

They ate lobsters in a shack on the waterfront. The woman who brought their food smiled at Boden and he found himself lonely and thinking of his wife, Mary. After supper Shred went along the street to a bar, and Boden took a walk.

It was light far into the evening in this State of Maine. Boden walked along the waterfront street. He followed the road up a short hill past the houses of lobstermen with stacks of pots in their yards, and he looked at their lives. He was soon walking northwest out of town, following the coast along the edge of Penobscot Bay. More small houses through the trees. You could buy land for reasonable money here, he thought. He imagined working one of these little saltwater farms, with a meadow going down to the rocky water's edge, and the Camden Hills dark against the red sky across the bay every evening. Get a simple boat to work alongshore. He could do it. It was not too late to settle somewhere and start again. He might make enough on this job, to come back here and get a toehold.

But it would be starting again without Mary, and still he did not know how to do that. She had to stay close to New York for the work she had found illustrating books for a publisher; work she had come by after years of submission and rejection. But without his own ship to run, New York had proven a cold harbor for Boden. There were as many jobs for sailing ship masters as there were for moon rocketeers, but he had aimed his whole life at that role, read himself into it with books, contrived a way to do it, and grown to feel it was something he did well. Beached, with his ship lost to him, he found he had trained and inclined himself into a rare redundancy.

He went out every day to look for any work at all. He had not been able to sit at home idle or fretting while his wife drew and painted in the next room, although over and over she insisted that, until things got better, she could make enough for two. He went out of the house when there was the certainty of no work (although his ideas of what work he might do changed as time went on). And even had there been any work, in too many places his sour fame had preceded him: along the waterfront, people had read or heard of the captain who'd abandoned his own ship. Finally he had taken the job his cousin Howard had been offering him at his printing shop in Brooklyn, and Boden had spent a week wearing a suit and tie and feeling useless and confused and growing ashamed at being the object of his cousin's charity. He quit. And then home, for all its warmth, became the location of his unendurable shame, and in the end he had crawled away. He grew to despise himself for his shame, and then to punish himself, he denied himself what he loved.

Boden didn't believe he could hold a job with Schenck for long, but a trip north might lead in some way he couldn't yet see to some other more permanent job on the water. He didn't know what, but his hope, still alive, was that he might still find a way to go home.

IN THE MORNING, a telephone call came to the Lookout Hotel for Boden. Through a crackling like frying oil, Moyle came on the line far down in New York.

"There's a boat down here you might want to look at. You found anything up there?"

"Nothing. What have you got?"

"It's what you want. Wood, built for ice work. She's a sealer out of some place in Norway. Come down here from Greenland to be sold. Nobody told 'em we got a depression, but they got one too. She's going cheap."

"Where is she?"

"Brooklyn. Up the Gowanus."

"Good shape?"

"Fair enough. Not too old. But strong. You won't see many like her."

"What's her name?"

"Isbyorn. Something like that."

"I'll be down the end of tomorrow, have a look at her the day after. Will she stay put?"

"She's going nowhere."

"I'll come for you in the car Friday morning."

Over breakfast in the same place they had eaten supper, they decided Shred would take the ferry to Halifax, see what was there, and return to New York by boat and train. Boden would drive south to look at the Norwegian boat.

"I been cooped up indoors with this leg for weeks," said Shred, who was happy to go on to Halifax. "I need to keep moving for a while."

HE DROVE ALL THE way through New England in two days, Maine nearly the half of it. A far different pace from the poking, harbor-spotting sort of Sunday drive he and Shred had taken. He ate on the move and stopped at a tourist court south of Boston in the late blue twilight of the first night.

It was strange to haul up at Meyer's Hotel at five-thirty in the afternoon and park outside his own door on South Street. He ate an expensive steak and drank two glasses of beer at Rolfe's Chop House around the corner on Fulton Street, went back to the hotel and made himself have a bath, and climbed into bed at seven. His body still carried the hum of his long drive. When he fell asleep, he had driving dreams of pushing the car through another town. He woke again and lay a long time thinking about Maine and how beautiful it was up there. Later in the night he dreamed he was back aboard his ship, the *Mary Boden*, all canvas set, running through the ice too fast, at automobile speed, great bergs tearing past close alongside but miraculously not touching, and yet the ship was driving down a narrowing lead into thicker ice, and up ahead lay the impenetrable pack, and he could not turn her or stop her because the wind at his back was too great.

* * *

AT NINE THE NEXT morning he picked up Moyle at a diner on Flatbush Avenue. They drove south to Sunset Park. Signs in Norwegian were painted in restaurant windows: KEITTOKIRJA—5¢; SILLI PERUNAT—7¢; LIHA PULLIA—10¢.

"This guy's Scandahoovian. They're all Scandahoovian down here," said Moyle. He said the sealer they were going to see had done five seasons in the Arctic and then come down to a Norwegian American family in New York as part of an inheritance from the old country.

They stopped at an apartment building at Forty-third and Fifth and Moyle went inside. He came out with a man younger than Boden, wearing a brown suit. Nordahl, said Moyle. They got into the car and Nordahl directed Boden north again up Fourth Avenue to the Gowanus Canal. The boat lay rising and falling against a rotting wharf behind a warehouse. Nordahl led them aboard.

Boden paced off the deck: about a hundred and twelve feet long, thirty of beam. A workboat, but she was clean, even handsome. She had a large wheelhouse aft, and a cuddy forward leading to the crew's fo'c'sle. Her fir decks appeared recently scrubbed clean. She had some new paint on her. Her mast, which would carry a steadying sail but functioned mainly as a hoist and derrick, and the massive oak bitts forward had been oiled, and the wood glowed.

Nordahl ran off the main details. She had been launched in Tromsø, Norway five years ago. Her hull built up of nine layers of wood, the outer skin being greenheart for the ice, the whole of the planking twenty-two inches thick, riveted and through-bolted to frames ten by twelve and ten by fourteen inches. Steel plate covered the bow and forefoot. Her engine was a two-hundred-horse Bolinder diesel, with tankage giving a range of fourteen thousand miles, or seventy days at full speed.

"Well, we can go below," said Nordahl, who had the best poker face Boden had ever seen.

There were four double cabins aft, grouped around the saloon. A serviceable head. A bulkhead separated saloon from engine room, which ran the full beam amidships. Forward through another bulkhead, the galley, and then the crew's quarters, holding twenty berths, and the crew's head. The plain pine tongue-and-groove paneling everywhere was painted white, with oiled pine trim. It was not fancy, not yachtlike, and Boden liked it.

He looked over the engine. Then he dropped into the bilge forward, midships, and aft, noting the massive scantlings of the ship's construction and finding no rot. She was sound. Once he knew that, he became aware of the feeling he only sometimes got when he made the acquaintance of a ship: a mix of admiration, affection, and something oddly tender. If he took her to sea and got to know her, and she performed well under difficult conditions, the feeling could expand into a form of love, and a relationship could form that might resemble an ideal marriage. If he was lucky, a man might come across a few such boats in a lifetime.

Up on deck, Boden told Nordahl he thought the ship would be suitable for their purposes; he would recommend it, and probably bring others back to look it over again. He asked if Nordahl would consider a charter for the summer. He would, but he would rather sell. He wanted twelve thousand dollars.

"That might be high," said Boden.

"You don't see another one like her on this east coast," said Nordahl.

They shook hands and drove back to Nordahl's apartment and dropped him off.

"What do you think?" said Moyle as they drove back up Fourth Avenue.

"It's a good boat."

"You think your big man'll like her?"

"I have no idea. But if he wants to go north, that's the boat. There's nothing else."

THAT SAME AFTERNOON HE drove to Newport to talk with Schenck. He had telephoned him about the *Isbjørn*.

"Good job!" Schenck had said over the phone. "Come on up and we'll talk." And he gave Boden directions for finding Aquitaine Castle.

As he drove north again along the Boston Post Road, the Connecticut towns blurred and he drove automatically. He thought the whole time about the *Isbjørn* and what he would have to do to her to take her north. He thought about how she would respond in thick weather. He was conscious of the deep excitement of preparing for sea again, of the sense of using himself in his best capacity, which he had almost despaired of ever doing again. Stout and sound and suited for the ice as the vessel was, Boden knew it would take all of him, his whole mind and heart and all his sailorly skill, to take her into the high Arctic with a man like Schenck aboard.

He had once believed there was nothing in life he did better than command a vessel at sea. Over and over he had tried to relive every moment in the sequence of events leading to his abandoning the *Mary Boden* and he wanted to believe that he would do the same again. Sinking as he left her, she should have sunk, but he had been wrong. An irrevocable mistake that had branded him a Jonah—as much to himself as to anyone else. He knew things would not be right in him until he again took a ship to sea, and he thought this was almost certainly his last chance.

IN HIS BLUE SUIT, brown derby on his head, Clement Shred sat in Charbonneau's Blue Moule Bar in Lunenburg, throwing back as much of a locally renowned rotgut Nova Scotian whiskey as he could before catching the boat to Halifax, and from there the steamer to Boston.

Through the window beyond the bar, ranging around Lunenburg's harbor, lay the Charbonneau empire. The phonebook hereabouts along the Nova Scotia coast was thick with C's. The Charbonneaus made workboats for which there seemed a considerable demand; and they also made every last item you could bolt onto a craft: Charbonneau lignum vitae blocks, the Charbonneau windlass, the famous Charbonneau worm gear connecting helm and rudder; there was a Charbonneau bronze foundry, a Charbonneau galvanizing plant, a forge, a sail loft, a ropewalk, all owned by Charbonneaus and kin. They turned out stoves, anchors, bolts, nails. You name it, somewhere out there around Lunenburg, a Charbonneau was knocking one out this minute. This Canuck clan had prospered in a wonderful fashion, wholly unlike the equally widespread but dwindling strain of Shred in the far south. Shred admired it all and it made him feel that he had sprung from a lower order of Creation.

Home now to City Island and her indoors. He picked up his full glass and drank half of it, and involuntarily squeezed his eyes shut. He had been happy on the road. A traveling man, staying in hotels, breakfast, lunch, and supper on expenses. A man with a noble mission: find a good ship. Happiest he had been, he realized, since those days after he left Fairhaven and traveled south in his skiff, seeing the world.

Back to his job, the nature of which still confounded him: a marine rabbit's foot for the boss was the best he could figure it. And home to Hezzie and her unhappy view of the world.

He stood up, drinking off the last of the Canuck moonshine, put too much money on the bar, and staggered outside.

ARTHUR SHOWED BODEN INTO the smoking room. In a moment Schenck came in. He was tanner than when Boden had last seen him in Greenwich, and, if possible, more energetic.

"Great job!" he said. "Hope you had fun too." He handed Boden a check for two hundred dollars more than was owed to him. "I put a bonus in there because you did a great job, and you found a ship. I knew you would."

Boden could hear it. He knew everything was wrong.

"I'm sure you'll want to come down to New York to see her," he said, and he knew the answer before he heard it.

"No need. We won't be using her. I found another boat to go in. Come on out."

Through a long high foyer beneath chandeliers, then out onto a patio. Rolling lawn fell away to the rocky shore and a small cove. And the ship.

"There she is," said Schenck. "*Lodestar*. How do you like her?"

Thinking about it, Boden was not surprised. Schenck was only being true to form.

"You can't go in that vessel."

"Why not? Look at the size of that thing."

He knew, as he started, that it was useless. "It's the wrong shape, it won't take the ice—"

"She'll do great! Thirty miles per hour! Get up there in three days. I just bought her. I'm taking her up into the Arctic as far as we can go. It's all set. I'm going to take pictures and *Motor Boating*'s going to do a spread of *Lodestar* up there in the ice with all the polar bears for the Christmas issue. I think she'll be the biggest ship that ever went up there, and certainly the first yacht. It's going to be a hell of a thing."

"That boat will not be safe in the Arctic. I could not be responsible for your welfare."

"Well, Captain Percival thinks she'll do fine."

"Who is Captain Percival?"

"He's the captain aboard her now. He came with the boat."

"I was under the impression that you wanted me to skipper the vessel you took north."

"We talked about that, you're right. And if we'd've gone in this boat you found down in Brooklyn, that's the way we'd've done it. But Captain Percival came with *Lodestar* and he's been on her for years, and knows the boat inside and out."

"Has he sailed in the Arctic?"

"No, but he got his stripes in the Royal Navy in the war. Sunk a bunch of German ships and got a chestful of medals. I think he knows his way through a tight spot. He said he's going to treat any icebergs like a kraut cruiser!" Schenck put his hands on his hips and laughed.

A minute later Schenck was still talking, and Boden heard him again.

". . . I want you to come with us. You've been up there. There's no substitute for that. I want you aboard and I'll pay you well. What do you say?"

"No, thank you. It's an unsafe venture in such a vessel. It's not built for the ice and if you get into ice you may not get out—"

"I'm bringing dynamite. We get caught in any ice, we'll blow our way out."

"You might as well bring firecrackers. In any case, I doubt you'll be able to insure that vessel for such a trip."

"I got insurance already. Lloyds of London. They'll insure me to the North Pole as long as I pay their goddamn premium. I'm telling you, it's going to be a great trip, we're going to be in the Christmas issue of *Motor Boating* magazine, and we're going to shoot every animal in sight. This is going to be a hell of a trip. I want you to come along."

"No thanks."

Boden declined a ride and walked to Newport station. He took a train back to New York.

CHAPTER 8

S CHENCK SENT *LODESTAR* AND Captain Percival
down to New York to outfit the ship for its cruise north.
Fortunately, the ship had been built with steam-sup-
plied central heating piped into every cabin, into the bridge and
saloon, and the crew's quarters forward. Schenck, who
thought that summer in the Arctic could be no colder than
spring on Lake Superior, and Captain Percival, who had told
Schenck how he had chased the Hun through the Shetlands in
frightful March weather, both agreed that the interior of the
ship should be toasty up north in August.

Lodestar was dry-docked for a week in the Brooklyn Navy
Yard—the only dry dock south of Bath large enough to accommodate her. She had not been dried out in Bath yet this year, so
her hull below the waterline was painted with antifouling copper, her sacrificial zinc anodes were replaced, her propellers
buffed. From there the ship steamed to City Island, where she
lay alongside the St. Clair docks, and men began to swarm all
over her. Canvas spray cloths were made to lash along the rails
during heavy weather; locker boxes for extra line and gear
were fixed to the foredeck. Schenck wanted to bring both Rivas, *Monte* and *Carlo* as tenders, for they were smarter than
Lodestar's own launch, and additional davits were installed
amidships to carry the two boats. Two pulling boats of different sizes, a fifteen-foot Whitehall, and a small eleven-footer,
were stationed in new chocks on the foredeck to ensure maxi-

mum independence for a full complement of crew and owner's party—Schenck did not want to wait aboard the ship for boats to return from some jaunt ashore if he or anybody else spied a polar bear or walrus floating by waiting to be shot. Maximum mobility, he told Percival. He was pleased that the Englishman had been through the war, and he instructed him to prepare the ship as if for battle.

THROUGH EDDIE RICKENBACKER (WHO declined Schenck's invitation to join his safari without hesitation), Schenck arranged to have lunch with Dr. Vilhjalmur Stefansson, president, and several members, old arctic hands, at the Explorers Club on Central Park West. He wanted to hear from them what game he might expect to find. These august gentlemen thrilled at the notion of an arctic safari, thought it a splendid prospect for bagging unlimited quantities of good-sized game, and asked Schenck to write an account of his safari for the Members Journal upon his return. Implicit in this, Schenck believed, was the possibility of becoming a member of the Explorers Club himself; something he had never given a thought to, but from the instant he set foot in the club and saw its walls of old parchment maps and stuffed beasts and oil paintings and leatherbound volumes of expeditionary journals, became his most cherished ambition. Carl Schenck, Explorer. He became determined to show the members what a safari could be.

The Explorers gave him a tour of their club, which was furnished with famous artifacts, including Peary's dogsled, his sextant, and the reindeer coat he had worn to the North Pole. They were able to acquaint him at first hand with some of the wildlife he might encounter: a ferocious 1400-pound polar bear shot by Dr. Stefansson reared nine feet high on its hind legs beside the entrance to the library. A pair of Eskimo-scrimshanded walrus tusks thirty inches long looked disappointing to Schenck after his earlier hopes of elephant tusks. But as the gentlemen moved into the dining room, Schenck looked up and nearly tripped. He felt himself weaken and grow dizzy, and all his hopes of big game trophies were instantly concentrated and crystallized into one desire: suspended from the dining room ceiling were the twin twenty-foot long arcing jawbones of an arctic bowhead whale. Such jawbones, Dr. Stefansson told Schenck, were larger than any other single bone from any animal that had ever lived upon the earth, including, it was thought, the largest of all animals, the blue whale.

"Let me get this straight," said Schenck, planting himself directly in front of the tall, elegant Dr. Stefansson, and pointing his finger upward. "The jawbone of this bowhead whale, which is up there swimming around in the Arctic right now, is the biggest thing you can get out of any animal now or ever, is that it?"

"That is correct," said Stefansson.

"Bigger than a dinosaur?" Schenck's eyes grew fierce behind his rimless glasses.

"Than any dinosaur!" Stefansson laughed, along with the other members. To a man they were charmed by their luncheon guest's pugnacious bantam manner, and his hunter's pithy concern for what truly mattered. They recognized him: he was one of them; splendid membership material.

"But you can't bag your whale with a Mauser, Carl," chuckled one of the Explorers.

"You leave that to me," said Schenck.

The men laughed, and a few clapped him on the back.

Stefansson presented Schenck with a copy of a monograph entitled *An Arctic Sojourn*, written by one of the club's members, Dr. Griffith of Chicago, who had spent a month in the Canadian Northern Territories. The little book, Stefansson told him, described the habits of the animals he could expect to encounter and would prove useful for his hunting.

The Explorers and their guest ate Kodiak bear steaks recently flown to New York from Alaska by a member. After lunch they screened Robert Flaherty's famous documentary *Nanook of the North*, for which Dr. Stefansson provided an exciting ad hoc commentary. But Schenck could not taste his food, nor afterward remember much at all of his visit. He could only remember looking up at the two giant bones.

WITH THE CHANGE OF hands, Captain Percival needed to replace a number of *Lodestar*'s crew.

The ship's engineer, Eddie Jenkins, a short, middle-aged Welshman, who had seen naval action during the war, stayed on. The left side of Eddie's face had been burned in an engine room fire aboard HMS *Grappler* during the blockade of Constantinople, and the accident left him with a tight, permanent, one-sided grin that made most people like him on sight. He loved steam engines and thought *Lodestar*'s two Bath-built turbines were the finest he had ever been given. Like beautiful twin locomotives they were, in polished brass, bright steel, green and black enamel. The great thousand-gallon copper boilers, copper condensers, and glass level gauges, gave the middle of the ship the appearance of a compact brewery. Eddie Jenkins kept it all clean enough to charm a spinster and working smooth as a clock. He could watch the two turbines at work all day long, and he was happiest in dungarees in his engine room. He did not care what happened topside or where she went, but when he went ashore, he blinked at the larger world like a hatchling and thought it marvelous. When he found himself with a stretch of shore leave, he sought out hills, the greener the better, and took himself off for epic walks, grinning twistedly at nature.

His engineer's mate, Raymond Strick, a tall youth from Bangor, Maine, a sometime automobile grease monkey ashore who had joined the ship during a refit in Bath, stayed on with him. He had little to do in the engine room because Eddie Jenkins took care of most things himself, so Ray also acted as relief fireman, shoveling coal into the engine fireboxes with firemen one and two, whose job was to shovel coal and nothing else. Fireman No. 2 quit when the ship reached City Island, so Percival was looking for a replacement to work with Fireman No. 1, who had stayed on—Dick Iams, another Maine man, from Ellsworth.

The ship's cook and nominal doctor, Roland Duhamel, a Frenchman with a wife, children, and grandchildren in Carteret, Normandy, wanted to stay aboard. He had worked as a boulanger and pastry chef aboard the French liner *Rade de Brest* and served vol-au-vent with a flourish that had delighted Mrs. Dudley Carroll. He liked having his own galley, and he found the demands of intermittent cruises on a yacht easier than the daily grind of turning out a thousand baguettes and brioches aboard the *Brest*. He could also stitch up a wound as neatly as he cut dough with a pastry wheel, and he enjoyed preparing bitter medicinal potions from herbs and weeds and making people drink them. Despite having crossed the Atlantic forty-seven times between Cherbourg and New York, Duhamel had an eccentric picture of the ocean's shape and the location of the landmasses at its edge. He knew that Québec was farther south on the globe than Paris, and that palm trees grew in places on the west coast of Scotland, far to the north of Normandy. Therefore the prospect of a voyage to the Arctic, which lay, he reasoned, between Canada and Scotland, did not bother him. It was not his job to drive the boat, but to prepare the cuisine, which he would do anywhere.

Topside deckhand Bill Fisher stayed aboard. A large, open-faced, red-haired man in his thirties from the seedy outskirts of Newport, he had worked around yachts since leaving school at fifteen. He lived the life of Riley, he told friends at home when he saw them, traveling between Florida and New England, eating like a Rockefeller, with girlfriends in every state along the Atlantic seaboard. You bet he was staying aboard.

Two of the four remaining deckhands did not want to go north, and quit, leaving Avery and Watts, two skinny Maine boys of nineteen, both from Bath, grown-up together and best friends. They reported to Bill Fisher.

The ship's steward, who cleaned the cabins, made the beds, and helped Duhamel in the galley, also quit. In City Island the word went out and men began to arrive at the yard in hopes of finding a berth on the big yacht bound north.

Gar Chamberlain Jr. had got on well, he thought, with Captain Percival during his two-week stay aboard *Lodestar* with Critchell Emmett as a guest of the Carrolls. He had spent much of that time watching, then occasionally helping the crew when they let him. When he could, he had talked deferentially with Percival, whose beard and uniform and history of naval action, and his habit of staring at you with cold blue eyes, and above all the calm absoluteness of his captaincy, had impressed Gar as they had Schenck. He thought Captain Percival was the most extraordinary man he had ever met. Finally he had asked him for a job. Percival had been surprised, and instantly rejected the notion of a young Brahmin playing dilettante aboard his ship, but when Gar told him frankly of his circumstances, and his ambition to make a life aboard boats, he said he would give it some thought. Then came the sudden change of ownership—without any warning, but never a surprise in the rich man's navy—and the need for crew.

Percival asked Schenck if he had any objections to hiring young Chamberlain on a trial basis. Schenck had none; he would be pleased to help the boy out, he told Percival, and they chatted briefly about Gar's change of fortune. Schenck had been savagely pleased to see Gar Chamberlain Sr., who had blackballed him from the Round Hill country club, reduced to ruin and his only boy casting around for such work. Schenck was more than happy to be the one to take on Gar Jr., and pay his paltry wage. He liked the boy.

Before *Lodestar* left Newport, Captain Percival told Gar he would take him on for a trial period.

"Your greatest hurdle will be your background," he said, staring the boy down. "You're soft. You're not used to work. You're a party boy. I won't have you drinking cocktails with the guests, or becoming anyone's pet. My crew stays forward and does not mingle aft when off duty. That doesn't mean you can't be your charming self, or become popular with the owner and his party and get yourself a good tip. But I won't have a special crewmember. Every man must do his work or he's of no use to me, or to the rest of the crew, who will be waiting for you to slip up. I've seen you in the boats and around the ship. You may feather your oars and tie a pretty sheepshank, but your enthusiasm and Bristol fashion ideas will take you only so far. This job is all about service. It's running and fetching and playing nanny to the party aft. It's doing as I say, no matter what. Too much boaty know-how will put you athwart me. Different ships have different longsplices, and if you once disagree with me or question me, I shall fire you immediately and set you ashore at the next port. I shall ride you hard, but fairly, and if you can take it, the job is yours."

"Thank you, sir," Gar said, intimidated and thrilled in equal measure. It was the first job interview of his life, the first acceptance of himself for his merits rather than his money or background—despite them, in fact—and he had made it, so far. He was given a set of *Lodestar* uniforms that were found to fit him, dress and working whites, and dress blues, and he appeared on deck outfitted for service.

At once, his relationship with Captain Percival changed utterly. While Gar had been a guest aboard the ship, Percival had been remote but cordial to him. Now he became colder, and much closer. He assumed the intimacy of a tyrannical father, and in the beginning, Gar misunderstood him. During *Lodestar*'s docking at the Brooklyn Navy Yard, at the end of their day's run down from Newport, Gar was standing beside Bill Fisher, head deckhand, his first moment of being unsure of what he was supposed to do. Percival was ready.

"Belay that line," Percival said to Gar.

Gar did not know the meaning of the word *belay*.

"Chamberlain, belay that line!" Percival shouted. Gar picked up the line in question, still unsure of what was needed.

"Tie it off!" said Bill.

Gar wound the bitter end of the line around a cleat.

"My God, what sort of nancy boy are you?" Percival continued, shouting at him, striding forward across the deck to push his face into the boy's. Before Gar lowered his gaze, he saw the captain's left eyelid twitching spasmodically. "When I say belay, you belay, and smartly! If you can't follow my orders immediately, you can clear off my ship!" Percival turned and walked away across the deck, leaving Gar shocked and white.

Later, when the docking was completed, Bill came below and found Gar sitting on his bunk, smoking a cigarette, still white, and shaking.

"What's the matter with you? You sick?" Bill spoke with a thick Rhode Island accent.

"No, but I guess I better go before he fires me."

"What do you mean?" They had talked about boats while Gar had been a guest, and Bill was happy for Gar and himself when Percival took him on.

"Captain Percival obviously thinks I stink. I better take off now before things get worse."

Bill laughed. "Are you kidding me? He's only riding you.

He's got to push you down first of all, get rid of any of your fancy ideas about yourself, turn you into a piece of shit, and then he'll build you back up the way he wants you. That's what they all do, except maybe he's gonna throw you a little extra crap because you come from aft, instead of through the hawse'le like the rest of us."

Gar shook his head. "No, I don't think he likes me."

"What do you mean, he don't like you? What are you, a girl? This don't have nothing to do with him liking you."

"But he wouldn't talk to me like that unless he didn't like me."

Bill looked at Gar more closely. "Nobody ever talked to you like that before? Right?"

"Yes, goddamn it!" Gar yelled. It was either that or cry.

Bill started giggling. "Ah, Jesus! Boy, you got another kind of education coming. Look, he don't mean nothing personal by it. He don't give a shit about you, see? He's breaking you in. Don't pay attention to the bark, just do what he says and you'll do fine. Listen, if he decides he don't like you, you're gonna know about it!"

"You think so?"

"Yeah. Now quit worrying about it. Come on, let's go ashore and have a beer."

Captain Percival filled his crew slowly. He was busy aboard the ship and at the suggestion of his new boss, he interviewed Clement Shred, found him sufficiently knowledgeable, and used him as a filter. Applicants saw Shred first, and if he thought they knew their stuff, he made appointments for them to meet with Captain Percival. From these people, Percival made a shortlist.

Shred did not like the Englishman. The man acted like a duke. All that gold swirly scrambled egg he wore on his uniform and hat. And that little tug he was always giving his shirtcuffs while he walked around. Shred was sure the fellow had to spend close to an hour in front of a mirror every day to get that beard and mustache trimmed like some piece of fancy hedge. But the boss thought he was bottletop cream so it didn't matter what Shred thought. Wouldn't be him going to sea under such a man, with Schenck pushing him on, and in such a craft. Shred had no wish to go anywhere in a boat with Schenck again. And not beyond Long Island Sound, not with Ben Pine of Gloucester at the wheel, would he care to travel in such an eggshell-thin make-pretend rich man's fool ornament of a ship. Not with Noah poring over God's charts in that dovetailed glass-walled wheelhouse.

So Shred was all ten parts flummoxed when Moyle came to see him at the yard and told him he wanted to sign on.

"They're going up to the ice," said Shred.

"That's what I hear."

"In that thing?"

"It'll be lively, and the grub'll be okay."

"Why don't you stay in Brooklyn and eat yourself to death?"

"That's what I'm doing. If they make it north, I want to see it. And if they don't, I want to see that too. You get me in to see that English fucker."

Moyle made the cull. Percival thought he was consumptive and too old, but then he thought Moyle would not give out before the trip was over, and he was a Cape Horner. That stood for something. Probably harder than anyone else he might have aboard. The old breed. The sort that would freeze onto a piece of gear and break in half with it before whining about anything. And Moyle had worked in the yard, he could paint and carpenter, and could probably throw in a wiresplice behind his back.

"Mr. Moyle, would you come aboard right away?" asked Percival. "I have some work I want done forward. The people in the yard here will do the work, but I want you to oversee it, and report to me."

"Yes, sir."

IT TURNED OUT, NOT surprisingly, that Gar Jr. had done some shooting. Not big game, but deer in the Adirondacks, quail in Massachusetts, waterfowl on the Chesapeake. He knew his way around a gun, he knew the form. Schenck decided the boy could help him with the ship's armory. With Captain Percival's consent, he brought Gar up to the house in

Greenwich one afternoon after he and Mrs. Schenck had returned from Newport, to prepare for their coming safari.

They were joined by two men from Abercrombie and Fitch of New York: Mr. Sutton, Abercrombie's armorer, from whom Schenck had bought his guns for his African safari, and who was going to look over his current arsenal and make further suggestions, if necessary, for arctic game; and Mr. Julian, who would suggest suitable clothing for a northern expedition. Both men had brought samples with them. Schenck had Arthur bring all his guns and a tray of iced tea into his library.

"Gentlemen, my crewman and expeditionary assistant, Mr. Gar Chamberlain Jr."

Gar, in his dress whites, shook hands with the men from Abercrombie's, and Schenck was pleased. Young Gar had the right appearance and touch for this sort of thing.

The four men stood sipping glasses of tea in the middle of Schenck's mahogany-paneled gentleman's library, a room of great tomes, maps, hunting paintings, Oriental rugs, replete in every aspect except for the heads and hides of the large animals Schenck so desired to put on the walls. Mr. Julian, the clothier, seemed not to care for guns, but the other three men handled the rifles, opening and closing breeches, sighting along the barrels.

"Ah, yes," said Sutton, picking up a rifle. "Beautiful. Holland & Holland 500/465 Royal grade hammerless ejector. A magnificent rifle. This is the one we ordered for you, isn't it, Mr. Schenck?" The English rifle was handmade and cost more than the Chevrolet automobile Boden had driven to Maine.

"Yup." Schenck had been disappointed that Holland & Holland no longer made rifles of the same bore as used by President Roosevelt. The 500/450 ammunition had been discontinued after it was used in weapons owned by insurrectionists in India. But he was happy to learn that the replacement 500/465 bullets were larger.

Sutton was a small, balding, bespectacled man, and would have looked like a minor functionary in an insurance firm, but he was suntanned and wore a beige linen suit which gave him a vaguely tropical air, and he handled the rifle with authority. He looked closely at the filigreed engraving on the lockplates, which were a variegated silver and gray-blue color from the color-case-hardening process that used bonemeal charcoal. "This is outstanding engraving, Mr. Schenck. You know Holland & Holland's engravers take about two hundred and fifty hours for each rifle. This one, I have to say, is the best I've seen. How did you get on with this rifle in Africa, Mr. Schenck?"

"I hardly had a chance to shoot a goddamn thing in Africa. I had a difference of opinion with that cocksucker of a white hunter Bennetts set me up with. Mrs. Schenck and I came home early."

"I'm sorry to hear that, sir." Sutton opened the breech and looked down the barrels. He frowned. "You should clean and oil this gun, Mr. Schenck." A trace of reproach in his voice. "It'll last a lifetime, but it'll be useless if it's not taken care of. In fact, I was going to suggest that you don't take this with you on this trip, sir. The moisture and salt air won't be any good at all for such a fine rifle."

"I'm taking it. If it gets wrecked I'll buy another one. But we need some more anyway. I want my man Chamberlain here to be well armed. What have you got?"

Sutton opened an oak-and-leather brass-cornered gun case. "I'd recommend this, sir. The 9.3-millimeter Mauser, built by Sauer. We could mount a Zeiss four-by sight. A particularly nice French walnut stock. Very reliable, and tough in the elements. Easy to strip down and clean. This is a workhorse weapon, sir. A longer range than your double-barrel, and more suitable for general game. Your Holland & Holland is really a little big for anything short of elephant or rhinoceros."

Schenck hefted the rifle, then lifted it to his shoulder and drew beads around the room. Then he passed it to Gar. "What do you think?"

Gar looked over the rifle appreciatively. "It's a beautiful rifle, sir."

"Think you'll be happy shooting that?"

"Yes, sir!"

"Okay, I'll take it."

"Very good," said Sutton. "And will Mrs. Schenck be accompanying you again, sir?"

"Yes she will. She didn't get a chance to shoot anything in Africa, either."

"What does she shoot, Mr. Schenck?"

"This one."

Sutton picked up the rifle. "Oh, yes. Springfield thirty-ought-six. Is Mrs. Schenck happy with this rifle, sir? It's heavy for a lady, I would have thought."

"Let's ask her. Arthur!"

Immediately Arthur opened the library door and came into the room. "Yes, sir?"

"I need Mrs. Schenck in here."

"Yes, sir." Arthur withdrew.

While they waited, Sutton discussed ammunition. "I presume you'll be hunting *Phoca barbata* and *Odobenus rosmarus*, sir?"

"What?"

"Seal and walrus, sir, I beg your pardon."

"If we see it, we'll shoot it. Right, Gar?"

"Yes, sir."

"You'll see both of those, I'm told," said Sutton. "I took the liberty of telephoning one of our customers, Mr. Lynch of Philadelphia, before I came out today. He was in the Arctic a couple of years ago and did some shooting. For both of those animals he recommends a spot either just above the ear, or between ear and eye. And for the walrus, which he said has a skull like steel plate, he advised steel-jacketed bullets with a sixty- to eighty-grain charge."

Mrs. Schenck came into the library.

"Good afternoon, Mrs. Schenck. How nice to see you again," said Sutton. He picked up the Springfield and handed it to her. "How did you get on with this rifle?"

"Is this the one you got for me, Carl?"

"Yes, cupcake. It's the one you had in Kenya."

Mamie held the rifle as if it were a log. "Well, I never shot it."

"How does it feel to you, Mrs. Schenck?" asked Sutton.

"Gosh, I don't know. It's not like a hat, is it? Should I say snug? Or smooth? How do I look with it? Do help me, Carl. What's the right answer?"

"Do you find it heavy, Mrs. Schenck?" asked Sutton.

"Compared to what? Will I have to carry it far, or will there be Eskimo porters, Carl?"

"May I suggest you try this one, Mrs. Schenck?" Sutton opened a case and handed her a smaller rifle. "6.5-millimeter Mannlicher Schoenauer. A shorter-barrel model. Small and light, not a great range, but perfectly accurate within, say, a hundred and fifty yards."

"Is this a peashooter, Sutton?" asked Schenck.

"No, it's a powerful weapon without doubt, Mr. Schenck. Quite able to stop a bear."

"You like it?" Schenck asked his wife.

"It's darling, Carl. It's really me, isn't it? I can see myself stalking all those bears like Annie Oakley. Here." She handed it back to Sutton. "Now do you need me anymore?"

"We have the clothing to look at," piped up Mr. Julian, who had remained well away from the rifles, and been forgotten.

"Okay, let's see it," said Schenck. "What do we wear up there?"

Mr. Julian moved quickly, opening cases and laying a series of outfits across the leather chairs and couches. Then he stood before them, his hands clasped together. He set the scene.

"In the far north, even at the height of summer beneath the midnight sun, you will find it exceedingly chilly. There will be ice and snow and wind at all times. Warmth and dryness are equally important, and a combination of garments will be required to ensure this." He turned and picked up two union suits, one white, the other red. "A suit of long underwear should be worn underneath anything at all times. These come in various colors and weights. I recommend several sets of each."

"Each color?" said Schenck.

Mr. Julian smiled. "Why not? Each weight, I meant. Over this might be worn an English Vyella shirt, a woolen sweater," he held up samples of these before laying them across his arm, "and then the first of our outer garments, our chamois golf jacket, which you will probably find indispensable." This too was added to the growing armful. "Finally, a Burberry windproof of Norwegian 'parka' design. This is the same article that is worn by polar explorers and mountaineers."

"Mm-hmm," said Schenck. He glanced at Sutton, who appeared uncomfortable.

Mr. Julian held the ensemble up to view for a moment, then carefully draped it over a chair.

He turned to face them again. "Every day you will face twenty-four hours of sun beating at you from above, and reflecting its rays at you from the ice below." He pulled a pair of round, dark-lensed glasses from his vest pocket and put them on. For a few seconds he faced his audience without speaking; enigmatic, inscrutable.

"I like those!" said Mrs. Schenck.

"Our spectacles made of Calobar glass by the American Optical Company will protect the eyes most admirably. You may have them ground to your own eyeglass specification, with bifocal."

"Let me see those," said Schenck, and he put them on over his own spectacles and peered around the room before removing them.

Mr. Julian continued. "For footwear there is really no choice. I recommend what everyone wears when they venture into the cold and icy: Bean's of Maine hunting boots." He drew a boot out of a case and held it up. "Rubberized around the foot, waterproofed leather uppers. A woolen sock over lighter woolen hose worn underneath."

Schenck took the boot from him and examined it. "Good. I like them."

Mr. Julian moved to another chair, where other samples were ready for him. He picked up two pairs of breeches.

"For pants, we have several choices. You may wear woolen breeches, which will be warm—until they become wet, and then they'll make you quite miserable." He tossed the woolens onto the chair and held up the others. "The waterproof Dux-Bak trousers are preferable." He laid these down, and turned back to the group. "But for very cold weather, nothing has proven better than these." He turned away, lifted a sample off the chair, and turned around.

"Oh, yes!" exclaimed Mamie. "I absolutely must have a pair of those! Two at least!"

"What the hell are those?" barked Schenck.

"Reindeer pants," said Mr. Julian. He held them up to his waist, and moved his leg slightly beneath them. They had the color and luster of brown mink, but were not as full.

Sutton, holding a rifle, looked away, his face coloring.

Mr. Julian continued. "We've sold a number of these to customers going fishing in Alaska and the west, and they've proved very popular. But they are really designed for arctic travel. They are modeled after the clothing worn by the Eskimo, and by Captain Peary and others. We have a reindeer jacket also, though that might be too warm in the summer. But the legs, which generally are provided with fewer layers, need something special. Particularly standing around aboard ship. These will keep your legs marvelously warm."

Schenck stared at Mr. Julian and the reindeer pants.

"Give me those things," he said, snatching them from Mr. Julian. He slipped off his jacket, pulled the reindeer pants on over his suit trousers, and looked around the room.

"Divine!" shouted Mamie.

Schenck put the Calobar glasses back on, picked up the Sauer Mauser, and struck a pose.

Mamie began shrieking. "Like one of those tycoons at a dude ranch! Where's your ten-gallon hat?"

Mr. Julian and Gar grinned. Sutton appeared uncertain, though willing to put a good face on it.

"I'll take them! Some for Mrs. Schenck too. And get Arthur a pair. And I want stuff for all my crew. New slickers. And those hats, what are they?"

"Sou'westers?" said Mr. Julian.

"Right. The hats, those Maine boots, and rubber boots for my crew, whatever sailors wear, and socks, sweaters, warm coats, warm pants for the whole crew. Everything they need. Speak to Chamberlain here. Gar, get what you need for everybody, and some spares. I want everybody warm. Nobody gets cold. Got it?"

"Yes, sir."

"And, Sutton, let me have all these guns. And send me some

shotguns for birds. The up and down ones, what do you call them?"

Sutton did not understand.

"Over and under barrels, sir?" suggested Gar.

"Right! They're good, aren't they? And I want those bullets, the steel ones for the seals and walruses. And send me enough of everything. I don't want to run out of ammo up there. Let me have five thousand bullets."

"Yes, Mr. Schenck," said Sutton. "Thank you, sir."

CHAPTER 9

HE WAS SMELLING THAT smell again.

He knew it was not real, that it was something happening only inside his brain, fooling him into sensation. But he smelled it, and it was always the same: a scorched, bitter, poisonous fume. Sometimes it would go on for days, no matter where he was, coming back when he thought he had left it behind. He had smelled it all his life, when things began to cave in.

This time it began while he was on the train to Montclair, and by the time he reached his mother's house it was strong. It filled his head and he could not escape it, as if trapped inside a burning house.

Marcella, the colored woman who looked after his mother, told him the doctor had just left but would be back in a few hours. She also told him she had called Mary, who had said she would be there later in the afternoon. Boden went in to see his mother.

He thought she was already gone. Her mouth hung slackly open, the eyelids were slightly parted, the eyes beneath appeared dry and unseeing. But he heard her breathing, a shallow, irregular effort.

Marcella brought him a cup of coffee.

"Thank you, Marcella."

"You're welcome, Mr. Will."

"What did the doctor say?"

"Well, he give her some pills and he said she doesn't feel no pain."

"And he thinks she's dying?" He knew it without asking. He could see it, but he needed someone to tell him plainly in those words.

"Well . . ." Marcella was uncomfortable with it put like that. "He said there was nothing more he could do, except make her comfortable, and he didn't think it would be going on like this too long." Marcella left the room.

He sat down. Slowly he drank the coffee. He had always felt his mother knew he was there, and who he was, even if she was confused about what he was saying. It wouldn't matter; she would see him and know. He didn't feel that now. She had slipped away. But she was still alive and he believed she was no longer confused. She was somewhere else and he wondered where and what was flying through her mind that was now released from confusion and pain. Maybe she was a girl again, light on her feet, thrilled by some long-ago girlish thing. But she was gone forever from him, and he felt the void of his future.

When he went out to the kitchen, Boyd, Marcella's husband, was there. They said hello and Boden thanked him for the way the house and yard looked. Boyd and Marcella were already grieving, and drawing comfort from each other. Boden was surprised at how easily and deeply they felt what was happening to his mother. He wondered if they felt worse than he did. In the last few years they had spent more time in this house and with his mother than he had.

He poured himself more coffee and went into the living room. The same furniture, the same old pictures he had seen all his life. The framed photographs. The photograph albums he had looked through a hundred times until they had shown a past so far from his present he could no longer believe he had ever been there.

He went upstairs and looked through the two bedrooms, one of them his boyhood room. Now spare rooms for a visiting son and his family. But he had produced no children, and left his wife, and in twenty years had spent only a few nights in this house where his mother had continued to live after his father had died. Here were the Currier & Ives prints from his boy-hood still on these walls: *The Mississippi Steamboat, The American Farmer, The Chicago Fire.* And books read by him long ago. Everything up here was old. The cords on the lamps were frayed, the gutta-percha insulation cracked, dangerous. He thought about what would happen to it all. He hoped Mary might take some of the books or pictures away, or Boyd and Marcella. It would all go away somehow, and the house would be sold, and soon there would be no trace of his mother or his father or himself, once a small family together in New Jersey, soon more forgotten and lost to time than a carpenter's pencil mark deep inside a wall that might someday, years into the future, be seen by someone when this small old house was torn down.

Upstairs in the stale rooms where time had stopped, he smelled what would not go away.

At five, Dr. White arrived. Boden had only met him twice. A young man, younger than Boden, who had recently taken over the practice from the older Dr. Wilkinson, who'd always had cigar ash on his lapels, whom Boden had liked. Dr. White was smart and tidy, professionally grave. He checked her pulse, felt her forehead, opened her eyelids wider, and shined a light at the pupils.

"Is she dying?" Boden asked him.

The younger man looked him over before replying. "Yes, I believe so. I'm very sorry. But she's in no pain. She's peaceful."

"How long?"

"I doubt she'll last through the night."

"What do I do when she dies?" Boden knew what he meant, but when he heard himself, it sounded quite different.

"Marcella has my telephone number. Just give me a call and I'll come over and we'll take it from there."

"Okay. Thank you."

Dr. White spoke to Marcella and left.

Boden went out for a walk around the neighborhood. The link to this place, his first place in the world, was about to be severed. It had the look of a tableau.

When he came back there was no change.

Mary arrived a little before six. She was small and slim, a

size that seemed to him perfect, and now when he saw her, after long separations, she appeared more beautiful than he'd remembered. The features of her face were subtly asymmetrical: there were two sides to her. When they were first getting to know each other, it had taken him an unusually long time to fix this face in his mind. By the time he did, he'd grown to love it. Now he noticed gray in her thick, nearly black hair, something he'd never seen before. With dismay, he thought, We're growing older without each other.

Her face was white as she smiled and said hello to Marcella and Boyd, and then said hello to Boden, with her eyes filling up, before she went into his mother's bedroom. Boden felt a great relief. Seeing her and hearing her voice made him feel that everything would somehow be all right; the way he had once felt seeing his mother. He didn't worry that after his mother died and he was alone in his room back in the city it would be much worse for having been with Mary and then being without her.

He went into the bedroom and they sat there together talking about Dr. White and what he had said, and then about Mary's mother and her sister Janet. He asked about her work and she told him she was illustrating a new book for a Scribner's author. That was wonderful, he said, and meant it, and Boden felt she was getting further away from him than ever. Mary asked him about his job going north on the boat, which he had told her about, and now he told her it was off. She stared at him for a moment and then looked away.

Boyd had brought some chicken, and Marcella fried it and baked some potatoes and served them supper in the kitchen at seven. Boyd wouldn't let Boden give him any money for the chicken. Mary asked Marcella and Boyd to join them, but they thanked her and said they would eat later.

When they finished supper it was still light outside, and they took a walk through the quiet streets. Mary told him that Jerry Burke was renting her mother's spare room downstairs. Jerry had been Boden and Mary's neighbor when they'd rented their house in Long Beach, when Boden had had his ship, and in those days Jerry had been a stockbroker. Now he had finally found a job as a porter for the Long Island Railroad. Jerry had always been a funny guy, and talking about him now as a porter and imagining him on a railroad car made them both laugh. Boden wished they could stop time and walk like this forever.

When they returned to the house, his mother was the same. At nine, Boyd said goodnight and went home. Boden wondered how their marriage worked with Marcella living at his mother's house. Marcella's sister came in to give her a day off now and then, but she had lived here full-time for the last two years. He wondered if Boyd spent many nights in the house. However they worked it, he was grateful to them.

His mother seemed to be dying with every breath, yet she hung on through the night. Mary stayed in the bedroom and dozed in a chair. Around eleven, Boden went upstairs and lay down on a bed.

He could not sleep. He wished Mary would come upstairs and lie down with him, but there was a terrible gulf between them now. She had tried to cross it and pull him back, and now he could see she was not going to do that anymore. She had become stronger, and he felt more lost to her than ever. He ached to run downstairs and lay his head across her thighs as she sat in the chair and say, "All I want is to be with you," but he knew that what had made them unhappy before was still there, and it would be the same again. Still he wished she would come upstairs and lie down with him. He curled up on the bed with his boyhood pictures and books around him and felt like crying, but he was only able to do that now in dreams.

Hours seemed to go by and he was unable to sleep. He could no longer stand it lying there in the dark smelling the scorched acrid fumes that filled his head. He got up and went downstairs. In the bedroom, his mother's breathing seemed louder, less frequent, more labored. Mary was asleep in the chair. He went into the kitchen and drank a glass of milk. He could hear Marcella snoring lightly in her room off the kitchen.

He sat down at the kitchen table and started reading the *Paterson Journal* that Boyd had brought with the chicken.

He did not know what it was that woke him up. It was becoming light outside. He rose and went into the bedroom. Mary was sitting on the bed. She looked up at him. He walked to the bed and kneeled down beside his mother. She took one breath, a short, tremulous gasp, and let it go, the softest whisper. They waited, very still. He heard the clock ticking on the bedside table and looked at it: ten to five. Like a boy, he looked around the room and wondered if his mother's spirit was watching him.

LATER IN THE DAY, after he had seen Dr. White and the undertaker, Mary made him come back with her to her mother's house, where she was now living again in her old room upstairs. Her mother, Betty, and her sister Janet seemed happy to see him. They told him they had read in the paper about Schenck's record-setting boat run to Florida against the Havana Special. He stayed for supper. At seven they heard Jerry Burke come in downstairs, and Janet went down and brought him up to see Boden. Jerry had put on a lot of weight since he had been a stockbroker. He was very sorry, he said, about Boden's mother, and was respectfully serious for a while. He started telling Boden about his job on the railroad. He stood up to show off his uniform.

"Pretty slick, huh?"

"Jerry, do your routine for Will," said Janet.

"What?" said Jerry, pretending not to know.

"You know! Go on!"

"Nah."

"Yeah, come on, Jerry," said Betty, laughing, showing wonderfully white dentures.

"Oh, leave him alone, Mom," said Mary, although she was smiling.

Jerry stood up, and shouted. "All a-*board! All aboard for Mass-a-pequa! Babylon! West Islip! Patchogue! Bellport! Shinnecock Hills! Hampton Bays! Southampton! East Hampton! A-a-a-and Monnnnnnn-tauk!*"

TWO DAYS LATER, MARY and her mother and sister came to the funeral in Montclair. Afterward, Boden walked them down the hill to the station. Betty and Janet walked on ahead, leaving Boden and Mary together.

"Will, there's no good time to tell you this, but I don't want to see you anymore. I've met a man I like. And he likes me."

"Oh. Who? Jerry?"

"No, not Jerry. He's a writer. I've been illustrating a book he wrote."

"Good book?"

"Yes. It's a children's book. He's published some others, with other illustrators, but . . . we're doing more books together."

"Sounds like a good deal. What's he like?"

"He's nice. He's heavy and he dyes his hair."

"Really? Why does he dye his hair?"

"Because he's older, and going gray, and I suppose he's worried about that. But he thinks I'm wonderful."

"Do you think he's wonderful?"

"We have things in common."

He saw their life, making their books together in a little house. And their children.

"So you want to marry him? You want a divorce?"

"I've got to make a life for myself. I can't go on with us like this. It's been over a year. You seem further away than ever. You seem lost, Will, and I don't know how to help you back. I've tried—"

"I know you have."

"I want to be happy. I want someone around who's good to me."

"Whatever you want, Mary."

"You know what I want."

He heard her crying, but he could not look at her.

At the station, Betty and Janet told him to be sure to come out to the Beach again soon.

He remained in Montclair for another two hours. He went to a lawyer's office and made out a will in which he left everything to Mary, except for a provision for Marcella. Then he walked along the street to a real estate broker's office and placed his mother's house on the market to be sold, leaving the name of the lawyer down the street as his contact. The broker told him the market was dead and he had no idea when the house might be sold. Meanwhile there were some outstanding taxes owed on the place.

Boden had a Coke and a chicken salad sandwich at Lake's Drugstore on South Main, where the counterboy was still Emory, who had served him black-and-white sodas when he had come in with his mother and father as far back as he could remember.

"Say, aren't you Willy Boden?" said Emory, who was a large old man with a collapsed face the color of unbaked dough.

"Yes I am."

"I remember you. You used to come in here when you were a kid."

"That's right."

"Well." Emory leaned his head back as if to read better and looked at the gaunt man with early gray in his hair sitting on the counter stool in front of him. "You haven't changed."

"Neither have you."

Boden's sandwich, like everything else now, smelled of burned paint.

BODEN'S ROOM WAS ON the fourth floor, on the northeast corner, overlooking Peck Slip and South Street, and the East River where it came sluicing into the narrowing gap between Brooklyn and Manhattan and made a hard right for the Upper Bay, roiling with current. Below his east window, the fishing schooners jammed the piers, and slid in and out of the river while being carried hard sideways at four and five knots in the tide. Below this window, from the middle of the night until a few hours after dawn, the Fulton Fish Market came to life, and he had always liked the noise when he heard it between dreams. Through both windows, north and east, the Brooklyn Bridge filled the sky, arcing over the river from its Manhattan tower a block up, and Boden had found the view from his window as beautiful as any postcard stretch of the Maine coast. He had lived in this room for more than a year, and it contained everything he now owned: his clothes, the gear in his chest, his books. The room provided a sink. A toilet and bath were down the hall.

When he got back from New Jersey, he lay down on his bed

in his suit. Twilight came and passed and he lay on his bed in the dark. He could not sleep nor think his way past the smell in his head.

A banging came at his door.

"Who is it?"

"Moyle."

He got off the bed and opened the door. Moyle stood in the hall, his face sunken gashes of dark beneath the bare bulblight of the hall.

"You feel like a beer?" Moyle asked him.

"Okay."

South Street was quiet in the dark blue evening. Lights moved through the bridgework over the river, up against the sky. Still too early for fish, the schooners showed no men, and groaned at the river pilings.

"You been to church?" asked Moyle, glancing at Boden's suit.

"I was over in Jersey at my mother's funeral."

"Your mother?"

"Yeah. You know what they are, right?"

"Someone who gives you a goddamn glass of milk and never lets you forget about it."

"That's right."

Moyle said nothing more until they were sitting at the bar in Morahan's. They ordered two beers and shooters, and both drank half the beer right off.

Then Moyle said, "You figuring on going north on this boat?"

"Schenck's boat?"

"That's the one."

"No. He's got a captain."

"So what?"

"I don't go as crew. Why? You're not going, are you?"

"Goddamn right I am."

"You're crazy. The boat's all wrong. The skipper doesn't know where he's going. Schenck's a madman. It's going to be a holy disaster."

"That's the way I see it too."

Boden laughed. He looked at them both in the mirror. "Why are you going?"

"I'm finished here," said Moyle. He downed his beer and wiped the foam off his mouth. "What've you got going?"

"I was thinking about killing myself."

"Then this is for you."

He laughed again, and then let himself think of what it was like up there: the beautiful severity; the wildflowers coming up through the tundra desolation; the drunk-seeming blaze of the northern lights. Above all, the ice: the fantastic bergs, some of them the size of Central Park; the rivers and deltas of glacial ice so big and so slowed in time's aspic that his own brief mortal concerns fell away to insignificance until he felt washed clean. The same thing he felt at sea.

"You don't want to be skipper of that pisspot," said Moyle. His emphasis of the last word sent him into a rattling cough. He expectorated and spat. "Let that candyass English fucker make a mess of things. You and me'll go along for the ride and see the sights."

Moyle raised his shot glass and threw it back.

"Now that you put it that way . . ." said Boden. He lifted his glass and swallowed his whiskey.

CHAPTER 10

SHRED WAS PUT IN charge of ordering of every item of gear required for the ship's passage north.

He was provided with an office at the St. Clair Boatworks on City Island. He sent men to fetch furnishings from other rooms and disused spaces around the shipyard, and they came back carrying a desk, a lamp, a filecase, and a chair that swiveled and reclined. A telephone was installed. When he had arranged all these items to his liking, Shred sat down in his chair, reclined, and put his feet up on his desk. He picked up his telephone and listened to its faraway underwater burbling tone. After two years of working at the St. Clair Boatworks, he seemed at last to have found his place.

He was amazed and obscurely troubled when Boden presented himself and asked for an interview with Captain Percival.

"There's no proper job for you on this boat," Shred told him. "They're only looking for a stoker now. You don't want to be aboard this one anyway, let me tell you."

"I don't care what the job is. I want to go."

Percival had filled his deck crew, he did not want a seaman. When he met with Boden he told him he only had space for a second fireman, and he doubted that would interest him. But Boden said he would be happy with that. He was taken on.

Back in New York he paid two months rent on his room at Meyer's Hotel, and left them Mary's name and address on

Long Island. He moved aboard *Lodestar* in the middle of July and joined the rest of the crew getting her ready for sea.

SHRED'S OFFICE BECAME THE center of great activity. In addition to interviewing likely crewmembers, he spent considerable time talking into the telephone in his search for ship's gear. One item in particular had been difficult to track down, but Westcott & Peabody Shipchandler's on Broadway and Cortlandt Street finally located what he was looking for. A reconditioned model, available for $2300, including a supply of its essential appurtenances, was in the hands of their agent in Boston. Shred sent a truck for it. Then he went aboard *Lodestar* to see the work going on in the bow, and once again felt the odd mix of hilarity and alarm at this proposed addition to the ship's gear.

Moyle, overseeing the job, first took him belowdecks. The yard carpenters had doubled up all the oak deckbeams in the forepeak, and added steel knees between the beams and the shelf, through-bolting at every joint. They had put oak blocking running fore-and-aft between each deckbeam. All this had created an interlocking honeycomb structure beneath the foredeck. The yard's design team had come up with the idea to run steel strapping vertically down the forepeak's aft bulkhead between the deckbeams and the keelson, to assist in transferring load from the deck to the keel. It all looked finely done, thought Shred, but still toy-boat flimsy, and he would have been happier to see two stout oak bitts rising from the keelson and going up through the deck, like a solid tree trunk to anchor the busy branching structure around it, rather than the steel strapping.

"What do you think?" he asked Moyle.

"It'll make a rare sight," said Moyle.

The truck from Boston arrived. Schenck drove into the yard several hours later and came aboard the ship. He stood with Captain Percival and watched as the yard's crane lifted the crated item onto the strengthened foredeck and the crate was broken away from it. Schenck strode forward. Men gathered around to stare.

"What the hell is that?" said Eddie Jenkins to himself,

watching from the engine room companionway as the owner walked around his new toy, and grabbed its handle and swung it around on its swivel base. Jenkins had been too busy with his engines to pay much attention to the deckwork forward.

Boden appeared, black with coal dust, out of the nearby coal scuttle hatch. He was working with a yard gang building extra bunkers below. He already knew what was coming aboard.

"Harpoon gun," he told the engineer.

"Harpoon? What the hell for?"

"To shoot a whale."

The Welshman stared at the white grin and amused eyes in Boden's black face. "With that thing?"

"It'll do the job. It takes a four-inch shell and shoots a projectile loaded with a bomb on a ten-second charge."

"From aboard the *Lodestar*?" The engineer paled.

Schenck finally stood back as the yard men, directed by Moyle, clustered around the harpoon gun, jockeying it into place, with the help of the crane, right in the bow, over the teak pad built for it on top of the reinforced deck.

Schenck turned to Captain Percival. "Our speed will be swift, our aim true, our strike deep and sure! We'll bag our whale, will we not, Captain?"

"We shall do our best, sir." Percival privately resolved that in the event of a whale chase he would personally take the wheel and keep the lightly constructed ship clear of any possibility of a strike. You did not tell a man like Schenck he could not do a thing; you said yessir, nossir, three bags full sir, and then you thwarted him with obfuscation, cunning, and if absolutely necessary, temporary deafness. In his career as a yacht skipper, Percival had dealt with many rich and willful owners, men who told him to steam his ship into some impossible or ridiculous situation. He had learned to control them. He would control this owner too.

The harpoon gun's swivel base was bolted down through the teak pad, the deck, through the network of doubled beams and blocking below, with eight one-inch-diameter bronze bolts. *Lodestar*'s bow railing had been removed on both sides far enough back to permit the swinging of the harpoon gun through a wide, unobstructed arc. The harpoon gun, with its short thick snout atop a fire-hydrant-sized base, looked like a squat cannon. Sitting right in the bow, it now gave *Lodestar* the look of a gentleman's personal warship.

With the gun came its harpoons, six of them, in two boxes of three. Not many to set out with, but they were presumed recoverable once they were cut out of a retrieved and butchered whale. Each harpoon was four feet long, weighed one hundred and sixty-five pounds, and carried at one end a crude, heavy, barbed point, threaded at the very tip to receive the sharply pointed fused bomb that would explode seconds after burying itself inside a whale. With the harpoons came a box of twenty fused bombs. And another box held twenty four-inch shells.

The harpoons, heavy enough to require two men to carry each one, were stored in deck boxes. Schenck gave instructions for one harpoon to live in the gun's barrel, ready to fire. He liked the look of its hideous barb. The bombs and shells were turned over to Gar, who stored them in the guest stateroom aft, that had been designated as armory for the duration of the voyage. In here he stored the gun cases, the sight cases, and the cartridge boxes delivered by Abercrombie and Fitch: 2500 rifle cartidges; 2500 12- and 20-bore shotgun shells; and a small case of dynamite sticks. Bill helped Gar lift and move the boxes, and Captain Percival checked that their greater weight was kept as low down and as far inboard as possible. In practice this meant the gun cases were stored upright in closets, and the bombs and dynamite and ammunition boxes were stacked beneath the twin bunks.

Schenck's man Arthur was accompanying his employer on this northern cruise. Arthur's position in the Schenck household was exalted; he had lofty dignity, he was fastidious. It was clear to him and to everyone else that he would not be bunking in with the fo'c'sle crew. He would require a cabin to himself. But *Lodestar* had been built as a short-run commuter, with accommodations for a minimum number in the owner's party. Arthur was afforded his privacy, but he slept above bombs.

AS THE SHIP WAS made ready for its voyage north, Shred watched the preparations with disturbed emotions. He could see plain as paint it was a fool's venture. A rich man's fair-weather craft outfitted with guns and dynamite and harpoons heading out for the Grand Banks, Newfoundland, and points north of there, rough and dangerous stretches of ice-choked water. It was foolish and he was working as hard as he could to help them on their way.

He worked long hours in his office, frazzled by increasing bits of paper, going through lists of provisions with the French cookie, ordering coal and steam hose and two hundred fathoms of new stud-link anchor chain, ordering this and ordering that, chasing up their delivery, and staying late through the long light of the summer evenings. Like him, the ship's crew and the men in the yard all worked late to get *Lodestar* ready for departure.

Evenings now, when he knocked off work, he joined the crew at Ivorson's hole-in-the-wall. They had become shipmates already, and Shred listened to them talk of the coming voyage. Boden told them of his voyages north on the *Arundel* and his own ship, the *Mary Boden*, and of the Eskimos, whole families of them, who had come aboard and spent days on the ships, with their kids climbing through the rigging, and the sealskin clothes and bone beads they wore and their carvings in stone and their bone and tusk scrimshaw, and the whaleships and whale stations and whales and bears and walrus he had seen. They all hoped to see the same things from aboard *Lodestar*. They talked endlessly about the ship, how unsuitable for such a trip she was, and yet how fine she was too, sweet in her lines, and built like the best. They talked about the French cook's food and all agreed they were lucky to have him.

Then Shred would go home.

"Good evening, dear," he said every night as he came through his front door.

"Oh, it's him, is it? Did you lose your way, poor feeble man, or plain forget you have a wife at home making your supper? You stink of drink again! Don't you! Stink of illegal drink! You're a criminal!"

His supper would be on the kitchen table. Hezzie would have eaten hours earlier and washed it down with a bottle of pop. Corned beef hash if he was lucky. Nowadays, with money to spend, Hezzie no longer cooked his old favorites: finnan haddie, chowder, cod any which way, bacalhao simmered in milk with hot sauerkraut. She bought cans of the stuff she saw advertised in her magazines: the red, bait-wormy-looking spaghetti; the meatballs and stews congealed to something nasty-looking after hours on the table or in the refrigerator. Hezzie had lately been saying again that she wanted to return to Fairhaven.

Shred did not want to go back to Fairhaven. He had gone too far now, and seen too much. He remembered how he had felt rowing down to New York in his skiff. And driving up to Maine, and going on to Nova Scotia and seeing the Charbonneaus of Lunenburg. He understood: he had traveled now, and if you traveled beyond a certain everyday point, you never really came all the way back.

LATE ONE AFTERNOON IN the third week of July, *Lodestar* pulled away from the St. Clair Boatworks in City Island and steamed the short distance up Long Island Sound to Greenwich.

Captain Percival barked orders from the bridge, and the deck crew coiled lines, removed fenders, and ran industriously up and down two hundred and twenty-five feet of deck. Joey had moved his gear aboard from the *Tally Ho!* and was acting first mate, which had rankled Bill Fisher. Joey and the other five deckhands wore their dress whites.

The engine room crew, Eddie Jenkins, Ray Strick, Dick Iams, and Will Boden, were below, wearing dungarees, getting up steam. Iams and Boden had been shoveling coal and building the fires all day. Despite vents and fans, it was blazing hot in the firerooms. It would be good down here in the cold up north.

In his galley, on the way to Greenwich, Roland Duhamel prepared the evening meal—cold roast pork, fresh Suffolk County baby asparagus and new potatoes, ice cream and strawberry shortcake—with the help of the new steward, Mr. Newton.

Mrs. Schenck had found Newton through an agency that supplied temporary domestic help. She had asked for someone who could help out in the kitchen, serve food, make beds and clean, and Newton had seemed more than suitable at his interview. He was sixty years old, an extremely short man (which Mamie always felt was good in a servant), a little heavy, but he had a noble and disproportionately large head, framed with waving white hair, square and jowled and august as an old-fashioned senator. He would look perfect moving about the ship with such compact dignity, Mamie thought. When she told him the job would be aboard a large yacht for a cruise of four to six weeks, he had been quietly enthusiastic. Mr. Newton (she was unsure if this was his first or last name, but he responded well to the prefix) came with excellent references from families in Westchester and Fairfield counties.

Shred was aboard for the run up to Greenwich. He wanted to feel the ship move in her element, and he wanted to see her off. Captain Percival gave him permission to come along as a passenger.

And he had nothing else to do. His busy office was quiet, his wastebasket full, his part done. Schenck had not given him another job and Shred supposed he would wander about the yard idle and uneasy until his boss returned.

He felt an unanticipated thrill as *Lodestar* pulled slowly away from the City Island dock. Clear of the land, she turned and gathered way, and began moving east up the Sound. He strolled up and down the long decks and watched the water flowing past the hull in a creamy froth. A folly perhaps, but she was fine. He saw that now as he had never seen it before. So perfectly tuned and vibration-free were the two steam turbines that he felt borne across the water as if on a Zeppelin, smooth and sure, with barely a hum from beneath his feet, but that hum felt wonderful. He had never known anything like it. He was won over by the ship.

At five, the ship let go her anchors off the Schenck property on Field Point. It was too large to come alongside the dock, where *Tally Ho!*, down from Newport, was now moored. Shred said goodbye to Moyle and Boden and some others and got into a launch going ashore. He sat facing aft, watching the ship as he drew away.

*   *   *

THE LAUNCH WENT BACK and forth for an hour, ferrying baggage and more food from shore. Boden stayed below, banking coal in the fireboxes. The crew continued stowing and making ready for sea.

Later, through a fireroom porthole, Boden saw the small final group leaving Schenck's dock in the launch and coming across the water: Arthur, Schenck and his wife, and the daughter. Boden remembered the few minutes when she had brought her snipe in to that same dock and he felt a sudden lift of spirit. It had not occurred to him that she would be accompanying her father on this voyage—he had forgotten about her—but she was aboard and going north with them. He felt unexpectedly light and thankful for the presence of women aboard the ship. He watched the launch through the porthole until it passed from his view along the hull. Then he was working the grates beneath the cinders, banking up a thick, incandescent blaze, hearing nothing but the roar of the fires, breathing in the clean cinder smell he associated with railroad travel, and shoveling coal again with Ray. Boden felt the ship turning around him and the turbines start to race. He took another look out the porthole and saw they were moving past the poorer Stamford neighborhoods on the shore side of the railroad tracks across a wide sweep of flat water. Then, he guessed, came Noroton and Darien, villages he remembered from the Post Road on his long drive to Maine and back.

He became aware of a clear joy filling him.

THE SHIP ONLY WENT a short distance and anchored while it was still light off the Norwalk Islands.

When Boden went forward to shower in some of the hot water he had been making all afternoon, he found Shred sitting on a bunk in the empty fo'c'sle.

"Clement, what the hell are you doing here?"

"I dunno, really." Shred seemed dazed. His brown derby was still on his head. "I got ashore back there in Greenwich and was saying goodbye to the boss and he says, You're sure you don't want to come with us? and I says, okay then, and I came back out."

"What about Hezzie?"

"I telephoned her," said Shred, looking away, and slumping further into himself.

"Well, you don't look none too happy about it. We can get you back ashore here easily. You can catch a train right here in Norwalk."

"Oh, I guess I'll hang on."

"You can get off anytime."

"I guess."

"Well, I'm glad to have you aboard, Clement."

Shred nodded uncertainly.

THE GREAT YACHT LAY tiderode in the still evening, its bow pointing east. The elliptical fantail aft deck, where Mamie and Harriet sat in large wicker chairs, was open to the west and bathed in peach-colored sunlight. Around them, deeply varnished wood glowed a tawny molten shade, and the bleached teak decks held a rose blush. Far down the Sound, the Empire State building could still be seen, a faint gray spire against the pinkening sky.

Mamie was reading from a stack of magazines. Harriet had lately taken up watercolors and had brought a box of paints and tablets of thick paper with her; now she tried to paint the scene to the west, and she was pleased with her first results. The faded wash of the colors seemed just right.

Mr. Newton, wearing a short white jacket over black trousers, appeared with two cocktails. He placed them on small glass-topped wicker tables beside each woman's chair.

"Thank you, Newton," said Mrs. Schenck.

Newton nodded his head and withdrew. He was happy with his new job, and the prospect of his summer.

Mamie sipped her drink. "Oh, this is wonderful. Isn't it? Harriet, I'm so glad you decided to come with us. You needed a break. I could tell."

Schenck came out of the saloon carrying a rifle case.

"Target practice!"

He laid the case on a wicker divan and opened it. Gar was behind him with more rifle cases and boxes of ammunition.

"Oh, Carl, please! It's a glorious evening. I'm in heaven. You're not going to spoil it now with explosions."

"I'm not going to spoil anything, cupcake. You lie there and look beautiful, but when young Gar Jr. has the scope on your new rifle, I want you to take a shot at that island."

Schenck held up his Holland & Holland. Its walnut stock and and smoky color-case-hardened steel, engraved with trumpeting elephants, gleamed in the low warm sunlight. He walked around Mamie's chair and held the rifle in front of her. "Take a look at this thing!" he said.

"It's the bee's knees, isn't it, darling?"

"You bet!" He loaded two cartridges and moved to the rail. He lifted the rifle to his shoulder and the barrel moved slowly across the nearby island. It stopped, pointing at a seagull standing on a rock. Schenck fired.

"*Good heavens* what a noise!" said Mamie, turning the page of her magazine.

The seagull lifted its wings and skittered sideways, but did not fly away. Schenck fired the second barrel and the seagull took off.

"Mamie, it's your turn. Pop off a few shots so Gar can set the sight for you."

"Bliss while it lasted." She put down her magazine and stood up. "What do I have to do?"

Gar handed her the small Mannlicher.

"See that small bush near the shore there, Mrs. Schenck?"

"Yes, Gar, I see it."

"Hold the rifle up, and pull the stock right into your shoulder, because it's going to kick back at you. Like that. Now look through the scope."

Mamie squinted. "Yes, I see the bush."

"Good. Center the crosshairs on it. Hold your breath, and squeeze—"

Mamie fired.

"My God, what a noise!"

"How'd that feel?" Schenck asked her.

"Well, what am I supposed to say? Swell? Peachy?"

Gar adjusted her sights through several more shots before Mamie announced she had had enough. She went below to change for supper. Schenck continued firing. The explosions of the 500/465 cartidges sounded like cannon fire. The still air was full of the hot gunpowder smell.

"Harriet, you want to try a shot?" asked Gar.

"No, thank you."

"Come on, Butch!" said Schenck. "Young Gar will make a crack shot out of you."

"I don't want to."

"Harriet, I want to see you shoot." There was a certain tone now.

Harriet put down her paintbox and pad and stood up.

"Have you ever fired a rifle before?" Gar asked her.

"No," she said sullenly.

Gar handed her the Mannlicher. They moved to the rail. Gar showed her how to hold the rifle, how to aim, how to squeeze the trigger. Then he demonstrated the working of the breech and how to load. Harriet finally put the loaded gun to her shoulder.

"See the bush—"

"I want to shoot the bell," said Harriet, aiming for the Norwalk Harbor red Number Two buoy beyond the nearby island, and she fired.

The bell rang.

"What a shot!" yelled Schenck. "Was that a lucky shot? Shoot that bird. See it? A hundred dollars if you hit the bird."

Gar reloaded the rifle and handed it to her again. Harriet held the rifle, looking at it for a moment, before putting it to her shoulder. In the Zeiss sights she found the gull pecking at mussels ringing a large rock at the tide line. She fired.

The gull smashed against the rock. Feathers blew into the air and fluttered down over a wide area.

"Jesus," said Schenck. He was so surprised he didn't know what else to say.

The next morning the ship headed north.

CHAPTER 11

SCHENCK WANTED TO GET north fast. Up and back, he told Captain Percival, who ran the ship at twenty knots, a sustainable two-thirds of its maximum speed. The wind was light from the southwest, astern, and the sea over which the yacht flew appeared flat and lightly ruffled.

They passed Block and Cuttyhunk and the Elizabeth Islands and sped across the top of Martha's Vineyard and below Monomoy and up the forearm of Cape Cod until land fell astern with the evening and was raised again at Cape Sable, Nova Scotia, at dawn, twenty-two hours after their departure from Norwalk. All that second day they ran at speed along the Nova Scotian coast.

Harriet stood at the ship's rail looking at seacoasts she found herself recognizing. The high smooth pink and gray granite slabs of cliff and headland and scattered clumps of bouldered moraine reminded her of the paintings of Rockwell Kent. The tall firs at the rock edge and the lonely unadorned houses that from seaward appeared bright and deeply shadowed cubes of white and red and gray made her think of N. C. Wyeth.

The second evening they sped past Cape Breton and entered Cabot Strait and the Gulf of St. Lawrence still in daylight, for they were now far north of where they had been the evening before. The ship steamed due north until high Newfoundland was sighted to starboard and brought abeam, then again the course was northeast along that sheer plateau-sided coast,

looming black and foursquare against the milky night. Before
the third dawn, they passed through the Strait of Belle Isle and
once more into the Atlantic, and finally north into the Labrador Sea, already a thousand straight birdflight miles northeast
of New York. The weather remained fine.

The crew were split into two watches, four hours on and
four off. For the deck crew—Joey, Bill Fisher, Moyle, Gar,
Avery, and Watts—this meant a man at the wheel, a man on
watch in the bow, a third man standing by and making rounds
of the deck. The three men off watch could sleep below, or
relax on the foredeck out of sight of the owner's party.

Captain Percival was on call at all times. He was found
mostly in the wheelhouse, standing to one side of the helmsman and scanning the sea ahead, abeam, and astern, or outside
on the bridge wings port and starboard of the wheelhouse, or
standing at the chart table behind the helmsman; charts, pilot
books, tide tables, and his crew in front of him; watchful, vigi-
lant. There were periods when Percival was absent from the
bridge, perhaps in his cabin below, but then the helmsman
would find him again at the edge of his vision, silent and alert.
The Englishman gave the impression of never sleeping, and if
not present, then about to reappear.

For the engineer's crew, a sustained run meant life nursing
an inferno and its twin turbines. The two firemen, Boden and
Dick Iams, spelled each other, working four of every eight
hours through the day and night tending the fires. They shoveled coal into buckets and tossed the bucket loads into the
fireboxes. Back and forth with the buckets in the fireroom,
shirtless, covered with coal dust and streaming pink rivulets of
sweat. They spread the fresh coal with a hoe over a molten bed
and built up the fires until they were banked thick and level
and glowing. Then they might be able to take a break for
twenty minutes until it was time to shovel and carry coal and
bank up the fires again. The fireboxes roared with the doors
open, and the heat blasted out like a smelting works, and when
they went topside for a breather, the summer air felt icy.

Engineer Eddie Jenkins would not leave his engines for more
than an hour at a time. There was no relief engineer. He had
long ago learned to sleep around regular visits to the engine

room, and he could go for ten or twenty years or until he died on such a schedule. His engineer's mate, Ray Strick, found Eddie appearing in the engine room throughout the night, frequently remaining and fiddling with valves or simply sitting with his engines. "All right, then?" Eddie would ask Ray, his eyes taking in the dials and the readings in the valves, and the hum of the turbines, and Ray's alertness all at the same time, and then he would say, "Good lad." And he might go away again for a short time, or into the fireroom. Like the captain, he seemed ever present.

Duhamel the cook and Mr. Newton had their hours of duty: mealtimes, and their preparation and cleanup, and between-meal feedings and drinking, and for Mr. Newton cabin-cleaning and bed-making. Then they might relax, but when anyone astern wanted anything, they responded to electric bells, or requests relayed by Arthur. Arthur directed their efforts with the longstanding knowledge of the Schencks' preferences.

Schenck was all over his new ship. On the bridge he peered through binoculars at the sea ahead, and watched the helmsman change course, and he steered himself sometimes to feel the linkage between the wooden spoked wheel and the rudder one hundred and eighty feet aft. He told Captain Percival to notify him before every change was made in the ship's course, partly because he liked to be up on such developments, and also because he liked to come onto the bridge and take the wheel and swing the ship onto its new heading. He got Captain Percival to show him where they were on the chart, and where they were going, and why his captain had chosen his route. He blew the ship's piercingly loud steam-powered horn whenever he came near it.

He walked up and down his 225 feet of teak decks and looked at every piece of wood joinery, every varnished panel in the teak superstructure, every door and companionway hatch and brass handle, every polished bronze cleat, stanchion and wire, flag halyard and eyebolt and block-and-tackle on the davit falls, and his twin Rivas, *Monte* and *Carlo*. All of it the best, top-notch stuff. And it all belonged to him, bought with his self-made wealth, and he loved that about it most of all.

He liked to go down into the engine room. He was a man

who understood machinery, and loved the sight of man's clev-
erness expressed in the power and beauty of machinery as only
a man who has made a fortune inventing such machinery can
love it. The steam engine is the greatest visual wonder of beautifully arranged interconnecting oil-shining racing metal parts
man has ever put together. A charging buffalo of snorting
metal. Its power can be felt simply by looking at it. Any boy
will stop and stare at the outsized workings of a steam locomotive, and thrill to his building-block hammer-banging boy roots
when that locomotive is rushing along a railway platform, but
the view then is so fleeting. Aboard *Lodestar* two of these
beautiful and mighty steam-driven machines were bolted down
and racing in place. The turbines were far sleeker than older
crank and eccentric steam engines, and they thundered and
spun like nothing else. Schenck could walk up to them and
around them and watch as long as he liked the blurring rushing, rocking, stroking, cyclical interconnected pattern of motion racing and blending into a smooth organ drone of noise
and vibration. And he liked to watch the men in the fireroom,
lit by the glow from the firebox doors like a poster for the new
Soviet Industrial brotherhood, shoveling coal and building the
fires around the clock, the dronepower that was the vital but
cheapest and most easily renewable component of Schenck's
machines.

Mine, he always thought. The biggest toy he had ever
owned.

When not roaming about his ship, Schenck enjoyed sitting in
the saloon reading the monograph *An Arctic Sojourn* by Griffith of Chicago that had been given to him at the Explorers
Club:

> One will not find the eider duck far out at sea. His
> nest will be perhaps upon an island located quite near
> the mainland; but it must be isolated, for if it is not, the
> cunning foxes soon find the nests and raise havoc with
> the birds and their eggs. Sometimes a nested island will
> perchance become connected to the shore, as by a con-
> centration of floe ice. If this occurs, sly Reynard takes
> advantage of the temporary bridge. . . .

*The coastal cliffs provide nesting havens for incalcu-
lable numbers of shore birds. They do not fear Man,
being quite unacquainted with him, but in visiting them
we were always careful to disturb them as little as possible. Their courage and faith win one's heart. It must be
difficult enough to sustain life in such a climate, let
alone raise and educate a family!*

Raise and educate a family! That killed Schenck. A terrific
book, he told Mamie, urging her to read it. Funny as hell.

HARRIET TOOK CONSTITUTIONAL WALKS around the
ship several times a day. She was surprised the first time she
found Boden on board, the afternoon of their early morning
departure from Norwalk. He was filthy, wearing a coal-dusted
singlet, smoking a cigarette at the rail near the engine room
door halfway down the deck. They said hello.

"You dinged-up your boat yet?" Boden asked her.

She smiled. "Maybe a little. I was in Newport for a few
weeks and I was sailing there. Are you a member of the crew
now?"

"Fireman," he answered with a smile, and a glance down at
his shirt. "I'm shoveling coal."

"But aren't you a captain?"

"When I can find a ship."

"You don't mind working like this?" She was suddenly embarrassed for him. He needed the work, she supposed. How
awful.

Boden grinned. "Nope. I like coal."

Harriet laughed, although she was not sure he was joking.
Was it humiliating for him, being a coalman now instead of a
captain, or did he really not mind? He appeared cheerful.

"And I wanted to make the trip," said Boden. "How about
yourself? It'll make a pretty cold vacation."

"I wanted to see the north. I thought I might paint some
pictures."

"You're an artist?"

"Oh, no. Well, I'm trying to paint watercolors. And I like
pictures of the sea."

She was wrapped in a thick, oversized cardigan, a long skirt, and tennis shoes. Boden's thin singlet rippled in the wind and Harriet could make out every muscle across his chest and back and up and down the arm that he raised and lowered as he smoked his cigarette. His muscles were not large, but they were as hard and defined as the drawings in an anatomy book she had looked at. She could imagine all the rest of him.

He asked her, "Have you ever seen Rockwell Kent's picture, *Toilers of the Sea?*"

"Yes! I saw it at the Whitney. I love that picture!"

The wind blew her bob off her face and he saw her milky complexion and brown eyes opened wide. "I used to do that, what they're doing in that picture."

"The fishermen? You were a fisherman?"

"Yes. When I was a kid. They're hauling dories. I used to haul a dory on the Grand Banks. The sea in that picture is right. He's got the swell."

They talked about paintings and the sea for a few more minutes and then Boden excused himself to go below to the fire-room.

STEAMING NORTH, SCHENCK'S THOUGHTS now turned to game and shooting. He stood at his harpoon gun in the bow and gripped its handle and swiveled it around, aiming at waves and imaginary whales. He noticed, standing right up in the bow, that the ship's speed brought him upon all kinds of marine life fleeing the oncoming monster, or rushing joyfully to meet it. He kept his newest weapons—the Mauser bought for Gar's use, the Griffin and Howe over-and-under 20-bore shotgun—and his Thompson submachine gun that had proved such fun in Africa, sitting on a settee in the saloon permanently dedicated to that use, loaded and ready to fire, so he could dash in at any time, pick up a weapon, and be back at the rail firing within seconds.

On the second day, Schenck brought Harriet up forward with the new Mannlicher rifle he had bought for Mamie. She hit more than he did right away, and then she hit almost everything she fired at. They shot at the porpoises and dolphins, tuna, swordfish, and sharks gliding beneath the surface and leaping into the air through rainbows of their own making. They shot at gulls and guillemots and petrels with the Griffin and Howe. Schenck took to spotting and pointing for her.

"Good!" Schenck said at every hit. "Good!"

Harriet grew thrilled at her unexpected excellence.

After her first day of shooting, she lay in bed in the humming dark of her cabin and saw again the eruption of tissue she had caused, time after time, on some arcing glistening fishback with the squeeze of her finger. Part of her felt sorry for the animals she had sent twisting down into the dark water. But she had made them hers, and she liked that.

SHE WOKE LATER WHEN her cabin door opened. Her father sat on the bed beside her.

"My girl's a crack shot!" Schenck patted her shoulder approvingly, as he would a dog. "My little girl made me proud today." He went on patting her for a moment.

Then he leaned over and kissed her cheek.

Harriet felt the mustache whiskers on her face, smelled the familiar whiskey breath. She stiffened.

BODEN HAD BROUGHT HIS sextant, sight reduction tables, a nautical almanac, his old page-warped arctic pilot book, and a few charts. He knew the rate of loss of his wristwatch, and he had checked its time to the second with a radio before leaving Connecticut. He might be only a stoker on this voyage, but he wanted to know where he was at sea, and what stretch of shore he might be looking at. From the deck, looking down at the water passing along the hull and the wake astern, he could estimate the ship's speed, and he could guess much of their route, confirmed by glimpses of the coast. With this information, he maintained a dead reckoning plot in his head.

In the Gulf of Maine, north of George's Bank, he shot a round of star sights at twilight and marked on his chart a position inside the hundred-fathom curve over Cashes Ledge, northeast of Cultivator Shoal, north of Georges Shoal, west of Browns Bank. He knew this piece of ocean better than his old neighborhood in Long Beach. Fogbound and drifting hereabouts, he had many times "armed" the lead—packed tallow or some stiff grease into the hollow at the bottom of the sounding lead at the end of the fathom-marked lead line—heaved it overboard, brought up a dusting of the seafloor, and determined his rough position from its nature and depth. More gravelly as you went north up toward the Bay of Fundy until you reached rock and weed, sandier over Georges Shoal, muddier and deeper on Browns Bank. He had sailed through this spot of ocean for twenty years and seen it in every state of weather, and his feeling for these waters was made up of those memories, and his fish's-eye view of the contour and composition of the seafloor, and his memory of the man he had been then. To be here again gave him a sweet sense of being in his own right place.

Captain Percival had also taken sights, in the morning and again at midday, wielding his sextant briefly on the bridge wings, and then returning to the chart table at the wheelhouse for several minutes of calculation before marking a spot on the chart.

At the helm inside the wheelhouse, Gar had watched both men, and their techniques appeared quite different. Captain Percival took no more than a moment to peer through his instrument's monocular before coming back inside to work out his position. Boden took longer, swinging the sextant slightly, pendulum-fashion, while adjusting it. Shooting the stars at dusk, he spent four or five minutes aiming it in different directions and looking at his watch before he turned and disappeared down the forward companionway.

Gar longed to learn the abstruse secrets of celestial navigation, and to join the exclusive club of seamen who could find their way about the world by observing the sun and the stars. He thought about asking Percival to instruct him, but the captain remained a forbidding figure. He had become far friendlier with Will Boden in their after-hours drinking on City Island. Aboard ship, their watches coincided, they ate at the same time at the fo'c'sle table.

"Will, would you teach me how to use the sextant?" Gar asked him on the second day, when they were off the Nova Scotia coast.

"Sure. Let's take a noon shot tomorrow. That'll be a few minutes before one P.M. I'll be on the foredeck."

But the next morning they steamed into fog.

During the night, the ship had passed through the Strait of Belle Isle and turned north into the Labrador Sea. The air had been cooling steadily ever since leaving Long Island Sound, and the steam-piped central heating had been turned on back in the Gulf of Maine. An hour into the Labrador Sea, the temperature on deck dropped from 48 to 39 degrees. Gar lowered a brass thermometer on a wire over the side and pulled it out reading 36 degrees. The sun rose at four A.M. after a clear night of cobalt blue twilight that obscured all but a few winking stars. The brown and blue fjords of the Labrador coast lay sharp on the portside in the low morning sunlight. High sheer cliffs rimmed green at the top with stunted trees swept back from the rock edge. It looked to be a clear day, but without warning the ship passed out of the blue morning into dense fog, as sudden as entering a room.

There was no wind. The surface of the sea became a flat pewter sheet that vanished into mist only yards beyond the ship's perimeter.

Captain Percival ordered slow ahead and speed was reduced to eight knots, but within the ship's curtailed circle of visibility, where it seemed to float through a cloud, and the only visible element beyond the ship was the white ploughed water curling down the side of the hull, this speed suddenly appeared break-neck. The ship's horn was blown every minute, the sound fading away into the fog, and the man in the bow listened for any answer. The ship streamed with moisture, drops fell every-where, rivulets ran down the varnished cabinsides, the bleached teak deck turned dark.

Boden came up on deck from the fireroom for air at eight that morning and was dismayed by the ship's speed. He knew that the south-running Labrador Current off this coast was the main conveyor of the great bergs making their way into the Atlantic. They came south out of Davis Strait as stately and thick as the shipping out of New York harbor. He knew that an average of 7500 bergs annually broke off the twenty Greenland glaciers north of Disko Island and were carried north by current up the west coast of Greenland into Baffin Bay, where they became fixed in the winter pack and were released again in summer to drift south through Davis Strait and on down the Labrador shore. Five hundred or more acre-sized and larger bergs passed south every summer through the waters they were moving north in right now. It was a one-way highway of ice, and they were steaming into it blind, against the flow. There was no way to tell what lay in front of the ship. This was madness.

Boden stood paralyzed and—rare for him aboard any ship—irresolute. He was a stoker, his position was below. The management of anything but the coal in the fireboxes was no business of his. He could not run, as all his instinct told him to do, into the wheelhouse and make them stop the ship. He walked forward to the bow and looked ahead into the fog, imagining the appearance of the berg that must be out there. Avery, wearing a streaming black slicker jacket and a water-beaded wool watch cap, was the bow lookout. He stood beside the cannon-shaped harpoon gun, which seemed to be producing water like a leaking fire hydrant.

"Thicka fog!" said the boy, working his shoulders under his jacket.

"Yes, fog," Boden replied. Avery was from Bath, well acquainted with fog, but apparently unperturbed at coursing headlong through it. Boden supposed the boy had faith in his captain.

He looked aft to the wheelhouse and saw Percival standing behind the glass windows staring ahead. What on earth could the man be thinking? It would be warm in the wheelhouse with its hot radiators, and warmth carried the illusion of safety. Boden had left his coat below in the fireroom, but he found he could not leave the bow. He could look aft only a moment before he had to turn and look forward again. He began shivering violently.

He glanced at Avery. "Anybody tell you to look out for ice?"

"Sure. Ice or anything else."

"Has the captain been up here?"

"Here? On deck? Not since I been here. I just come on at eight."

"Who'd you relieve here?"

"Mr. Moyle. He was here when I came on."

"What'd he tell you?"

"He said to keep a good lookout and blow this horn if I see anything." Avery held up the cheap rolled-brass one-note horn that would trumpet a warning to the bridge if blown.

Boden looked ahead again, then turned and walked quickly aft over the wet deck to the fo'c'sle companionway.

He came down into the open space that constituted the crew's saloon: shelves with books and magazines along the hull on both sides; to port a large table framed with settees where they took their meals. A passageway through the aft bulkhead led through the ship, first past the captain's cabin, then aft to the engine room and fireroom.

Forward of the crew's saloon, four cabins, two to port, two to starboard, each containing four bunks up and down, were partitioned off against the hull. Nicely appointed for a gentleman's crew, but tight in the narrowing bow.

Moyle was sitting on his bunk in his cabin, starboard side, sipping a mug of coffee. Boden stood in the cabin doorway.

"This is crazy, heading into fog like this. At any speed."

Moyle glanced at him, a trace of a smile as he raised his mug.

"You got to tell him," said Boden. "He might hear it from you. There's ice all over the place here. If it were clear we'd see it. He doesn't—"

"He's the captain," said Moyle.

Moyle's bunk lay against the thin paneling fastened to the inside of the hull's steel frames. The seawater could be heard sluicing inches from Moyle's head.

"It'll come through here like rock through eggshell."

"This side or the other," said Moyle. He put his mug on the shelf beside his head, next to a coffee can, and stretched out on his bunk.

Boden said, "He might hear it from you."

"He's the skipper. I don't tell him anything. Fuck him."

"What about everyone else?"

"It ain't my call."

Boden stepped back up to the deck and looked forward
again, his eyes straining ahead, knowing he would see nothing
until it was barely ahead of the bow. If then.

He turned and climbed the steps to the wheelhouse door and
knocked.

Captain Percival opened the door. He stared at Boden.

"Excuse me, Captain. I've sailed in these waters and I believe
there's a good chance there's ice—"

"Thank you."

Percival shut the door.

Boden retreated down the steps. He went down to the fireroom and filled the coal buckets. He shoveled and raked the
cinders, and stoked the fireboxes and banked the fires in a
savage rhythm, and slammed the firebox doors.

Perhaps an hour later, the ship reduced speed again. Boden
heard and felt the turbines being throttled down. He wanted to
run topside and see why, but he restrained himself. He tended
the fireroom until Iams came down to relieve him at ten
o'clock. Then he went up on deck.

Visibility was zero. When he looked fore and aft from the
engine room companionway amidships, the bow and stern,
both just over one hundred feet away, were invisible in fog.
Streamers and clouds of it floated past his face down the deck.
The ship was now ghosting through the water at barely steerageway. A proper speed. He reflected that it might have happened sooner if he had said nothing to Percival, and he resolved to keep his place in future. Let the war hero run it as he
saw fit. Boden knew that luck at sea was perversely on the side
of the happily blinkered sailors who had no idea of what was
stacked against them. If he stayed out of the captain's way,
they might all come through it without incident. He went forward to shower.

THE OFF-WATCH CREW were all below in the fo'c'sle, either in their bunks or in the crew's saloon, trying to stay warm
and dry. Men came below from their watches and shed their
streaming oilskins and hung them over the radiators along the
aft bulkhead. Rubber boots stood in a line near the compan-

ionway, and wool socks lay steaming on the radiators. The atmosphere below was a warm, cheesy fug.

Shred sat at the crew's saloon table, his derby on his head, reading one of Joey's crime magazines. He looked up as Boden came through, nodded, and returned his attention to the magazine. He felt ill at ease seeing Boden black with coal and rimed with sweat. Shred's position aboard *Lodestar* was as vague and supernumerary as it had been at Schenck's boatyard. Captain Percival had not included him in the watch roster. He had come aboard at Schenck's invitation and was treated by everyone forward and aft more as a guest than as a crewmember, yet he ate and bunked in the fo'c'sle and stayed there while they all went about their routines. He slept through the nights and spent his days wandering around the forward part of the ship, keeping out of the captain's way, talking with whoever had time to talk to him. Gar had provided him with half a bunkful of the cold-weather clothes that had been purchased for the whole crew: a heavy sweater, peacoat, socks and rubber boots, slicker top and bottoms, a sou'wester. Shred wore these as conditions demanded. He felt the miles passing beneath the hull and knew he was moving north at an unprecedented rate. Nova Scotia and the Charbonneau-packed town of Lunenburg, his recent benchmark for the extreme edge of the world, had passed by in a flash some time ago, and he was now moving into unimagined distance. He was not surprised by the fog when it arrived, feeling he had traveled sufficiently far to reach an otherworldly place, and he was ready for anything—gargoyle creatures and ice palaces—when the air cleared.

Gar lay in his bunk trying to sleep, but Moyle, on the bunk immediately below him, was expectorating with deep, bubbling heaves, bringing up gobs that he spat with a hollow ringing sound into the coffee can he kept on the shelf beside his bunk and routinely emptied down the head. Gar could tell how full the can was by its shoaling resonance when Moyle added to it. Part of him rooted for each effort, hoping Moyle might finally empty his lungs with one last great bottom-scraping evacuation, but there was no end to it. Gar had been listening to him do it ever since Moyle came aboard.

Gar was exhausted. He was still unused to the four-on and

four-off routine. During the second night, on his watch as helmsman, he had nodded repeatedly at the wheel, mesmerized by the compass binnacle's small island of light and numbers floating disembodied in the dark wheelhouse, and jerked himself out of it each time terrified that Captain Percival would see him. Once he thought Percival must have seen him, for he was nudged awake by some throat-clearing noise the captain made behind him at the chart table. He felt heartened at the thought that Percival might have noticed and been so lenient with him.

He was still having trouble making up his lost sleep while off-watch during the long daylight hours. Moyle's hacking bothered him, and now he was troubled by something else. He had been in the wheelhouse when Boden knocked and mentioned the ice and Captain Percival shut the door in his face. Gar believed in Captain Percival. The captain's demeanor carried an unquestionable confidence. He seemed to know his ship and direct its operation with absolute certainty. But as they steamed through the fog, Gar felt blind, instinctively apprehensive of what might lie ahead unseen, and he had been relieved when Boden came to the door and said what he did. Relieved but disturbed, because he could see no other possible response from Percival than the one he had made. The captain could not be instructed, could have no suggestions made to him, by anyone except Schenck, and even an owner was on delicate ground telling his captain how to manage his ship. The captain was the final authority in matters of seamanship. Gar knew and understood this, but in the fog, moving at a speed that precluded any possibility of the ship's timely response to whatever might appear ahead, his own crawling scalp had told him that Captain Percival was wrong.

HARRIET BECAME DISORIENTED IN the fog. Below in her cabin, or in the saloon, or on the aft deck, if she did not look up or out beyond the rail, she retained a sense of direction, a feeling for the coast at some remove to her left, of the open sea to the right, and north ahead. But looking into the fog, she lost her inner compass and the world reeled around her. The ship appeared at times to be turning left, or right, or to be going around in circles, and she couldn't believe it was still heading in a straight line. Without a horizon to refer to, she couldn't tell if the ship remained on an even keel, and she felt dizzy. Then she went to the rail and held onto it to steady herself, and looked down at the water. It was moving by so slowly now that it seemed solid and constant, and she felt better. But looking up again, there was nothing to sight against the ship as it floated through the gray mist. It was a strange sensation. She didn't understand how the ship could be steered through so obscure a medium, even if the wheelhouse compass provided a theoretical direction. She wondered how the captain and his crew knew what lay through the fog beyond view, and she was comforted by the thought that they understood what she did not and that she was safe.

She came out on deck frequently through the foggy morning, fascinated by it, and by her new sense of dislocation. Constantly she thought she saw shapes in the diaphanous murk. And the regular blast of the horn surprised her each time she heard it, alerting her as if auguring what might appear at any moment through the fog, what she could almost see that remained out of sight.

She looked for Boden along the dark wet deck, but it stretched emptily away forward into the fog and gave her the feeling that she was alone on the ship. Once she descended the steep stairs to the fireroom, but she found Iams carrying coal buckets. "Help you?" he said, his eyes unnaturally white in a coal-dusted face, and Harriet replied she was just looking around. She climbed up the stairs again and went back into the saloon.

AFTER HIS SHOWER, BODEN tried to nap in his bunk, but he was restless below. He wanted to see where they were and what was going on even if he could see nothing. He put on a wool sweater and carried his coat up on deck.

The fog was still thick. But with no wind blowing and their progress nearly stopped, the air outside was no longer an icy blast. The commotion of their speed—the rushing cataracts of water, the throb of the engines—was gone. It was cool and damp and quiet on deck. The horn continued to blow once a minute. Boden moved to the rail near the bow and looked out over the few yards of visible water into swirling wrack.

"Captain Boden!" Schenck appeared at the rail beside him. "How are you enjoying our trip?"

"Very pleasant so far, sir."

"And what do you think of her?"

"An impressive vessel."

"She's the best! How about this fog? Think it'll lift?"

"At some point."

"Can't make much progress like this. You come this way when you were up here?"

"Yes, sir."

"Was it like this then?"

"Foggy."

Schenck laughed. "You know where we are?"

"I have an idea."

"What's ashore here?"

"Not much in the way of settlement. It's forested—"

"Any animals?"

"Probably what you'd find in Maine. Deer, moose—"

"Moose? With the big racks, right? Horns?"

"Antlers, yes."

"Think we could get ashore here?"

"You'd have to ask your captain, sir."

Schenck laughed appreciatively. "What do you think of him? Knows his stuff?"

Boden looked around in the fog. "He got us here."

Schenck laughed again, harder, and slapped Boden's arm. He walked aft along the foredeck and climbed the steps to the wheelhouse.

AT ONE O'CLOCK, NEWTON served the Schencks lunch in the dining room. This was at deck level, forward of the saloon, and they sat beside large windows that gave them a view of the gray featureless world beyond the rail. Despite the fog, it was bright as day inside the dining room, but Mamie found the cloud view so gloomy that she had Newton turn on all the inside lights. He had barely served the cassoulet when the bow lookout's brass horn was heard clearly in the dining room.

Schenck left the table and went outside to see what was happening. Harriet followed him. They found Gar, Shred, and Boden on the foredeck. The engines were throttled back to idle. Captain Percival stood on the bridge wing outside the wheelhouse door.

"It sounded like an animal," said Bill Fisher, who was all the way forward, standing beside the harpoon gun.

They all listened. A minute passed. Bill blew his horn. In answer, a noise came distinctly out of the fog from ahead, and to port, the direction of land.

"It's a dog!" said Bill.

They all moved forward to the port rail, the place their ears told them was closest to whatever was ahead.

"Maybe it's a seal," said Gar. "I saw one at Barnum's circus. They bark just like a dog."

Schenck walked forward and took the horn from Bill. He blew it loudly. An angry barking came back.

"It is a dog," said Boden.

"There can't be a dog out here," said Gar.

"Sure there can," said Boden, grinning. "All the time."

Captain Percival descended the steps from the bridge with Watts.

"Give him a hand will you, Boden?" called Percival.

"He wants us to take a sounding," Watts said as they walked forward. They pulled the long lead line out of a deck box. Three hundred feet of half-inch hemp marked every ten fathoms, wound on a large reel; the weight was a twenty-pound cylindrical bronze casting, green with age and service, the name *Lodestar* cast into one side. Very pretty, but no hollow in its base for the navigator's fisheye wad of tallow. Watts held the reel up over the rail with both hands so the line would run freely, and Boden dropped the weight over the side. It disappeared, the line angling aft, for the ship still had way on.

"No bottom at fifty fathoms, Captain," Boden called aft. He knew they were over the Labrador shelf, a long shallow gravel plain paralleling the coast from Belle Isle all the way north to Cape Chidley at the entrance to Hudson Strait, the hundred-fathom line averaging ninety miles offshore. Percival should have known it too, he thought. But no harm in throwing the lead.

Schenck blew the horn again and the dog's barking returned, prolonged, and closer. Then shouts and men's voices and laughter came out of the fog, so close ahead that the persistent invisibility seemed impossible, a trick.

"Jesus Christ," said Watts, looking at Boden. "Are we about to run ashore?"

Boden smiled at him, amused. "Not quite yet."

"Hello!" Schenck yelled.

" 'Allo!" came back, with renewed barking.

Lodestar continued its slow forward drift. Everyone stared into the fog, held by the voices now heard clearly at conversational volume.

"Portuguese," said Boden. "Codfisherman."

Then through the mist a piece of the fog grew darker, and resolved into something like the soft-edged shadow of a familiar shape: a ship. They all watched it acquire definition, a curving sheer and three masts, but it was a long minute before they could make out the men aboard it and the dog standing on its hind legs at the bulwark in the waist, staring outraged at the approaching apparition, and barking furiously. And then the ships were gliding alongside each other. The schooner, a little over a hundred feet long, was becalmed; it carried lower sails—main, foresails, and staysails—all made of heavy flax, stained dark with tea to fight mildew, crudely patched, saturated with damp and hanging limp. On *Lodestar*'s deck, Harriet could make out the warp and weft of the flax cloth.

The fishermen, prepared for any other vessel, gaped at the sight of the yacht twice the length of their own ship and they fell silent as it materialized. The people on *Lodestar* stared back at them as the two vessels slid past each other at a distance of twenty yards. Only the dog made noise, barking hysterically.

"*Boa tarde!*" yelled a man from the schooner, finding his voice. The other men aboard the schooner—there were only four of them—began yelling the same thing, and the dog continued barking.

"Hey!" shouted Gar, waving, and Watts and Bill and Boden

all yelled out hellos. Everybody waved back and forth across the narrow strip of water.

"Are they biting?" Schenck yelled, waving too.

Shred knew they were there for cod, and he knew how they ate it. *"Bacalhao!"* he shouted.

"Sim, sim! Bacalhao! Muito bom! Bacalhao! Bacalhao!"

"What's bacalhao?" asked Gar.

Shred turned away from the schooner and stared at the boy. He had talked to Gar and knew a little of his background. He knew that Gar had tasted the better things in life. "You don't know what bacalhao is?"

"No."

"Dried and salted cod. And a portugee way of cooking it. You boil it in milk with butter."

"Is it good?" asked Gar.

"I'm partial to it," said Shred, imagining a bowl of bacalhao.

Now the men on the schooner saw the yacht's American ensign hanging wet and limp at its pole at the stern, and shouted their appreciation of this fantastic vision from the land of plenty that fulfilled their wildest expectations.

"America! Hello hello! I want money please! Take me to America!"

Boden felt a breath of wind on his face. As the ships slid past each other the air began to brighten. The outline of the schooner hardened. The water appeared in widening sunlit patches around the two vessels, patterned with traces of a light breeze. Within minutes the fog rolled clear, tumbling away across the sparkling blue surface of the sea like clouds of pollen. Suddenly, aboard *Lodestar*, they could see for miles, and they saw the schooner's dories, little bobbing peapod shapes dotting the ocean all around them.

"Look!" said Harriet, beside Boden. "The Toilers of the Sea!"

Boden turned and saw her staring out across the water at the painting they both knew come to life. Then she looked up at him, her face alive.

"That's what you did?"

"That's it."

"They're from that boat?"

"Yes."

"What are they fishing for?"

"Cod."

She looked back at the dories. "The Toilers of the Sea. And now I know one of them."

Boden looked down at her and was suddenly moved by her keen face smiling up at him.

The deck trembled as the throttles opened and the ship began to move slowly ahead through the dory fleet.

Schenck blew the brass horn as they passed near a dory, and the doryman waved back, staring at the ship.

"Butch! Let's go finish lunch," he called to Harriet. He gave the horn back to Bill. Harriet followed her father aft.

Boden leaned against the rail looking out over the sea and the dory fleet. He counted seventeen of the sharp little craft spread out over the eight-mile-diameter circle of ocean he could now see from where he stood on the foredeck. Some were no more than dark suggestions of an object up near the edge of the horizon. They might be five miles from their mother ship, the schooner. A whole day—a long day up north here at this time of year—sitting jigging in your boat in sun and fog, air temperatures in the sixties some days, and some days in the thirties. Everything you needed through that day you carried in the dory with you: wooden tub of line and hooks, wooden bucket of bait, oars, a scoop bailer, a small grapnel anchor and its line no matter where you were; your own basket with a bottle of water, some bread and cheese, and perhaps meat or a piece of dried cod, tobacco to chew or smoke, your knife and compass, and a whistle to blow when they lost you in the fog. No life jacket—Boden had never seen such a thing aboard a fishing schooner. No use, for you'd be dead of cold in such water long before you tired of swimming.

It was a dory's flared buoyant peapod shape that was your best chance of survival, and all you had to do in all weather was keep the water out of her. A doryman's bailer was his lifesaver. You sat on the flat bottom, for there were no thwarts in the dories because they all nested inside each other in stacks on the schooner's deck. You wore thick black oilskins and got wet through no matter what. Your hands got the worst of it.

The work made gloves impossible. You baited your hooks, maybe five hundred of them on a three-thousand-foot line, and rowed your line out and then hauled it in, pulling the cold flapping fish off the hooks and baiting the hooks again with pieces of icy herring from your bucket. Boden had always been thin and felt the cold, and his hands numbed fast. He got frostbite often and was too concerned with keeping his fingers to make a good doryman. But he remembered it all now in that way you remember your simpler bad times before you had any idea how much worse it could get. Plain physical discomfort, which he was hardly aware of anymore, had been his only problem then; he had his whole life in front of him and knew he would go on to some great success. That was what was supposed to happen to the young who dreamed of great or noble things in America, as Boden had once dreamed.

As the ship gathered way and he looked back on the dory fleet, he saw a white and blue turreted shape about a mile from the schooner that did not clear away with the fog. An iceberg lay astern, barely off the path made by their wake. They had passed close to it in the fog.

BEFORE THEY BOTH WENT on watch at two that afternoon, Boden showed Gar how to take and work out a sight. Conditions were good. They had blue sky, a clear horizon line, and the ship moved across the flat sea almost without discernible motion.

He explained the operation of his sextant, a thirty-year-old instrument made by Hughes & Son of England, not much more complicated than a pair of binoculars, but its brass scale was not easy to read. He told Gar not to bother with any theory beyond understanding simply that the sextant measured the angle, in degrees and minutes, between the observer on deck and the sun or star above and the true horizon. Boden pointed one arm up at the sun and the other horizontally at the horizon. This angle. Gar nodded, seeing clearly, and feeling his fear of incomprehension fall away. Boden showed him how he rocked the sextant pendulum-fashion to make the orb of the sun seen through the eyepiece swing in an arc over the horizon, grazing its lower limb on the distant swell at the bottom of the arc, to make sure of true verticality. Boden took a reading and Gar took two, and they consulted Boden's watch each time.

Below in the crew's saloon he showed Gar how the nautical almanac gave them corrections to apply to their sextant readings for the refraction of the atmosphere and the height of their eye above the sea as they stood on the foredeck, simple additions or subtractions of degrees and minutes made to the original sextant reading. Boden's watch gave them time to the second, which they converted to the time at Greenwich in London, and the almanac gave them the Greenwich Hour Angle and the Declination for the sun at that time on the day of their sight. This gave them a figure, the Local Hour Angle, to take to the book of Sight Reduction tables at their approximate latitude and appropriate Declination, where they found more figures.

"Got it?"

"Sort of."

"Don't worry about what any of it means for now," Boden said. "Just do it in this order. Make a worksheet and go through it. We end up with this, an azimuth, or compass direction, and this, a distance."

With his parallel ruler running from his chart's compass rose, Boden penciled a line off the Labrador coast.

"We are somewhere on that line," he told Gar. "We have a good idea where from our dead reckoning, but we can take another sight later this afternoon, when the sun has moved sufficiently to give us a new azimuth and cross the two lines, bringing the first line forward in the direction and the distance we've traveled since we took the first sight. That'll be our position, give or take a few miles."

Gar's two lines, when they had worked them out, were within five miles of Boden's line. He was amazed and thrilled. How it worked remained unclear, but he saw that by simply following the procedure with a worksheet, the mysterious business of navigation by celestial observation was something he could do. He was on his way to being a navigator.

"Holy cow," said Gar.

"It's just practice. Take a sight whenever you can. Percival might have some English method that's a little different, so ask him if you can do it with him too. His way might be easier, for all I know. Ask him to show you. Here." He handed Gar his sextant case. "You're welcome to use this, as long as you don't drop it overboard."

Gar took reverent hold of the once-varnished, scarred and dented box with brass corner plates and bronze carrying handle. "Jeez, Will. Thank you. I'll take care of it."

At two, Boden went below and relieved Dick Iams. They were steaming hard again and the furnace needed feeding. He shoveled and raked and banked for four hours, with a few breaks topside for the duration of a cigarette.

GAR REPORTED TO THE wheelhouse. He was placed on lookout in the bow, going forward and taking the horn from Joey, who had done 1789 jumping jacks in an hour. Because it was always cold in the bow and the view ahead relentlessly unchanging and the lookout's senses, if he were not doing jumping jacks, tended to dull quickly, the position was relieved every hour, rotating with another man on his watch.

When Gar was relieved at three and came back into the wheelhouse to take the helm, he asked Captain Percival if he might follow the captain's taking and working out of his sights.

"No, you may not," said Percival evenly. "I am not here to help you; rather, it's the other way round. And when you're not helping me I want you out of my way. Nor are you to spend any of your watch time studying navigation, other than whatever you might passively deduce in the course of your duties."

Once again Gar wondered if the captain had taken against him for some reason. He had to remind himself of incidents when Percival treated the other crewmembers similarly to hold on to his feelings. Fuck you, Jack, he thought.

"However," said Percival. And let it hang a moment. "When you have confirmed your positons with Mr. Boden, when you are quite sure of them, you may mark them—neatly, and in pencil—on my charts here in the wheelhouse, as long as you don't rub out my marks. Do this in your off-watch periods only. You may use my dividers and parallel rule. You may also refer to my pilot books, tide tables, and lightlists here in the wheelhouse, but do not remove them."

"Yes, sir! Thank you, sir!" Not such a bad old fuck.

THE AFTERNOON REMAINED CLEAR and Percival had the ship running again at twenty knots. They saw more ice. By the change of watch at 1800 hours, floes of bergs of all shapes and sizes were in sight all around them and more appearing ahead. Several times the ship was steered around large group-ings. At 2000 hours, the captain changed course, heading far-ther offshore. He had been reading in his pilot books himself and, in the thick blue British Admiralty publication *Ocean Pas-sages of the World*, of the counterclockwise flow of ice north along the coast of Greenland, across the top of Davis Strait, and south down the Labrador shore. It seemed that it might be better farther away from land.

As the sun slowly lowered, the ice floating in the sea took on the hues of the long and spectacular sunset. Red, pink, orange, and coldfire-blue castellated bergs lay along the entire horizon, glowing like embers in the dark sea.

The sun disappeared into the sea a little after eight. At nine Boden and Gar stood on the foredeck, ready to take star sights. Boden explained the several twilights and their meaning for a navigator.

"Between sunset and when the sun is six degrees below the horizon is the period called 'civil twilight'—what we've had roughly between eight o'clock and now. The sun's down but it's still pretty light. You can read by it. The sky's still blue and you'll only see Venus or a few very bright stars. 'Nautical twi-light' is when the sun is between six and twelve degrees below the horizon, and that's when we want to take star sights. That's when it's dark enough to see the stars we want, but still light enough to find a horizon through the sextant. Nautical twilight is great up here in such a high latitude, because it lasts so long, more than an hour tonight. Plenty of time to find stars, shoot them, write down our times. In the tropics it passes in a few minutes. This cruise is a good opportunity for you to learn."

And through the long nautical twilight, Boden pointed out

stars, showed Gar how he found them, and they each took sights of Antares, Betelgeuse, and Fomalhaut. Below in the crew's saloon, the three stars became three lines on Boden's chart, intersecting to form a small triangle.

"We are somewhere in that little triangle," said Boden. "The seaman's cocked hat, the English call it. And shooting three stars at the same time, giving us three lines, we have a triangulated fix right away, rather than waiting as we have to during the day for the sun to move in order to get a second bisecting line. Star sights are the most accurate and the best for the navigator to try for."

"What happens if it's cloudy?"

"Then your choices for stars are fewer, depending on what you can see, or, if it's overcast, you get nothing."

"Well, what if it's overcast and you don't see the sun or stars for days?"

"Then you have to fall back on dead reckoning, your speed and course since your last good fix."

Moyle sat at the other end of the saloon table with a cup of coffee, staring absently at the chart. The fog had affected his lungs; up his throat as he breathed came a bubbling sound like smoke passing through a hookah. Moyle didn't know how to navigate by sextant, but he understood perfectly the need for clear skies to fix a position.

He said to Gar, "You're beating west on a winter passage south of the Horn. You've got a westerly gale or worse in your teeth for a month, maybe six weeks. You make your boards, come about and come about, zigzagging for weeks, blown back by wind, set back by current, your ship making leeway she's never made before, and through that whole time you never see land and you never see sun or stars. Your DR plot looks like a scribble made by a monkey. What do you do?"

Boden laughed. Gar looked at them both.

"I don't know," said Gar. "What do you do?"

"You pray," said Moyle.

"Okay, but really? What do you do when that happens?"

"I stayed in my bunk when I wasn't out on that fuckin' yard."

"That happened to you?"

"I was there. Couple of times, but I wasn't the navigator, thank Christ."

"And what happened?"

"We come through."

Gar turned to Boden. "So, what's the answer? You're blind, right? You keep a dead reckoning?"

"There's no answer," said Boden. "Your DR is shot to hell by that point. All you can do then is take a negative or counterpoint fix at it. Map out the growing area of your uncertainty of position and try to stay outside of that. In the end it's instinct. Some men have a gift for it, a smell for where they are, made up of what they know and who they are and how much their mothers loved them and anything else you can think of. Probably more men have been wrong and lost their ships. I'd say it comes down to a feel for the information you're missing and how much you can be wrong. A hunch."

"And luck," Moyle said, and sipped his coffee.

"Yes. Only a landlubber will tell you there's no such thing as luck," said Boden. "Luck is the greatest factor at sea, but the only one you can't measure, or work to your advantage."

During the night, after his watch finished at two in the morning, Gar came quietly into the centrally heated wheelhouse. The captain was not present. Joey was at the helm, Watts stood by, Avery was in the bow. Gar walked to the chart table. Using Captain Percival's brass dividers and his heavy brass rolling ruler, he located the point on the open chart where 58°24′ north latitude met 57°37′ west longitude. He saw that on this chart he was three inches southeast of Hudson Strait, five inches south of the Arctic Circle, and Greenland lay four inches to the east.

He drew a neat penciled X.

CHAPTER 12

THE TRUE BREEZE FELL away with the dawn, leaving only the icy twenty-knot blast from dead ahead made by the ship's streaking progress. All day it steamed across a flat glassy sea, cutting it neatly as a tailor and peeling it aside in its wake. Despite the sun in the blue sky, the air was a frigid 38 degrees in the sheltered lee of the superstructure at the ship's stern.

Schenck appeared on deck in his reindeer pants. He wore them as naturally beneath his Burberry parka as if they had been gray flannel. Mamie, Harriet, and Arthur had also been equipped with reindeer pants, but Mamie would no longer go outdoors while the ship was at speed. Arthur's black skin turned an unbecoming moribund gray in the cold and he also now remained inside, but he nevertheless wore his reindeer pants as he served drinks and tended to the Schencks' needs. He said he felt too cold without them. (Mamie was convinced he was simply mad about them and allowed himself to wear them because he was far out at sea and nobody he knew, apart from the Schencks, could see him.) Harriet thought her reindeer pants might be fun at a fancy dress party someday, but now that it had turned cold she wore wool jodhpurs with Bean boots and an aviator's leather jacket over a heavy sweater when she went out on deck. The men on watch in the bow, with no shelter, would have been grateful for a pair of reindeer pants. They felt frozen long before their agonizing hour was up despite the new sweaters and wool pants and peacoats they wore beneath their oilskins.

During Gar's watch at the helm in the afternoon, the course was once again landward, and soon the line of icebergs that they had turned away from the day before appeared ahead again, stretching north and south across the entire horizon. First seen from miles away were the remnants of large tabular bergs, flat as mesas and some as large; then the smaller irregular bergs, calved sections of former mesas, grew visible, with shapes of spires and turrets, the size of mansions and houses and automobiles. As the ship neared the line of bergs, with open sea astern, the view ahead became more concentrated with ice and took on the appearance of a highway. The ship reached the point where it began to cross the road.

Once among it, Gar saw that the spread of ice was thicker than it had appeared from farther off. Floes trailed in long stretches like patterns of sargasso weed, with scraps and growlers filling in the apparent spaces between the larger bergs. Captain Percival, pacing now along the wheelhouse windows, ordered the ship slowed, then slowed again, until they were progressing at little more than steerageway. The smooth sea rolled with a swell that was barely perceptible except when it dipped and revealed undulating floes of bobbing rubble blocking the way ahead. Gar responded to the captain's directions, turning the wheel constantly to dodge and follow leads as they appeared and then closed off. He felt a tension rise in the wheelhouse as Percival's voice grew more than usually curt and Gar began to perspire. Despite the compass in front of him, he lost all sense of direction. His course was reduced to narrowing stretches of navigable water, and he soon felt trapped in a maze. He felt too, for the first time, a sense of the ship's vulnerability.

The open lead they were following, a narrow waterpath through the closing ice, turned, and then the way ahead dead-ended in a vast heaving plain of floes. Percival ordered slow astern to bring the ship to a drifting stop. Ice lay along both sides, right against the hull, moving up and down with the sea swell, but not pressing or appearing to scratch the paint.

Percival sent Bill outside onto the wheelhouse roof to look

for another lead. Bill called down that he saw no available open path but that a berg the size and shape of a Providence factory lay a quarter of a mile abeam, and was coming their way.

As they stopped, the speed of the approaching berg became evident. It was moving at about two knots, pushing aside all the smaller ice in its path. It came on purposefully, heading directly for them. It was blue, and appeared to glow and emanate some cold intent, and as he stared at it, growing larger with its approach, Gar felt the back of his scalp contract.

Schenck came into the wheelhouse. "What are you going to do about this iceberg?" he asked Percival.

"Avoid it. Let it go by and then find a clear lead in its wake."

The captain then telegraphed half astern to the engine room. A moment later a brief shudder passed through the ship and it began to move backward.

"It's going to go by in front of us?" asked Schenck.

"I intend it so," answered Percival.

"Good," said Schenck. He went outside.

As the berg approached, *Lodestar* began to move slowly backward, drawing the berg's path from amidships toward the bow. A shout came from Bill on the roof saying that the ice was closing in astern, they could not go back much farther. Percival telegraphed slow ahead and then all stop. The ship lay in its own slot in the ice. They all watched the great flat blue building-looking berg closing with the bow, on course now to pass just ahead. Percival went outdoors onto the bridge wing and asked Bill if he was able to see any indication of the berg's shape below its waterline.

"It looks like it goes in under the water, like it's all been eaten away at the waterline and below."

Captain Percival said nothing, but fixed his gaze on the berg. Gar wondered if they were far enough back for it to pass without some underwater part of it reaching out and snagging the ship's bow. He noticed the men of the off watch coming up from below to see the iceberg pass. The crew clustered in the bow. Gar looked back at the berg, its own square bulwark bow drawing level with theirs. The bows crossed. It began to slip by like some unheeding blind blue undersea monster.

Gar's eye was drawn to the crew moving suddenly backward on the foredeck, leaving Schenck alone in the bow. He saw Schenck's arm fly forward. He did not understand until the enormous percusive *Bang!* made him jump. He saw a shower of ice fly up off the berg.

"Good God," said Captain Percival.

Schenck had thrown a stick of dynamite onto the berg.

AS SCHENCK PULLED ANOTHER stick out of the box at his feet, a hand closed around his wrist so hard he dropped the stick—or it was taken from him. Boden took it. He released Schenck's wrist.

"Excuse me, sir. I don't want you to get hurt. We don't need any dynamite now."

Boden's words and tone, loud enough for the crew behind him to hear, were respectful. His face was seen only by Schenck. For just a moment, while Boden lifted the small case of dynamite and put it under his arm, Schenck was too surprised to speak.

Then Boden turned and walked aft with the case.

Schenck watched him go, then turned to watch the berg sliding by.

The crew saw Schenck's head nodding. Then they heard him begin to laugh.

Boden walked all the way down the deck to the stern and dropped the case of dynamite overboard. He watched it sink.

"CHAMBERLAIN, HARD A-STARBOARD. Make for the opening there." Percival pointed to the open water left in the berg's wake, and telegraphed slow ahead, while Gar turned the wheel all the way to the right—north, he saw, as the ship began ponderously to wheel about the compass card.

Schenck came into the wheelhouse. "Stop the ship. I'm going ashore."

"Ashore, sir?" said Percival.

"I want to walk around on this ice."

"That would be rather tricky, sir—"

"Damn tricky, eh, what?" Schenck mimicked the Englishman's clipped accent. "But you'll have to figure it out, old chap!"

Schenck left the wheelhouse. Percival turned away to scan the horizon.

"Jesus! Captain—"

Percival turned and looked along Gar's outstretched arm. Schenck was climbing over the rail. As they watched, he lowered himself until his legs were out of sight below the hull. Then he let go the rail and disappeared.

Others on deck had seen him drop over the side. Avery, Watts, and Shred rushed to the rail. They saw Schenck getting to his feet; he had rolled over on landing. He stood and walked about on the flat ice, appearing from above to balloon out like a top with the bulk of his reindeer pants. He was sliding astern as the ship was still moving forward.

In the wheelhouse, Percival telegraphed all stop, and came out on the bridge and ordered Watts and Avery to lower the smaller rowboat. Everyone was watching Schenck, now abreast with the aft saloon. The ship trembled as Eddie Jenkins below ran the props hard astern.

Harriet had come on deck with the sound of the explosion. She climbed into the boat as Watts, Avery, and Shred lowered it. But there was no clear water to float it, and it dragged and thumped over the ice as the ship slowed. Harriet got out and stood on the ice.

Watching from the bridge wing, Percival yelled through the open door at Gar to keep the helm hard over to starboard. As the ship came to a stop, its starboard slant opened up a narrow vector of water near the stern. Avery and Watts jumped down onto the ice, released the boat's tackle, and began dragging it toward the opening water.

Schenck was now twenty yards astern, calling for Mamie. She appeared on the aft deck and saw her husband standing on an ice floe across a widening gap of water.

"Good heavens, Carl! What's going on? What was that noise?" She saw the boat coming aft alongside the ship, and then she saw Harriet, who had not joined her father but was standing still on the ice looking up at her. "What are you both doing?"

"Out for a stroll!" called Schenck.

Lodestar finally stopped. The two deckhands pushed the boat into the water and pulled it by its painter along the edge of the floe. When they reached Schenck, he turned and headed away across the ice. Watts and Avery looked back at the ship, then followed him, pulling the boat out of the water and dragging it behind them. After a minute, Harriet walked along the rowboat's gouged wake.

Shred moved down the deck, involuntarily following the figures, stopping forward of the canopied aft deck, where Mamie stood, where the crew did not venture unless the ship was docking. Moyle, Boden, the engineer, and his mate had all come up on deck from below. Captain Percival and Gar stood on the bridge wing. The ship's complement watched the four figures moving away on the ice, dragging the ship's boat after them.

"Where are you going?" shouted Mamie, for everyone watching.

"Having a look around!" came back Schenck's reply.

THEY RETURNED AN HOUR later, Watts and Avery poling the boat with the oars through a narrow open lead in the ice. The ship's ladder had been lowered. As they came alongside, Harriet handed a large bundle over to Boden, who stood at the ladder's lower platform. It was a seal pup, quiet, blinking, looking around with unperturbed curiosity. Harriet came up the ladder behind him and took the seal in her arms. She went aft to show her mother.

"Oh!" shrieked Mamie. "It's absolutely darling!"

Harriet put the seal down. It heaved itself across a foot of deck and stopped, rolled onto its side, and gazed at its new surroundings. It looked up at Harriet and her mother and blinked.

"Oh, it's dear! Where's its mother?"

"I don't know. It was just lying on the ice. It didn't move away."

"Look at those eyes! It's looking right at me! I can't believe it! Will it let me touch it?"

"Yes. It's completely tame."

Mamie bent down and took one glove off. She carefully reached out and ran her hand along the seal's side. "Oh my God. A living coat."

"Well, you're not wearing it."

"Of course not! How could anyone kill such a dear creature!"

Harriet went forward to the galley and returned with some pâté. The seal sniffed at it and moved its head away.

Then it barked.

THE GREAT BERG LEFT a canal through the ice that was navigable. They followed it north for several miles and a lead opened to the west. In another hour they had passed through the ice highway and were heading northwest once more. Ice was still visible everywhere around the ship, but widely scattered and separated by large areas of open sea. Their speed remained slow, eight knots, and Bill stayed on the wheelhouse roof, frozen and clinging to the mast, looking for smaller bergy bits that might lie in their path, awash and hard to see.

LATE IN THE AFTERNOON, his watch over, Gar sat in his bunk reading Boden's arctic pilot book.

Watts and Avery were playing slapjack at the fo'c'sle table. "The Boys," these two were called by their shipmates, for their exuberant behavior, and for the fact that they both came from Bath and had grown up together and were as comfortable and offhand with each other as two brothers. They occupied the moment without any burdens of regret or hope, and although they were Gar's age, they seemed to him far younger and infinitely, sometimes enviably, simpler. They liked to play slapjack for hours, forgetting the people around them, slapping cards down so hard and fast that Boden, Gar, and Moyle had at various times told them to keep it down, knock it off, shut the fuck up. They were polite boys and always quiet for a short time afterward. Then they forgot themselves.

It was at the edge of Gar's mind now to ask them to pipe down, but he was too enthralled with the pilot book, with the spare horror of its descriptions of inhospitable coasts, to pause.

Then Joey came below and told Gar that Captain Percival

wanted to see him. He closed the book, pulled on his new peacoat, and climbed up to the wheelhouse.

Percival was white, and began to shout. "What the bloody hell have you messed up my chart with?"

Gar's stomach turned icy. Before he could answer, the captain—who was not as tall as Gar—grabbed him by the shoulder and thrust him toward the chart table. With his other hand he forced Gar's head down until his face was inches above the chart and his neat pencil marks.

"What is this damned nonsense?"

"Sir, I thought you said it was okay—"

"*If* you knew what the bloody hell you were doing! These marks bear no relation to our position! Do you see my positions? Here. Here. Here. Look at your positions! What do you mean by marking my chart like that? You and your friend Mr. Boden are out by a hundred long miles!"

Percival picked up his dividers with a shaking hand and measured the distance between the most recent position Gar had marked on the chart and Resolution Island at the entrance to Frobisher Bay, off the southeastern point of Baffin Island.

"One hundred and twenty miles, according to you two navigators."

He seized Gar by the arm and pulled him across the wheelhouse and out the port door. "What the bloody hell is that then?"

Land stood up across the sea to the west. It shimmered slightly over the flat horizon, but its outline was bold and unmistakably close.

Gar could not speak. Part of him registered surprise at seeing land so close, but his mind had shut down with Percival's assault, and he could make no sense of what he saw.

"Would you be so good as to come back here with Mr. Boden," said Percival. He opened the wheelhouse door and shoved Gar out.

Two minutes later both men came into the wheelhouse. Boden was sweat-streaked and sooty with coal dust. Gar had briefed him, and Boden now looked at Captain Percival with lively interest. Gar stood slightly behind him.

"What is that piece of land out there, do you suppose?" Percival asked Boden, pointing out the window.

"That's Resolution Island."

"Really? A hundred and twenty miles away by your reckoning."

"Give or take a few miles. How far away do you make it?"

Percival was affronted by the direct question. "Rather closer than that! More like thirty miles away!"

"It's a mirage," said Boden.

Percival stared at him, his eyes bulging. "Are you actually trying to make fun of me?"

"No, Captain. I'm telling you I believe that's Resolution Island, about a hundred and some miles away, well below the horizon in fact, but we're seeing it because its image is bending over the curve of the earth, forming a mirage, a common feature of arctic waters when—"

"Shut up!"

"I may be wrong. Where do your sights put us, Captain? I'd be glad to compare our methods." Boden glanced toward the chart table.

"You can keep your sextant and your methods below deck from now on, Mr. Boden! This ship needs only one navigator. Now get off my bridge!"

"With respect, Captain, I'll continue to keep track of our position for my own pleasure. If you want to compare our results let me know." Boden pointed out the window. "That's Resolution Island, over a hundred miles away, visible to us because of atmospheric distortion."

When he turned to leave, Schenck stood in the open doorway.

"So who's right?" Schenck asked, his eyes taking in the stance and every spark of contact between the two men.

"Excuse me, sir." Boden moved past Schenck and out the door.

"You lost?" Schenck asked Captain Percival.

"No, sir." Percival stared blandly at Schenck. "Hardly. Mr. Chamberlain, you may go below."

Gar left the wheelhouse.

"So what's that piece of land there?" asked Schenck.

"Resolution Island, sir. No disagreement about that. Merely a damn sight closer than they imagine, and they've been messing up my chart with their scribblings."

"Show me the chart."

They moved to the chart table. Percival indicated the island off the southern tip of the greater mass of Baffin Island.

"Okay," said Schenck, looking at his captain, and Percival would not meet his eyes, but kept his gaze on the view through the wheelhouse windows. "And where exactly are we now?"

Percival glanced down and briefly tapped the chart roughly on his own penciled position, halfway between Gar's mark and the island, his fingertip covering an elastic sixty square miles. "Right here, sir. Will you excuse me a moment?" He went outside onto the bridge wing and trained his binoculars on the shimmering land across the sea.

An hour later a southerly breeze set in and the profile of land wavered and vanished, and the ship once more appeared to be far out at sea.

At the same time, to the northwest, fine off the ship's port bow, and forward of the position of the vanished Resolution Island, a white glare appeared in the blue sky. Everyone who looked forward now saw it and wondered aloud what it was. Boden saw it when he came off watch and he told Bill Fisher he thought it was the ice blink of Terra Nivea glacier on Baffin Island: the reflection of the white mass in the atmosphere above it. Word passed through the crew that Boden thought it was a glacier.

Later, as the glare drew abeam, Captain Percival gave the helmsman a new course, due west, and the ship now headed directly toward the white glare. As the sun dropped lower in the sky, the horizon grew faint, and the air above the sea appeared to thicken into diffuse particles of pink and blue. Then gradually the color paled away, and before anyone could see it coming, they were once more in fog.

IN THE MISTY TWILIGHT, most of the people aboard *Lodestar* became aware of a change.

At sea, the body viscerally registers the loss of stability that it takes for granted on the hard unmoving earth; this undermines a voyager's most primeval sense of security. The Schencks at dinner first sensed only an ease in this subliminal anxiety. Boden, Moyle, and Shred in the fo'c'sle, Duhamel in his galley, Captain Percival in the wheelhouse, all realized that the motion of the ship was losing the hardly felt rise and fall of the ocean swell that is always present at sea even during apparently flat calms. Unless a ship is no longer at sea, but close to land.

After dinner, Harriet pulled her parka on over her leather jacket and went out on deck. The fog around the ship appeared white and bright, suggesting a clear twilight somewhere not far above. A cold southerly wind was now blowing across the water onto the ship's side and around Harriet on the aft deck, and as she breathed it in, she smelled a peaty dankness.

The ship, she saw now, looking at the water, had reduced its speed and was moving at its slowest pace again. She walked forward. She saw Boden and Gar talking together on the foredeck. Near them Watts and Moyle were taking soundings, heaving the weight far forward and pulling the line back in as the ship moved over it.

"Thirty fathoms," Watts called back to Captain Percival, who stood on the port bridge wing. The captain wore his Royal Navy hat and camel duffel coat, and held his binoculars at his chest.

Harriet approached Shred, who stood at the port rail. "Are we near land, Mr. Shred? I think I can smell it."

"I believe so, Miss Schenck." He tried sniffing the air, without evident result. "We're on soundings now and I heard there's land to port and up ahead somewhere." Shred was wearing his new peacoat. His brown derby was pulled down low on his head and fog glistened on his red face.

"What land? Where are we?"

"Ah, well, I guess it'll be some northern bit of Canada, Miss. You'd have to ask young Gar, or Captain Boden. They been navigating and looking at the charts, and they must know."

"Is Captain Boden a good navigator?"

He glanced at her. A young girl who could know nothing about a man like Boden. "Oh, I think so, Miss. He's considerable natural at it. He's not just a stoker, you see. He's a ship's master in his own right."

"Oh, I know. He went with my father to Florida. Why did he come as a stoker?"

"Well . . ." Shred now believed he understood perfectly why Boden had embarked on this ill-begot voyage: for the same reasons he himself had come along. Every reason in the world not to, and in the end he had to come. But Shred was unable to explain this in any way that might make sense to this girl, or to himself. "I guess he wanted to come, Miss."

"Doesn't he have a family who will miss him?"

"Captain Boden? I wouldn't know about that, Miss."

She watched Boden and Gar. They seemed to be getting along well. Gar looked different to her now—better in some way. He looked happy.

"Will we see the shore in this fog, Mr. Shred?"

"Why, that's the main question, Miss. That's why we're poking along here at what I've come to feel in a very short time is an inconsiderable speed, and why they're sounding nonstop now, and why everyone's staring themselves fish-eyed into this fog. It could come popping out ahead any minute, you see." As he spoke, Shred was squinting into the depthless mist, turning his head slightly back and forth.

"LAND!" YELLED BILL, AT nine o'clock.

Everyone looked and found it portside, to the south, a hole in the blue mist through which they saw a dark rocky outline topped with snow, an indeterminate distance away. More holes appeared in the fog, billowy rents showing glimpses of a sharp land; more the view from an airplane descending through cloud. The holes grew as streamers of mist stretched and separated, and minutes later the fog was gone.

Ahead and along both sides of the ship a raw scene lay exposed. To the south, on the portside, high jagged coasts of rock, mantled with snow, rose to mountains deep in twilight shadow, their skyline sharp against the pale sky. Shale and glacial moraine littered the cliff-edged shores. *Lodestar* appeared to be passing between two rock- and snow-bound islands that she might easily have hit in the fog. Ahead, beyond a small Milky Way of rocks scattered completely across the water between the two islands, a fjord cut into the land. At its head, the frozen tableau of a glacier rose nearly three thousand feet from the sea: a mountain-sized ice river on a scale that made all the lethal foreground disappear. Surrounded by dark rock and dull snow, the glacier shone with a sepulchral luminousness. The ice, clear against the deepening blue sky at its upper reaches, fell into impenetrable shadow at its base far up the fjord.

The bow lookout, Watts, and everyone else aboard, could see nothing below the surface of the water, only an inverted picture of their surroundings in the mirror of the sea, shot through with the pink and orange that edged the sky. The ship, as surrounded by rock as it had been by ice, trembled underfoot as the propeller shafts reversed, and came to a drifting stop.

Schenck entered the wheelhouse, where Captain Percival was bent over a chart. "I say, old chap! Where the hell are we?"

Percival straightened up. "Off the southeast coast of Baffin Island, sir."

"Off the southeast coast of Baffin Island. I see. 'Off the northeast coast of the United States, sir,' he says, with New York City on the bow."

"Well, sir—"

"My fault, sport!" said Schenck. "Let me make myself a little clearer." He stuck out a hand, pointing through the wheelhouse window. "What's the name of that rock there, Captain?"

Percival looked carefully through the window. Then back at Schenck. "Half of these islands are unnamed, sir. I haven't been here before, as you know. But I should say we're right about—" With a finger he tapped the chart. "—here, more or less."

"Which is it, old chap? More or less?"

Percival tried staring at him, but Schenck popped his own eyes open and rolled them at Percival. He made a sound like an owl.

Percival, who was anxiously uncertain of the position of the ship, now experienced a much stranger vertigo. "I am working on establishing our position, sir."

Schenck smiled at him, and went outside. He looked forward, then stepped down into the fo'c'sle and found Boden
and Gar at the saloon table bent over a chart and the open
pages of a large, stained, ripple-paged blue pilot book.

"Captain Boden, sir. Do you know where we are?"

Boden was about to suggest that he ask his brass-buttoned
naval hero, but seeing Schenck's face, which was unusually
flushed and excited, he decided not to.

"We're between Gross and Potter Islands—here." He
touched the chart with the point of his dividers. He moved the
brass points along a pencil line from Davis Strait. "We were
here this afternoon when we turned west and made about
ninety miles before the fog slowed us down. We passed north
of Edgell Island, here, in the fog at about eight this evening. I
was going up on deck now to see if I can find this summit—
here on the chart, called Sugarloaf Hill in the pilot book—and
take a bearing off that and the glacier. That's Terra Nivea
Glacier, twenty-eight hundred feet high. You can generally see
it from everywhere off this part of Baffin Island. When I get a
bearing off these two points, I'll have an accurate position for
you."

"Have you been in this place before?"

"Not this spot. Over the peninsula on the south shore, and
across Frobisher Bay. But the glacier can usually be seen from
anyplace hereabouts. It's a good landmark. A bearing off that
and off this hill," he tapped the chart, "should pinpoint us."

"Then let's go find that hill."

On deck, Boden raised to eye-level a small brass compass
held in his hand. A prism on its glass face provided a horizontal eye-level reading. He took bearings on the conical hill to
port, then turned to starboard, facing the glacier high above
them, the dominant feature of the landscape. Gar was carrying
Boden's sextant, and Boden now took it from him, giving Gar
the compass to play with. He turned back to the hill and aimed
the sextant at it for a few moments. "Okay, let's go below."

As they stepped down the fo'c'sle companionway, Gar
looked up and saw Percival in the rear of the wheelhouse looking out at them.

On his chart, Boden drew lines along the azimuths he had

read from the glacier and the hill. Schenck bent over the table watching the process. "We should be here," said Boden, looking up at Schenck, tapping the spot where the lines intersected: in a rock-strewn channel between Gross and Potter Islands.

He opened his nautical almanac and placed it on the table between himself and Gar. "To confirm that, we know from the pilot book that Sugarloaf Hill is a thousand feet high. A sextant angle—" Boden held the sextant in the light and read the scale. "—of a known height will give us a horizontal distance off the base of that height. That distance is—" He ran a finger down a table on an almanac page. "—seven and a half miles." With his dividers he picked off seven and a half minutes of latitude at the side of his chart. Sticking one divider point on the center of Sugarloaf Hill on the chart, he brought the other point down virtually on top of the intersection of his bearing lines.

"We're here, Mr. Schenck."

"Good man! Where do we go now?"

"That's up to you and your—"

"Give me your best suggestion, Captain. I want to stop and go ashore. We're a bunch of dogs that need to take a leak. We got to get off this thing. Find me a good spot on your chart."

"Well, Noble Inlet, right here, looks good." Boden traced a route with the divider points. "We should turn around and leave Gross Island to starboard, and then head up the inlet. Here, off the base of Sugarloaf Hill. It's only about five miles away."

"Thank you," said Schenck. He climbed the steps to the deck.

The wheelhouse door opened. Schenck went straight to the chart table. "Captain Percival! Orders just in from HQ, old boy!"

Percival left the forward windows, where he was peering through his binoculars, and carefully approached the other side of the chart table. "Yes, sir?"

Schenck had found a pencil and was making a mark at the spot Boden had found. His voice was cheerful and controlled. "Looks like we're right here, old chap. Damn good luck! Might have steamed up here!" He stabbed the island on the chart. "Or right up the jolly old glacier! Now be a good fellow and take us back around this island and anchor us right . . . here." The pencil point broke. "Got it?"

"Whatever you say, sir. Of course, I can't take responsibility for your route—"

"Of course you can't, old boy! These orders come from the top! We do our duty." He bared his teeth at Percival and left the wheelhouse.

After a moment, Percival turned to Joey, who was at the helm. "Is he mad? What's he on about? You know him, don't you? You work for him."

Joey turned and looked at the captain with dead blank eyes and shrugged and looked away.

With soundings taken as they ghosted through the still water, and most of the crew at the foredeck rail looking for rocks, *Lodestar* turned and passed around the south of Gross Island, giving a wide berth to its rockgirt shore. It was after ten in the evening, but still light enough to proceed up the apparent entrance to the fjordlike inlet. Boden was braced for the submerged rock they would never see, but the ship did not find it. At eleven, still not dark, but the light failing at last, well up the inlet, they brought the thousand-foot cone of Sugarloaf Hill abeam.

"Let go!" called Percival from the bridge wing.

Moyle worked the windlass. The pawl released, the gypsy flew, the chain ran through the hawsepipe. A great metal clattering filled the silence of the inlet.

At once a large dark patch of the tundra inside the gloom at the base of the hill wheeled as a piece and began to move away. The muted sound of many hooves on a spongy turf came across the water.

Schenck ran down the deck and disappeared through the saloon door. A moment later he reappeared with a rifle and went straight to the rail and began firing. The heavy-bore reports echoed across the still water up and down the high-sided inlet.

CHAPTER 13

SCHENCK WAS UP OUT of bed, in and out of his cabin, all night.

"Carl, what is it? What are you doing?" Mamie asked with sleepy exasperation.

"Nothing. Go back to sleep."

Harriet's seal began barking. A sharp, braying, unending, *arrh!arrh!arrh!arrh!* It came from the other side of the thin mahogany bulkhead.

"I can't stand this!" said Mamie. She got out of bed and went into Harriet's cabin.

Schenck went up on deck. He peered through the boreal glow of the arctic night for the ninth time to look for the caribou ashore. He pictured their antlers. Their noble taxidermied heads sprouting great branching tines up the walls of his library. His shots had driven the herd over a ridge at the side of Sugarloaf Hill, and he worried all night that he wouldn't find them again in the morning. The sky began to lighten at two. At three, the bloom end of nautical twilight, he dressed.

FORWARD IN THE FO'C'SLE, a single electric light in the deckhead lit the aft end of the crew's saloon. One man at a time was on anchor watch, rotating at hourly intervals, while the rest of the crew slept their longest stretch since leaving Connecticut.

Joey woke to a form bending over him. His mind flew to

167

scenarios of victims murdered while they slept, their bodies twisted into the death shapes in the photographs. He sat upright quickly.

"Who's that?"

"Me," said Schenck. "Where's Chamberlain?"

"The other side, Mr. Schenck. First cabin, top bunk."

Schenck left the cabin. Joey lay down again, his adrenaline pumping, the muscles across his stomach and chest twitching. He thought how easily Schenck might have murdered him while he slept. It disturbed him, although he knew Schenck had no reason to kill him. He could fire him.

"LET'S GO," SAID SCHENCK, shaking Gar out of deep sleep.

Gar had been on anchor watch two hours earlier. He looked at his watch and could make no sense of what was happening.

"Time to go hunting!"

"I thought we were going at nine o'clock, sir."

"They'll be in Greenland by then. It's getting light now. Let's go."

The preparations were mighty; everybody was woken up. Schenck found Duhamel in the cabin he shared with Newton. He woke them up and told Duhamel what he wanted for breakfast, and why:

"I want meat! Bacon, ham, sausages for everybody going ashore. A whole pig's worth, snout, hock, and tail. A side of beef; I want steaks. And stacks of flapjacks and gallons of maple syrup. A hundred scrambled eggs. Forty pounds of home fries. And I want cowboy coffee I can drink with a fork. I want American food this morning, Monsewer, got me? Grub for a charge up San Juan Hill. I'm going hunting! I'm going out there to kill beasts! I want to be strong!"

Standing beside Dumhamel, wearing a former employer's hand-me-down Sulka pajamas, taken up at the hems, and an old cashmere cardigan, Newton watched Schenck give his breakfast order. He had looked through the saloon windows in the lingering twilight before going to bed and beheld the landscape with terror. It bore no relation to the gentle scenes of Block Island and Nantucket he had pictured when he signed on for a summer cruise aboard a yacht. He understood, deep in his belly, that they had somehow, very quickly, reached the end of the world, an awful primitive place where Mr. Schenck was an authority beyond all accountability. They would all do what this man wanted and there would be no stopping him. Newton was afraid.

Gar dressed and gathered rifles from the closet and boxes of ammunition from under the bunks in Arthur's cabin. A hunting party was formed: Gar, Boden, Joey, Bill, and Watts would accompany Harriet and Schenck ashore. (Mamie told her husband she had no intention of tramping about the tundra, but preferred to wait aboard until a polar bear or walrus floated by the ship.) Gar filled four canvas fishing satchels with cartridges. Bill Fisher had his own rifle, a Winchester. From his sea chest, Boden took a Colt revolver and stuck it in his peacoat. Each crewman carried a knife.

The sun rose at four. There was no hint of fog. The air was still cold as night, unmoving and clear. The water in the fjord displayed an undistorted inversion of the surrounding shore, rising to the skyline and the glacier. On deck, Boden and Moyle lowered the two pulling boats and sculled them round to the ship's ladder on the portside. Ice as thin as isinglass had formed on the water in the inlet and around the ship during the night, but broke easily beneath the oars.

Despite the early hour, the shore party soon found their insides churning with a sharp hunger, for the whiff of Duhamel's frying pig and boiling coffee and burning toast filled the ship as they dressed and worked, and hung in the frosty air on deck, and, to varying degrees, they were all feeling the trembling onset of blood lust. Schenck and Harriet breakfasted in the dining room aft, the crewmen forward in their saloon. The menu was identical for both groups: everything Schenck had asked for, and Duhamel added bread, toasted and butter-saturated pain d'épices, and hot chocolate.

While they ate, a light wind came up from the northwest, the direction of the glacier at the head of the inlet. Flat floe ice that had not been carried out to sea but borne up the inlet on tidal eddies, and islands of glacier-calved bergs, began moving down the inlet.

Captain Percival interrupted Schenck's breakfast to tell him of the approach of the ice, and that he felt they must raise anchor and move immediately before a berg fouled their anchor chain or stove in the hull. He had aleady pulled Eddie Jenkins, Strick, and Iams from forward and sent them aft to raise steam.

"We'll go ashore," said Schenck, waving a forkful of dripping flapjacks at Percival, "and you come back later and pick us up."

"I don't believe you would reach the shore, sir, and it may prove impossible to return here. Perhaps you'd care to see for yourself."

Schenck went out on deck. A new terrain of ice fields, gorges, and steeples had filled the water around the ship since he had last been outside, half an hour earlier. More was coming, drifting down the inlet, crowding their anchorage. As he watched, a piece of the ice shaped like a wide flat mushroom, the size of a bus, grazed the yacht's anchor chain, spun slowly around it, and whirled in stately pirouette past the bow. The visible danger to the ship was apparent, even to Schenck with his determination to go ashore right now. He looked around for Boden and saw him nearby, also watching the ice.

"You think we should get out of here?"

Percival was standing beside Schenck. He looked away.

"That's your captain's call," said Boden.

"He says we should leave."

"I agree with him."

Schenck turned to Captain Percival. "Well, let's get going." He walked aft.

Percival could not look at Boden. But he said, "Get those boats out of the water."

The windlass's gasoline donkey engine was started, and the chain hauled in.

Harriet came forward. She spoke to Avery, who was at the rail watching the chain come up. "Have you seen my seal?"

"No, miss."

"Has anybody seen my seal?"

Nobody had.

*   *   *

TWO HOURS LATER THE ship was ten miles offshore in Frobisher Bay. Fields of floe ice drifted nearby but not in concentration. The ship lay with its turbines idling. The weather remained clear, the breeze light.

At seven, Mamie joined Schenck at the rail.

"I should be exhausted after a night like that, but I can't stay in bed when it's this light. If I read, I fall asleep. It's too hot down there, Carl, and I'm not supposed to open that darn porthole. I feel like some potentate lying in bed in the middle of the day, but it's only seven o'clock. What are those things over there?"

"What things?"

"On that slab of ice over there—oh, look, Carl! They're moving!"

"Where?"

"There! Oh, my gosh, they're plopping into the water! They're more seals!"

He saw them now. Their heads were reappearing in the water alongside the floe, eyes staring at the ship. They swam directly to the hull, ten feet from where Schenck and his wife stood on deck. They bobbed in the water, staring at the Schencks. They were adults, much larger than Harriet's pet.

Mamie said, "Now these look exactly like dogs! Like Labradors, but without ears! Aren't they adorable! Harriet, come and look!"

"Phoca barbata!" Schenck went into the saloon and reappeared with his Holland & Holland.

"No! Carl! Not here! I can't stand it! You will *not* shoot one of those doggy creatures right here while it's sitting there looking at me with a face like that! I won't have it!"

"You'd like the coat, though."

"That's not fair. Go hunt them somewhere else, please! Go away on a boat and shoot them. Not here!"

Schenck lowered the rifle. "Whatever you say, puss." He took his rifle into the saloon.

Mamie started whistling, and the seals' heads rose higher out of the water and stared at her, appearing astounded.

"Look at them!" said Mamie. "Helloooooo! Hello there!"

Schenck came back out. He was carrying his book, *An Arctic Sojourn*. He stood beside Mamie and began reading.

" 'This charming little creature, with its round intelligent-looking, puppylike face—' "

"But exactly! They're absolutely dear!"

" '—makes its home among the floes. When the sun is shining, hundreds of the plump little chaps can be seen, disporting themselves in the water like youngsters at camp, or napping on the ice.' "

"They do look just like children down there, swimming about and looking up at us. Why, they're water babies! I've never seen anything so darling in all my life! You're not really going to shoot them, Carl?"

"I didn't come all this way to toss them crackers."

"Well, not around here, please. I want you to be far away from me when you shoot them. Hel-*looooooooooh!*" Mamie began whistling again. "Read me some more."

" 'The word *napping* is used advisedly, for they never sleep longer than a minute or two at a time. A brief period of slumber, and then the little head is raised again, and the inquisitive fellow carefully inspects the whole horizon, not unlike a wise-looking prairie owl. Its great enemy is, of course, the polar, or ice, bear. The bear is just as intelligent as frolicsome Phoca, and its tremendous appetite must be appeased if Bruin is to survive.' "

"What a marvelous little book!"

"Yes. Here, you read it," said Schenck, handing her the book. "Frolicky there has someone else to worry about now."

Schenck went forward and found Bill on the foredeck. He sent him up onto the wheelhouse roof with a pair of binoculars and told him to find a floe with seals lying on it.

Bill raised the binoculars, and began to turn slowly. "Right over there, sir!"

Schenck had his own binoculars around his neck. He took a look. Then he gave orders.

The fifteen-foot Whitehall was lowered. Avery and Bill brought it round to the ship's ladder. Schenck stepped into the bow. Harriet stepped down the ladder carrying the Mannlicher and sat in the stern. Gar gathered ammunition for the Holland

& Holland—which Joey took from him when he learned
which rifle it was for—and for his own gun, the new Mauser,
and the Mannlicher. He sat in the stern beside Harriet, and
Joey sat with Schenck in the bow. On the center thwarts, Avery
and Bill dipped oars and pulled for the floe where Bill had seen
seals. It was about six hundred yards away.

As they moved away from the ship, Schenck said, "Look at
that boat, willya? God, she's beautiful!"

And they all looked and saw he was right. Sitting by herself
on the blue water, *Lodestar* loomed as big as a liner. But unconstrained by the need to fill herself with people, she was
stretched out to accommodate solely the idea of speed and
matchless beauty on a new scale. She was also unconstrained
by the practical considerations of her medium, the sea. She was
picture-perfect, yet strangely so, like something out of a dream.

At four hundred yards, the seals on the floe noticed the boat.
They lifted their heads and watched as it grew closer. Schenck
lay down in the bow, resting his rifle barrels on the hull.

"Nice and easy," he said to the rowers.

The boat glided closer. Three hundred yards. Two hundred.
The seals had seen them, but appeared simply curious; heads
raised and turning, examining the oncoming object from every
angle, they remained otherwise still. Schenck nuzzled his cheek
against the French walnut stock and squinted through his spectacles. He was waiting until he was sure of a good shot.

The explosion from astern surprised him. He jerked his trigger reflexively, the rifle loose in his arms. The stunning blast of
the Holland & Holland obliterated the other noise; the rifle
thumped into his shoulder, and the boat rocked. Schenck saw
the seals break and scatter, and without a chance of aiming, he
impulsively pulled his second trigger.

He sat up, his glasses askew. Blood began dripping from a
cut on his cheek. He turned and saw Harriet lowering her rifle.

"Jesus, Butch! Wait till you have some chance of hitting
something!"

"I hit it," said Harriet.

Schenck looked and saw the single seal lying on the ice. "I
shot that one. They were all moving after you fired."

"Actually, I think Harriet got that one, Mr. Schenck," said Gar. "I saw it."

Harriet glanced at Gar with a suggestion of a smile.

"Really? Well, where'd mine go?"

The Whitehall's bow hit the ice. Schenck hopped onto the floe, which floated in the sea with the ponderous stability of a laden barge. The others stepped out and approached the single dying, bleeding seal.

"You sure about this?" Schenck looked at both Harriet and Gar.

"He's mine," said Harriet, staring down at the dying, bleeding seal. "I shot him."

"Where the hell'd the rest of them go?"

"Down here," said Joey, pointing. The ice was pocked with holes about two feet across on the surface, widening conelike as they descended to the water less than a foot below.

"I bet they're still down there." Schenck aimed his rifle into a hole and stood still.

"There's one," said Bill.

Schenck saw the movement at the edge of his vision, but the seal's head vanished as he swung sideways and fired into the hole. He lowered his rifle and looked around, frustrated. Joey looked too, anxious to find a seal for his master.

"Okay, let's row around and see what we can find."

Bill and Joey pulled the seal across the ice and into the boat. The others climbed in and they rowed away.

Harriet sat in the stern and stared down at her seal.

THROUGH THE MORNING, *LODESTAR* followed the small Whitehall at a discreet distance. At intervals, shots came across the water: three distinct percussive signatures from the three rifles.

Boden spent the forenoon stoking in the fireroom, coming up on deck for spells, and sometimes he heard the shots and saw dark figures on a white floe a mile away.

The hunting party returned at lunchtime, the boat heavy and heeling with four seals. The carcasses were lifted aboard by the davit falls, swung inboard, and held suspended by the neck over the deck while Harriet and Schenck posed for Mamie's

Kodak. Held aloft by block-and-tackle, a noose around their elongated necks, the seals' heads were twisted to one side at unnatural angles, like hanged men. Chapman of *Motor Boating* had given Schenck two Gravlex 4 x 5 Series D cameras, with fifty packs of verichrome film, and after informal poses for Mamie's Kodak, Gar took photographs of Schenck standing beside the kills, cradling his Holland & Holland.

"Which ones did you shoot, Carl?" asked Mamie.

"Every bag that comes aboard is officially mine. But you'll never believe it. Your daughter shot three of these. Gar Jr. got the fourth. Butch, come here."

Schenck moved aside and Harriet crossed the deck and stood alone beside the seals. Hanging, stretched their full length, they were nearly twice her height.

"Look at the camera."

She composed her face, which became a grave scowl. Gar photographed until he thought he had enough, but Schenck told him to take some more.

The seals were lowered onto the deck.

"I want the skins," said Schenck. "Who knows how to skin a seal?"

Joey raised his hand.

"Have you skinned a seal before?"

"No. But I think I can."

"Okay. Go to it. But remember, we're making a fur coat for Mrs. Schenck out of these babies. No slips."

"Yes, Mr. Schenck."

Joey started hauling the seals up to the foredeck.

"Say, Joe, you want a hand?" asked Bill.

"No."

Joey found a degree of privacy forward of the large windlass. He pulled his Buck knife from his pants and opened it. It was the Sportsman's Special, oversized, the blade engraved with a picture of a bear, and he kept it barbershop-sharp. He had read about flaying and had a pretty good idea how it was done. And so it proved on the very first seal. He made an incision beneath the chin and carried it down to the chest, cutting experimentally deeper through the skin and the pearly-hued fat until he reached maroon flesh. Then, pushing his hand into this slit, he forced it palm down across the still warm body. He pushed the pelt over the seal's shoulder. The tight blubber-backed coat came away from the flesh with the steady pressure of his finger-tips, and slid over the backs of his hands so uniformly that it seemed to Joey as if he were undressing someone. But much better somehow. Nobody came forward and bothered him. He took his time.

After lunch (the Schencks ate cold squab and carrot soup while watching the distinctive shapes of bergs drifting past the dining room windows), Schenck, Harriet, and Gar went out again, rowed this time by Boden and Moyle. Joey remained behind, still flensing on his sticky and darkening patch of the foredeck.

BODEN WAS HAPPY ROWING. So natural did it feel that he believed he could row a boat on down Davis Strait, across the Grand Banks, down the African or the Brazil coast, down the Atlantic, through the Southern Ocean until he was rowing back up the other side of the world again, and continue on forever. Moyle sat astern of him, both facing aft, so that he looked over Moyle's head, past Gar and Harriet in the stern, up Frobisher Bay to the piebald rock and scree and ice shores of Baffin Island. They rowed after floes, through leads between them, intercepting small fields of ice drifting in the bay as Schenck directed their changeable course, searching for nap-ping creatures to slaughter. Boden and Moyle pulled hard or rested on their oars, and drifted between wind and tide and ice. The weather remained fine and sunny.

Schenck excused Gar from rowing duties. He told the boy to keep his eyes peeled for game and be ready to shoot. Schenck wanted to shoot as many animals as possible and to astound the members of the Explorers Club with the number of his kills. That would be, like Roosevelt's African safari, the only true indication of its success.

So Gar looked around, but he also watched the two seamen in front of him pulling at their oars with the skill and economy of long practice. Neither feathered his oars, that slick forward flick of the wrist that swept the blades horizontally like wings through the air at the end of the stroke, as he had been taught to do rowing shells at Yale. They took shorter strokes than he had learned to do, leaning forward and pulling backward less, yet they pulled with power and in perfect concert with each other's rhythm through every maneuver and change of course. Gar envied them what they knew about boats and the sea, and guessed romantically at their hard-boiled schooling.

"Will, how many times have you come up here to the Arctic?" he asked.

"Three. Once with Newbold McKenzie aboard his boat *Arundel*, in the early twenties, then twice in my own ship."

"Where do you like it best here?"

"I like it all. I guess the farther north, the more I like it. I like the fjords along the east coast of Baffin Island. But I spent the winter of '20–'21 aboard the *Arundel* about fifty miles north of here, and I have good memories of this place."

"You spent the *winter* here? On a boat? Was it wrecked?"

"No. McKenzie loved the Arctic and he wanted to spend a whole winter here. He had the *Arundel* designed and built to overwinter. Her hull was shaped to ride up on the ice when it froze and squeezed in on it. It was a fine time. The ship was warm, we had plenty of grub, it was a good crew. We took measurements and observed the wildlife, we made trips all the way across the bay here over the sea ice. It was a great winter."

"This bay here? It's all frozen in the winter?"

"Hard as ground. It's a whole different place then. White, icy, dark, and pretty quiet except when the wind's screaming, or when the ice is grinding around the ship."

"How long was it dark for?"

"Well, we were just below the Arctic Circle, so we never had any days when there was no sun at all. But many days when it rose at eleven in the morning and set at two. For months, most of the day was twilight."

"Did that make you feel gloomy?" asked Harriet, who had also been watching him pull at the oars.

"No, I liked it." He smiled at her. "I thought it was beautiful. It wasn't dark so much as different shades of deep blue, and the sky around the horizon was always a pearly sort of pink and orange. But it got some of the guys down."

"Boy," said Gar. He thought it sounded like the best thing in the world.

"See much game that winter, Captain?" asked Schenck from behind his back, up in the bow.

"We saw it all, sir. Caribou coming and going on their migration. The white arctic fox. Gyrfalcons and snowy owls—"

"Bear?"

"Yes. Fair number of bear."

"Where was this?"

"We froze in just across the bay here. On the north side of Loks Land Island. About fifty miles over there." He nodded a direction.

"What's the farthest north you've been?" asked Gar.

"Bylot Island, off the top of Baffin, across Pond Inlet."

"And the game up there?" asked Schenck.

"Not as much as around here, sir. It's warmer down here always, so more small critters, and big ones feeding on them."

"And you say you like it better farther north?"

"It's less spoiled, and I like that."

"This is spoiled?"

"This is fine, but right up the head of the bay here you've got a settlement, with a Hudson's Bay Company post. And it's growing. There are sealers, Eskimos, traffic. We're here. It's quieter up north."

"I want to go up there when we leave here," said Schenck.

"There's too much ice."

"I've heard that from you before!" Schenck laughed.

They were quiet for a while, watching the ice on the bay.

Then Harriet said, "Mr. Boden?"

"Yes?"

"Where's your boat now?"

It was a moment before he answered. "I lost it."

"You mean it sank?"

"It almost sank. I had a crew of kids on it, and the ship got into trouble and we got off."

Harriet saw Gar making a face at her. She ignored him.

"So what happened to your ship?"

"Someone picked it up. Brought it into port."

"Didn't you get it back?"

"No."

"Salvage!" said Schenck, with a happy tone. "The law of the sea."

Two small seals drifted by on a large pancake of ice and Harriet and Gar shot them. No one felt like skinning them, and anyway Schenck wanted to haul them up in block-and-tackle aboard *Lodestar* to photograph himself beside them, so they pulled the heavy sausage bodies, each the weight of a grown man, into the Whitehall. The dead seals lay bleeding beneath the thwarts Boden and Moyle sat on, and blood began to pool in the bilge, washing thickly like oil over the floor timbers and frame bottoms as the boat rocked. After a few minutes, Boden asked Gar to start bailing the blood.

Boden first noticed the vee'd wake streaming from the object moving steadily through the water a quarter mile astern. White with a black dot at its bow. It was making for them and gaining. He knew without question what it was. He turned his head to look for the ship. It was a mile away.

Moyle turned his head and glanced at Boden.

"Yeah, I see it," said Boden. "Mr. Schenck, you see that thing back there gaining on us?"

"Where?"

Boden pointed. "Coming at us. See it?"

"I got you. What is it?"

"It's a polar bear. Mr. Moyle and I will give you a slant, and then please start shooting the water around it. Try not to hit it, sir. See if you can get it to alter course."

Moyle and Boden both raised their port oars and dragged their starboard blades, and the boat slewed sideways, rolling heavily with the weight aboard, giving Schenck an unobstructed shot.

"My god! I'm going to wait till it gets closer and kill it and then we can get a line on it."

"We can't tow it, sir, we're overloaded. We're in no shape to take on a bear. Gar, one of you, start shooting please."

"Aim near it?" asked Gar.

"Yes. Don't wound it. We want to make it go away, unharmed, unangry."

"I want it!" said Schenck.

Boden said, "Gar. Shoot."

"Hold your fire there, young man!" commanded Schenck.

The bear was two hundred yards away. Now a clear white deltoid face with a shining black nose and two black button eyes, distant spots, yet across the water came the clear locked fix of its gaze.

Boden leaned forward and grabbed Gar's Mauser. He raised it and fired. A geyser spouted from the water beside the pushing head. The bear looked, swung its head back to them, its interest unfaltering, and swam on.

Harriet fired. The shot was closer. The bear ignored it and came on, with purpose.

"Gar." Boden tossed the rifle to him. "All of you, shoot to kill. Shoot that head. Stop it. Kill it or it'll kill us. Mr. Moyle."

The two men dug in both oars and pulled hard, leaving the shooters an open bead. Schenck's Holland & Holland roared. Then again. The blast hurt their ears and rocked the slender, overburdened boat. Harriet and Gar fired, but the motion and pull of the oars sent the bullets wide. The shooters fumbled for cartridges and started to reload.

The boat was closing with a slab of ice. Boden and Moyle were forced into a hard crabbing turn around it. The bear held its original course, coming hard. As they pulled around the floe, ice came between them and the bear, and the bear was lost to view. Boden had broken a sweat. They were all turned, looking aft.

"Jesus Christ!" said Schenck.

The bear appeared on the top of the floe, coming at them in a rolling series of bounds, rippling, ivory, a rainbow mist flying off it in the sunlight. Its stare locked-on and certain.

"Shoot it!" yelled Boden. Schenck fired, the bullet going wild. Harriet and Gar fumbled with their bolts. Schenck's second barrel fired and missed.

Boden and Moyle pulled hard away from the floe, but found more ice forcing the boat up a narrowing lead. The bear ran off the floe, belly flopped, never lost its fix, and came on, twenty yards astern.

Harriet fired, and Boden saw the shoulder hit. The bear flicked its head to one side as if noting a bee sting.

The bow crunched hard against ice. Schenck, who had stood to shoot, fell backward, his shot blowing skyward. The bear reached the boat, raised a dripping, black-clawed paw the size of a chair seat, and swatted, smashing through the mahoganycoma] transom, pushing the bow up out of the water and forward onto the ice. They tumbled, kicked, and rolled frantically out onto the flat white, sliding away on their backs, kicking to push backward. The bear found what it was smelling, the dead seals and their blood, but it looked up at the wriggling creatures on the ice and smashed more boat aside and rose out of the water as if running up a slope, and it was on them. Gar sat up and lifted the Mauser barrel as Boden grabbed an oar and stood and began to swing over Gar's head. The bear knocked Gar's rifle scattering. The oar blade smacked its head as Harriet fired from fifteen feet. The bullet hit the chest. The bear lurched toward Boden, and fell heavily. Schenck stood and fired into the bear's back. The animal lay and shook.

They were all speechless, breathing hard.

THEIR PREDICAMENT HAD BEEN observed aboard *Lodestar* by Captain Percival through his binoculars. The ship had been steaming toward the marooned party and reached their ice floe minutes later.

While the hunters were being pursued by the polar bear, Mamie had been lying in the sun on a wicker chaise on the aft deck, wrapped in a blanket, reading *An Arctic Sojourn*. The book's rendering of seals into "plump little chaps," and its other genial characterizations of the denizens of the Far North made the Arctic seem personable and intimate to her in a way it had not appeared in the view over the ship's rail. Dr. Griffith was also a dab hand at verse, providing vivid scenes that brought the whole dull white place into dramatic view:

> *The mountain tops rose bare and bleak*
> *Below them stretched a floe*
> *Engraved upon its soft white coat*
> *Tracks of Bruin in the snow.*

The lengthy footprints told a tale
Of wandering at will
Then stalking to the water's edge
Intent upon a kill.

But here the fresh trail ended
In a blood-stained ivory heap
This polar king, so gaunt and fierce
Forevermore will sleep.

A crash of cordite rent the air
Bruin dropped, and there he lay
Thus he, not his quarry, fell
A fiercer hunter's prey.

She had been comforted by the sporadic and increasing riflefire, sure that her husband and daughter must be having fun. She read on until she heard Schenck yelling to her from somewhere beyond the rail.

"Mamie! Come take a look!"

She laid down the book, pulled off the blanket, stood up and walked to the rail, and was astonished by the sight of boat wreckage, splashes of blood on the ice, and the excited people standing beside the great slain bear on a piece of drifting floe twenty yards away.

"Good heavens, Carl!"

"Look at this! He wrecked our boat! Harriet stopped him at point-blank range! Then I finshed him off!"

It took them half an hour to lift the bear off the ice onto the ship's deck. The tackles on the boat davits lacked the size and advantage to lift the half ton of dead weight. Boden rigged a three-part tackle between the ship's foremast and windlass and the bear was raised by inches as Bill, Joey, Watts, and Avery pushed oars into it to hold it off the rail cap at the deck edge. They had to unbolt a section of rail. Laid out on deck, the bear measured nine feet four inches long. The circumference of its neck was thirty-six inches.

Then the bear was hauled upright over the foredeck. In its hanged posture, the neck stretched far beyond normal appearance, the skin riding above the sloping shoulders like a poorly made suit. The head was twisted aside by the noose, and a long tongue hung out of the mouth. Black eyes stared upward. Schenck put on his reindeer pants for the photographs. Harriet would not stand beside her father in front of the bear. Gar took pictures of them separately with the Gravlex. Both short, they appeared to be half the bear's height as they stood beside it holding their rifles. Schenck raised one of the hanging paws and held it on his shoulder as if he and the bear were pals. Mamie loved it and snapped away with her Kodak when she could stop herself from laughing.

Joey had finished with the seals. The five skinned carcasses lay together at the edge of the foredeck like giant flippered pigs prepared for a luau. The deck had been sluiced with seawater and scrubbed clean. The sealskins lay around the foredeck drying in the sun.

"Good work, Joey!" Schenck was impressed. "You got a knack. You ready for my bear?"

"Yes, Mr. Schenck."

"Listen, once you got the skin off, get the Frenchman up here and you and him have a huddle about our supper. Everyone eats bearsteak tonight. And I want the heart. I'll talk to him, but you go get him when you're ready to start carving. Steaks, heart, whatever's good to eat. He'll know. Got it?"

"Yes, Mr. Schenck."

But Schenck's large-bore blast through the bear's back had torn through the heart and ruined its possibilities as a dish of any visual appeal. Duhamel could do nothing with it except to chop it up for soup.

After supper, Schenck ordered Captain Percival to return to the previous night's anchorage.

He wanted to go ashore in the morning and find the caribou herd. A bear—two of them—could be stuffed to stand in his library to greet visitors; more could be skinned to lie before fireplaces; seals could make Mamie a coat and for all he knew maybe they could be stuffed too. But Schenck wanted a caribou's head and high antler rack for his walls as much as another man desired a Rembrandt. He wanted to hunt caribou on the tundra on the model of the classic stalk of the African veldt. He saw it clearly: the caribou grazing, raising heads now and then as he drew noiselessly closer, rifle at the ready.

Despite calm conditions, sizable chunks of berg ice still littered Noble Inlet, and drifted with eddies of tide, and the anchorage, Percival stated adamantly, was untenable. The ship was turned and steered back out again to the more open waters of Frobisher Bay.

As the pale candy twilight came on, threads of green light appeared in the sky and began to wave and contort across the dim stars. Everybody except Mr. Newton came out on deck to see the northern lights.

Boden was looking skyward when Harriet appeared at the rail beside him.

"Hello," she said.

"Hello."

"It's like magic, isn't it?"

"It is magic."

They watched the sky in silence for a while.

"Good night," said Harriet.

"Good night." He looked down at her and she had not moved, but still stood beside him at the rail.

He looked up again and felt a tug on his arm, and out of the cold air warm lips pressed on his cheek. Then she was walking away down the deck.

The aurora borealis went on and on. Some of those who had rushed on deck fearing a fleeting apparition watched and watched as pale green and rose waves undulated overhead until it appeared the spectacle would go on all night.

At ten o'clock, in the deepening twilight, Watts was following the heavenly show reflected on the water, when he spotted a pearly, more definite shape swimming steadily on its own undoubted way.

"That's a bear," he said out loud, to no one in particular.

Schenck got his rifle and took up position in the bow. Joey climbed up to the wheelhouse with Schenck's instructions to take the helm, and the ship closed in pursuit.

The bear looked over its shoulder at the looming shape that might have appeared as an oddly dark iceberg, and changed its course, and changed again and again as the ship slowed and settled into a position fifty feet behind it and followed it no matter which way it turned. Finally, as Schenck had hoped, the bear found a floe to crawl up onto and turned and hissed at the bedeviling ship as it drew up, and from twenty-five feet, Schenck fired. The shot went low, into the bear's groin, collapsing it for a moment before it tried to roll upright and scramble for the water. Schenck's second shot, the rifle held steady on the rail, entered the side of the bear's chest and dropped it onto its stomach on the ice. It lay there, the side of its face against the ice, and groaned until it died.

They were two hours getting it aboard in the falling dark.

CHAPTER 14

BODEN AND MOYLE BROUGHT *Carlo*, the Riva, around to the ladder and filled it with anchor, lead line, extra line, iron mooring stakes and a sledgehammer, blankets, binoculars, flares, matches in small round screwtop waterproof containers, bottles of water, and wicker food hampers containing roast beef, ham, cheeses, bread, beer, four bottles of a Rothschild claret, strawberries, chocolate cake, sufficient linen, and in each basket a handwritten inventory of its contents. The rifles and ammunition remained in the saloon while another early morning hunter's breakfast was eaten.

The group stepped down the ship's ladder into the boat at five-thirty. The satchels of ammunition were passed down; rifles were held across laps. Hands pushed off. Joey drove the boat. Shred had come along this time, for a spell of shore leave, and to see something of the country. He sat in the back with Gar.

Mamie came on deck and waved. "Have fun!"

On the foredeck, Moyle, Avery, Watts, and the engine crew—Eddie Jenkins, Ray Strick, and Dick Iams—watched the boat head for the shore.

As he watched, Moyle felt disquiet. After a moment, he turned and looked back at the wheelhouse, but he could see only the glacier reflected in its windows.

They found a bend in the beach where the Riva could float in shallow water. Joey nudged the bow onto gravel and they stepped ashore off the bow. Bill threw a small grapnel anchor off the stern to hold the boat off and stop it grinding its varnished bottom and buffed brass propellers in the shallows.

Gar suggested they leave the food hampers in the boat; they were too heavy to carry any distance; they could come back to the beach for lunch. He covered the hampers with blankets. Joey, Bill, and Gar carried the ammunition satchels. Shred carried two canteens of water.

Schenck was wearing his new Dux-Bak breeches over shin-high Bean boots. Beneath his Burberry he wore the Abercrombie and Fitch hunting vest he had worn during his abbreviated African safari; it had twenty loops across the chest that he had filled with the 500/465 cartridges made by Kynoch of England. Over the vest he was wearing a fifty-cartridge bandolier across his chest like Pancho Villa in a newspaper photograph he had admired some years before. Four inches long, as big as fat thumbs, packing seventy-three grains of cordite powder, each cartridge weighed two ounces; the 140 cartidges on Schenck's vest and bandolier weighed nine pounds. His Holland & Holland rifle was thirty-eight inches long and weighed ten and a half pounds. Between the rifle and cartridges, Schenck was carrying twenty pounds. His Burberry parka, the canvas oiled and lined with wool, weighed six pounds. He wore his Calobar eyeglasses ground to his prescription by the American Optical Company. On his head he wore a wide flat tweed cap from Herbert Johnson of Bond Street, London.

"Okay," he said, facing inland, feet planted wide on the gravel. "Let's go."

The shore was flat and covered with gravel, spongy moss, and patches of weedy bog. They crossed the narrow coastal strip and headed toward the ridge over which they had watched the caribou herd disappear. The tracks—impressions of splayed crescent-shaped cloven hooves pushed deep into the moss and bog mud—were clear and easy to follow.

A short distance from the shore, they were stopped by a pure white spectral shape flying up out of a mound close by on the dun tundra. It rose in three great flaps and sailed through the air on broad wings. It was the size of a swan, and so close they could see the irises of its eyes. Schenck pulled the rifle off his shoulder and fired, one barrel after the other. The bird banked and continued flapping unhurriedly away.

Gar said, "Mr. Schenck, if there are any caribou around—"

"I know, you're right." He reloaded and shouldered the rifle. "What the hell was that, anyway?"

"A snowy owl," said Boden.

"An *owl*? It looked like a cat. A great big flying white cat."

"Did you think it was a flying white cat, Daddy?"

"Of course I did, Butch. I wanted to stuff it and present it to the Explorers Club. Schenck's Flying White Cat."

They moved well on the gravel, but as the land rose and came under the permanent shadow of the ridge, they began walking through soft snow, deep in places, so that their boots sank in and they stumbled up the rocky scree. It was half an hour before they reached the peak of the ridge, which had seemed near from the beach. The sun was already near its day-long zenith, and they were all hot. Schenck was sweating and breathing heavily, and Shred, carrying the canteens, had fallen behind and was some distance down the slope. A light breeze had begun to blow from the north, and cooled them as they stood on the ridge and waited for the canteens.

Below them the land fell away in a tundra plain broken by a series of boggy furrows and shallow rises, like a confused ocean swell, until it rose again seven miles south to a ridge several thousand feet high.

"There," said Gar, pointing.

The herd was smaller than it had appeared in the dusk two days before: perhaps forty adults, all with large antler racks, and fifteen calves. They stood in a loose group munching on the sedge around a bog, a quarter of a mile away, out of effective firing range. But as the hunting party watched, all the caribou suddenly raised their heads, noses high in the air, wheeled, and trotted off to the east, disappearing quickly between swells of land.

"They smelled us," said Boden. "The wind's at our back. It carried our scent straight down the hill to them."

"We need a goddamn truck," said Schenck. He was still catching his breath. "This could take all day."

"We'll have to flank them," said Gar.

"We're going to split up is what we're going to do. There's too many of us. I don't know what we smell like, but we must've looked like a bunch of Masons coming over the hill, and that would put the fear of God in anybody."

Joey immediately moved to Schenck's side.

"You're with me," Schenck said to Gar. "And you too, Butch."

"Then who's in the other group?" said Harriet. "And what are they going to do? Wander around by themselves with our ammunition?"

"Say, you're being pretty fresh today, young lady. Suit yourself. Who wants to be around you, the way you shoot? Captain Boden, would you accompany my daughter, please?"

"Be glad to."

They agreed that Schenck's group—Gar, Joey, and Shred—would follow the ridge to the east until they sighted the herd again, and then try to come around to the south and approach it from downwind. Harriet, Boden, and Bill would continue down to the bog where the herd had been and move south and then east, until they could also sight the herd to windward. They agreed to try to avoid shooting each other. Boden took a canteen from Shred and the ammunition satchel Gar was carrying that contained Harriet's 6.5-millimeter cartridges. The groups set off.

AWAY FROM SCHENCK, BILL Fisher grew chatty.

"Bobby Block, he's my buddy from Cranston, me and him used to take our twenty-twos down to the shore and shoot all kinds of things. One time we found these turtles crossing the road and we stuck them in the water and shot them as they came out. They came out real fast, 'cos they didn't like the water, and we'd try to hit the top of the shell so they'd roll over back into the water."

Harriet bore him in silence and moved ahead, far enough that no answer would be expected of her, carrying nothing but her small rifle. She moved lightly over the difficult ground.

Boden was undisturbed by Bill's chatter. After years in fo'c'sles and other difficult places with all kinds of men, he knew they talked to fill the air around them with their own sound, like an animal leaving spoor, to dispel the lonesomeness of any place and make themselves feel at home. Wherever they went, their chatter followed an unvarying pattern. First, they griped about authority, whoever it was who held them in the yoke of the moment, as Kruger and Mills had castigated Brant while they were chipping rust on the freighter in the South Bay. In *Lodestar*'s fo'c'sle the men had talked about Captain Percival and what a martinet he was. They had talked about Schenck and decided he was a nut, but they rather liked him. That settled, a commonality found, they brought out the graven episodes of their lives, like talismans they might have nailed above their bunks, tales of good times or disasters with some buddy or jerk that had hardened into their own enshrined histories, and they spoke them as incantations to charm strange places. They told their stories over and over like aborigines around campfires. Boden wasn't listening, and knew Bill expected no answer.

He watched Harriet. Beneath the thick sheepskin avaitor's jacket and woolen sweater, her small breasts were still apparent. Or he was somehow aware of them. Her small boyish bottom inside her jodhpurs as she hopped and walked surefooted over the uneven ground was really not like a boy's at all. She reminded him of his wife Mary.

As they approached the bog where the caribou had been, a cloud arose and engulfed them.

Bill started to say, "Holy—" And began flailing.

The air filled with tiny whines. Mosquitoes swarmed over their heads, in their ears and down their necks, into their eyes and mouths and nostrils. They swatted themselves and began running away from the bog, twisting and waving arms like lunatics. Some of the mosquitoes came with them, but the maddening cloud was left behind over the fetid bog.

Two hundred yards away they stopped, breathless, still waving their hands around their heads. They were perspiring, and smashed mosquitoes lay on their faces.

"Jesus H. Christ!" said Bill. "They're worse than they are in Maine!"

"Let's head this way," said Boden.

They put the northerly breeze at their backs and headed

south. The going was slow. The ground was more irregular than it had looked from the ridge. They found themselves walking up small mounds of peat, around hummocks covered with purple saxifrage, stepping across the fissures in the earth filled with pondlike greenery and melted ice that ran between the peat mounds in the same mosaic pattern as cracks in a dried mudbed. It was wet everywhere because the meltwater could never seep into the permafrost; it lay on the surface and bred the soggy mosses and sedges and the mosquitoes. They traveled with their eyes down, determining each squelchy step, looking up now and then to orient themselves to the land and each other. Mosquitoes whined but the cloud was behind them. The air smelled of the peaty ground odor and the perfume of the wildflowers and cloudberry and herbs and lichens crushed underfoot.

"*Goddamn!*" Bill said when the ground fooled him and he slipped and stumbled.

They walked south for an hour, and the ridge was still not a long way behind them.

"Well, let's try heading east," said Boden when they all met on a peat mound. "We don't want to get too far from the others." He had kept track of the sun's trajectory, and Sugarloaf Hill was still on their right, and now a little behind them, so they turned left and walked east. He had also noticed a high filling cirrus.

Bill fell behind. His rubber seaboots were no good in such gluey terrain. They got sucked off his wool-stockinged feet by the mud in the boggy cracks and the dense peat on the hummocks. He stepped out of them repeatedly as the boots stuck and stayed behind. Harriet stopped a long way ahead and waited for Boden to reach her.

"What'll we do? We're not going to get anywhere like this," she said to him. She was wearing her Bean boots.

Boden wore old shin-high lace-up leather boots, oiled over many years to water repellency with the sheep's wool grease and tallow found aboard any ship. He walked back to where Bill sat on a hummock with his boots and now his socks off, trying to wring the wet mud out of his socks, but they were as congealed and solid as if packed with shit. His bare feet were red with cold. The rest of him was smeared with mud and flattened bugs. He had been using his Winchester as a walking stick and it was caked with mud.

"*Damn* it! I'm sorry to hold you guys up, Will, but this is for the birds."

"You better go back, then. Keep the hill on your left and you'll hit the ridge and see the boat. Start on lunch. I don't know when we'll be back, but stick around the boat. Or maybe they'll see you on the ship and come get you. There's some weather coming, so don't wander off. Stay by the boat."

"All right. I'm sorry. What'll you tell Mr. Schenck?"

"I'll tell him I sent you back. Don't worry about it. You think you can get back okay?"

"Sure. I'll see you later."

"Clean that rifle when you can."

He walked back to Harriet and they set off again, heading east.

As they walked, rounding hummocks and fording water, they ranged alongside and behind and in front of each other.

A gull rose screaming from the ground ahead. It wheeled and dove and rose with sudden abrupt changes, agitated and disturbed.

Directly beneath the gull, a fox came into view, trotting alongside a stream. It carried a small chick in its mouth.

Harriet raised the Mannlicher and fired. The fox fell over kicking. The chick fell from its mouth and ran away screeching and flapping small fuzzy wings. The gull continued to dive and wheel overhead.

They walked forward. The fox saw them as they approached. Its mouth was wide open in a feral grin, tongue stuck out, panting hard. The wound was in its side, through the gut. Harriet fired again, into its chest at close range. The fox arched its back until it appeared its spine would snap, and then relaxed and died.

"What is it?" she asked Boden.

"An arctic fox."

"I thought they were white."

"They are in the winter."

"Oh."

Boden looked up at the gull, still crying overhead. "A Ross's gull. See its rose color? It's very rare. No one knows much about it. You saved its chick."

The gull swooped and hovered over a low mound, and Harriet shot it.

Boden watched her walking toward the mound, and after a moment followed her.

They found the gull still very alive near its nest, lying on its face in the spongy turf, its good wing flapping. The bullet had passed through the other wing near the shoulder. A chick was in the nest. The other chick, sprung from the fox's mouth, was still screeching, running and falling in circles nearby. The chick in the nest was completely quiet.

Harriet shouldered her rifle and picked up the Ross's gull. It became still in her hand and vomited two large shrimp across its rose-hued chest. Harriet took the shrimp in her other hand and held them over the chick in the nest. The chick opened its mouth and screamed and Harriet pushed the shrimp in. The wing-shot gull began to flap in her hand.

"Would you kill it, please?"

Boden pulled off one glove and took the gull from her and cradled it in his bare hand. He pushed his thumb against its chest. It died instantly. He handed it back to her.

"Thank you."

"What are you planning to do with the fox?"

"I could wear it. Would you skin it for me, please?"

Boden looked at the fox. Then he pulled out his jackknife and knelt down.

JOEY, ALERT FOR HIS master, his own blood up for a kill, spotted the herd first. They tramped out of a gulley, swatting the mosquitoes that were traveling with them, and the caribou were a hundred and fifty yards away, still moving at a desultory saunter along a muddy rill, grazing between steps, raising their heads and looking around as they chewed. It was the scene Schenck had imagined so clearly.

The hunters immediately lay down and wriggled backward into the cover of the gulley. They had left the ridge when it veered back toward the shore, and were down among the hummocks and small rises of tundra. The wind was at their side now, blowing across them and the herd, carrying their scent away. They were close enough for a shot from Gar's single-barreled bolt-action Mauser, but not from the Holland & Holland. The trajectories from the canted side-by-side barrels met at a point under a hundred yards; beyond that, the rifle was aimed by experience. Shred reached their hiding place finally and sat down gasping.

Gar started to say something, but Schenck hissed and chopped air. He was panting too. He slipped the rifle off his shoulder, then rolled onto his back, struggled out of his Burberry, and unbuckled his bandolier. Joey took the bandolier, buckling it around his waist and looking at it. Schenck struggled back into his parka and then lay on his back, catching his breath. The others waited.

He rolled onto his stomach and spoke in a harsh whisper. "I'm going ahead. You stay here. And stay down! And no noise!"

He pulled the sling over his head again so the rifle dangled on his forearms, and moved away on his elbows. They watched him go. He crawled heedlessly through the mud, between hummocks and peat mounds. Now and then, one of the animals raised its head and looked around as it chewed, and Schenck stopped and dropped his face onto his arms. Wet and muddy, he looked like a natural lump in the tundra landscape. There were always at least ten caribou with their heads raised, but Schenck had decided on the ones who would see him. He crawled on, gaining gradually on their slow aggregate saunter. He left a swath in the mud that filled with brown water.

Hidden by a roll in the ground, Schenck crawled to within sixty yards of the edge of the herd. With great care, he pulled the strap over his head, pulling his hat off as the strap caught it, and then he lifted the rifle, planted his elbows, and took aim.

From behind, they saw him grow still except for the slight wavering of the rifle barrels, and they waited for the report. He dropped his head and his back rose with a deep breath, and he raised his head again. He moved the gun, sighting in a different direction. He changed aim a third time. Gar tried to see which animal he might be aiming at now.

The noise was like a clean thunderclap. By chance, Gar saw an animal's hind leg just below the thigh erupt in blood. The caribou collapsed, rolling over on its back, three legs kicking air. The herd was off without a glance, wheeling like a flock of birds into an immediate gallop. Schenck fired the other barrel. The shot tore into the ground beside the wounded caribou, which was twisting its head around to see what had knocked it down, eyes rolling, its rack waving through the air.

As Schenck stood up, breaking open the breech of his gun and ejecting his shells, the animal found a position of brief repose lying still on its side. Then it heaved itself up into a sitting position, forelegs extended. The head bent forward in effort, twice, finding its lever moment, and suddenly it was on its feet, the wounded hind leg hanging quivering, almost severed but held by tissue and tendon, dripping blood steadily. The caribou saw Schenck now and turned its head in his direction, a glance merely of slight withering umbrage, and then hopped away after the rest of the herd. Schenck grabbed at his vest and pushed a cartridge into one barrel, snapped the breech shut, lifted the rifle, and fired. He missed, loaded again, fired, and missed again. The wounded caribou hopped quickly out of range.

"Let's go!" he yelled.

BILL HEARD ALL THE shots. Three from behind him. Then away to his left, east, one and two. Then three and four. Soft flat thuds from far away. He turned to look for either of the hunting parties, but he saw only the dull seaweed green and mustard terrain.

A little later he reached the top of the ridge. He was exhausted, and famished. The wind had changed, he realized; it had backed to the west, where solid opaque white cloud was rolling over the landcape. He noticed for the first time the fog that had come down. The top of Sugarloaf Hill was lost in it, and he could not see as he had expected to the beach or the boat below or the ship out on the water. Never mind, he knew they were there. He felt cold, the sweat from his struggle in the mud now clammy and chill under his clothes. He wished they were in Newport. He would rather varnish a quarter mile of rail in the sun than hump his ass through this freezing mud. He hoped to Christ Mr. Schenck would send the boat south to Miami again. Conch fritters at Turkey Jack's. And Cora, who might suck his cock again all winter. Cora was all right, except she had a real case on him and she was always asking him in a whining voice what was wrong, as though something about her was bothering him when nothing was bothering him at all except her whining voice. Nothing's wrong, Cora, for God's sake!

As he started down the hill toward the beach, he noticed the light snow falling out of the white sky on his left. He tried to hurry, making short sideways hops down the slope, but he slipped and fell in the snowcover over the scree.

THEY RAN AFTER THE herd for a few minutes until Schenck stopped, gasping. He raised his rifle, but he could see its barrel waving through too great an arc of space.

He turned to Gar. "See if you can hit anything with that goddamn thing!"

The herd was three hundred yards away, indistinct in the lightly falling snow, still trotting away. "If I hit anything at this range—"

"*Shoot!*"

Gar aimed in the direction of the herd.

"*No, don't!* You won't hit anything and we'll spook 'em. We'll let them relax." He looked at his rifle. "Jesus Christ, this thing weighs a ton. I need a fucking caddy! Joey!"

Joey hopped forward and took Schenck's rifle.

Gar had been looking up into the falling snow. He said, "Sir, do you think we should—"

"No, I don't. We keep going. If we stop now, we'll never find them again. Come on."

The herd was quickly lost in the obscuring snowfall. They followed the tracks. There was no sign of the injured caribou. It had either caught up with the herd—unlikely, for they had seen no blood in all the tracks on the ground—or they had lost it. In their flight, the herd had left the stream they had been following and galloped south, farther inland. The tracks led over firm ground, and the going was easier than it had been.

"What do you think?" Schenck asked Gar. "They're going to stop, or keep going?"

"Well, if they're like deer, and they're probably not as easily spooked as deer, they'll probably slow down after they've run a little way and start eating again. That's what I'd guess."

"Me too. We'll keep going, and let's keep quiet."

The snow was slanting across their path, carrying the scent of their sweat and muddy clothes away from the herd that had disappeared somewhere ahead.

Schenck set the pace, the others followed. Shred trudged a long way behind. At times he saw the group ahead fading in the snow, and then he tried to hurry. They went on for twenty minutes.

"Mr. Schenck," Gar whispered. "Look at these tracks. They're closer together and not as deep. I think they're walking now."

"Shhh! Me too. They're going to be right ahead up here somewhere." Schenck snapped his fingers at Joey, who came forward and handed over the rifle. Schenck opened it and reassured himself that both barrels were loaded, snapped it closed, and held it across his chest, advancing like a soldier on night patrol.

The snow thickened. Color faded out of the pinching scene, until they saw only the white tracery streaking down across a dim gray welter. Sound faded, as if each man were surrounded by cotton, and they heard only their own labored breathing, and far away their sucking footfalls. They came to another stream; the tracks followed its bank. They followed the tracks.

A hand gripped Schenck's shoulder, stopping him. Joey was at his side, silent, but his arm held out rod straight. Schenck looked.

"Good boy, Joey."

They were just dark shapes through a gauzy curtain. The caribou stood with the snow settling on their backs, grazing again at the water's edge. Three large animals were forty yards in front of Schenck.

He raised his beautiful Holland & Holland and fired.

* * *

BILL COULD SEE NOTHING beyond his feet in the snow. He knew he had crossed the ridge and started down to the beach, and he was somewhere between the ridge and the beach. He had tripped on the loose rock beneath the snow and fallen two or three times. He tried to remember how long it had taken to walk uphill from the boat to the ridge. Even falling, he seemed to be taking far longer to get down the hill. He could not tell if the ground beneath him still sloped. Thinking about that and looking down at the rocky ground, he swayed and almost fell over, but he stuck a foot out and stayed up. He knew if he made it to the beach he would find the boat. He would walk along the shore until he found it. He was not particularly worried, except he could no longer feel his hands and feet.

He was in the water. He realized it when it got above his knees, and then it felt for a moment like burning. He stopped and looked around for the shore. There it was, right behind him. He turned and walked out of the water back up the gravel.

Christ, there was the boat right there. Bull's-eye. He had started to feel a small pulse of unreasonable fear, being not really lost, but out of sight of things in the snow, but here was the boat finally; and a little ways off the beach, a few hundred feet was all, though obscured by falling snow, he knew the ship lay anchored. Everything was fine now.

He fell over again. Never mind, here we are, everything's okay now. He got up and made it to the boat.

The tide was lower, and the Riva was half out of the water. Filled with snow. No, the snow was only covering the blanket. He pulled the blanket aside and there was one of the picnic baskets. God, he was hungry. He sat down but fell into the boat. After a long struggle, he got himself turned around the way he wanted and pulled the blanket over his legs. He watched his hands trying to open the basket. His fingers were clumsy, he guessed because they were numb. He threw his arms around, slamming his hands against the leather seats. Finally he managed to open the basket.

A menu, for Christ's sake! He pushed the paper aside and picked up a ham sandwich, all Frenchified with great long thick slices of bread. It was stiff with cold, but he got it up to his mouth and bit a piece off.

He heard a noise, a droning. *Unng unng unng.* He realized he was making the noise as he chewed open-mouthed. Was it relief, or exhaustion, or because he liked the sandwich? A sort of moan in rhythm with his chewing. *Unng unng unng.* Out it came. Weird, but who gives a shit.

He could hardly taste the sandwich, and it was difficult to swallow. Too dry. He was dying of thirst, he realized. He scooped snow off the varnish into his mouth and chewed it with the sandwich. Oh . . . Oh God what a difference. That was delicious. The snow was melting in his mouth, beautiful wet, melting the sandwich. He was tasting the ham now, and the bread, and there was cheese in there, and mustard. He could taste it all now, a warm, wet, savory pap in his mouth. It was the best. God. *Unng unng unng.* He ate one sandwich and felt warmer and alive and hungrier, and started eating another, with mouthfuls of snow.

Out of the monochrome gray and white world a large shape in rippling ivory relief filled Bill's whole peripheral view to his right. He started to turn. *Unn—*

SHE HAD SMELLED THE rancid odor of a kill, not fresh, but close, and she came slowly, noiselessly, padding down the beach, her front legs characteristically swinging around each other, paws flapping, her larger rear legs bowed from her wide hips.

She saw the seal ahead, flopping injured-looking on a shiny rock, issuing a queer wailing bleat, sick and wholly unmindful of her approach, but eating. She smelled it and its rank kill strongly now, for she was approaching from downwind. She reached the final point of her approach and she bounded. The seal only saw her at the last moment, when she swung her paw and knocked its head with the same force she used for beluga whale when she caught one at a breathing hole, the force to kill immediately or stun senseless, the only force she knew.

The white seal with red fur at the head was like no other she had killed. The skin was loose and pulled apart when she bit into it to pull the seal out of the rock it lay in. When she got it onto the beach, she had to tear great loose flaps of tasteless skin off it before she found any flesh. A thin, sick seal. The only deposits of flesh were around the middle part, and it carried no blubber. She put one paw on the chest and bit and pulled open the stomach and found the rich organs and the hot bowels. She gnawed the flesh over the ribs and found more flesh beneath the loose skin around the top of the unseal-like legs, and she put the leg bones between her molars and crunched until they cracked, and she lapped the dribbling marrow, but it was a poor kill and left her hungry.

She nosed through the seal's kill in the hollow rock where it had been lying eating, finding small pieces of sharp-tasting flesh and other mush in a loose bush in the hollow rock. She dragged the bush out of the rock onto the beach and smashed it open and ate what was inside. The rock too was strange. She tried chewing it. It was no rock at all, but a movable thing that carried various smells, including the smell of food. She pushed it and pulled it apart, smelling more food and chewing pieces. She returned to the dead seal and pulled and chewed at it again. Then, looking for more substance, she loped off down the beach.

THE SLUG SIZED AND powdered to bring down a charging elephant hit the grazing caribou in the hip. It felt no pain. Only the enormous surprising shock of the kick from an unseen source, and it found itself on the ground. The herd bolted, fading immediately in the snowfall. The wounded caribou tried to follow them, but was unable to rise. It felt panic.

Schenck ran foward. He stopped eight feet from his first bona fide safari bag. He was trembling. He stared at the caribou.

"God, it's beautiful! Look at that head!"

The head and the stupendous asymmetrical rack with one broad-bladed brow tine were waving around as the caribou tried to rise, its eyes huge. Schenck raised the rifle to dispatch the animal, aiming at the brain, but he lowered, realizing that the great beautiful head was unblemished, and he wanted to keep it that way for mounting.

"How do I kill this thing without ruining the head?"

"The heart, sir," said Gar.

"Right."

He aimed at where he guessed the heart was, then he lowered again. "I want to eat the heart. That Frenchman's going to cook it for my supper. I want to save it."

They discussed the problem. Joey provided the solution. Joey, Gar, and Schenck, in that order, each grabbed an extremity of antler. The head jerked and pulled, but they stood on it and finally pinned it still. The forelegs kicked. Joey knelt on the neck. He took out his Buck knife and opened the blade. He felt for the great pumping neck artery, found it, and pushed the blade in across its flow, making a neat slit. The blood spurted out in a thick pulsing jet across the snowy ground. Joey watched it come through the slit, feeling the vein pump beneath his fingers. He moved his hand, putting it across the slit and felt the hot blood force itself between his fingers. He kept his fingers over the wound until the blood stopped and the caribou was still. Gar noticed this and thought it was strange.

The men got off the caribou and stood looking down at it.

"Joey. I want the head and neck off in one neat piece, just above the shoulder."

"Yes, Mr. Schenck."

"Then I want the heart and the liver. Neat and clean! And then maybe some steaks—I don't know." He turned to Gar. "Do they eat caribou?"

"I guess so. It's a sort of deer. It must be like venison."

"Venison steaks, Joey! Wherever they are in there, cut 'em out. You know what you're doing in there now, don't you?"

Joey looked up at Schenck and nodded. "Yes, Mr. Schenck."

They heard a shot. Dampened by the snow that fell thickly now, it sounded far away.

"That's my Butch!" said Schenck.

THEY WERE CLOSE TO the animal before they could make it out, motionless but trembling as it sat on the ground beneath a coat of new snow. It saw them, knew they were coming, but did not move.

Harriet stopped. She expected it to leap up and run away,

and then she would shoot it as it ran. Very slowly she pulled
the Mannlicher off her shoulder.

"It's hurt," said Boden.

They walked toward it. The creature watched them approach but still it did not move.

They saw its leg.

"Your father shot it."

"Or one of the others."

"No, your father. Look at the size of the wound. He shot it."

Harriet raised her rifle, breathed in, and held her breath,
then fired. The bullet entered the caribou's chest between its
front legs. It fell over and looked at the ground close to its face.
After a moment, its body began shaking. It shook for more
than a minute before it was still.

"You want to wear it?" Boden was carrying the fox pelt.

"You're being facetious."

"Eskimos wear caribou skins. Peary wore them to the Pole.
Your father wears reindeer pants—"

"You're still being facetious."

"A little."

"Well, I don't want to wear it. I wanted to put it out of its
misery."

The snow was falling thickly now. It lay on the caribou and
fell melting into the seeping blood across its chest and legs.

Boden said, "We better head back to the boat now. I hope
the others have, or we're all going to get lost in this snow."

He pulled his small brass handbearing compass out of his
peacoat, held it up, and looked through its prism.

THE HEART STILL PULSED as Joey cradled it in his bare
hands, amazed at its persistent life. It was hot, and weighed
about four pounds. He held it like a treasure. He thought, It's
like delivering a baby. Steam rose out of the vent he had cut
along the underside of Schenck's caribou.

"Let's get this stuff back to the boat," said Schenck.

Joey cut out the stomach, leaving the tubes at either end as
long as he could. He squeezed the stomach contents out and
knotted the smaller tube. They could tell the plants the caribou
had been eating, the same ones they had been walking over. He

pushed the heart through the bigger tube with some difficulty, though the warm, slippery blood lubricated its passage. He cut out the liver and the kidneys and pushed those into the stomach. The warm rubbery feeling of the organs in his hands was a familiar magic to him now, after flaying the seals and butchering two bears. He knotted the other tube and then cut off a large patch of the caribou's hide and wrapped it, fur out, around the heavy stomach ball.

They were all watching him, fascinated. "Joey, you're an artist," said Schenck. "I had no idea."

Shred reached them at last. He had followed their footprints in the snow. He was cold and shaking.

"We better head back," said Gar.

They started back in the direction they had come. The caribou's head and rack weighed a hundred pounds. Gar and Shred dragged it between them, holding onto the antlers, though Shred had no more strength, and lagged behind Gar. From the neck seeped a thin slurry of gore. Joey carried the precious furball. The herd's tracks, and the impressions of their own feet, were disappearing beneath the accumulating snow.

"This way, I think," said Gar.

BODEN SAW AND UNDERSTOOD the story before they reached the wreckage of the boat. He pulled the Colt revolver out of his jacket and looked around them. The snow was falling thicker, reducing visibility to twenty yards.

"Is your rifle loaded?"

"Yes," said Harriet, staring. "God, what is that?"

"We're going to stay close together. You keep looking around us."

"What am I looking for?"

"A bear."

"Do you want my rifle?"

"No. You're a much better shot. If you see a big white bear and it's heading our way, shoot for the chest."

She followed him. They reached the smashed boat.

"You stay next to the boat here," said Boden.

"Where are you going?"

"Just over here."

"Is it Bill?"

"Yes. What's left of him."

Harriet couldn't take it in. She stopped thinking of Bill. She continued looking around, but keeping a fix on Boden moving at the edge of her vision, just within the shrinking circle of what she could distinguish.

"I won't see anything in this snow," she said. "Especially a white bear."

"Keep looking."

She heard him grunting while he moved objects across the gravel. He took an oar and scooped a shallow depression in the gravel, dragged things into it, and pushed gravel over the top. She saw this while looking away, looking all around her.

"What happened to the boat?" she asked while Boden worked.

"The bear."

"Why?"

"Hungry, I guess. Looking for food."

She observed him walking a short distance from where he had been working and heard him vomiting. Then he returned to the boat and looked through it. He found an Abercrombie and Fitch canteen of water, and shook it. The water inside was not completely frozen. He unscrewed the lid and held it out to her. "It's clean."

Harriet realized she was terribly thirsty. She drank until the water numbed her throat with cold. Boden opened the canteen he had been carrying. He rinsed his mouth and spat, and then drank. The wicker picnic baskets were torn apart, pieces scattered, together with their silver flasks and salt and pepper shakers, napkin rings, and ivory-handled cutlery, inside the boat and over a wide area of beach. The boat was full of pieces of picnic food the bear had missed or dropped. Boden gathered these leftovers into a pile on a blanket, wrapped them up, and put the bundle on the gravel, next to the two canteens.

Then he inspected the boat. It was a lightly built craft, thin planking over narrow, closely spaced steambent frames; rigid and strong enough for boating on the Italian lakes, but not designed for bear. Nevertheless, the structure had held together well. The windshield was smashed, the wheel bent—it looked like a car crash. Holes had been punched in the hull, strakes splintered and torn, but none of it sufficiently grievious to render the boat useless. The bear's unintended crucial damage consisted of the holes stomped clean through the bottom of the hull. The boat would not float.

Boden looked out across the water. Snow was still falling, obscuring any view of *Lodestar*. It was settling on their heads and shoulders. Harriet was watching him now, between looking around them for bear, but the snow was now falling so thickly she would see no bear until it was close enough to touch.

"We're going to need shelter," he said.

"Shouldn't we go find the others?"

"We'll miss them in the snow. We don't know where they've gone. They probably don't know where they are now either. Eventually they'll try to head back here, if they haven't already, and they'll get lost. We should stay here and signal. Why don't you fire off four shots, not too fast, but as near evenly spaced as you can make them, firing, loading, and firing, so it doesn't sound like shooting for a kill. And in five minutes fire off four more. Hopefully they'll hear it aboard the ship, and maybe the others will too. We've got enough ammunition to keep that up for a while. We should have arranged signals when we split up, but it's too late now."

He stepped into the Riva and pulled up its seats, arranging them over the aft cockpit so they might stop some of the snow. There was space underneath for them to lie down on the bottom of the boat.

Harriet laid out cartridges on a rock, and began firing at regular intervals.

"WHERE THE FUCK ARE we?" said Carl Schenck, echoing the words most frequently uttered by Man, in his every tongue, since the earliest days of his snowblind northward groping. They had walked four miles since leaving the boat earlier in the morning, through bog and accumulating snow, and now the weight of his rifle, his Burberry, and the cartridges he still carried on his hunting vest, weighed him down. He'd had it. He wanted out.

Joey wore the bandolier, and walked stolidly behind Schenck, placing his feet in Schenck's footprints in the snow, carrying in his arms the package of organs wrapped in fur. Joey had always been told where to go and had never been required to ponder directions himself. He was sullenly disquieted to hear Schenck wondering aloud in this way. The single overriding characteristic of his boss was that Schenck always knew where to go.

But the snow had covered their earlier tracks, or they had slewed off their course. The snow had dropped a dense curtain around them. The few yards they could see appeared identical in all directions. They heard no sounds but their own footfalls, and these were floating puffs in the air, without the normal clues to say whether they came from up or down. They saw each other as hunched shapes surrounded by a white without depth or contour.

Schenck stopped. "Chamberlain. Do you know what direction we're going?"

"I'm not sure any longer, sir."

"Anybody else?"

From the rear Shred said, "We been dragging this head. It's made a wake like a boat in the water, but in the snow. If we could look back and see the wake going straight or in some other direction, why, maybe we'd know if we was off course."

"Mr. Shred, you're a genius."

They all looked back. The serrated edge of the caribou's neck, dragging coagulated lumps, had left a depression in the snow, traveling in a fitful line before fading into white obscurity yards behind them.

"Well, is that straight or not?" said Schenck.

Gar said, "Sir, if one of us walks back along the trail of the head and keeps shouting, maybe we can tell if the shouts start to move in one direction or another."

"Okay, let's try it. Start walking."

Shred and Gar let go their antler-holds, and the caribou's face settled into the snow. Gar walked back along their track. He disappeared in seconds.

"Start shouting!" shouted Schenck.

They heard Gar shout faintly.

"Louder!"

They heard him once more.

Schenck looked at Shred. "What direction is that?"

"I . . . I dunno, sir."

"Come on back!" yelled Schenck.

They waited.

"Come back!"

His shout was blown away.

Schenck, Joey, and Shred stood together and saw each other indistinctly. The blizzard was filling the air around them.

Schenck grabbed Shred's jacket and pushed his face close. "Go find him. But don't go far! Ten or twenty feet. He's got to be nearby. Keep your eyes on your tracks. Go look and come back!"

Shred nodded. He turned and walked in the direction Gar had gone. He looked down to follow the depression made in the snow by the caribou's neck, but he saw only featureless white, his own legs vanishing into it below his knees.

He turned and walked back against the slant of snow. He failed to reach Joey and Schenck.

THEY LAY TOGETHER INSIDE the Riva. Snow still fell between the seats he had arranged overhead, but they were out of the wind.

Harriet had fired her rifle until they had both become so cold and snow-covered that they had crawled into the boat and held onto each other. They lay beneath the two blankets with Boden's coat on top. He lay on his back and she lay on her side against him, her head on his arm that wrapped around her and held her close to him. They had crawled into the boat and clung hard to each other, shivering, but at last a warmth grew between them.

Harriet's face lay against his neck and she breathed in the smell of him with every breath. Her nose and her cheek and her lips pressed into Boden's neck as she breathed, and when she moved slightly, she felt the sandpaper rasp of his whiskers, and she moved now and then, pushing her face against him, to feel that.

Boden felt her too. He floated away from where they were, taking only the heat between them and the feel of this girl pressed against him and her face and hot regular breath on his neck. Periodically, thoughts about the others wandering somewhere outside in the snow came to him, but he knew there was nothing he could do now except stay alive, and he let those thoughts go. He dozed and let everything go but the warm shape of her against him, and her warm breath close under his ear. The sensation began to unlock feelings, and he let them come.

BODEN WOKE AS SHE was moving, agitated. Her hand was under his sweater. She moved it over his chest, kneading the muscles, down across his stomach and up again. A circular motion that stirred him. Her leg was clamped over his, her crotch pushing into his thigh, and her face came up to his, her breath tremulous and unsteady.

She began kissing his face. He reached down and caught her hand.

"No. Harriet. We can't do this."

"We can. I want to."

"I don't."

"Why?"

Suddenly this slaughtering child and her insistent appetite made him feel like a Ross's gull locked in her sights. But it wasn't that.

"I have a wife. We're not together right now, but I've been thinking we could be again, and that's what I'm going to try to do when we get home."

"So? She's not here now."

She tried to kiss him again but he moved away.

Harriet sat up and pushed against the seats overhead. Banked snow fell in over them. She stood and stepped out of the boat. Boden sat up and followed her.

The snow had stopped. Sugarloaf Hill was sharp and clear against a pink and blue sky. The sun was lower and far up the inlet on its long crepuscular arc to the northwest. There was wind now, and as before, when they had first anchored here, it had blown more ice down the inlet.

Boden turned suddenly and looked across the water.

The ship was gone.

CHAPTER 15

TWELVE HOURS EARLIER, MOYLE had followed the shore party through Gar's nearly new binoculars until its members had disappeared over the ridge. He was on anchor watch and remained in the bow. He liked the view; the severe landscape without a particle of superfluity in it appealed to him.

An hour later, smoking a cigarette in the bow, he felt the new wind. Slowly the ship swung around its anchor to face it. Moyle saw torn shreds of cloud tumbling down the glacier and felt the cold in the wind as it came off the blue ice and funneled over the water between the inlet shores. He watched the short curling waves rise on the water and come rolling toward the ship's bow. The anchor chain lifted slowly out of the water, extending forward through the chop as the strain came on it. The ship lay in fifteen fathoms, with seventy-five fathoms of cable veered. There was no great fetch up the inlet; if the wind backed to the west and southwest, coming later from the land instead of down the inlet, as Moyle's instinct told him it probably would, the ship would be protected by a windward shore. If the wind veered northeast, there were islands in that direction, and the anchorage would not be too exposed. They would lie comfortably through whatever blow was coming.

So he was unprepared when Eddie Jenkins came forward on deck and told him that Captain Percival had given the order to raise steam and make ready for sea.

"What'd he say about them ashore?"

"Nothing," said Jenkins. The musical Welsh accent made him sound the more amazed. "He just came down and told me to get steam up and make ready for sea."

"Make ready and stand by, or does he mean to raise and go?"

"He didn't say."

Jenkins looked at him expectantly.

Moyle sensed with deep unease why the engineer had come forward into the windy bow to tell him what was afoot and to wait, looking at him, as he was now. Moyle was no more than a deckhand aboard ship, certainly subordinate to Jenkins, who as engineer was the most important and senior member of the crew after the skipper. But Moyle's time at sea in many ships, in all weathers, among a rich stew of men, conferred a rank upon him that might lie ignored until the day there boiled up a need for it, and then men would look to the Moyle in a crew, no matter who he was, a man whose opinion in a time of crisis would be sought and taken as a natural law. It was a call.

"Well," he started to say, and was stopped by a deep spasm of coughing. "I guess I'll go ask him what he's planning."

Jenkins seemed relieved. "I'll come with you, then."

The two of them walked aft, the rising wind at their backs. They found Percival in the wheelhouse. He was standing at the chart table reading the blue cloth Admiralty *Arctic Pilot*, volume 3. He looked up as they came in.

"Are we leaving here, Captain?" asked Moyle.

Percival stared at him with his pet glare, as if to hammer Moyle or any questioning miscreant into the deck by the force of his eyes.

"I gave orders to raise steam and make ready for sea. Get on with it."

Moyle had been stared at before. "What about them ashore?"

Percival's stare blazed and suddenly relaxed when he saw he might have been staring at a cigar store Indian for all the effect it had on Moyle. "I understand your concern, gentlemen. I share it. We shall leave nobody marooned. However, the weather is getting up and we've been forced to leave this same

spot before. As a precaution, I want the ship ready for steaming should it become necessary to run for a lee. I'm sending
more food ashore in the event we do have to clear out. Thank
you, gentlemen." He returned his attention to the book.

"We'll have a lee shore here when this wind backs," said
Moyle.

Percival looked over at Moyle, not with his stare but for a
moment in plain hope of an answer he could believe: "And will
it back before it blows ice down upon us as it did before, Mr.
Moyle?"

"Maybe. We could wait and clear out—"

"Quite! Thank you, Mr. Moyle!"

They left the wheelhouse, descending the steps to the deck.
The first flakes of snow flew overhead.

"Well, I dunno," said Jenkins. "Wind's up. Seems reasonable
to be ready to maneuver. It's the seamanlike thing. We might
have to steam into it if it comes on hard. Or clear out if we get
ice."

"And them ashore?"

"Well, they'll be all right, won't they? I mean, they're
ashore." Jenkins held the seaman's assumption that folk ashore
were well out of harm's way. "If we had to clear out, well,
we'd come back for them, wouldn't we? He's leaving them
food." Jenkins nodded over Moyle's shoulder.

Moyle turned and looked across the deck where the boys,
Watts and Avery, were unlashing *Monte*, the other Riva, from
its davits, getting ready to lower it into the water.

"We're better off sitting here than moving around these
rocks and ice in a blow," muttered Moyle. But he knew it
sounded reasonable to be ready to move in thick weather, and
Jenkins was ready to see specious reason rather than go against
his captain. He was British navy, like Percival, and the tradi-
tions of rank and obedience ran deep in him.

"Well, he hasn't said we're going, has he?" said the Welshman, his national tic of rising inflection making his hopeful
assumptions sound so reasonable. "He's only preparing. I
mean, he's the old man, isn't he?"

They had come up against it, and flubbed it. Jenkins turned
away, and went below to the engine room.

Moyle watched the boys lowering *Monte*. Then, moving fast, he stepped down the forward companionway into the fo'c'sle. He found pen and paper on the shelf beside Gar's bunk and began writing.

A few minutes later Moyle appeared on deck at the top of the ship's ladder. He handed Watts the extra picnic basket Duhamel had prepared, and Watts stepped down the ladder and dropped into the boat Avery was holding with difficulty off the ship's side in the rising waves.

AVERY TRIED TO NOSE in to the beach, but the building wind caught the Riva and slew it sideways, the waves rocked it farther in, and the propeller hit rock. The engine stopped.

"Shit! Push us off!" yelled Avery.

Watts leapt overboard into knee-deep surf and tried to push the stern into deeper water.

"Jesus, it's cold!" yelled Watts.

"Push her out!"

"Well, gimme a hand! I gotta leave the food!"

Avery was trying to restart the engine. It rumbled, and he threw the throttle forward, and the boat leapt sideways, almost knocking Watts over.

"Hey, watch out!"

"Here!" shouted Avery. He threw the picnic basket at Watts. He had the boat going astern into the waves, which broke over the flat transom. The engine died again.

Watts left him trying the ignition and waded ashore. He ran heavy-legged to *Carlo* at the bend in the beach and threw the basket in. He ran back into the water.

The boat had been pushed sideways by the waves again.

"Push her off!" yelled Avery.

"Well, gimme some help!"

"I gotta start the son of a bitch! Push the bow around!"

Watts waded to the bow and pushed. Avery was pushing the ignition button and the engine was turning over but not catching. Watts had the bow almost into the waves when the engine rumbled and Avery gunned it. The stern came around and knocked Watts over. He fell backward into the water and went all the way under. He came up gasping, his wool watch cap gone, his mouth open, but he was too cold to make any sound.

Avery had the engine going and looped the boat around and came alongside Watts. "Get in quick or we're going to get pushed in again!"

Watts grabbed the side of the cockpit and tried to climb in, but his heavy new clothes weighed him down and he felt like ice, and had a hard time moving his arms. "I can't."

Avery leaned over and tried to pull him in, but he was too heavy. "Hold on. I got to get us out a little deeper and then I'll help you." He moved the throttle forward and the boat rumbled through the waves into deeper water.

"I can't hold on!" Watts thought he yelled, but his voice was weak. He started to slip off, but Avery grabbed his jacket. Avery let go the wheel and tried hauling Watts up. It was impossible.

"Get me aboard. I'm freezing," said Watts.

"Wait a minute, Jesus, I'm trying to do five things at once here!"

Avery got one of the boat's mooring lines and tried to pass it around Watts's chest, but he couldn't get it around him, Watts was too big, too wet, too low in the water, and then, as Avery was bending over him, Watts let go. He started to float away. Avery grabbed his sleeve. "Hold on, Freddie!"

"I can't."

Avery saw that the boat was being pushed back into the shallows, so he wound the line tightly around Watts's sleeve, and held onto the bitter end himself, which was easier to hold than Watts's arm. "Hold on! We're going back!"

He pushed the throttle forward until the line pulled through his hand, burning his palm. He pulled back the throttle and grabbed the line. Watts's arm was still tangled in it, held alongside the hull, his head above the water, so Avery threw a quick knot around the arm and wrapped the line around one of the boat's mooring cleats and pushed the throttle forward again. The arm was forced back but held, Avery knew, because he saw Watts's purple hand at the edge of the cockpit.

The boat was alongside the ship a minute later. Moyle had watched them and had gathered Iams and Ray on deck to help.

Captain Percival stood on the bridge wing above them, but Moyle told the men what to do. Iams took the boat's painter thrown up by Avery and ran it through a cleat, slacking it off as the boat drifted aft along the hull until it lay bobbing in the chop beneath the boat davits, and then he tied it off. Moyle lowered the block-and-tackle falls. Avery tried to get a line around Watts again, but Watts was entirely in the water now except for his head and the arm strapped to the line.

"Tie that fucking line to the hook!" yelled Moyle.

They hauled him up by his one arm. He was blue and staring dead when they laid him out on deck.

MAMIE AWOKE FEELING THE ship heel. She became aware of the rise and fall of a seaway. She had been lying on her bunk reading an Ellen R. Swinton romance and had fallen asleep in the close heat of her cabin.

"Carl?" she called out.

When no answer came, she rose from her bunk and left the cabin. She climbed the stairs to the saloon, swinging with the motion, but gripping the banister tightly. She met Arthur at the top of the stairs. He appeared irresolute and distressed.

"Where is Mr. Schenck, Arthur?"

Arthur was terribly relieved to confide in Mrs. Schenck. "He is still ashore with the others, Mrs. Schenck."

She looked out through the saloon windows at waves going by.

"Well, where on earth are we going?"

"I don't know, Mrs. Schenck. I heard that the captain thought we'd be better moving from where we were. Like how we left the other morning. I don't know where we're going."

It was immediately clear to Mamie what she had to do. "Get your coat on, Arthur. I need you to give me a hand."

Arthur went below. Mamie put on her Burberry, which lay on a sofa. Arthur reappeared wearing his new peacoat and his reindeer pants.

"Let's go."

"Your boots, Mrs. Schenck?"

Mamie was wearing her tennis shoes.

"Never mind. Come on."

They opened the door to the sidedeck. The noise of wind and waves was sudden and loud and reminded Mamie of the time she had flown to Newport by seaplane from Floyd Bennett Field in East Brooklyn and they had taken off after bumping for an absurdly long time across Jamaica Bay. The wind came from aft and immediately blew her and Arthur forward along the deck, which was fine. Mamie gripped Arthur's arm. He gallantly took the outboard rail, putting himself between her and the elements, and they made their way forward. The ship's narrow hull rolled with irregular lurches and they tottered heavily together from side to side between the superstructure and the delicate rail. In a few minutes they reached the wheelhouse. Mamie let Arthur go, grabbed both rails, and started up the steps. He attempted to support her from behind, holding one of her arms while crawling up the steps in the lee of her billowing Burberry. Mamie hauled them both up to the door and pulled it open.

Captain Percival, standing at the window forward of the helm, turned his blandest gaze on her.

"Where are we going?" she demanded.

"I was unhappy with our anchorage in the developing conditions, Mrs. Schenck. We were being threatened by ice. We are making for East Bluff, nine miles away, where we will find shelter."

"Well, in your unhappiness you forgot Mr. Schenck! I can't imagine what you thought you were doing. Now turn this boat around and go back and wait for him."

The captain's face transfigured. "Do not instruct me in the management of this vessel, Madam. The weather disposes in this instance, not you or I. We will return for your husband when conditions allow. Now kindly leave my bridge and go below."

Mamie was astonished. She had never been spoken to in such a tone by a servant, which was how she unequivocally saw the captain. "Now you listen to me, you rude man. I don't know what you mean by calling anything about this boat yours. This is my husband's boat—and mine for that matter. So do what I say this instant! And stop making that silly face and rolling your eyes at me! You don't scare me one bit."

Captain Percival came away from the window and faced her at rigid attention. He bellowed above the noisy buffeting of the wind: "I am the law while this ship is at sea! You will remove yourself from this place at once and go below!"

Mamie was momentarily rattled. She was aware that Arthur was somewhere behind her. She looked over at Avery, who appeared sick and white as he wrestled with the helm and kept his eyes on the swinging compass card.

"Okay, buster! You asked for it." She turned and opened the door and pulled Arthur outside. They descended the steps and fought their way back along the deck. They reached the saloon door and pulled themselves inside. Arthur shut the door behind them.

"That man is crazy!"

"Yes, Mrs. Schenck."

"Well, we have to stop him!"

"Yes, Mrs. Schenck."

CHAPTER 16

WHEN THE WEATHER CLEARED, the four women pushed the umiak into the water and climbed inside. They paddled out into deeper water. The three men carried their kayaks down the beach and stepped into them and pushed off from the beach without wetting their sealskin boots. They drew wooden rings over their heads and dropped them down to their waists, where the rings clamped their short sealskin jackets over the round holes in which they sat. They paddled after the women. The kayaks soon overtook the umiak, ranging ahead and offshore of the women's boat. The group paralleled the coast, moving south. The sun came out again. The new wet snow on the shore began to melt.

The offshore wind had blown the loose summer floe ice well away from the land, and the people were surprised and pleased to find walrus, who usually stayed with the ice, lying in the sun on the dark gravel beside a tidal stream that debouched into the sea from an estuary behind the beach. The gravel fan bottom in the shallows off the mouth of the stream was layered with nutrients from the estuary and a thick crop of clams, which had drawn the walrus. There were about sixty animals in the herd on both sides of the stream. They lay on their sides dozing in the sun or scratching themselves delicately with their flippers. The men in their kayaks reached the beach first, coming out of the water well away from the herd. One of the men had a rifle but he waited while the other two moved quietly to within fifteen feet of a large bull and threw their spears. The bull roared and the herd picked up and began hauling for the water, cows bellowing for their calves. The hunter with the rifle ran alongside another bull and shot it in the head at a range of eight feet. It stopped moving and began to die and he returned to his kayak to fetch his spear and throw it into the bull speared by the other two men. The women beached their umiak and yelled and laughed as they watched the men stabbing their spears into the dying bull.

The four women began cutting up the two walrus immediately. The killing done, the men sat on the bodies and ate pieces of meat while it was still warm. The women chewed pieces cut from their work. The flesh beneath the blubber was a rich maroon color. The women cut long strips of skin and blubber and pulled them off the carcasses and lay them out on the gravel. They scraped the blubber into fatty heaps and piled it onto several pieces of scraped skin and wrapped these up into balls. They rolled up the rest of the scraped hides and tied them closed with strips of flesh. The men now hacked the tusks out of the heads with short axes they had obtained by trade with the Hudson's Bay Company stores, while the women cut out the organs and solid deposits of the maroon meat. They chopped the ribs in sections off the spine. They carried the rolled hides and wrapped blubber bundles, the heavy chunks of meat and the rib sections, down to the water's edge, and they slid the umiak into the shallows before loading it, for they had half a ton of meat and bone and blubber to put into the wood and skin boat. The women did all this. Jaegers and glaucous gulls that had been hopping through the sleeping herd pecking at walrus feces, now wheeled and shrieked overhead, and dropped and hopped, fluttered, and backwinged around the men and women and the methodical butchering, snatching at pieces of meat and fat and dark coagulating lumps on the gravel.

The work was unhurried and took several hours. When they were finished, the men and women sat and continued eating for an hour. Then the men loaded their weapons and axes into their kayaks, and the women climbed into the umiak, and the screeching birds covered the stripped hulks of the two walrus.

They were all in their boats and paddling when one of the women saw the man on the beach. He was staggering, and seemed to be trying to follow them along the shore. He was waving.

The woman said, "Look! *Quallunaaq!*"

They turned and paddled back to the shore.

The *quallunaaq*, Clement Shred, collapsed on the gravel as the Eskimos came toward him. They could see he was all in and they were eager to save him. They stuffed bloody walrus meat into his mouth but Shred gagged and spat it out. Bread was the simple picture in his mind. Shivering uncontrollably, he said, "Bread. Please, bread. And water. And I'm cold."

"No bread, no biscuit, laddie," said the older Eskimo man, the one who had killed with the rifle. His English was thickly inflected with a Scottish accent. "No porridge. No finnan haddie. Walrus. Fresh."

A woman brought a caribou skin from the umiak and laid it over him, and then got beneath it with him and pressed her face against his. Another brought a skin waterbag and dribbled water into Shred's mouth. He grabbed at the mouth of the skin and sucked on it until he swallowed wrong and had a coughing fit. An Eskimo woman pushed another piece of walrus into his mouth but again he gagged on it and spat it out. One of the women gave him something green to try and he found he could eat it. It was delicious, like a soft, sweetish cheese, not dense like the meat. He got some water down and ate more of the green food. It was seal meat that had been packed in a skin with blubber for several years and fermented slowly in the cold to its present delicate flavor.

"What ship, laddie?"

"Out there," said Shred, nodding vaguely out at the water.

At this, the Eskimo men stood up and looked out to sea. They saw no ship.

"What ship?"

"The *Lodestar*."

"Whaler?"

"A what?"

"Whaler ship?" asked the Scots-sounding Eskimo, whose name was Tikiqtituq.

"No. She's a yacht," said Shred. His mouth was full and Tikiqtituq did not understand him.

"What kind?"

"A yacht. Pleasure craft."

"What kind vessel that?"

"For rich people. For fun."

"Fun?" The Eskimos talked among themselves for a minute. Tikiqtituq remembered the word *rich*, which had figured constantly in the preoccupation and goal of all the *quallunaaq* he had known. They had come here in ships, mostly from Scotland, to hunt whale and seal and grow rich. They had hired the Eskimo men and slept with their women. It had worked well for everybody. Everybody grew a little rich, but it had been ten years since the whalers last came. They had become rich enough perhaps.

It was clear to them that this *quallunaaq* was already rich because he was wonderfully fat and obviously did no work, but employed others to work for him.

Fun was a new word to Tikiqtituq, but this rich *quallunaaq* had come here to find it. "What fun you find here?" he asked.

"Fuck knows," said Shred with feeling.

Then Tikiqtituq laughed as if he had received happy news of an old friend. "Fucken right, mate!" He slapped Shred on the shoulder. He laughed with the others, saying *fuck* several times, and the Eskimos all laughed with him.

"Long time I hear fuck, laddie!" He laughed and pointed to the Eskimo woman who was snuggling against Shred and warming him. "My wife Mequ. Grand fucken, my wife!"

Shred turned his head, looked at the woman and then at Tikiqtituq, unsure of what he had heard, though the man's speech was clear. The Eskimos all laughed hard.

"I fuck you good, Sikatsi laddie!" said Mequ. She laughed and began to cover Shred's face with smacking kisses. Beneath the skin, her hand searched for his crotch. He tried to turn away, but she was strong.

Tikiqtituq pointed to one of the younger women. "Arnanguaq. Her father Sikatsi. Come here from Dundee."

The woman, Arnanguaq, looked fairer and less slant-eyed

than the others. She smiled invitingly at Shred, who struggled beside Tikiqtituq's wife. She said, "Sikatsi Dundee."

"Stop. Give over," said Shred weakly. He pulled a hand from beneath the skin and managed to push the wide face of the woman away. "Hullo! Listen!" he said to Tikiqtituq. "My people are back in there." He pointed inland. "You got to get them out. You take us back to our ship. My boss is a rich man. Rich! He'll give you money."

"You rich, I see! Dinna see you ship. No ship there, laddie."

"Well, it's out there! You get me back to the ship and you'll get money."

"How much mates ashore?"

"Six. Six more."

"What they do?"

"They're hunting."

"Hunting fun?"

"For some folk."

"You find fun?"

"Not me."

"Where?"

"What?"

"Fun!"

Shred stared at the insistent face looming over him.

"What fun?" Tikiqtituq repeated. "Make rich?"

"Yes. Find them and you'll get rich! Lots of fun."

Tikiqtituq spoke to the others. There was agreement. Tikiqtituq's wife and the other women returned to the umiak and began unloading it. Two of them started digging a hole in the gravel above the high-tide line. The other two men lifted the three kayaks out of the water and carried them up near the digging women. Tikiqtituq pulled Shred to his feet.

"I'm sick," said Shred, tottering, pulling the caribou skin around him.

"You tolerable, laddie. You come. We find mates. Then fun." He laughed and slapped Shred on the back. "Fucken right mate! Rich man!"

The women began burying the walrus meat. The men took Shred inland.

*   *   *

AS THEY CLIMBED TO the ridge, Harriet was silent. She stayed out of Boden's reach, too far away for him to help her over the bigger rocks. She would not look at him when he turned to look back for her. She kept to her own path up the slope, so that when he stopped to wait for her she drew level with him yards away.

What Boden had told Harriet beneath the boat had been creeping around the side of his thoughts, but it was the first time he had declared to himself that he was going back to his wife. Now it was all he could think about. And whether she would have him back. His brain filled with the picture of Mary and her older man with the dyed hair, and their intimacy. He saw it, and their shared life of colorful books which was progressing far to the south in New York.

He turned to scan the water. The ship was nowhere in sight.

It was easy, now the ship was gone and he was stranded far away in a cold place, to think that all he wanted was to go home and be with her. He had forgotten why if he were in New York he wouldn't run to the train and find his way home. But that was all he wanted now, and all he wanted to know. He was desperate to find the ship.

He understood why Percival had decided to leave, but the wind had backed and blown the ice offshore, and the inlet was now clear. There was still no sign of the ship. It ought to have come back.

Bill Fisher was dead, chewed up by a polar bear, and Boden was afraid for all of them now. He knew if they did not get aboard the ship before nightfall they could die. He looked at his watch: it was past eight in the evening; they had been ashore over fourteen hours. The snow had fallen for perhaps three or four hours, and Schenck's group had been without shelter. If they were not already lying in a drift dying of cold, they would not make it through the coming night unless they were back on the ship.

He turned again, noting Harriet below him, and looked out to sea. The sky had cleared beautifully. To the northwest, where the weather had sprung up, he could see the rocky coastline in sharp definition narrowing all the way up to the head of the inlet, where the deep blue ice faded into the dark water that now lay in shadow. To the northeast, across fifty miles of the ice-clutter of Frobisher Bay, he could see a rose band of sunlight on a long mountain skyline, cold and clean and lonely. There was no sign of the ship. Boden felt a swell of rage.

He reached the top of the ridge and looked down as they had earlier in the day when the group had split up nearly in this same spot. Below lay the bog where they had seen the caribou herd, the route he and Harriet and Bill had taken. New snow covered the tundra four inches deep. He waited for Harriet and when she reached him he asked her to fire off four evenly spaced shots. He held the cartridges and handed them to her as she shot and worked the bolt-action. Four shots off in twenty-five seconds.

THEY HEARD SHOTS; HEAVY charges. The Eskimos pulled Shred up a rise and they saw two more *quallunaaq* below on the other side. One of them, short like the man they pulled with them, was firing his rifle. The other sat shivering on the ground beside a caribou head and a ball of fur.

The Eskimos approached.

"Mr. Shred! My God, you found help! Good job! We've heard rifle fire, so the others aren't far away."

"Good day," said Tikiqtituq.

Schenck grabbed his hand and pumped it. He looked at the other Eskimos and saw they were all younger than Tikiqtituq, the undoubted leader. "Good day to you, sir! Carl Schenck. I am a personal friend of Robert Flaherty. Robert Flaherty, perhaps you know him. Nanook of the North. *Nanook!*"

"Nanook?" said Tikiqtituq. "Many Nanook, Jack."

"Good! Now then, I want you to help me find my people and return to my ship. I will pay you well!"

"Pay me money. We find fun for you."

"Fun?"

"What fun?" said Tikiqtituq.

"Is he saying fun?"

"Aye, Sikatsi. Where?"

"What?"

"You look fun."

"I look fun?"

"Yes! Yes! We look!"

"Is the man nuts?" Schenck asked Shred.

"I dunno, sir."

"Fun!"

Schenck moved close into Tikiqtituq's face. "Forget the fun for now! We find my people, we go to my ship! Big ship!" He pointed in the wrong direction. "To the sea! Lots of money in my ship! Let's go! Joey, get up!"

"Where ye captain, mate?" asked Tikiqtituq.

"Our captain's aboard my ship."

"We talk with captain."

"I agree! Let's go see the captain! Let's find the ship anchored in the ocean! And we find my daughter and the others. Listen!" He raised his rifle and fired. The Eskimos winced. "Now listen!"

A moment later came an answering shot, not far away. In the direction of the low sun.

"See? We find them. Then we find ship. You two—"

Schenck pulled Tikiqtituq and another Eskimo, whose name was Angutidluarssuk, to the caribou head lying in the snow. "—you carry this. Let's go!" He walked away, heading northwest. He fired again into the air.

A SHORT WHILE LATER one of the Eskimos cried out and pointed up to the rim of a slope. Schenck saw the two figures.

"Butch!" He threw down his rifle and ran uphill as they came down. He hugged his daughter.

Boden walked to the group of men. He said hello to the Eskimos and shook their hands. He looked at the caribou head, and then at Schenck.

"Where's the boy?" Boden asked him, afraid. "Where's Gar?"

CHAPTER 17

GAR HAD TURNED AND shouted "Here!' and walked on a few feet and shouted again. By then he could no longer hear Schenck shouting back at him, and he decided he had come far enough. He turned around and walked back.

Missed them, he realized a minute later. He turned around and followed a skewed reciprocal of the blind course he thought he had been taking.

Later he began firing his rifle. Feeling for shells in his coat pocket, he remembered that the Mauser ammunition was in the bag with the Mannlicher cartridges he had passed to Bill when the group had split up. He had only what was left of the handful he had put in his pocket. He counted three. He stopped shooting.

For another hour, perhaps, Gar tramped an unseeing zigzag through the falling and settling snow. Several times he came across suggestions of footprints filling up, his own or others, he could not know, but he followed them until what was left of his sense of direction told him he had gone too far from where he had first become lost.

Finally he stopped. He stood still and listened to his breathing, the only sound in the world now, along with the somehow audible settling of large snowflakes on the earflaps of his old checkered hunter's hat. He was cold and he was tired.

He saw nothing at all beyond the white tracery around him

and he remembered nothing in the stunted tundra landscape that could provide shelter. He could sit down or stay on his feet and keep walking. He pictured himself as a snowdrift and saw that he was dead in that picture, and Gar suddenly realized he might die today. He pulled up a sleeve and looked at his Rolex wristwatch, which seemed curiously sharp and easy to read when he held it up in front of his face. The air in the occluding snowstorm was strangely bright. It was only a little after two o'clock in the afternoon. He started walking.

At first he worried about where he was headed: the only possibility of survival seemed to be to reach the coast and get back aboard the ship. But he could think of no way to determine his course. He decided any direction was better than sitting down. He walked slowly, without urgency; if he was heading away from the coast, he was in no hurry. He gave up hope of finding anyone, and he thought he might be better off without Schenck. He thought he would try to walk until it grew dark, which he knew would be at least eight hours away, or until the snow stopped. He had no real idea the distance they had covered stalking the caribou. Just keep walking, he told himself.

At home today he might have played a few holes of golf. Benny, the pro at the club, had told him his game could amount to something if he paid attention to it. The trouble was, Gar played golf because he loved going to the club, and the game was what you did there before the best time: settling into the clubhouse bar at the end of the afternoon. That was his best game. He had been thrilled to come on this trip, but it wouldn't have happened if he'd been able to stay home and play golf and sail and drink like every other summer.

He thought of his father. A month ago, right after he came home from his Newport cruise with Critch and the Dudley Carrolls, it appeared one morning that Gar Sr. had suffered a stroke. He had stopped, like a clock run down, on his way through the living room after breakfast. Not in a chair, but standing up, the view ahead gone out of his face, his eyes seeming blind. Gar and his mother had led him upstairs to bed. They called Dr. Nelson, who came right over. The doctor used his flashlight, stethescope, and little rubber hammer.

"There's nothing wrong with him that I can find," said Dr. Nelson. "He's upset, naturally. Give him a couple of days. He'll be fine. He's only fifty-two."

That evening Gar Sr. let go his bowels in bed. He never moved. After the second time, the next day, they started wrapping him in towels pinned at the side like big diapers. Gar had driven to the drugstore in Darien to buy the biggest pins he could find. His father didn't get out of bed before Gar left to go north three weeks later. He still ate; he wouldn't raise food to his mouth, but he opened it if a fork or spoon came near, so they fed him by hand in bed. His bowel movements were regular. And he could reach out and turn the dial on the radio beside the bed. He evidently liked to listen to *Stoopnagle and Bud*. Gar's mother was beside herself, and he hated to leave her, but he was glad to move aboard the ship and be out of the house.

His father had gone to bed owing seven million dollars. It was a hell of a break for his mother. Where they would go after the house sold was a question he had tried to push away. A room in Stamford? And some laundry bill with his old man's diapers. Where would the money come from?

He thought of Schenck and all his money. The Crash hadn't touched him; it seemed to have left him better off. Schenck had more and newer cars than anyone else. He was building boats. He had bought the place in Newport only a year ago. And he took *Lodestar* off Dudley Carroll faster than you could play a hand of poker.

Gar's thoughts came around to Harriet. They'd hit it off so fast two summers ago. She had been so swell, and pretty, ready to go anywhere and do anything. She'd been good about letting him do what he wanted; and she'd wanted it as much as he had. She had amazed him, and he'd wondered where she'd learned to do all that stuff. Girls talked about it maybe, was what he'd figured. Then she had shut him off like a faucet. The quiet girl with a small round mouth and large eyes who walked up and down *Lodestar*'s deck and shot with such deadly skill was nothing like the Harriet he had known. He guessed he still had a thing for her. Gar wondered where she was now in this blizzard, and he hoped she was okay.

He saw a hole without scale or shape open up in the white ahead, and he lost his balance and fell over. He managed to avoid falling into the hole, which turned out to be water, a puddle close up to his face, with a mud smell, the snow falling into the water and melting at its edge. Gar stood up and moved forward slowly and found more puddles, and depressions everywhere around him. A boggy pond, with caribou tracks all over it. Was it the same bog they'd seen from the top of the ridge? And if it was, what edge of its irregular perimeter had he reached? Christ, he wished he had a little handbearing compass like Boden's.

Gar tried to remember what he had seen from the ridge beside Sugarloaf Hill when they'd all climbed up from the beach. The bog down the hill below us. The caribou at one end. They smelled us and took off. They disappeared behind a rise at the other end—the left edge when seen from the ridge. A peat mound, regular as a midden, large enough to hide from view a line of trotting caribou. If this bog had such a mound, it might be that bog, and if he found the mound he could find Sugarloaf Hill and the coast. Unless it was a different bog with a similar mound, but he let that go.

Gar started off again. He found a rise of solid white ground and climbed over it and around it and saw that its edge pushed into the bog like a blunt ship. He fixed a tentative geography in his mind and turned away from his one landmark and set off into the featureless white.

He soon found the tug of gravity pulling heavier, and he was able to lean into the ground without falling. He decided he must be climbing. He grew warm again. Later, the ground fell away and he leaned back and went down a hill. Now large stones broke the snowcover and small ones loosened beneath his boots. He could see the shapes and found he could focus on the irregular surface, and he got the feel of it and went down without falling, until the ground leveled out again. Then, as he walked away across what seemed flat, he felt tundra moss under his boots and the ground was once more opaque white and vanished a few yards ahead in falling snow. The snow was lighter, he thought, but still an effective curtain. The coast, he thought now, was somewhere nearby, but once he left the only feature he could make out—the hill behind him—he would become instantly lost.

Gar stopped and sat down. His watch said five-thirty. He would wait fifteen minutes and then stand up and jump around to keep warm.

He woke suddenly from deep, absolutely gone, sleep. He had been dreaming; some vivid warm-colored place, and . . . But it faded with his first deep breath. He remembered he was no longer in the fo'c'sle but out on the tundra lying alone in the snow, and it was all real. He sat up and saw the sky was clear and pale twilight-shaded. It was as if there had been no blizzard at all, except for the new snowcover over the ground. He was cold but not severely, and, the damnedest thing, he had a terrific hard-on.

He had heard a shot, he realized. In the dream, or had he really heard it? Gar stood up and looked around.

Coming down the hill earlier, he had pictured it so clearly: in front of him the coast, and somewhere off it the ship, and Sugarloaf Hill to his left and the ridge had come down behind him, but now he saw nothing ahead but tundra plain and low hills. Nearby, a rocky defile, almost a chute, rose a few hundred feet between two round, snow-covered hills. He must have come down the defile. The glow of the late sun lay beyond more hills a few miles across the plain.

He had no idea where he was.

Then he heard a shot again. Distant, but sharp like a firecracker, and piercing the squeezing loneliness that gripped him. He was not sure what direction the shot had come from—over the hills to the right he thought—but he pictured the people firing it—Schenck, Harriet, Boden—somewhere over the tundra not far away. They were looking for him.

Gar picked up the Mauser at his feet and pulled a shell from his parka pocket, loaded, and raised the rifle high into the air with both hands and fired. He heard it echo off the rocky defile now behind him and fly away through the air. Hear that, please! He started walking fast over the flat ground, facing now what he had first thought of as the right-hand hills. He wished to Christ he had a compass with him.

No shot came back answering his. He walked faster. Should

he fire again? He had two more shells. What if they were moving away? But if his first shot had gone unheard, another one
now would be no better. He told himself to wait, and get
closer. He began to run.

He was out of breath and gasping when the ground began to
rise. He could no longer run, but pushed his legs ahead as if
wading through thigh-deep water. The hillside was grassy beneath the snow, and he slipped and fell forward and crushed
his fingers under the rifle. They were already cold and numb
inside his gloves, but they hurt like hell at the same time. He
got to his feet and slung the rifle across his back and started up
again, sometimes on all fours when the ground came within
reach, and he pushed at it. He found a rhythm with his breath
and hands and feet and moved steadily up the hill. He climbed
above a shadowline into sunlight. The snow became wetter
and heavier, clumped like mashed potatoes. Gar's legs and
hands became wet through, and beneath his woolen undershirt
he was pouring sweat. More plants grew up here in the late day
sunshine, wildflowers that had bloomed months earlier and
were already developing overwintering buds to open at the onset of the next year's spring and make the most of their short
season, and Gar grabbed at them to pull himself up.

But as he came over the top and the view beyond opened up,
nothing looked like he had imagined it would. No coast, only
more plain and bog and waves of mounds and hillocks. Far off
beneath the low sun, miles away to his left, was a single tall
hill, maybe Sugarloaf Hill, but he was so far from where he
had thought he was that he felt a cold rush of bewildering fear.
He pulled the rifle off his back, loaded it, and fired. The sound
echoed until he could only hear it in his mind, and he waited
for an answer until he knew it wouldn't come.

There was a square rock nearby, the snow melted off its top.
Gar sat down on it. He was scared, and wished he was sitting
in an armchair in the bar at the Round Hill Country Club, or
home in bed, with his father pooping into his towel diapers
down the hall. He felt like crying. He wasn't prepared for this.
He wanted someone to come and save him.

A cold shadow moved over him and he shivered, aware of
his damp, clammy undershirt. He looked and saw that the sun

had gone down below the tall hill several miles away. It was eight-fifteen, civil twilight. At ten or so it would be full twilight—dark until about four, when the sun would come up again. At no point in the night would it get really dark. That made Gar feel not so bad.

He looked again at the tall hill a few miles away. It was regular and spirelike, the tallest land around. He pictured the chart again, Will's chart on the fo'c'sle table, and he saw it quite clearly. There was only one hill like that within miles of this spot on the coast off which they had anchored. That was why it was there on the chart, a pimple of inked strokes with its name beside it, the predominant feature in the landscape here for the sailor to note. Gar couldn't have wandered more than four or five miles, tops, in the last few hours in the blizzard. That had to be Sugarloaf Hill.

Will had explained to him (drawing the earth on a piece of letter-writing paper, dotting a slanted axis through it, and drawing the sun way off to one side) what happened during the day in the Arctic: at midday the sun was due south, as it was from the Pocumtuck Yacht Club on Long Island Sound and everywhere else in the northern hemisphere. Up here, if you were far enough north to see the sun at midnight—on the Arctic Circle at latitude 66-and-a-half degrees north, or higher, on June 21 or later—it would then be due north. It went around in a circle all day, from north to south through east and west. Here on the southern tip of Baffin Island, they were at 62 degrees north, and the sun was dipping below the northern horizon for about seven hours in the middle of the night. It went down in the northwest and came up in the northeast. Sugarloaf Hill, therefore, on a line between Gar and the lowering sun, was northwest of him.

He pictured the chart again, and remembered the anchorage, the view from the deck, the run ashore in the boat. The shore had trended in a nearly straight line from northwest to southeast—

Gar got off the rock and squatted down and drew a line in the snow. The hill had been southwest of the anchored ship—a fingerpoke in the snow. The reciprocal direction, the direction in which the coast and the ship lay from the hill, was northeast.

They had tramped southeast from the hill after the caribou—
he drew a line in the snow paralleling the line of the coast.
Squatting there in the snow beside the flat rock, he stared at his
squiggles for a while, going back in his mind over what he
thought he had done.

Gar stood up. He decided he had wandered inland through
the blizzard. The coast had to be—he looked down at his
snowy map, and he pointed his left arm at the hill to the undoubted northwest, and stuck the other one out at ninety degrees—the coast *had* to be over *there*. Down this hill, across a
mile or so of ground, over those hills beyond, keeping Sugarloaf Hill always ninety degrees on his left. He thought it all
through again and started down the hill.

AN HOUR LATER HE stood on the beach beside the water. It
might be gravel and severe of aspect, but Gar knew beaches.
He knew their slant. He felt relieved, much happier, no longer
lost in a strange landscape. He was just down the beach a few
miles from where they had come ashore.

He couldn't see the ship because the sun had gone behind the
mountains up the coast north of Sugarloaf Hill, and the land
beneath the skyline was lost in dark blue shadowed mist, out
of which the sea materialized only a mile or so from where he
stood. But surely there would be lights on the ship and he
would see them? Maybe not. But he believed he could see the
top of the glacier, or at least where it lay, from a luminous
patch in the air above the shadow of land where the sea faded
in the direction of the inlet. The ship, the Riva with the food
hampers, they were all up there. Gar started walking along the
shore.

A few minutes later he saw an object come out of the blue
mist up the beach ahead. Far enough away that he could see
nothing but the pearly whiteness of it, and yet some swinging
aspect of its movement made the back of his scalp contract.
Gar stopped and he saw the white round shape become motionless at the same time. For a moment he questioned himself,
but then the white ball elongated as it rose up on its hind legs,
and he saw its hip-heavy, slope-shouldered figure. It dropped
and came on.

Gar turned and trotted back down the beach in the direction
he had come. He scanned the land in front of him. No tree, no
rock, no deceiving bush; no cover at all but a line of grass and
moss at the top of the beach, then flat snow-covered tundra
stretching to the smooth hills he had come over. The snowy
rise of the hills would slow him down and there was no shelter
there or beyond, but he would never reach them in time anyway. The beach at least felt familiar, and Gar didn't want to
leave it. He looked behind him: he could make out now the
side-swinging flap of the bear's front legs, a black nose, the
black-dot eyes. He started running.

He tried not to look back because he knew it slowed him
down, but what he saw made him run faster. And then he grew
so afraid his lungs seemed to lose all their space and he felt he
could no longer breathe. He was getting nowhere, and reaching an end, too fast. He stopped, trying to catch his breath, and
turned around to see the bear. The bumpy paw-flapping trot
changed as he looked into a steady, shambling bound. The
bear did not appear to hurry, but it was closing the distance
faster. Its black eyes and whole interest focused on Gar, the
black nose point of the wide head aimed at him, almost unmoving at the front of the rippling, bounding body.

He felt for the last shell in his pocket, trying not to hurry or
fumble, found it, and loaded the Mauser, and stood with his
chest heaving convulsively. He was desperate for one deep
breath. Seeing the bear come on, growing bigger than a buffalo, Gar didn't think any one bullet was going to stop it, even
if perfectly placed. This was really it, he thought. What would
he do? Try to fight? Sit down and put his arms over his head?

Then, to his amazement, his life passed before his eyes. It's
true, Gar thought, it does happen. He saw it at the end of a
long tunnel, as if through the wrong end of a telescope: the soft
pampered boy who always had it too easy, given toys, given
everything, but ignored and made into a soft spineless man of
facile talents, good at golf and yachting and mixing highballs,
fashioned only to follow his pooping father into bed—but now
yanked from that fate to be eaten like a hot dog. It was all so
pointless. His life a waste . . .

A scream tore out of him. Angry, feral, loud. Gar didn't hear it. He was running at the bear screaming incoherent words, no longer aware of fear, only terrible, primordial anger. The bear slowed. Still a hundred yards away, Gar came on, stooping to grab gravel and hurl it toward the bear, raging and crying. The bear slewed its course toward the water and stopped abruptly. It raised its head and watched Gar for a moment, and then with a roll, turned and began trotting away, looking back at him over its shoulder.

Gar ran after it, screaming and throwing gravel, until the bear resumed its rolling bound and began to put some distance between it and its pursuer. Gar saw it getting away. Beside himself, not thinking at all, he stopped and raised the rifle and fired. The loud shot and the jolt of the rifle broke his anger. He saw he had hit the animal and he was sorry.

The bear went down on its side, crashing in a heavy, sprawling somersault. It recovered in a sudden fluid roll onto its feet, and stopped. It raised its head and Gar heard its pained, unmistakably angry, howl. The head looked and saw him, bellowed again, and the bear turned its body, moaning, and started back toward him.

It began with a charge, but fell again, and howled. It was maimed. Gar saw the blood in the white fur of the rear leg. It rose and came on again, its movement now a dipping, lurching, painful trot. But it was fast enough, and Gar was afraid again.

Once more he ran and was pursued. The bear's speed, dragging its rear leg, was slower and tortured, the wound maddening it with every step. He heard it behind him, bellowing and moaning.

At first Gar seemed to put new distance between himself and the bear. He ran away down the beach, the gravel and small stones smooth, with little in the way of washed-up flotsam that could slow him down. He looked back and the bear seemed farther away than before, but it still dipped its painful trot, which forced its head into a lurching bob, and he could see that the bear's eyes remained fixed on him.

Eight or ten minutes later, perhaps half a mile down the beach, Gar's breath gone again, his running was growing desperate. The bear had gained on him and the distance between them was closing. He could hear the animal's breathing now, a deep bronchial moaning that sounded as strong and regular as a locomotive.

Gar turned and tried yelling again, rushing a few precious yards toward the bear, but it was a feint, tentative, and without any of his earlier fury, and the bear came on, snorting and staring at him. It wasn't going to stop, Gar realized. It was going to run him to earth. He ran on, but his thighs felt as if spikes had been driven into them, and all the heat was gone out of his body. He ached and was exhausted and he knew the bear would be on him in minutes if he didn't fall before then.

He stumbled a few paces, bent over to the point of falling, and almost pitched into the gravel, but his legs pushed him on and when he raised his head he saw the men in front of him, too dark to make out anything but the squat bulk of them against the dark blue sky.

He tried to yell "Help!" but it came out a breathless wheeze, and he fell onto his hands and knees in front of them. One of them raised a rifle, the other a spear, but a third figure came forward out of the gloom and spoke.

"No! He's mine."

Gar recognized the voice and looked up to see Schenck standing over him, feet planted, the bantam stance resolute. What he saw in Schenck's face made him believe he was saved: the eyes were invisible behind the blue reflection of the sky in his spectacles, but Gar knew that Schenck was ready, absolutely unafraid, the whole force of him focused on the oncoming bear. Gar watched and it seemed slow and beautiful: Schenck raised his Holland & Holland, bent his cheek to the walnut stock, waited. The other men began shouting, and then came the big-bore explosion.

CHAPTER 18

LODESTAR HAD STEAMED SOUTHEAST in the driving snow. She began to roll badly. For all of her 225 feet of length, and the great weight of her teak superstructure and high wheelhouse, and her rich appointments, she carried only a shallow seven feet of draft. She had no purchase on the water beyond what was necessary for a run down the sheltered waters of Long Island Sound.

After two hours, Captain Percival turned the ship north, into the weather, and reduced speed to slow ahead. They drove into wind and waves for two hours and then came about, rolling past thirty degrees as the ship presented her beam to the swell, and headed south for two hours. The ship held station thus, steaming slowly back and forth through the day, corkscrewing between the waves when she ran north and south, and rolling dangerously to the edge of her righting moment when she turned and exposed her beam to the rising seas. In the falling snow, visibility shortened to a hundred yards.

Duhamel staggered into the wheelhouse to remonstrate about conditions in his galley. Unable to serve meals, he brought sandwiches to Mrs. Schenck and the crew. Things were falling and crashing aboard. Pilot books flew off their shelf above the chart table. Lying on his bunk in his stateroom, Arthur heard boxes of harpoon bombs shifting and thudding beneath his mattress. The Riva lurched and banged in its

davits, despite extra lashings, threatening to break free or
wrench hardware out of the deck.

By late afternoon, waves had risen to fifteen feet and were
breaking, sweeping the decks fore and aft. The long narrow
hull was wracking and twisting and emitting ominous groans.
Inside the wheelhouse, Captain Percival began to look upward
at the crumbling wavetops. He decided to run for shelter and
turned the ship west, hoping to pass around the bottom of
Baffin Island, seeking a lee from the northerly wind and waves.

Early in the long evening twilight the blizzard moved away
over the sea, and shapes of land hardened under the lifting
clouds on both sides of the ship. Two and a half miles north,
off the starboard beam, high land tumbled seaward and
stopped abruptly at a six-hundred-foot black rock wall that
dropped sheer into deep soundings. Aft and to port, less than
three miles to the south, a group of flat-topped islands spread
across the sea, breakers exploding into white spume at their
edges. The ship had passed between the high land and the islands in a thick curtain of snowfall, and standing on deck looking across the water, Moyle didn't ask himself whether Percival
had dead-reckoned his way into this five-mile strait with un-
common skill, or blind-threaded a needle by fool's good luck.

Moyle went below to the fo'c'sle and rested his elbows on
Boden's chart. It was a British Admiralty chart, dated 1897,
with finely engraved views of certain notable features printed
along one edge. Moyle was no navigator, but a sense of place
at sea had come to him over the years and now he decided that
the high land to the north was East Bluff, the southeast point
of Baffin Island, and the islands on the port quarter were the
Savage Islands. The chart gave a view of the flat-topped Sav-
ages that strengthened his belief.

In the wheelhouse, Captain Percival drew the same conclu-
sion from an identical chart, and detailed descriptions of the
coast given in his Admiralty *Arctic Pilot* book, 2nd edition,
1915. He held on to his westerly course, hoping to put Baffin
Island between himself and the still high wind and sea. He was
anxious to find shelter before the weather closed in again. He
did not consider returning to the inlet they had escaped.

The chart showed an indentation of the coast, named Trying

Inlet, twelve miles west of East Bluff. The Admiralty pilot, collating information derived largely from logbooks written by whaling masters, described this indentation:

> *Trying Inlet is a short, steep-sided, narrow inlet which affords good shelter for small craft in depths of 4 to 13 fathoms. Fresh water can be obtained from a small waterfall on the West shore half a mile within the entrance. A small trout stream flows into the head of the inlet.*

Good shelter was a rich suggestion in a volume whose style ran necessarily to severe caution. Percival knew that by *small craft* the pilot book meant fishing, sealing, whaling vessels, most of which would be dwarfed by *Lodestar*. However, depths were more than adequate, and an inlet of at least half a mile or greater was implied. The description made Percival think of Scotland, where he had been stationed during the war. He pictured a peaty burn at the head of a heather-bound loch. He had cruised aboard a destroyer and seen it maneuvered regularly in and out of narrow lochs. This sounded much the same. Running inland to the northeast, high enough to feature a waterfall, the inlet would provide shelter from wind and sea in a northerly blow.

At nine in the evening, the sky still pale blue and clearing above the flying scud over the shadowed Baffin mountains, the watch changed. Avery was relieved by Moyle, the only other member of the deck crew now aboard. The two of them had steered off and on all day, napping below when they could, for in the blizzard there had been no use for a lookout in the bow.

"I want you forward for now," Percival told Avery. "We're going into anchor."

Avery had appeared white and ill and remained speechless since Watts had been winched aboard in the morning, though he had steered a passable course through difficult seas during his long stints at the helm. He was twenty-three, tall and thin in a wiry, muscular way, and his body was still far stronger than his mind. He turned from the wheel when Moyle put his hand on it, and left the wheelhouse without a word. Moyle watched him walk along the center of the pitching forward deck and take up station in the bow. The boy put one hand on the rail and faced forward.

South Reefs is a group of islets, up to 160 feet high, and rocks extending 1 and a quarter miles offshore from a point 8 miles WSW of East Bluff.

Percival made them out ahead. Swirling eddies and lines of curling tide rips were visible in the water off South Reefs, and he instructed Moyle to hold well offshore. Fifteen minutes later, a cleft between two rocky cliffs drew apart and deepened, and a view of dark still water in the shadow of the cliffs opened up. Percival rang for very slow ahead, and told Moyle to make for the narrow entrance to Trying Inlet. The high bulwark edge of Baffin Island rose out of the sea as the ship approached the crack in its wall. Moyle wondered if there was turning room inside, or if they'd have to moor between cliffs, like locking through the Erie Canal, and back her out bouncing off the walls when they left. Percival called down the blower to the engine room for Strick or Iams to come up and help Avery sound as they went in. Iams appeared on deck and went forward, and the two of them got the light harbor lead line out of a deck box.

The long ship passed between the high cliffs as if into a railway cutting. There was no warm Scottish heather nor any soft contour visible as they came in. It was a sharp gash in the rock, too steep for snow. Gulls, murres, dovekies, and guillemots wheeled and screamed up and down the inlet walls between the water and the clifftops, and perched in ledge nests. A thin waterfall spattered down the rock on the left western wall. The ship was suddenly remarkably quiet and still, riding evenly over smooth water. Two or three times a minute the water heaved up and down a few feet, lifting the ship gently as the ocean swell moved in and out of the inlet like a vast inhalation and exhalation. The wind was gone, except for a low howl, blowing across the gap in the land high overhead.

In the bow, Iams called the soundings out and Percival stood on the bridge wing beside an open wheelhouse door.

"Nine fathoms . . . eleven fathoms . . . eight fathoms
. . . six fathoms . . . seven . . . six fathoms . . ."

Half a mile inside the entrance, the rock walls sloped away
less precipitously and the water widened out, providing room
to swing to an anchor. Katabatic gusts dropped down the
slopes at the head of the inlet and came across the flat water
with a dark mottling disturbance.

"Five fathoms . . . four fathoms . . . five . . . five . . .
six . . ."

Percival directed Moyle to steer a tight loop around the head
of the inlet as the men on the bow sounded, and they all grew
familiar with the contours of the bottom. Iams called back to
the captain that the lead felt soft on the bottom and it came up
clean, indicating sand or gravel, good holding.

Finally Moyle knew goddamn well where the anchor should
go, but he was silent as the bow rode over the spot, and they
drifted on. He wondered if the captain was taking his sweet
time because he simply could, or if Percival was deliberating
because he lacked the clear thing Moyle had inside him that
said, when any ship came to that spot in any harbor, "Now!"

It was another loop, as Percival stared about and stroked his
pointed beard and ruminated, before he called to Iams and
Avery to ready the windlass, and finally barked, "Let go!"
Chain rattled through the hawsepipes and Percival telegraphed
slow astern. In the engine room below, Eddie Jenkins pushed
and hauled at levers and spun valves and made the screws
rotate counterclockwise and the ship moved backward,
straightening out its chain and turning over the anchor until its
flukes bit and dug into the gravel bottom and the ship stopped.

IN THE GALLEY, WHEN order had been restored, Duhamel
began to prepare a late supper for the captain and crew, and
Arthur, and Mrs. Schenck. His iceboxes were keeping wonderfully cold, the cook thought. The ice was melting far slower
than it normally did around Long Island or in Maine waters.
He still had several hundredweight of beef, twelve hams, a
crate of pork chops, dozens of chickens, and a quantity of
plump guinea fowl and game hens. Cold guinea fowl was in
fact on his menu calendar, prepared back in Connecticut, for

tonight's supper, with asparagus, and a light soup. Summer evening fare. But it seemed wrong now, as so many of his menus did here in the Arctic. Something else was wanted, he felt, after a long and terrifying day of blizzard and peril at sea, so he began frying fresh dark bearsteaks and pommes frites.

Mr. Newton, who appeared to have forgotten how to shave and make a creditable toilet, and now shuffled about like an old man, and refused to go outdoors, and kept his head turned away from the views through the windows, and gripped rails and handholds tightly even in the stillness of the new anchorage, went aft to set the dining room table for Mrs. Schenck and to ask her what she would like to drink with supper.

But he couldn't find her.

EDDIE JENKINS WAS RAKING coals in the fireroom. He had let Ray go forward to sleep when the anchor was down and he was tending to things by himself. Down here in the engine room and in the fireroom everything still made sense to him. He maintained the order and beauty of the mechanical relationships down here, he kept his turbines spotless, he stayed nice and warm, and he could always have a bit of a singsong, and no one to mind. Let them do what they liked topside, go wherever they fancied. Though he'd just as soon Mr. Schenck and the others got back aboard and they all buggered off home as soon as possible.

He loved to sing, Eddie Jenkins, like any Welshman. He had sung in the chapel choir as a boy, and gone to the eisteddfod in a charabanc. Hymns, he loved most. He had a clear alto voice, high as a boy's, and he sang as he raked the coals, glowing all lovely like the inside of an Aga. "Immortal, Invisible," he sang now, the 19th-century Welsh hymn, and it brought to his mind pictures of the Brecon Beacons, and the glorious country up and down both banks of the Usk, and the farms and meadows and slag mountains above all the mines between Crickhowell and Abergavenny. He had run all through that hilly land winter and summer as a boy and always found his way home.

After the third verse, he heard clapping behind him. He turned and saw Mrs. Schenck.

"Mr. Jenkins the engineer, is that right?" she asked.

"Yes, mum."

"Well, you have a marvelous voice."

"Thank you, mum." He widened his burn-twisted smile.

"Would you do me a favor, Mr. Jenkins?"

"Yes, mum, whatever I can."

"I'd like you to put those fires out, please."

EVERYBODY WAS HUNGRY, AND they ate all the bear-steaks and fried potatoes Duhamel put before them. They ate large bowls of hot apple pie and whipped cream for dessert. They drank coffee.

AFTER SUPPER, AT MIDNIGHT, Mrs. Schenck appeared at the wheelhouse door. She opened it and looked in at Captain Percival, who sat at the chart table reading his Arctic pilot. She was bundled up in her parka and her reindeer pants. She wore a fur hat.

"I want to go ashore," she said. "Would you please have the launch brought around to the ladder."

Percival looked surprised. "Might I suggest you wait until morning, Mrs. Schenck, when it will be lighter."

"It's perfectly light out," said Mamie. "I haven't been off this boat since we left Greenwich, and I'm going ashore now."

The captain leaned back in his chair. "Mrs. Schenck, my crew, shorthanded as they are, have been up all day, working through, I'm sure I have no need to tell you, rather frightful conditions. I daresay most of them are asleep. It would be inconsiderate to say the least to wake them now to launch the boat—"

Mamie turned and looked down the steps to the deck, where Moyle and Dick Iams had appeared. "Why look, here's someone on deck now. Would you men mind awfully getting the boat to take me ashore?"

"Whatever you say, Mrs. Schenck," Dick Iams called out. He and Moyle crossed the deck and went aft, where the Riva hung in its davits.

Mamie looked back at Captain Percival. "They're very nice men, aren't they?" She smiled and went down the steps.

A few minutes later, Percival heard the rumbling of the launch alongside. Then the noise faded and grew distant and was gone.

A katabatic gust came down Trying Inlet and buffeted the wheelhouse windows briefly before it too passed.

Percival suddenly shivered. It was damnably cold in the wheelhouse, he realized. He reached out to the radiator beside the chart table and was dismayed to find it barely warm. He rose and crossed the wheelhouse and picked up the engine room blower. He blew into it, then called for Jenkins. There was no answer.

He went outside, down the steps, and strode down the deck to the engine room companionway. He stepped down into the engine room.

"Jenkins? Jenkins!"

There was no answer. The turbines were quiet. The engine room was warm, but not hot. Percival walked through to the fireroom. It was unaccountably peaceful. No noise at all. He pulled open a firebox door. It was dark inside; a warm oven heat escaped. The few remaining coals on the grate had been spread out to burn down, and had gone out. He looked at the door and saw that the air baffle had been closed. He opened the other firebox and saw the same thing. He looked up at the boilers and the pipes and valves and levers, none of which held the remotest clue of function for him.

He returned to the deck and went forward and down the fo'c'sle companionway. He shouted:

"Jenkins! What the bloody hell are you playing at, man!"

There was no reply. Percival threw open the doors to the bunk cabins. He turned and ran out of the fo'c'sle.

He went into the galley and out again. He threw open the door to the saloon and stepped inside. He ran aft and down the staircase to the owner's and guests' cabins. He came back up the stairs and went out through the door to the aft deck, and then he ran all the way up the deck and down into the fo'c'sle again, throwing open the doors to every cabin and the crew's head, and he ran out and down the deck and back into the saloon. He stood shaking and gasping, trying to breathe. It was growing cold in here too. Suddenly he turned.

A small figure hovered nearby. A penitent, crumbled posture, the great statesman head bent, the gaze scattering over the floor, occasionally flickering toward the vicinity of Percival's knees.

"Good evening, sir," said Newton. "Can I get you anything?"

"Where the bloody hell is everybody?"

"They've just this minute gone out, sir. They didn't say when they might be coming back. Will you be needing me anymore this evening, sir?"

"Where do you think you're going?"

"I thought I might retire for the evening, sir."

CHAPTER 19

O N THE FLAT GROUND above the beach, the women had erected a shelter made of old canvas, patched with sealskins where the canvas was frayed and holed. It was supported by long hoops of baleen. Most of the lost and tired *quallunaaq* lay asleep in it.

Beside a smoky, popping, grass-and-walrus-blubber fire on the beach below, two of the women, Mequ and Iterfiluk, and their men, Tikiqtituq and Angutidluarssuk, were gathered around the great *tôrnârssuk* shot by the older *quallunaaq* who wore glass before his eyes. He had claimed the heart, which had been roasted on the fire, and he had eaten half of it before crawling into the shelter and going to sleep. A long strip of haunch had also been hung over the fire and then cut up for the other *quallunaaq*, who wouldn't eat the meat raw. *Tôrnârssuk*'s hide lay spread out on the gravel to be scraped in the morning.

Before they slept, Tikiqtituq and Angutidluarssuk and their wives were going carefully through the spread-eagled carcass while it still held warmth. They were looking for information. The contents of *tôrnârssuk*'s stomach would tell them what it had eaten recently, and what game they might themselves encounter in the close vicinity. And the condition of *tôrnârssuk*'s entrails could give up signs for interpretation. An engorged entrail could mean an approaching season of plenty. Or it could mean that a season of plenty might produce shit. It de-

pended upon the state of the entrail contents, and upon interpretation, and the investigators all had their own ideas. They
pored through the creature's split-open cavity and pulled out
of it long segments of the thick veined tubes and lay them on
the gravel and slit them open and ran the offal through their
fingers and tasted it while they chatted and argued their points
of view.

Joey had squatted near them for a while before going up to
the shelter to sleep, watching them go through the bear. He
envied their deft familiarity with deep anatomy, and he added
to his own knowledge of the inside of a bear.

The other Eskimo man, Inuiyak, and the daughter of Dundee, Arnanguaq, lay under caribou skins in the lee of the upturned umiak a little way along the beach, content to let the
others read the signs. The northeast wind was dying down and
it was peaceful on the beach.

Boden sat near the fire, staring into the flames. He was tired,
but he had slept and been warm beside Harriet during the
blizzard, and now he felt he couldn't sleep until he figured out
how to find the ship and what exactly he would do when he
found it. They might all be dead or freezing to death if the
Eskimos hadn't found them. Percival had abandoned them,
and Boden couldn't keep from his mind an image of what he
might do when he got close to the Englishman again. The man
was lethal. And then there was Schenck. Somebody had to stop
this madness and take them all away from here, if that was still
possible. If they could find the papier-mâché ship and get it
home without sinking. In the morning, they would start back
up the beach to the smashed boat, which would be where the
ship would come back for them—if Percival hadn't cracked it
up on some rock or iceberg. They would have to wait there and
hope, and if the ship didn't come, the Eskimos would probably
help them make it over the ridge to the Hudson's Bay Company post at Lake Harbour. They had already talked about
that with the older man, Tikiqtituq. From there, at some point,
a ship could get them south maybe as far as Halifax.

And the writer who dyed his hair was wooing Mary. Time
was running out.

Cries of wonder broke from the Eskimos. They had removed

the stomach and opened it on the beach. Churned among its dark viscid lumps they had found a sign. They wiped it against their clothing and held it up to the firelight, and then brought it to Boden. He took it between thumb and forefinger, and in places he could read what had been written:

12 sandwiches ham
Cheeses Camembert, Port Salut
6 btlles Mouton Cadet '18

The paper was torn and soft and dissolving into pulp, the penciled words bloated. But readable.

Boden looked over at the forty or fifty pounds of gore lying beside the emptied bear and realized what he was seeing.

"Writing!" said Tikiqtituq, staring at him. "What's he mean, Jack? Fucken hell!"

"It's a picnic list," said Boden. He handed the paper back to the Eskimo and rose and walked down to the water. He put his hands into the icy water and washed them. The bearsteak turned in his stomach. He splashed his face and took deep breaths.

Tikiqtituq squatted beside him at the water's edge. "What?" he asked intensely.

"The bear ate our lunch."

When he stood and looked back at the group, they were staring at him. They had found writing in the stomach of the bear. They were astounded and would not believe the words came without profound significance. They waited for him to explain the message.

"We came ashore in a boat. We had our lunch—food—in the boat. The bear came along and ate it." He shrugged.

Iterfiluk, who was still poring through the bear's last meal, now exclaimed and raised an item in her hand. They all looked. It was another hand, or part of a hand, ending in shreds of gristle near the wrist, missing the thumb and index finger, and well-chewed.

"This something your food, Jack?" said Tikiqtituq. He spoke to the others and they laughed.

"There was a man at the boat."

Tikiqtituq spoke. The others looked grave.

"Bad lucky chap."

The Eskimos began examining and debating the rest of the stomach contents.

GAR HAD FALLEN ASLEEP sitting up beside the fire, with bear meat in his mouth, and one of the Eskimo women led him up to the tentlike shelter above the beach, laid him down and put a skin over him, and left him. He was fast asleep when Harriet came in. She lay down beside him. Later Joey and her father and Clement Shred had come into the shelter and lain down on the other side of Gar.

Schenck talked of the bear and how glorious the kill had been, how the beast had stood up on its hind legs despite one leg being wounded and made a noise like a trombone, and then raised its paw to cuff him the moment before he shot it, and how his shot had spun the animal around and knocked it over. Schenck talked about it in the dark, reliving the kill until he fell asleep.

Harriet couldn't sleep. She got up and left the shelter. She looked down at the scene of Boden and the Eskimos and the splayed-open nine-foot-long skinned carcass and its viscera spread out beside the smoky fire, and she turned away. The air around her was a deep blue, and Harriet walked away down the beach.

Inuiyak startled her when he rose up from the water's edge and approached her, but he saw she was frightened, and he smiled and spoke strange words quietly to her. His teeth were very white and even. He was a small, wiry man, only a few inches taller than Harriet. His black hair fell below his shoulders. He took her hand and led her back along the beach, but when she saw he was taking her back to her shelter, she pulled him to a stop. She let him hold onto her hand. Inuiyak turned and led her the other direction. They reached the upturned umiak and he kneeled down and pulled her down with him and covered them both with a caribou skin. Beside him, Arnanguaq opened her eyes, saw Harriet, and smiled. She giggled and said something to Inuiyak. She reached across him and touched Harriet's face and spoke words in her own lan-

guage that meant *face as white as the moon*, and then she
rolled away, turning her back to them. The cold fur of the
caribou skin brushed Harriet's face and she looked up at the
stars in the indigo sky.

Inuiyak leaned over her. Heavy hair smelling of meat fell
into her face. He had a powerful smell. Like an animal, Harriet
thought. She moved her head closer to him and breathed it in.
His hand moved across her chest as he found her breasts and
squeezed them. The hand moved down over her stomach and
squeezed between her legs over her Dux-Bak breeches. Harriet
reached down and unbuttoned her pants and pushed them off.
She felt the fur of Inuiyak's bearskin trousers against her thighs
before he pulled them down and pressed against her. His hand
went between her legs, which she spread open as wide as she
could, cool fingers sliding into her and then out, spreading her
wetness up and down. Harriet took hold of his penis, surprisingly hot beneath her palm and fingers. Her thumb found the
tip wet and she moved her hand up over it, spreading the wet
film until her hand was slippery with it. Her legs went around
him and her hips pushed against him. Inuiyak rolled on top of
her and pushed into her. She pushed back and they found a
rhythm. Her hands found his buttocks, small and hard like a
boy's, and she felt the muscles bunch and relax. His sealskin
coat was pushed up between their chests, and she raised her
arms and ran them over his furry back. She thought it must be
like this with a wild animal, and the spasms came on and her
hands dug into the fur and pulled, her legs squeezed around
him as she lifted her hips and shook and jolted against him. She
heard him moan as his rhythm faltered and his feet pushed on
the ground as though he were trying to crawl over her, and her
hands pulled hard on his buttocks and Harriet could feel the
spurts and the wild animal's warm semen filling her.

Hunkered down on the flat ground above the beach, Joey
could hear the sounds they made and he saw how they moved
beneath the skins.

MEQU, TIKIQTITUQ'S WIFE, FOUND the other sign
among the thick soup of the bear's last meal.

She woke Boden, who had fallen asleep beneath his blue coat

and a skin beside the fire. He didn't want to read any more of the lunch menu, but as Mequ held the torn paper close to him, he could see by the dawn light that this was something else. Reluctantly, with thumb and finger, he took it from her. It had not been written in lead pencil in the regular looping hand of the cook, but by someone else, in an ink that had dissolved away in the bile of the bear's stomach. There was a faint smeared wash of shapes readable only as having once been words. But through its violent passage, the paper had retained a compacted fold, and when Boden pushed another finger into the fold and opened it up he made out two words, close together, and at the same time he knew the writing was Moyle's. He read: *seeking*, and *lee*.

CHAPTER 20

"I'M COMING WITH YOU!" said Schenck.

He stood on the beach biting cold chunks of roast bear meat from a piece he waved in his hand and chewed with speed and force. The sun was up. The day looked clear. The women were loading the umiak.

Boden said, "You're not. I don't want you with me."

Schenck threw the meat into the water, planted himself before Boden, and poked a finger at his face. "If you think I'm going to let that limey cocksucker run off with my ship and my wife and then sit around on the beach here until he decides to come back—well, by Christ, I'm not going to!"

Boden stepped forward fast, putting his face close to Schenck's. His voice was low. "Bill Fisher is *dead*. That's as much my fault as anybody else's, but I don't want any more to follow him. Someone has to go back up the beach and stay with the boat in case they come back—"

"Then you stay."

"No. I'm going to Trying Inlet. And I don't want you with me." He turned away and walked to Gar. "Gar, I'd like you to come along."

Schenck felt Boden's resolve. His immediate instincts were to throw himself against him—against any man with resolve—to test him. But he also recognized the rising up of a man to a moment that was peculiarly and only his, and Schenck saw

252

that if he put himself against Boden now, he would be over-powered.

Boden told Gar to pack bear meat into two ammunition bags, then he turned to Shred. "Clement, you'll be okay here. Keep your eye on the girl. Stay near the boat."

"Oh sure," said Shred. He liked the Eskimos. He liked some of their food now. And he was afraid of leaving the water and becoming lost ashore again. Land was a muddle to him, but on the water, Shred felt, a man always knew where he was, good or bad.

BODEN HAD BEEN TO Trying Inlet with McKenzie. Whalers had used it, setting up their tryworks ashore, where they had boiled heaps of blubber down for oil. It was the only harbor of refuge around the southeast tip of Baffin Island, the only place a ship might have gone to find shelter from the northerly gale that had blown the day before, but it would have been difficult for the ship to have found the place, and bad seamanship to make for any shore in thick weather. He was counting on Percival for the last quality.

Boden had something like a chart in his head and could find on it East Bluff and the Savage Islands and Gabriel Strait and Resolution and Edgell Islands, places he had looked for, raised out of the sea, and passed by. He remembered them and their configurations in the sea, and the bearings from one to another. But like Clement Shred, the territory inland of a known shore was a blank to him, or at best a vaguely remembered snapshot of a hill or a lake. His compass might help him navigate his way over land, but mountains and difficult features could set him athwart his course like an unseen current, and he knew he could become lost or delayed. He had never gone inland from Trying Inlet, and the land hereabouts was unknown to him.

But Tikiqtituq had worked with Scottish whalers for more than ten summers, and he talked about those days as he and his wife Mequ led Boden and Gar toward the high land they had to cross to come down to Hudson Strait, ten miles away, three thousand feet up and then down. In Trying Inlet, Tikiqtituq had flensed whales, tried blubber, and his wife of those days, Nivisinark, had made clothes for the *qallunaaq* men.

"I work for ship *Loch Scavaig*. Captain Jimmy Smith, Sikatsi man from Oban." Tikiqtituq rolled out the names with a burr as native as any son of Oban. "Saturday those days they pay me sugar, coffee, tobacco, whiskey. All we wanted."

At first they crossed bog and flat ground. Tracks ran everywhere in the recent snowfall, small patterns made by fox, squirrel, lemming, and mice. After a few miles they began climbing a boulder fan, the debris fallen from the hogback ridge of Meta Incognita Peninsula three thousand feet above. Yesterday's snow was already melting in the morning sun, and turning slushy underfoot. Boden and Gar began to sweat in their woolen clothes; they removed their outer jackets and tied them around their waists.

When they reached a fast-flowing stream twenty feet wide, Tikiqtituq and Mequ sat on the ground and removed their sealskin boots. Mequ's were much higher than Tikiqtituq's, more like hip boots, and when she had taken them off she wore only short foxskin panties below her coat, and then she removed those. Tikiqtituq pulled off his fur trousers. Boden sat down and began unlacing his boots.

"We wading across?" asked Gar.

"Go in water unless you bird, Jack," said Tikiqtituq with a broad smile.

Pulling their coats high above their waists, naked below, holding boots and trousers, Tikiqtituq and Mequ waded into the stream. The white men watched the water climb to Mequ's wide pale rump, which dimpled with the cold. At its deepest, the water came above their crotches. Boden pulled off his pants, held his clothes in his arms, and followed. The water was liquid ice and he felt his breath stop, and he had to start it again. In the middle of the stream, he let out a loud whoop and felt better. He walked stiffly out on the far bank and turned to Gar, who was looking at him. Boden grinned.

"You're going to love it," he called. "But don't rush it. The current's strong, watch your footing."

"Oh my God," said Gar as he went in. The water was rushing against his legs with tremendous force, splashing up his thighs. He tried to feel the stones along the bottom with his feet, but his legs immediately felt like wooden poles. He looked down as the water rose and saw his penis shrunk to a little blue thing, like a newborn baby boy's. His testicles had risen into his body, and his scrotum was crumpled to the size and appearance of a purple walnut. He looked up and saw Mequ and Tikiqtituq watching him, laughing. When he came out on the far bank, he could hardly move, but he walked around with Boden and the two Eskimos, holding his clothes modestly before him, waiting for the blood to return and his legs to dry. The Eskimos were still laughing at him and he felt happy.

AS THEY CLIMBED HIGHER, Boden looked far out over the sea, northwest up Frobisher Bay and northeast and east, past the Savage Islands and Edgell Island and Resolution, out to Davis Strait, in every direction the ship might have gone, and he saw no ship.

The spine of the peninsula was several thousand feet above them, and as they climbed, it seemed they might reach it that afternoon. But at eight hundred feet, they came into the long shadow of a steep ridge above and began to cross a nearly level snowfield that lay over hard ice. Their legs sank to the knees into soft, wet snow. In two hours they covered half a mile. Rills of meltwater ran over the hard ice beneath the snow. The Eskimos' sealskin *kamiks* remained dry, but the white men's boots and their wool and canvas breeches grew freezing and saturated.

In the middle of the afternoon, Mequ gave a shout and pointed back in the direction they had come. Two figures were following them. Boden could see it was Schenck and Joey. He told Tikiqtituq to keep going.

At six they made camp on a flat col, a sunny spot covered with gravel and some grass and moss and a few small yellow flowers.

"I make fire," said Tikiqtituq to Boden and Gar. "You go pick grass, Jacks. Bring me grass like these."

Tikiqtituq pulled sheaves and clumps of dried brown grass out of his and Mequ's boots—insulation—warm and only a little damp from the perspiration of their feet. He pulled the dried grass apart, fluffing it up, airing it out, as if it were clumps of cotton wool, until he had a sizable bundle of it spread out on a flat rock. He didn't use the fresh grass Boden and Gar brought back to him, but laid that out on the gravel in the sun. From somewhere about his person or coat or the thong-tied roll of skins they had carried with them, Tikiqtituq produced thick brown tufts of dried moss, which he lay on the bundle of dried grass, and small bacon-sized strips of desiccated walrus blubber, which he arranged carefully over the moss. In his hand appeared a small gunmetal Ronson cigarette lighter. It had no wick or fuel, but he held it close to the grass and thumbed the wheel; sparks flew and tendrils of grass ignited. The grass crackled and became a bird's nest of flaming twine, and the moss settled down into it and began to glow, and the blubber melted oil into the moss, which soaked it up and burst into a smoky flame.

An hour later, Schenck staggered up to their camp, supporting Joey. He dropped Joey by the fire and sat down himself, breathless and unable to speak. Schenck's clothes were dry, but Joey's were wet and it was evident that he was freezing to death. His eyes were half open, but he seemed unconscious.

The Eskimos unrolled a caribou skin and lay him on it. They pulled off all his clothes, and then Mequ took off her clothes and lay down naked beside Joey, hugging him. Tikiqtituq lay another caribou skin and their coats over the top of them, and turned to the other three men.

"One sailor take off clothes lie here or your friend die."

Boden, Gar, and Schenck looked at each other.

"It's not looking good, Joey," said Schenck.

Gar was elected. After a long moment of watching Mequ clasping onto Joey's white body, he stripped to his underpants and crawled beneath the caribou skin. Joey's body felt like a turkey taken from an icebox, and Gar recoiled from it for every reason. He turned on his side and pushed his back against the cold meat and pulled the caribou skin over him and tried to conserve his own heat. Mequ's hand moved over his arm and gripped him, locking the three of them together.

They roasted bear and walrus meat over the fire, and drank from canteens filled on the snowfield. Joey came slowly back to life and ate and drank a little. Everyone fell asleep after they had eaten.

While it was still light, Joey crawled out from his warm berth, taking a caribou skin with him, and rolled up in it close to the dying fire.

CHAPTER 21

THEY WENT ONLY A short distance up the coast before they reached the smashed Riva on the beach.

Shred went in the umiak, the women's boat, with Harriet and the two paddling Eskimo women, Iterfiluk and Arnanguaq. Inuiyak and Angutidluarssuk paddled in their kayaks, one of them towing Tikiqtituq's kayak. They ranged ahead of the umiak and dropped behind and talked across the water with the women in their queer glottal tongue. They all seemed to smile and laugh a great deal, and occasionally they looked at Shred and he wondered if they were laughing at him. Harriet was still wearing Inuiyak's sealskin coat, and she was paddling, not as well as the Eskimo women, but with a steady unobtrusive stroke that made her seem—to Shred's good eye for such a thing—part of the crew. With the coat and her thick dark hair and small neat body, she could nearly be taken for one of them, he thought, and he envied her.

It seemed to Clement Shred that he was as useless as ever. Except for the activity of the last month, he had been lost, absent, idle, or plain confused throughout the two years of his employ at the St. Clair Boatworks. He had been useless aboard the ship, invited as an afterthought, and he had come only because he had felt so unrooted ashore; but he had filled no position, and wandered the deck and skulked in the fo'c'sle like a stowaway. Now, sitting in a skin and whalebone boat, surrounded by cheery strange-yammering natives, moving along a bleak arctic shore, he felt he might have fallen through space and come to rest on the moon. There's no place or reason for me anywhere, he thought, not with self-pity, but considerable dismay. Why did he ever leave Fairhaven? Even with dwindling little to do there, at least he had been a part of the place, no less than any bush that had grown up from seed blown along the Acushnet. Travel had appealed to Shred when he first set out rowing in his skiff. He remembered his night on a beach somewhere, marveling at it all. Maybe if he had never stopped but gone on rowing to Florida . . .

All the time he was thinking this, Shred's eyes had been going over this Eskimo boat, and finally he gave himself up to the pure admiration of it. It was a considerable clever thing. Skins of some sort sewn together neat as oar leathers, pulled tight and lashed with sinew around a delicate structure of long arcing rib bones and fronds of baleen. Greased tight, light, and easily rowed, the only water coming in was the odd splash from overside. It was wide and not too pretty, but who was looking? It carried a good load: all these women and himself and their skins and cunning Eskimo doodads and devices, and a great ripe heap of blue meat.

As he looked around the boat, he glanced over at the woman with the name that sounded like a duck's quack. The Dundee girl. She turned her head and smiled at him. She'd been smiling at him since they found him on the beach. Not the ready dumb grin of the family defectives folk at home brought out on Sundays for church, who stood around after service showing their gums to anyone looking their way; this Eskimo woman seemed to gaze at Shred as if he might have grown or changed in the last fifteen minutes: she took him in with a long look, and smiled as if she'd found something. He knew she wasn't laughing at him. Already Shred liked her; he couldn't help it. She was the one who'd been feeding him the green cheesy stuff he liked. He'd found himself glancing her way often, then oftener, to see if she would smile at him, and she did, in her strange and wonderful Eskimo way. He had forced himself to stop for a time during the morning, and later, when he looked across the boat at her, she turned and smiled at him and Shred smiled back. He couldn't help it.

She made him feel it was perfectly all right if he was without an identifiable purpose in the world.

THEY SIGHTED THE RIVA in the early afternoon, and the skin boat was run ashore a clean distance away down the beach. They all knew what had happened there. The women made camp again. Harriet fell in with them, doing as they did.

Inuiyak and Angutidluarssuk hauled the kayaks high up near the grass, pulled off their short sealskin paddling jackets that closed with the hoops over the kayak's hole, and walked up the shore over the harder gravel close to the water to see the wreckage. Shred went with them. The snow from the blizzard was all gone, melted through the long day, and the dark rock on the beach gave off real warmth.

They had all heard Boden's spare account of what he and Harriet had found. The boat looked almost itself from a distance, but by the time they reached it Shred could see that two men in a boatshop would produce a new boat complete with five coats of varnish far quicker than picking this one apart and putting it back together. In New England its hardware would be unbolted and the rest of it broken up for stove wood. But to the two Eskimo men on the treeless tundra shore, unhampered by notions of boatshop economy, it was twenty-four-carat flotsam. They looked at the splintered strakes and twisted rivets and the broken backbone, and saw glories.

"Captain take boat away?" Inuiyak asked Shred.

"I don't think they want it," Shred answered. And then added, "But don't tell anybody I said so."

The Eskimos rocked the boat back and forth, lifted the engine hatch, and peered inside.

"Good whaleboat!" said Angutidluarssuk.

"Oh my, yes!" Shred found himself smiling at the delicious thought of the two Eskimos, harpoons raised, hunting in the Riva. "Any whale sees you boys coming in this rig, he'll head for the bottom right off."

Shred walked on and came to a cairn, a long pile of stones. A broken piece of oar stood up like a stunted post at the high end of the stone grave. His smile faded as he thought of the red-haired Rhode Islander whose remains lay beneath the stones.

He looked up and down the shore and turned and walked back to the camp.

HIGH ABOVE THE DEEP shadow at the head of Noble Inlet, the glacier glowed blue through the long sunset, the last spot in all the dark surrounding range beneath the pale sky to give up its light. The Eskimos rolled after-dinner cigarettes and smoked around the fire.

Inuiyak shared a cigarette with Harriet. Arnanguaq, who had been smiling at Shred all day, rolled and lit one for him. He nodded politely at her as she handed it to him. She sat beside him as they smoked and smiled at him and he grew uncomfortable. He was guessing that Angutidluarssuk and Iterfiluk were paired: she was picking lice out of his hair while they smoked, flicking the bugs into the fire, in a way that bore the smack of wifely attention. And last night, while the others had butchered the bear on the beach, Shred had seen Inuiyak bedding down beside the skin boat with Arnanguaq, who was now sitting next to him smiling in a way he could no longer misunderstand. Both Eskimos seemed to have forgotten about each other and turned their attention to their guests. He wanted to ask Harriet if she knew the score, but she was sitting real close to Inuiyak in the most natural fashion, and Shred was too embarassed to bring it up. He seemed, in fact, to be the only one in the dark about things. Everybody else was smoking away as relaxed as could be.

He tried to do just that. He looked appreciatively at his cigarette, sucked too deeply at it, and was struck with a fit of coughing. Arnanguaq began pounding his back with tremendous force, saying cooing things to him. She hit him so hard while he was bent over his knees that he fell sideways, and suddenly the woman was climbing on top of him, pounding him and laughing, her hair falling into his eyes while he gasped for breath. Then she started tickling him, her fingers nipping his sides like crab pincers, and he writhed beneath her, gasping, coughing, and amazed.

Iterfiluk shrieked, got up, and jumped onto the rolling pair. Her hands tore at Shred's clothes until she found his bare stomach, and then she tickled him viciously. Inuiyak and

Angutidluarssuk launched themselves at the cluster of legs and arms and shrieks and tickled the women. After a moment's hesitation, Harriet leapt onto Inuiyak and began tickling him. Everybody was screaming and shrieking. Beneath it all, crushed and fighting for air, Shred was thinking he might have misunderstood all the smiles and attention, that anything he guessed about them might be wrong, because Eskimos were, without doubt, the strangest people in the world.

But he was beginning to like them.

Soon they all lay on their backs, laughing and catching their breath. Then Angutidluarssuk and Iterfiluk moved away until they were formless shapes low on the beach in the half dark. Inuiyak spoke with Arnanguaq and stood up and pulled Harriet to her feet and took her away down the beach beyond the umiak.

Shred sat up and watched as Arnanguaq smoothed the gravel beside the fire and lay skins over the smooth area and then removed all her clothes and sat on top of the furry bed, half pulling a caribou skin over her. Shred stared and then looked away. Then she leaned over and pulled off his derby hat and he looked and saw she'd put it on her head and was smiling at him, inviting him to look at her, and he gave up and looked and looked. In all his life he had never seen another naked woman but Hezzie, and he hadn't cared to look at her too often. He had never been with or touched another woman. The only representations of the naked female he had ever seen were illustrations of the scriptures, when angels came down to earth to attend miracles, and they always came in thin blowy robes. Arnanguaq appeared like an angel, oddly wearing his derby hat, and the moment seemed miraculous. She looked at Shred and spoke to him. He couldn't move. She reached to him and pulled him over onto the skins. She talked to him, touched his face, got him out of his clothes and pulled him down beside her, and covered them with skins.

Then she took him to heaven.

CHAPTER 22

B EFORE MIDDAY TIKIQTITUQ AND Mequ brought
them onto a path used by migrating caribou that led up
over a low col between higher ridges, and they crossed
the peninsular backbone and saw Hudson Strait, blue with
wide patches of calm, stretching away into the indistinct south.
Somewhere half a mile below, hidden by the curving bulge of
the land they now descended, was Trying Inlet.

In the early afternoon, Mequ spoke and Tiqiktituq stopped.
"You hear?" he said.

So they stopped and listened. There was a southerly uphill
breeze rustling the grass and wildflowers that grew much more
abundantly on this southern slope of the peninsula. It carried
the scent of flowers, and something else.

"Yes!" said Tiqiktituq.

Then they heard it: a voice pure like a boy's, singing, floating
uphill on the breeze in the clear air. They stood still, trying to
determine a direction. Words came up over the flowers:

> . . . and did those feet, in ancient times
> walk upon England's mountains green . . .

"It's 'Jerusalem,'" said Joey. He had recovered well, and
eaten pounds of meat at breakfast.

"What?" said Schenck.

"It's a hymn, Mr. Schenck."

Boden remembered he had gone to church with Joey at Smith Island down on the Chesapeake when they came up from Florida, and Joey had known all the hymns.

They shouted down the hill, but no shouts came back. The singing faded in the wind and then came back. Then it stopped.

"It stopped!" said Schenck.

"It's the end of the song," said Joey.

They shouted again and there was no response.

"Right then!" said Tiqiktituq. He set off again along the caribou path. Mequ followed, and the others walked after them. The path wound in long switchbacks down a slope so steep that the route immediately below was always out of sight, so they expected to meet the singer at every turn. But an hour went by, and they heard no more.

"We lost them!" said Schenck.

"No worry, Jack. Happy chap down here. Or else flying bird sing your song."

"The man's full of native wit," said Schenck.

Then Eddie Jenkins appeared around the bend below them, Moyle and Ray Strick behind him.

"Ah, there you are then," said Jenkins, as if he had been looking for children hiding in a house.

"Good Christ, Jenkins! Where the hell is my ship?" Schenck yelled at him. "Where's my wife?"

THEY SAW THE SHIP later in the afternoon, when Jenkins and Tikiqtituq led them off the caribou path at seven hundred feet and down a thinner grown-over trail that went around the base of an escarpment of rock, and the inlet came into view below. The ship lay peacefully, swung around on its anchor, facing the breeze that funneled up the inlet from the entrance.

At seven they reached a swale above the head of the inlet, a shallow depression into which binoculars on the ship could not see, where Mamie, Arthur, Avery, Dick Iams, and Duhamel were camped. They were suffering a minimum of discomfort. Two nights earlier, when they had all left the ship, they had also towed *Lodestar*'s last remaining boat, the eleven-foot rowboat. In the few hours before their midnight departure, they had filled it with boxes of food, wine, beer, coffee, awnings, blankets, and bedding. Duhamel had packed a valise crammed with a castaway chef's irreducible *batterie de cuisine*: many knives and a sharpening steel, shears, several pots and pans, coffeepot, spatulas, graters, strainers, corkscrew, matches, and more. Avery had grabbed the shotgun from the rack on the fo'c'sle bulkhead, and found some shells. Dick Iams and Moyle had both brought pistols. Jenkins had filled bags with coal, because his thinking ran to fires, and he had seen no trees or wood ashore, and brought shovels and rakes from the fireroom. Ray Strick brought a small toolbox. They had taken the cushions off the wicker chairs and chaises on the aft deck. Mamie brought a toilet case with powder and lipstick, and she had thrown into it her Ellen R. Swinton novel and *An Arctic Sojourn* by Dr. Griffith of Chicago. She took a pair of binoculars from the saloon.

Ashore, once they had found their snow-free, grassy, private-seeming swale, they had erected a tentlike canopy with the awnings, using four eight-foot oars in a line as poles, wrapping the awning guylines to rocks. Dick Iams had shot some ducks and Duhamel had roasted them for lunch. When Schenck's group reached the camp, Mamie was reading on a pile of cushions; Duhamel was making toast over the glowing coalfire, and Arthur was pouring tea. It was late for tea, but still broad daylight, and Mamie was waiting for it to get darker before they ate supper. She leapt up and ran to her husband and hugged and kissed him. She took a handful of his jacket and twisted it and said, "Where's Harriet?"

"She's safe, sweetheart. She's just the other side of the hill. We're going to go pick her up now." He told her about the writing in the stomach of the bear, the prodigious charging beast he had brought down, that they could only guess where the ship might have gone, that Harriet and Mr. Shred had stayed behind with more Eskimos in case the ship returned.

"The boy Watts was drowned," said Mamie. "That fool captain is unfit!"

Piecemeal, the two groups exchanged their recent histories. Boden learned that Moyle had put a note in the extra food basket sent ashore. He told them what had happened to Bill Fisher. Avery sobbed as he told them what happened to Watts, and Schenck manfully embraced the boy. Mamie said Mr. Jenkins had told her that one man alone could not operate the ship, certainly not without an engineer, so she had proposed to him and Moyle and the others that they all steal ashore with a few necessities, and leave Percival trapped aboard, and it had worked perfectly. They had spent the night on the beach and the next day found this spot and made their camp. Then Moyle and Jenkins told how they had loaded young Ray with food and water and set off the next morning—that morning—hoping to find them, and when Boden asked how they had any idea where to go, Moyle said Jenkins had looked at the contoured land within the coastal perimeter on Boden's chart and declared he could find his way over the hill.

Mamie said, "Now Carl, you've got to remove that man before he gets anyone else killed! Put him in the bilges and then let's go get Harriet and for God's sake go to Nantucket."

"IT'S MY BOAT!"

"You come any closer, I'll knock you down," said Boden. He had left his heavy coat up at the camp and wore only his turtleneck sweater above pants and lace-up boots.

So in the monochrome half light, Schenck watched Boden and Gar and Moyle get into the rowboat and push off into the dark calm water.

He picked up a rock and threw it into the water.

Then he climbed back up to the rim of land above the swale, where everyone else ashore had gathered to look across the water like disadvantaged spectators of a distant event. They watched the rowboat leave its beetle wake on the mercury surface and disappear into the pooling dark around the ship's hull, and they waited. Ten minutes, perhaps a little more.

Then across the still water came a sudden tearing ratchet noise. It was over in a few seconds, echoing around the inlet, when they realized it was the tommy gun.

Half a minute later they saw a flare appear on the ship's bridge, glowing a moment before falling to extinguish in the water.

Shortly afterward a single shot. They waited and heard nothing more.

*   *   *

IT WAS AS DARK as it was going to be, and darker still in the gloom of the inlet, but Boden knew that if Percival trained binoculars on them he would see them coming. He sat in the rowboat's bow, facing forward, and rested his eyes unfocused on the darkest section of the ship's hull just above the water, the way he aimed his gaze above the horizon at sea at night to detect any hint of land or loom of light below. That way he would see all he was going to of any movement on deck. He saw only the still silhouette of the dark ship on the water growing larger as they approached. Gar rowed more carefully than he had ever done at Yale, making no splash, as Boden had directed him, dipping the oar blades and raising them with no more sound than water squeezed from a cloth. They had buttered the bronze oarlocks and the oar leathers, and with Gar's mindful deliberation through every stroke they moved almost silently toward the ship, but still Boden knew Percival would hear them if he was listening and waiting for them.

The ship wore no lights at all. No hum. It sat quiet as a plague ship, lifting slightly in the ghost swell that rose and fell in the inlet. The ladder had been raised, but Boden would not have used it for the creak and stretch of its falls. Gar came in under the fantail stern and Boden and Moyle raised their hands to the cold iron, and the rowboat stopped. Boden reached for the closed loop of the bronze fairlead at the deck edge and pulled himself high enough with one hand to grab the stern rail with the other, and he climbed up over the rail and stood on the deck. Moyle followed like a monkey. Boden took the painter from Gar, tied it low on the rail, then Gar passed him the Mauser and climbed up after it.

Boden and Gar went forward along the starboard deck. Moyle stayed abreast of them on the port side. They saw no movement through the saloon, dining room, and galley windows, only each other peering across the ship. They climbed port and starboard wheelhouse steps and Boden opened the door and went inside, leaving Moyle and Gar on the bridge wings. He looked around the dark, cold space, made sure it was empty in all its shadows, and came outside. They came together forward of the wheelhouse and Boden stepped care-

fully down the engine room companionway. He pulled from
his belt the flashlight he had brought from camp and shined it
through the dark. The engine room and fireroom still held a
detectable warmth. There was no one down there.

They found Percival asleep in his cabin below the galley. The
captain woke into the flashlight's beam.

"Get dressed," said Boden, from somewhere much closer
than the flashlight across the cabin. "Dress warm."

Percival's hands moved beneath the blankets, and Boden's
Colt revolver appeared in the beam of light close to Percival's
face, his thumb clicking back the hammer. Percival at once
became still. Boden's other hand reached into the light and
pulled the blanket away. Percival was already wearing a white
turtleneck sweater and navy trousers. His hands were fisted
and held over his chest.

"Get up."

Percival sat up and swung stockinged feet out of his bunk.
Still held in the beam, he looked blindly around. "You're taking my ship with force. This is mutiny. An act—"

"Shut up and get dressed."

"What are you planning to do with me?"

"I'm going to demote you."

"Are you putting me ashore?"

"No. Now get dressed."

Percival reached for his shoes, black with toe caps. He pulled
them on and tied the laces with calm hands. He stood up and
pulled on his jacket, one of the three identical suit jackets he
always wore: double-breasted, brass-buttoned, Royal Navy
Commander stripes above the cuffs. He brushed his hair and
put on his white, black-visored dress hat. A ship's master, to
the tiny muscle that twitched his lower left eyelid.

The door to the fo'c'sle was bolted on the other side. They
took him up on deck, Moyle ahead, Boden and Gar behind,
and went forward along the port side toward the fo'c'sle companionway. But as they reached it, a figure came up out of the
dark from below, a small hesitant shaking figure holding
Schenck's Thompson submachine gun.

Moyle said, "Newton, put it up, it's us, you fucking idiot."
He put his hand on the tommy gun's magazine and pushed it

aside as Newton squeezed the trigger. A short shattering burst spewed skyward out of the gun. Shoulders instinctively hunched and heads turned away. Percival ducked and started running across the deck. Moyle punched the large slack face before him and wrenched the gun away as Newton crumpled to the deck. Then they all looked to Percival.

He had crossed the deck and was leaping up the wheelhouse steps on the starboard side. Gar lifted the Mauser and Boden reached out and pushed the rifle down. Percival opened the wheelhouse door, went inside, and slammed it behind him.

Holding the Colt at his side, Boden started up the portside steps. He heard Gar behind him and said, "Stay down here."

So Gar stepped down and back two paces, to where Moyle stood looking up at the wheelhouse. They saw Boden reach the top of the steps and put his hand on the door handle, and then, through the windows, they saw Percival from the chest up move into view and his hand come up as Boden opened the door, and they saw the flash and heard the igniting bang and the instant searing expellant rush, partly contained inside the wheelhouse, which filled immediately with sulfurous smoke, and Boden appeared kicked backward to the bridge rail, his chest erupting with incandescent flame, his arms raised around his head. The rail stopped him, but Boden seemed to writhe over it and dropped into the water.

"Jesus!" cried Gar, running down the deck, looking into the water.

Percival strode out of the smoke onto the bridge wing, the ship's wide-bore Webley Very pistol in his hand. He stood erect, chest puffed out, snorting through his nostrils like a horse. His eyes bulged. He stared down into the water at the drifting, spectacularly dispatched mutineer, and then he stared aft at Gar, who was climbing over the stern rail, dropping into the rowboat. He looked off at the shore. Then abruptly he turned and noticed Moyle, who stood twenty feet away, hand raised and pointing at him. Holding a pistol, Percival realized, as Moyle fired.

"NUTS TO THIS!" YELLED Schenck. He ran down to the shore. Joey followed him, and as they struggled to pull the

Riva over the gravel, Tikiqtituq appeared and suddenly the boat was sliding into the water. Tikiqtituq pushed off hard and climbed in last.

"Nossir, you're staying here!"

"I come! I see your captain!" said the Eskimo. He sat down in the upholstered backseat and looked about for a paddle.

Schenck looked at him, turned away, and said, "Get us out there, Joey!"

The engine grumbled beneath Tikiqtituq, who stood up and was thrown back into his seat as Joey pushed the throttle forward and the boat leapt.

The ship's ladder was down, and Boden lay on its platform above the water, the chest and shoulder of his sweater burned black. Gar crouched over him. They got him into the front seat of the boat and then Moyle walked Percival down the ladder and put him in the back beside Tikiqtituq. Moyle climbed in facing him. The Eskimo stared at the captain, who did not appear to be badly injured, although the upper right arm of his uniform jacket was soaked with blood. Once he was aboard, the boat sped back to the shore.

It was immediately apparent to Tikiqtituq what had taken place. Murder in any culture was a commonplace, but the removal of a captain from a ship horrified him. He understood mutiny. The *quallunaaq* had removed the power that governed them; they had become capable of anything. As soon as they reached the shore, where the whole group was waiting for them, he trotted over the gravel and climbed up to the camp. Mequ was asleep. He woke her and they rolled up their skins and ran away up the mountain.

CHAPTER 23

THEY BROKE CAMP IN the morning and ferried everything back to the ship. Moyle, Gar, and Avery got the boats aboard and the ladder raised. Eddie Jenkins found his boilers and pipes still warm, for the short night temperatures had not fallen below freezing while they had been ashore. Ray Strick and Dick Iams made the fires and built them up while Jenkins bled all the pipes and radiators, and by midafternoon they had made steam; the cold air in the ship was warming up and there was pressure sufficient to drive the turbines.

At teatime, Schenck gathered the remnant crew in the saloon and told them they were leaving immediately to get his daughter. He asked them who would man the ship and find their way back around Baffin Island. No one answered.

"I'll do it myself," said Schenck, "if I have to. But I'll bet all of you know better than me how to take a boat from one place to another, and one of you is better than the rest of you. So who's that?"

Jenkins spoke up. "I reckon Mr. Moyle could do it if anyone could."

Schenck moved to Moyle and stood before him. "Mr. Moyle, what do you say?"

"I'm no skipper. And no navigator."

"Would you be any worse than our recent captain?"

Moyle looked sour—that is, sourer than usual. "I reckon I

271

can get us back around the corner while the weather holds. Then let's see."

Moyle told Gar to start the donkey engine for the windlass and bring in the cable, and he put Avery in the bow.

He climbed alone to the wheelhouse and stood at the wheel and looked forward along fifty narrow feet to the bow, which now pointed directly down the inlet toward the entrance. He had handled her, and he was not overawed by her. She had a wheel and engines, and he could make her cut water and go. And he would, too, and keep a hold of her before he again saw any man stand her into danger. He spun the wheel three and a half revolutions until it stopped hard over and spun it two and half the other way until it stopped and spun it back three turns to put the rudder amidships. Through the window he saw Avery straighten up from leaning over the bow rail, and look back at the wheelhouse and give him a thumb. Moyle yanked the telegraph to slow ahead, and below, Jenkins sent up his acknowledging ring. Presently he felt the thrust of the screws. Moyle returned his hands to the wheel. The sides of the inlet rose and narrowed and he put himself between them, where he wanted to be.

HE WENT DOWNSTAIRS INTO the basement of the house in Long Beach, where he kept his tools and sea gear, and found it empty, all cleaned out, as you might come into an empty room in a house for sale. Neat and broom clean. But near the stairs he found thumbtacked to a wall four or five curling photographs. He pulled the rusty pins out and wiped the obliterating dust off the pictures and found himself smiling back at the camera: pictures Mary had taken of him, his happy self, of not so long ago, but now another man altogether. He felt a great ballooning inside him, rising up like a wave.

Then the wave broke, fell in on itself, washed away. He cried with great wracking sobs, and it felt like a damburst to let it go. He cried so hard his shoulder hurt.

Morphine dreams. He rose out of one and fell into another.

You're a selfish boy. I've had it with you. I've come to the end of my rope. His father went up the stairs, and somehow he knew what was coming, but he couldn't get around him, the

*man in the suit moving slowly up the stairs was too big. An
implacable force turned against him, no matter what he said or
did now there was no stopping what was to come. This big
stolid vengeful man bent on punishment went into his room
and took his models, the paddle steamer, the speedboat, the
Wright Brothers' plane, and the glue tubes and paint pots and
his sable brushes. The way he picked them up and pushed them
into a pile in his arm, breaking the airplane's wing and the
paddle wheel. He turned and went downstairs with Willy following, shouting, I'll be better, I promise I promise I promise.*

*In the backyard his father made a pile and poured kerosene
from a can, yellowing the paddle steamer's white paint. He
tried to grab them and run away but his father held his hand so
hard it bruised, while he lit a cigarette and took a few hits and
said, You don't play ball with me, I don't play ball with you,
and threw his butt on the pile. The kerosene made bright
flames and the paint wrinkled and rose in bubbles before it all
went black. Thick smoke stinking of the peculiar conflation of
wood and glue and paint and sable bristles burning together
swirled around them in the backyard and went up his nose.*

*The smell stayed with him for days. It filled his head and he
took it wherever he went. The stench of ruin and crushed hope.*

AT SEA AGAIN. HE felt the roll of the ship. Real pain now,
in his shoulder, and no dream. He opened his eyes and saw the
cabin ceiling. Lower, the raised paneling of the bulkhead
planed by a craftsman's hand to just shy of unerring perfect to
reveal it as the work of a man's hand and declare the beauty he
could fashion. Beautiful useless ship, Boden thought, and then
he remembered it all.

The ductile magnesium had splashed into his sweater as liquid fire, and lodged there in the melting scrim, and continued
to burn underwater until it was chemically exhausted, although Boden had clawed at it and burned his right hand and
fingers too.

They'd carried him up to the camp and laid him beside the
makeshift kitchen, where Duhamel and Mamie conferred over
treatment. They cut his sweater off, and then his pants, and
removed his boots and put blankets over most of him. His left

upper chest and shoulder appeared blackened as if with coal dust, the flesh crusted around pitted craters, flayed off in roasted strips, and it gave off a smell part chemical, part meat. As Mamie and Duhamel worked on him, the skin wherever it remained unbroken rose into sausage weals and bubbles and straining pastry-sized blisters that filled with serum. Duhamel poured olive oil over the whole burn area and laid a linen napkin on top of it. Having spent his life around flaming ranges aboard ships, he was not unnaturally well acquainted with the treatment of burns, but this one had him making distressed sounds and muttering over and over.

Boden had been conscious through it all; in the water burning, hauled out of the water, delivered ashore, carried up to the camp. He watched them bent over him. The stench filled his head. He caught sight of the chef's doctor's bag.

"Frenchman, you got any morphine?"

"Oh yes, of course!"

"Then for Christ's sake give me some."

"Of course! I'm sorry!"

"Give me two. Now."

"All right, I know." And Duhamel had produced a syringe and snapped two vials of morphine, and sent Boden off to his twisted fiddler's green.

Now he was back. In some cabin aft. He could see blue sky through the porthole over his bunk. The turbines were humming at medium speed. He felt no wave impact, only the slight regular lift and fall and an irregular suggestion of a roll. His mind formed a picture of oily calm over invisible patterns of swell, and the subsiding memory of a cross sea.

He lifted his left arm, and the pain, which had been dull, soared. He flexed fingers and bent the arm slightly and satisfied himself that the muscles and tendons were working. He knew what had happened to him; he would have weeks of pain and suppurating scabs and he would be left with scars, but he would heal. He reached up with his right arm to pull the bedclothes off and saw that hand bandaged and remembered why. He propped himself up on his right elbow, and was able to move his legs over the edge of the bunk. The burning tore across his left chest and shoulder, but he pushed through it, because more than any pain, he was dying to know too many things to lie still and wait. It was what he saw when he looked down at himself that made him despair.

"Oh fuck," he said. He was naked.

MAMIE STOPPED HIM IN the saloon when he came up the staircase wearing sheets and blankets. She tried to take him back to bed, but he would only sit down and ask for his clothes, so she sent Arthur to fetch her husband. When they realized Boden was not going back to bed, Schenck had his pants and boots brought from the fo'c'sle. Arthur helped him dress.

Schenck said, "Our Mr. Moyle shot him, right after he turned you into a circus act. Got him in the armpit. I think he was hoping for a better shot."

"Where is he?"

"Percival? Up forward, in the forepeak. He's patched up and he's quiet. I think he got scared."

"Who's on the bridge?"

"Captain Moyle. What do you think? The old geezer's got sand."

"Yeah."

Boden couldn't wear a shirt or sweater or his peacoat, so Arthur wrapped his top half in blankets, and when he was decent Mamie returned to the saloon and pinned one of her shawls around him.

"You look interesting, Mr. Boden, I must say. Like an Indian chief, possibly," said Mamie.

"Thank you, Mrs. Schenck."

Boden stood up, opened the saloon door with his bandaged right hand, and went out on deck. The ship was past East Bluff and steaming up Frobisher Bay. Ahead off the port bow, Terra Nivea glacier sat embedded on its mountaintop like a blue-green opal. The sea was calm, as he had pictured it. The weather looked as though it would hold.

Schenck followed him out on deck.

"When you feel up to it, Captain, I'd like you to take over. I want you to be *Lodestar*'s skipper. I should have taken you on as skipper from the first, but—what do you say?"

Boden was unable to speak. He started forward.

But Schenck moved around him and stood once more in front of him, blocking his way.

"This is the plan. We pick up my daughter. We take aboard a few Eskimos, we head out—" Schenck's eyes locked on to Boden's. "—I want a whale. I want you and those Eskimos to find me a whale to harpoon—"

Boden's burned right hand, unbandaged but covered with some grease, appeared from beneath Mamie's shawl. Schenck watched it rise to one side as if to see in what direction Boden would point with it, and then it moved fast across his face, slapping him hard as it passed.

Boden said, "We'll get your daughter and then we're going home. No whale. No more hunting. No more dead boys. And you, sir, stay out of my way."

He turned away from Schenck and walked forward.

Schenck put his hands to his face again and pulled them away and stared at the grease on his fingers.

IN THE MILD, STILL, sunlit evening, *Lodestar* glided into Noble Inlet. Boden stood in the wheelhouse directing Moyle at the wheel and nodded through the window at Gar when he wanted the windlass brake released, and the anchor went down near where it had before. From the ship, the umiak and the Eskimos' ragged tent were visible on the beach, and farther alongshore lay the broken Riva and the rock cairn Boden had made to mark Bill Fisher's grave.

Schenck, Mamie, Joey, and Gar went ashore in *Monte*. There was nobody visible on the shore until the boat gently nosed into the gravel, and then Angutidluarssuk and Iterfiluk and Arnanguaq and finally Shred appeared on the grass above the beach, all of them breathless, appearing to have run to the beach from somewhere inland. The Eskimos stopped at the grass, and Shred, panting, staggered down the gravel to the boat. Schenck was the first to jump ashore. He carried no gun.

"Glad to find you well, Mr. Shred. Where's my daughter?"

"I . . . I dunno, sir." Shred looked around at the Eskimos. "I think she . . . she went off somewhere with one of . . . with the other fellow."

Mamie came up to Shred. "She went off with an Eskimo man?"

"Yes, ma'am . . . they, they went away, and . . ."

"Went where?" barked Schenck. He was turning a blotchy color. "When will they be back?"

"I dunno, sir. Neither way. They didn't say. They were . . ."

Schenck turned and looked over the Eskimos, finally staring at the remaining man, Angutidluarssuk. "She's with the other man?"

"Yes, sir."

"When did they go?"

Shred turned again as if to ask the others. "Well, sir, I was . . . they were . . . I guess this morning."

"What did she say, man!"

Shred shook his head. "She . . . I didn't—"

"Do they know?" Schenck walked past Shred up the beach. "Where is my daughter! Where is she!"

The Eskimos looked at him; not blankly, not inscrutably, not unkindly, but with a calm, solipsistic curiosity.

Schenck crunched fast across the gravel until he stood in front of Angutidluarssuk. "I remember you. You went whaling with the Scotchmen. You understand me. I know goddamn well you do!" He pulled a wad of hundred-dollar bills from a pocket of his hunting vest. He shook it before the Eskimo's face and pointed inland with his other arm. "One hundred dollars, you take me find my daughter!"

"Forty dollars," said Angutidluarssuk.

Schenck barely paused. "Let's go!"

"No!" shouted Mamie. She ran to her husband and grabbed his vest with both hands. She spoke fiercely. "You're not going, Carl! Gar will go, and Joey! They'll find her! You're not leaving me again!"

Schenck looked at everybody, Gar, Joey, the Eskimos, then back at Mamie. "All right."

Gar returned to the ship for food, water, and his Mauser and ammunition. While he was gone, Schenck questioned Shred again.

"Did you look for them?"

"Yes, sir. Well, we looked around this morning."

"What were you doing just now, when we arrived?"

Shred appeared uncertain, and slightly ashamed. "I don't really know, to be sure."

"What do you mean you don't know?"

"I think we were playing, sir."

"Playing?"

"Yes, sir."

"Playing what, Mr. Shred?" asked Mamie.

"Oh my. I believe it was a sort of catch, ma'am."

"Catch? Do you mean as in 'let's play *catch*'?"

"That's it."

Mamie looked at the Eskimos. "How do they play it?"

"Well, I run and . . . they catch me."

"And then one of them would be it? And you ran after them?"

"No. It was only me that ran. I ran off—"

"And they caught you."

"Yes, ma'am."

"Hmm." Mamie looked at Shred and the Eskimos. "Was it fun?"

Shred looked briefly around at his playmates. "Yes, ma'am."

Gar soon returned, rumbling in to the beach. He approached Schenck. "Sir, will you be—"

"I can handle the boat," snapped Schenck. "You bring Harriet back, Gar. I don't care what she says. She'll say anything sometimes. You bring her back no matter what you have to do. Do you understand me?"

"Yes, sir. I will. Don't worry."

Gar gave Joey a bag containing food and water. He kept the gun and an ammo bag. Joey was looking at Schenck.

"You go with him, Joey. You help him bring my daughter back."

"No matter what, Mr. Schenck," said Joey.

"That's right, Joey! No matter what!"

When he saw they were ready, Angutidluarssuk looked at Schenck and said, "Forty dollars," and he walked away down the beach to the south. Gar and Joey followed him.

"Jesus Christ," said Schenck. Then he yelled. "Gar! Find out how high he can count! That's what he gets if you find her and bring her back here! Teach him some arithmetic!"

"Yes, sir!"

Schenck declared they would return to the ship. He would send Avery back with the launch to wait at the beach for Harriet.

"Push us off, will you, Mr. Shred? I'll get her started and then you can hop in."

"Yes, sir," said Shred, as he watched Schenck and his wife turn and walk toward the boat.

Then he realized this was it, he was leaving. He looked at Arnanguaq, who seemed to know the same thing, and she was crying. He walked across the gravel to her.

"Goodbye," he said, looking at Arnanguaq's wide, weeping angel's face. A sudden lonely desolation filled him. The world tilted and no longer looked the same, and he could see no further than the next few moments.

"Mr. Shred!"

"Yes, sir."

He wanted to say something to Arnanguaq, but even in English he could think of no words. He took off his hat and put it on her head. She raised her hand and laid it on the hat.

"Shred! Come along!"

Schenck was standing in the boat waiting for him, his wife seated beside him. Shred walked down to the water and pushed the boat off. Schenck started the engine and Shred clambered in awkwardly, getting his feet wet and trying to avoid wetting Mrs. Schenck. Schenck backed the boat out into deeper water, turned it around, and made for the ship.

Mamie turned around in the front seat and looked at Shred, who sat on the wide, upholstered backseat, looking ashore. "You gave that woman your hat, Mr. Shred. Did you make a friend of her?"

"Yes, ma'am. I guess so."

"How sweet!" she said sincerely.

"Mr. Shred is a man of many skills," said Schenck.

Clement watched the two Eskimo women growing smaller on the shore. Very quickly the only way he could tell them apart was that one of them wore his hat.

*   *   *

IT WAS NOT FAR. The sun had set, but there was still a warm glow to the air and few stars had appeared in the pale sky overhead when they reached the river that cut through the beach, the place where the Eskimos had found the walrus herd. The two pinniped skeletons, cleaned of all meat by now, lay on the gravel looking like museum specimens.

Angutidluarssuk pointed out the kayak drawn up into the grass, and they found Harriet and Inuiyak beside a smoky blubber fire on the sandy estuarial bank up the river behind the beach.

"Go away!" Harriet said as they appeared. She wore her sealskin coat. Her face and hair were smeared with grease. She looks just like one of them, Gar thought.

"Harriet, we're leaving—"

"I'll catch up with the boat somewhere else." Harriet had wriggled closer to Inuiyak and sat beside him.

"Harriet . . . we're going back to New York now—"

"Well, I'm not!" she shrieked at Gar. "I'm enjoying myself for once in my fucking life! I'll go when I'm ready!"

Both Eskimos were looking between her and the white men now, fascinated.

Gar was unsure how to proceed. He wondered if he would have to drag her away, if he could physically do that, and if the Eskimos would interfere.

"You can't make me leave," said Harriet, calmer, but strong and sure.

"I can," said Joey. He had hung back by the kayak and now walked forward with Harriet's Mannlicher. He raised it and aimed it at Inuiyak, who immediately rolled away from Harriet and stood up, ready to flee, and began talking fast in Eskimo.

Joey said, "Your father says come back. You come or I'll shoot him." He nodded at Inuiyak.

The Eskimos were talking excitedly to each other and In-uiyak walked to Harriet and pulled her to her feet and threw her down on the sand in front of Gar.

"No! I want to stay with you!"

She crawled back to Inuiyak and put her arms around his legs, but he leaned down and began cuffing her head.

"Hey!" yelled Gar.

She cried and raised her arms to ward off the slaps, but Inuiyak pulled one of her arms aside and smacked her hard across the face. Harriet screamed. He pushed her down again in front of Gar.

"Hey, cool down!" Gar shouted angrily.

Inuiyak, still talking, walked back a few steps.

Harriet crawled after him. "I want to be with you!"

Inuiyak rushed forward and kicked her leg. Harriet screamed and curled up into a ball. Gar yelled again angrily, and Joey stepped forward, jabbing the rifle. Inuiyak retreated quickly. The two Eskimos were still talking fast and anxiously to each other.

"You take her now," Joey said to Gar. "I'll keep them here while you go, and then I'll come." He pointed the rifle at Angutidluarssuk, motioning unmistakably for him to move closer to Inuiyak. Angutidluarssuk moved. Both Eskimos were extremely obedient, although making frantic noises now.

"Hey! Shut up!" Joey yelled at them.

Gar slung the Mauser over his shoulder and tried to get Harriet to her feet. She screamed. Joey moved close to her. He bent down and yelled at her: "You go now or I shoot them! See! Look at this!" When Joey saw Harriet raise her head, he swung the rifle at the Eskimos and fired.

The two Eskimo men fell to the ground. Joey walked toward them, loading fast. They were yelling loudly, beseeching. "I told you to shut up!" He put the Mannlicher's barrel against Inuiyak's head. The man twisted his head away and his voice only rose. "Get her out of here!" Joey shouted at Gar.

Gar pulled Harriet to her feet and dragged her over the grass toward the beach. Joey watched them go, keeping an eye on the prone men who were still jabbering, imploring, half crying. When he saw Gar and Harriet reach the beach and their heads disappear below the grass, he turned around and looked down.

"I told you to shut up."

Joey raised the rifle and brought the stock down on Inuiyak's temple. That shut him up. Angutidluarssuk started to rise and

Joey smashed the stock into his face. He grunted and put his hands to his face and tried to roll away, and Joey raised the rifle and brought it down on the side of Angutidluarssuk's skull. He brought it down on Inuiyak's head once more. Neither of the two Eskimos spoke again.

It was amazingly quiet.

Joey walked a few steps away. His heart was pounding and he was breathing hard. He looked all around the wild tundra and back at the two bleeding Eskimo men on the ground. He realized they were his now, and he could do whatever in the world he wanted to do with them. He knew exactly what he was going to do. He felt that his whole life up to now, and all the years of reading, and the perfectly designed culminating experience of the last few days, had prepared him to do it well.

He lay the rifle down.

AVERY HAD FERRIED SCHENCK'S bearskin and caribou head, which had begun to stink, out to the ship in the Riva. The bearskin was stored in the deck box forward with the rolled-up sealskins and the other two bearskins. The caribou head was hoisted onto the foredeck. Schenck had Mamie photograph him standing behind it, framed by the sweeping antlers. Then it was lashed to the forward rail, like a theatrical prop. Avery returned to the beach, and when Gar arrived with Harriet, he took them out to the ship.

Avery headed back to the shore in the Riva when he saw Joey trotting up the beach.

Joey was carrying the Mannlicher and a small heavy bundle wrapped in an Eskimo's dark wet foxskin shirt. As he approached, alone, making for the boat nudging into the shore, the Eskimo women, awaiting the return of the men, began shrieking at him.

Joey pointed the rifle at them. They were unfazed and ran toward him as he climbed into the boat.

"What's going on?" said Avery.

"Get going!" said Joey.

The boat backed away from the shore as the two women screamed after them. Then they turned and began to run down the beach toward the south.

CHAPTER 24

THE NEXT MORNING, AFTER breakfast, *Lodestar* put to sea.

As the anchor came home tight against the hawsepipe, Gar spun the worm gear wheel engaging the windlass brake and spun another wheel to disengage the gear on the gypsy. Then he shut down the donkey engine.

Gar loved operating the windlass. Such an arrangement of design, a partnership between one item of gear fashioned so perfectly to aid the working of another, of which there existed so many arrangements aboard a ship, profoundly appealed to him. The beauty of mechanical hardware and the arrangements between separate pieces and the way they brought order to a vessel and aided its operation, was a strong part of what pulled him to boats, from the smallest rowboat propelled by oars in simple but unimprovable bronze oarlocks, to *Lodestar*'s windlass and the way it dealt so neatly with its many tons of heavy chain. There was no abstraction to a boat and its gear and their interdependent function, nothing at all of the world in which his father had worked and come so suddenly and unexpectedly to grief. There had been no neat visible fitting together of things or their coming apart around his father to forewarn him that anything was amiss. Gar Sr. had not known the true nature of what was failing in his world until another man telephoned him to tell him that he was ruined, that he must sell his house and all he owned, that he was diminished and bore no relation to the figure he thought he had been a moment before the phone call. Gar was determined that would never happen to him.

Only when he was finished on the foredeck did he remember that Captain Percival was in the forepeak, only inches beneath his feet, and would have heard him at work, his feet moving overhead, a close witness to the whole operation of retrieving the anchor and chain, but having nothing to do with it, confined and powerless. Weeks ago, cruising Block Island and the Vineyard and Newport as Critch's guest aboard the ship, Gar had watched Captain Percival stand on the bridge wings and bark orders and he had thought the world of him. Percival, he realized, had experienced much the same reversal as his father.

He walked aft down the deck and helped Moyle fit the covers over the Riva, and they tied the rowboat's oars to its thwarts, and they threw extra lashings around both craft to hold them still and secure through any weather.

Lodestar passed through the small islands at the entrance to Noble Inlet and headed southeast once again. The wind was still light today, blowing over southern Baffin Island from Hudson Strait and the southwest. The weather was fair, and the sea in the lee of the land was flat and dark blue. To port, farther offshore out in Frobisher Bay, there was enough breeze to make a fine weave of small dappled unbreaking waves, and a tide rip threw up a long white curling line in the blue water, and ten thousand gulls, terns, and fulmars wheeled and dove and cried in the air all along the line. The tundra bogs and peat hills where the shore party had become lost fell away off the starboard side and dropped quickly into the water until only the cone of Sugarloaf Hill and the high snowfields and the peninsular ridge some of them had climbed over could still be seen, and all that too began to slip into the water, and more and more they were at sea.

IN THE WHEELHOUSE, AVERY steered the changing courses given to him as Boden moved around behind him taking bearings and changing charts and now and then stepping out into the sun on the bridge wings to look up and down the ship and scan the horizons.

Boden meant to leave the Savage Islands to starboard and pass through Gabriel Strait into Hudson Strait and from there into the Labrador Sea and follow the hundred-fathom line down the Labrador coast six hundred miles and pass through the Strait of Belle Isle into the Gulf of St. Lawrence before the weather changed. Once through Belle Isle, they would be safe from ice, he could find holes in which to weather anything that might blow up, and they would be only two days steaming to New York.

Boden took no joy from his new command. He was overcome with shame and cold grief over the death of the two boys. He avoided Schenck when he could; he did not let himself think about Percival locked away forward. He felt sick of the sea. He was as lonely as he was burned. All his ambition now lay in getting the ship home and himself on the train to Long Beach and his wife. He allowed himself no thoughts or hope beyond that.

The burns across his chest and shoulder had become a single unified weeping lesion that made a soggy unwholesome tea-colored mess of the clean sections of ripped sheets Duhamel used twice a day, or whenever Boden would let him change the bandages. The pain came and went like a tide. A degree of infection had set in, and he had begun to run a fever. He took aspirin but no more morphine, so the pain at times was difficult to think through, but he could count on what he thought. Or so he thought. And he knew he would not be able to stay on the bridge and pay attention to the ship and its course—in short, he would not remain fit for command—without longer periods of rest and sleep below than he would have liked. But he was confident of his core crew: Moyle, Shred, whom he had put on the watch roster, and to a lesser extent Gar, were, he felt, capable of keeping the ship on course and out of trouble. More importantly, he trusted them to come to him before acting on their own. Joey he could count on to steer.

At noon, Shred came into the wheelhouse and relieved Avery at the helm. The ship had left the Savage Islands astern and was well into the wide waters of Hudson Strait. The wind had backed to the southeast, bringing it dead ahead, and increased to fifteen knots, and raised a small, breaking chop, but *Lode-*

star's needlelike bow cut through it with barely a tremor felt on deck. The wheelhouse barometer was very high at 1031 millibars, and the sky remained clear with a scattering of small cumulus clouds. Boden decided the wind would hold steady and fall off in the evening. It all looked right. Button Island, which they would pass before heading down the Labrador Sea, was sixty-five miles and five hours ahead. He allowed himself to sense his fatigue and pain, and he made himself go below to his bunk in the fo'c'sle to still his flaming shoulder and throbbing head and to try to sleep while such benign conditions held.

IT WAS THE FIRST time Clement Shred had steered the long blade of ship, and its response to his touch was something outside his experience. There was no trembling live feel to the wheel, with which a sailor could gauge and anticipate a response from his craft; in that sense the helm could be called dead. But a spoke moved an inch or two either way translated so precisely to the rudder under the water one hundred and eighty feet aft of where he stood, that a change of course of two or three degrees on the compass card could be made and accurately maintained. And this sensitivity came without nervousness; the helm was so steady the ship would hold on with no correction, no touch at all, for long minutes at a time. For a while Shred gave himself over to the pure marvel of it. With thumb and forefinger, he edged the spokes port and starboard and watched the nose ahead move as surely and smoothly as . . . nothing he knew. He had never driven an automobile and had no frame of reference beyond other boats. However, he had seen airships passing above Long Island Sound, and he thought steering one of those through the sky might be something like taking the helm of the *Lodestar*. He glided down through Hudson Strait.

But as miles passed astern and he got used to the helm, a heavy feeling grew and settled on him. Arnanguaq's face and body filled his head and his chest, and he felt something else outside his experience. That Eskimo talk she spoke, looking into his face all night, touching him all over—he'd understood her plain as day in some wonderful fashion, and never in his life been more comfortable with a fellow creature. How was that? What was it between them? And had it been the same for her? He thought so. He knew it somehow for certain.

Mad pictures flew through his brain: he saw himself cutting the lashings of the rowboat and throwing it into the sea and himself after and rowing all the way back to her. To do what? The voices of native ridicule came into his head clear: "Lordy, lookit you, Clement! Where'd you get them furs?" And he tried to imagine Arnanguaq working a church jumble with the ladies of Fairhaven. He felt a strange desolation. Mile after smooth mile he felt worse.

He became aware of Schenck calling up at him from the deck directly in front of the wheelhouse. Pointing ahead and slightly to starboard.

"Do you see it, Mr. Shred?"

He certainly did all of a sudden, now that he stopped his daydreaming and looked. An iceberg. Not a big one. A castle-shaped thing. It was all by itself, as far as he could make out, among the short cresting waves. No way to tell its size off in the sea there, a mile or two ahead. No scale to figure it by. Size of a house maybe, depending on the house. Shred saw that their present course, the one Boden had given him, would take them maybe a quarter mile clear of it.

"Do you see it?" Schenck called again.

Shred nodded, and said "Yes, sir," not loud enough for anyone outside the wheelhouse to hear.

"Then take me over there," called Schenck. He turned and started forward to the bow, where Joey and Avery stood looking off at the berg.

Shred blinked. He looked down at the steady compass card and saw he was on course. That was the course.

"Can you hear me?" Schenck called. He had stopped and was pointing again. "Take me over there, Mr. Shred!"

In the bow, Joey and Avery both turned and looked back at Schenck, and up at the wheelhouse.

Shred left the helm and walked out onto the starboard bridge wing. "It's off our course, Mr. Schenck. I'm supposed to hold one forty—"

"It's bang on our course, Mr. Shred! It's right ahead of us!

I'm telling you to bring me a little closer! Don't argue with me!"

Shred went back to the wheel. He looked down at the compass. He looked up through the windows at the iceberg which now appeared closer, but slightly farther to starboard. Where it should be. He looked back at the compass. The course was unchanged.

"Jehoshaphat, Mr. Shred! Don't you understand me?"

Joey came away from the bow and ran lightly aft and bounded up the wheelhouse steps. He reached the helm and pushed Shred away hard, sending him tottering backward into the rear of the wheelhouse. Joey planted his feet wide and twitched the wheel, and the bow came around slightly, without any sensation of change in the ship's onward humming rush. Shred edged forward, staying well away from Joey, making for the door, but Joey turned from the wheel and came at him. He grabbed Shred with both hands and threw him backward. Shred's hip caught the edge of the chart table and he fell to the floor. Sharp pain flashed through his side and he stayed down where he had fallen. He propped himself up and sat slumped against the chart table and watched Joey staring intently ahead out the window, making adjustments to the wheel.

A moment later he heard some shouting; Boden's voice, urgent.

Then the explosion forward.

CAPTAIN PERCIVAL'S NEW QUARTERS in the forepeak— *Lodestar*'s nearest equivalent to a ship's brig, accessed only by a lockable door—were not uncomfortable. Forward of the fo'c'sle, it was a long sliver of a compartment narrowing to a point at the ship's stem, the forwardmost space belowdecks, where bosun's stores and sundry supplies were kept in long shelves along each side of the hull. But a seven-foot-long, eighteen-inch-wide shelf on the starboard side had been cleared of boxes and fitted with a mattress and bedding. There was an electric light in the deckhead. Percival had been supplied with books from his captain's cabin. Food was sent in regularly; he was brought aft into the fo'c'sle twice a day, where Duhamel changed the dressing over the wound in his armpit; and he was taken to the head as often as he requested. He found he needed to urinate now with unaccustomed and humiliating frequency, pounding on the locked door to the fo'c'sle every few hours and escorted to the head like a bad schoolboy by whoever was off watch. Precautions on these excursions were light, for although his gunshot wound was clean and not serious, it was extremely painful, and his arm was held in a sling, and he was not inclined to overpower his escort and mount an attempt to take back the ship. He was afraid of Boden and Moyle, afraid they would hurt him again if he misbehaved. His confinement, he and his shipmates understood perfectly, was more in the nature of a punishment.

Percival had cried himself to sleep several times on his shelf in the forepeak. Until Mr. Dudley Carroll had sold *Lodestar* to Mr. Schenck, he had been very content, and had hoped to keep his position indefinitely. He had saved some money. It was the largest ship he had ever commanded, and in the yachting game, size, like pricks at school, counted for everything. His record had been blemished before, but he had always managed to wipe it clean, or lie outright, or run far enough away. Certainly in America so far this had worked. He had become adept at passing himself off as a former British Navy Commander, with his Edward VII beard, his suits and Royal Navy duffle coat, his forbidding demeanor and mix of naval and nautical jargon, and his accent which, to American ears, sounded authentically upper class. He had lost boats in the Solent, run a yacht onto the rocks off Cannes, skimmed money off chandlery bills and been dismissed when his fraud came to light, but that had all been in England and Europe. Until now everything had gone so well in America, but he was horribly certain this episode would prove unusually difficult to put behind him. He might have to relocate to some distant place. *Lodestar* was a famous yacht, and her skipper's forcible removal would inevitably be talked about from Bar Harbor to Palm Beach. The immediate future looked grim.

A clang of metal rang through the forepeak. It was telegraphed through the deck by the eight one-inch bronze bolts fastened to the reinforcing steel strapping that crisscrossed the additional blocking and deckbeams and formed part of the interconnected matrix of the newly strengthened deck beneath the harpoon gun.

Percival lay on his shelf and looked up. He heard more noise—he heard shouting too, Schenck's voice, but the man was always shouting. What he heard now was different, metallic, and it came so clearly down into the forepeak that he could visualize precisely what was making it.

He stood up, and looked at the whole structure over his head. He had spent a good deal of time aboard ships, navy vessels and yachts. He might have suffered a few mishaps, but he knew a thing or two.

He turned and began pounding on the door to the fo'c'sle. He started to yell.

"Stop him! Somebody stop him! The man's a maniac! *Get me out of here!*"

BODEN HAD WOKEN TO Schenck's shouting, and was out on the deck before Percival began pounding on the door. He came up through the companionway and saw Joey through the wheelhouse window, and then he looked forward.

He saw the iceberg and Schenck crouched over the harpoon gun, one hand gripping its swivel handle, other hand on the firing lanyard. Avery stood behind him. A harpoon without a bomb screwed to its tip protruded from the gun's barrel. The hawser bridle was still attached to the gun's muzzle. Schenck was swinging the gun slowly to starboard as the iceberg, about fifty feet wide and thirty high, came abreast of the bow.

"*Do not fire!*" Boden roared, starting forward.

Schenck turned and saw him, ready as a bad boy with his answers. "There's no bomb! No whale! No problem! I bought this goddamn thing, and I'm going to shoot it!"

Schenck looked forward again and jerked the lanyard.

The four-inch shell—the same size of ordnance that had proved so devastatingly ineffective in the trenches of France—came with the percussive blast most people can only associate with military parades or fireworks. Schenck, Boden, and Joey up in the wheelhouse watched the harpoon fly over the water, the steel hawser snaking in the air behind it. It hit the iceberg and vanished in a shower of ice and water vapor. The hawser fell into the sea. The ship ran on at thirteen knots.

The harpoon lodged in the ice.

The steel hawser ran out across the bow from the squealing reel through-bolted beside the harpoon gun.

"Turn into the berg!" Boden yelled up at the wheelhouse, and waved his arm. Then he ran forward and tried to grab Avery, but the boy stepped away from him, afraid. "Get out of here!" Boden yelled at him, but Avery stepped farther away and held onto the bow rail. Boden grabbed Schenck—both hands came out from under the shawl—and dragged him aft. Schenck tried to fight him off, but tripped and fell and Boden didn't stop pulling, dragging him back across the deck away from the bow. Still the ship ran on and the hawser reel spun, and the iceberg was now falling aft down the starboard side, farther from the bow.

"Get back here!" Boden yelled at Avery, who stood alone now right in the bow, looking back, afraid.

Joey tore out of the wheelhouse and down the steps and ran forward, but before he reached Boden, still hauling Schenck aft, the steel hawser rose from beneath the waves like an erupting line squall, throwing shards of water off its entire length, stretching between the ship and the iceberg with a low hum that rose in tone as it lifted and pulled aft down the starboard side, slicing through the rail, until it grew taut with a loud whine. Avery dropped to the deck and grabbed hold of a stoutly bolted-down bronze bollard.

For a second the ship began to pull to starboard. Then with a splintering noise the reinforced section of deck over the forepeak tore away in one piece, the way a roof comes off in a hurricane. It went sideways, taking bow rails, harpoon gun, hawser reel, and Avery with it, one edge of the structure ripping through the thin iron hull, and crashing into the sea. Green water flooded into the torn hull, which seemed to dig downward, and more water toppled into the hole over the forepeak.

Boden lifted Schenck as if he had been a teddy bear, grabbed Joey, who stood still, dumbstruck, staring at the piece of deck moving away in the waves.

"Take him aft!" he yelled at Joey, and pushed both of them away down the deck.

He ran up the steps into the wheelhouse. He yanked the telegraph to stop and spun the wheel all the way to starboard. Then he looked forward to see what would happen.

As the bow came around, still plowing into the sea, water filled the forepeak, and the weight brought the ship down fast and steeply by the head. He thought she might dig in and keep going if Jenkins didn't stop her in time, and if she did that, she would drive right on down and go altogether under in seconds. The open hole in the deck, a full twelve-foot-deep vector aft from the stem, was dropping into the waves. Not rising. She was going under. Boden turned and saw Shred standing beside him, staring stupefied out the window, held by the spectacle. When he looked forward again he saw the *Mary Boden* awash and foundering, so real and vivid that for a moment he forgot which ship was going down, and when he remembered, he could not believe it was happening again and began to founder himself. Was he the Jonah?

Then Boden felt the bow lift slowly, but miraculously, and he saw the water level inside the hole over the forepeak subside, and he knew the bulkhead had given way and water was flooding aft inside the ship.

WHEN THE HARPOON GUN'S shell fired, Mr. Newton was in his bunk in the fo'c'sle cabin he shared with Duhamel, where he had spent every moment except for essential excursions to the head since they had come aboard at night and shot the captain. The gigantic bang of the shell drove him deeper into his bedclothes. As deep as he could go, pulling the pillow over his head, and he would not get out of bed again until they reached Long Island Sound.

But he couldn't shut out the sudden screeching, rending groan that sounded like a train crash that came from somewhere immediately beyond his feet, so loud and frightening he couldn't help raising his head to look, and the instant he did so he saw an utterly fantastic embodiment of the die-hard landlubber's worst nightmare of the sea: the wall at the foot of his bunk splintered apart and a cataract of icy water engulfed him.

He was pushed deeper into his bunk than he had ever managed to go by himself, flattened as if beneath a waterfall. He opened his mouth to cry out and freezing water came in. He heard only roaring now. Then he was no longer pinned but rose and floated a moment before the watery train wreck took off with him at terrible speed through splitting bulkheads, swirling doors, splintered paneling, tables, someone's legs, a maelstrom of debris, into a foaming pocket of air where he could only expel water instead of breathe, and then the whole unbelieveable weight of the sea smashed him through another wall and he became light as a feather and was borne far away like a dandelion seed.

THE WATER FLOODED AFT, rose, and burst through the ultimate commuter flyer's thin bulkheads, through the fo'c'sle, the head, storerooms, the captain's cabin, until it reached the engine room, where it rose more slowly as the bow came up and the sea was no longer pouring in through the hull and the foredeck.

Eddie Jenkins remembered the battle of Constantinople and the fire inside the *Grappler* that scarred his face, and he grabbed Ray Strick and threw him at the ladder and pushed him upward. He opened steam valves as fast as he could reach and spin them, and shut his Bath turbines down as the cold water rose and hissed over the hot metal. He ran aft into the fireroom where the rising water had turned black and oily with coal, and he picked up a shovel and turned his face aside as he nudged the catches on the firebox doors, which blew open as if cannonshot under the force of steam building in the boxes as the water rose over the glowing coals. Then he clawed up the ladder, and he and Ray both reached the deck unharmed.

THE WATER LEVELED OUT through the ship, moving aft through the bilge, no longer high enough to rise and break through bulkheads. In the owner's accommodation aft, it climbed quickly above floor level.

Harriet had remained in her cabin with the door locked since Gar had brought her aboard. She had not come out for food. She had not gotten out of bed except to lift up the carpet and raise a floorboard and squat over this convenient hole above the bilge. As she watched the water come up over the floor, her mother began to pound on the door, calling for her to open up. Harriet pulled the covers over her head. Then Mrs. Schenck called Arthur. An axe came through the upper panel of the door, smashing a hole large enough for Arthur to reach in and turn the lock. He opened the door and Mamie waded in and sat down on Harriet's bunk.

"What's the matter with you, darling? Your father and I are worried about you. Anyway, you can't stay in here. Arthur's going to carry you, so you won't get wet."

Arthur came in and lifted the small bundle of blankets. She was little larger than a child. Her hands came out and wrapped around Arthur's neck and he carried her up to the saloon, where there was no water and, for the moment, everything appeared quite normal.

AS THE SHIP SLOWED, Boden held the wheel over and she came around until the southeasterly chop was on her port side. He straightened her out and she lost way and drifted with the wind and waves on her port quarter. He pulled Shred to the wheel.

"Try to hold her like that," he said. "Keep her off the wind." He looked at Shred and added sharply, "Got it?"

Shred nodded. "I got it."

Boden left the wheelhouse. Gar stood on the foredeck, staring forward.

"Get the rowboat into the water!" Boden told him. "Give me a shout when you're ready. Get Ray to help you, and both of you see if you can spot Avery."

Gar nodded, grateful for action. He ran aft.

Boden walked forward until he stood beside the windlass and could look down into the forepeak. The rip in the starboard bow, a V with its edges splayed outward like two petals, stopped five feet above the waterline. It appeared to have been started by the hawser slicing a clean downward cut which was then split further and widened by part of the torn deck and its gear being pulled out through it. Now on the lee side of the ship, no water at all was coming through the rip. He looked to port, the weather side: with the ship effectively hove to and drifting at a knot or two off the wind, it left a broad calm slick to windward, over which the three- to five-foot southeasterly waves tumbled and broke harmlessly. The wind was still only fifteen knots. Not even spray was coming over the deck to fall into the forepeak. The situation had stabilized.

Eddie Jenkins came and stood beside him, staring down at the damage. Boden briefly told Jenkins what had happened, and asked about the engines.

The engineer's face was covered with an oily film, his branded half smile at counterpoint with the expression in his eyes. "There's water halfway up the blocks. Water over the fires. The generator's gone. And my bilge pump is packed up too. You might fix her in a shipyard, but not out here."

They heard a groan and saw Dick Iams, soaking wet, hauling himself out of the fo'c'sle companionway. He started crawling aft across the deck with his head lowered as if he were being fired upon. They crossed the deck and rolled him over onto his back. They found no blood or broken bones. He appeared to be unhurt but in shock.

"Get him aft into the saloon, Eddie," said Boden.

He saw Gar and Ray still unlashing the rowboat and yelled at them. "Hurry with that boat! Cut it away!"

Then he looked down the fo'c'sle companionway. The ladder was gone. He sat down with his feet hanging, put his right hand on the hatch coaming, got ready to feel the scabs and bandages tear away from his burnt chest and shoulder, and swung himself down into knee-deep water.

The entire forward part of the ship appeared changed, a different vessel altogether, double its former size without its partitions, the sleeping cabins gone, swept away with the whole of the forepeak bulkhead, except the two oak posts beneath the windlass, which anchored that item and transferred all its strain to the keel.

Most unnaturally, and inimical to the way of ships, blue sky hung above the whole deckless forepeak, exposing it to bright daylight. The place was awash with wreckage: splintered lengths of doors and paneling, mattresses, bedding, books, suitcases, his own chest, cans of paint and varnish, sodden unrecognizable bundles, all floated around his legs like harbor flotsam, or were jammed and smashed together into thickets of boards and wrenched bolts and bent nails, wedged into corners, hooked on torn woodwork, filling gaps in the half-smashed aft bulkhead.

"Gimme a hand," came a voice from a corner aft. It was Moyle, dripping wet, blood streaming from an eyebrow gash. He was upright and holding onto a heavy heap. Boden waded back and saw that Moyle was holding Percival, keeping the lolling head above water.

"Fetched up back in his old berth," said Moyle. He horked and spat into the water floating through what had been the captain's cabin.

"Is he alive?"

"He is. But not that one." He nodded to a corner where most of the wreckage seemed to have collected, strainerlike, around the half-rent engine room bulkhead, a mass of boards, doors, and the built-in solid mahogany desk, bunk, and furniture from the captain's cabin, all wracked together and some of it wedged so tight and high up that it appeared to defy gravity.

Boden saw the wood and other debris but nothing else.

"Up," said Moyle.

High up under the deckhead, atop the wreckage as though spearheading its impossible passage through too small a hole, two short splayed legs stuck out halfway through the bulkhead. A rag of torn wet silk was wrapped around one leg. Boden waded aft through the open passageway until he came to the engine room door, which was open, and went inside. He looked forward. The front half of Newton's body protruded from a hole in the top corner of the bulkhead. His large head had changed shape: it was flattened at the forehead like the effect once desired by certain Indian tribes who bound rocks to the foreheads of their infants. Otherwise it appeared undamaged. The arms were pinned back somehow. The mouth was agape, the eyes wide open in a bug-eyed stare. Newton looked like a large grouper caught while trying to swim through the bulkhead. Boden went back into the fo'c'sle and they dragged Percival to the foot of the companionway. Moyle pulled him-

self up on deck, disappeared, and came back with Eddie Jenkins and Ray Strick. Together they hauled Percival up on deck.

Boden looked at Moyle's cut. "You okay?"

"Sure."

"You got a cut."

Boden touched his own brow in the corresponding place.
Moyle prodded and felt his injury. "I'll live."

"How are you feeling?"

Set deep in his bloody, oil- and coal-filmed face, Moyle's
eyes were abnormally large. "Woke up."

BODEN AND GAR PULLED the rowboat back and forth
between the drifting ship and the deltoid section of the foredeck, which now floated a quarter of a mile away, and they
saw no sign of Avery. Boden's arm, shoulder, and right hand
all hurt like hell, but as they rowed, the pain dulled and he
nearly forgot about it, and felt mostly the sadness that was
filling him, displacing some of his anger.

He scanned the rising wave faces all around him for a head
or the heavy half-sunken line of the boy's long back, and grew
certain it would be better not to find him, for Avery would be
dead in the water this long, and better left where he was. The
briny would not let a body grow foul but would quickly see it
unraveled to its smallest thread and its tissue dispersed wide, as
a living part of the watery world. A gift to the sea. Boden had
long hoped he would die at sea, that his body would not be
found and brought ashore to fester in dirt. He had at times
considered the opportunity provided by the center span of the
Brooklyn Bridge, high above a hard-running ebb. A body
dropped from there would be swept downriver past Governor's Island, maybe down the Buttermilk Channel, past Ellis
and Bedloe Islands and out into the Lower Bay within an hour.
He had imagined himself passing between Sandy Hook and
Rockaway Point on his way down the Ambrose Channel and
out to sea past the light vessel, to become the sustenance of
creatures who traveled along the continental shelf or rode the
Gulf Stream across the Atlantic to Europe. That was the way
to go.

Gar was weeping in front of him. Boden held both oars with his left hand and placed his right on Gar's back.

As they turned and rowed back and forth, he caught sight of the ship. She was beam on to the swell now, stalled and rolling, the sun catching her enameled black hull, the varnished superstructure, the brass fittings and the bronze. The gash in her bow and the lost section of deck had not spoiled the line of her sheer. She still looked beautiful in the sun on the blue sea. Awfully beautiful. She was almost certainly on her last course, making slowly for her rock or harbor of ruin. The people who had brought her here would try to save themselves at her cost, one of the bitter rules of the sea. She would be abandoned to lean over on some shore and grow dull and lose her shape and settle and blister and corrode and rot into dissolution. A skeleton to be forgotten and found again long hence and wondered at.

After an hour they gave up looking for Avery and pulled for the ship.

FORTY HOURS—TWO SHORT periods of sunset, a long day, and two mornings later—*Lodestar* was again closing with the southern shore of Baffin Island.

The fine weather had held and the wind had remained in the south, falling light through the two short nights and breezing up again during the day. Boden had directed Moyle, Gar, and Dick Iams to rig an awning between the foremast and the windlass, making a fluttering trapezoidal sail that had added a knot or two to the ship's drift and pulled her downwind and a few points to the west; as far west as Boden could coax her. One hundred and thirty miles west-northwest of East Bluff lay Lake Harbor, with a Hudson's Bay Company post, an Anglican mission, and a telegraph station; a place he'd sailed into twice before, now their nearest and best hope of safety and transportation back to the world in the south.

But the ship would not make it that far. Tides ran strongly in the strait, with the weight of a continent's riverwater and meltwater flushing out of Hudson Bay, and the ship had been set east of the course she had been able to follow. She was coming to the end of her last ride. Within a few more hours

Lodestar was going to come ashore somewhere on the rocky coast dead ahead, at the place where the tide and the wind, little affected by Boden's efforts, would combine to land her.

Boden sat at the chart table in the wheelhouse and read through sections of the Admiralty *Arctic Pilot* again to reacquaint himself with possible landing sites. It made grim reading:

> *Between East Bluff and Pritzler Harbour 45 miles WNW, the tidal streams run with great strength. It is not advisable to approach within 3 miles of the coast or off-lying islands without local knowledge.*
> *The coast from Pritzler Harbour to Cape Weymouth 64 miles WNW is for the greater part fronted by many islands and very dangerous rocks and shoals. There are no easily accessible harbours along this part of the coast.*

Of necessity, Boden read about the harbors, however difficult of access:

> *Wight Inlet, 26 miles WNW of Pritzler Harbour, is a long, narrow and foul inlet, which nearly dries out.*
> *Balcom Inlet has numerous dangers in the approach and cannot be entered at all states of the tide; it is reported that, towards low water, heavy seas against the ebb break to the bottom.*
> *Barrier Inlet is narrow and hazardous even for small boats; constrictions in the channel create inward rushing reversing falls during the flood tide.*
> *Shaftesbury Inlet, 62 miles WNW of Pritzler Harbour, is fronted by islets, shoals and rocks for a distance of 3 miles to seaward of the entrance; strong tidal streams set across these hazards.*

Hazardous and inaccessible it might be, Boden had contrived to bring the ship to within a few miles of Shaftesbury Inlet. There had been no reasonable hope of a safe harbor east of there, and he saw, as the land loomed ahead, that he would not get the ship farther west. Shaftesbury Inlet seemed the only possibility for getting her grounded inside a harbor rather than foundering at the base of the coast's sheer cliffs, or impaling her on take your pick of rocky islets. No voice inside him said, "For what? What do you care?" A vessel brought into the most marginal harbor meant a better chance of safely getting her people off, but if there had been nobody aboard he would still have done all he could to bring her in to any kind of shelter rather than see her crack up on a rock or shoal. He knew no other way.

"The inlet itself is deep in mid-channel and free from dangers and affords well-sheltered anchorage in suitable depths."

Once inside, the ship could be anchored and they could disembark into her boats and all of them could reach the shore safely.

If he could get her in. High water would be in an hour, he knew after days of watching the tide. The stream now was light. There would be perhaps another hour of slack before the ebb began to flow with a force that would carry the ship. The wind was still in the south, pushing the ship directly toward the high, forbidding coast. Shaftesbury Inlet appeared as a narrow cut in the high land ahead. An ungrouped throw of rocks and small gray islands lay directly in a line between the ship and the entrance, but a preponderance of these lay to the east of dead ahead.

In the wheelhouse, Boden took the helm and asked Shred to go find Gar and bring him up. A minute later Gar came up the steps into the wheelhouse. He looked through the windows at the inlet ahead.

"How are you doing?" Boden asked him.

Gar was no longer recognizable as the boy who had come aboard *Lodestar* in Newport. He had lost weight. Dark whiskers shadowed his face. He had thought he was going to die and lived. Several times. He looked ready to fight for his life.

"I'm okay. How about you?"

"I'm all right. I want you to go aft and tell them to be ready to abandon ship instantly. If we have to get off, we may have to go fast. They bring nothing but the clothes they're wearing. Get Schenck's rifles and bring them up here to me. I don't care what he says, Schenck is not to have a gun, do you understand?"

"Yes."

"Take Iams with you if you like."

"I'll be fine."

"Good. Then get Jenkins and Ray to help you lower the ladder and get the boats ready to drop. Ask them to stay with the boats, because we're going to be loading them. Put one rifle and ammunition inside the rowboat. The rest up here."

"Right."

"Something else," said Boden.

"What?"

"Keep Schenck away from me."

"I can do that."

"I don't want to see him up here. You understand?"

"Don't worry." Gar started out the door.

"Gar. You've done good."

Gar looked at Boden. "Thanks, Will. So have you."

Boden sent Shred to tell Duhamel to prepare baskets of food and water. He told Moyle, Shred, and Iams to remain on the foredeck to handle the sail. He went out on the bridge and shouted down to the galley for Duhamel to send him up a jug of water. He knew his mouth and throat were going to dry.

As the tidal stream slackened, Boden brought the wind as far as he could onto the port quarter without stalling the ship's forward momentum. By the time the stream stilled, the ship lay a mile west of the entrance, three miles offshore. It drifted on, with the wind flapping the jury-rigged sail, heading directly toward the land. Its present course aimed it straight into the sheer rock wall west of the entrance.

Soon the ebb was apparent. The ship began to slip sideways, east, toward the rocks a mile away along the starboard side. At the same time, it continued its languid windblown forward progress.

Duhamel came out of the galley door beneath the starboard bridge wing and stood on the deck, where he had rarely been seen. The Schencks (except for Harriet), Joey, and Arthur stood at the rail aft. Jenkins and Ray stood near the Riva in its davits amidships. Moyle, Shred, and Dick Iams gathered near

the windlass, aft of the hole in the deck. All watched the closing shore. Arrival was certain, imminent, and unstoppable, but
its quality, whether gentle or fearful, could not be determined
yet. The calm aspect of its approach sharpened its fascination.

The tide strengthened. Once the sideways-pulling stream
grew stronger than the ship's slow poke forward, an odd
change of perception occurred on board. It appeared to the
watchers on deck as if the ship had stopped and the rocks and
small islands and the land itself had begun to come at them
with a gaining speed. It felt as if all control had been lost and
the ship were as hapless as a leaf washing down a stream, and
they weren't far wrong. A group of rocks fast approached the
starboard side and passed close astern. The water swirled
around the rocks like river rapids. Other small rocks, sticking
up alone in the water, looked as if they were powering forward
through the water, leaving wakes behind them.

In the wheelhouse, Boden saw that if he held on, the ship
would be swept past the inlet. The drag of the current on the
ship's long underwater profile was overpowering the faltering
drive from the jury sail. Heading downwind reduced windforce
by the amount of the ship's slight forward speed, and the awning flopped and spilled wind. The ship needed a shot of acceler-
ation, and a few minutes of resistance to the tide.

Boden left the wheel and stepped out on the bridge wing. He
called to the men forward. "I'm going to head up. To port.
When we start to come round, hang on those lines and flatten
that sail."

"Trim her for a reach?" Shred said.

"Exactly."

Moyle nodded.

Back at the wheel, he had to wait agonizing minutes to allow
a large rock to creep up to the ship's bow. Its bearing held
steady; it appeared to be on a collision course. The men forward watched it come with growing consternation, glancing up
at the wheelhouse to see what Boden would do. Boden
watched hoping for some change in bearing, but the rock came
at the bow in an unwavering straight line. Finally there was
nothing for it but to pull the wheel to starboard, the last direction he wanted to steer, hoping to swing the bow off inside the

rock. But the bow came around too slowly, and he thought of icebergs and their seven-tenths below the surface and wondered at the shape of this rock below the water. Then the point of the bow was past the rock and he spun the wheel to port.

There was a bump, very soft, no noise. So gentle he thought the bow would ride off, but it stuck and the tide began to pull the stern around. The hull caught on some underwater footing of the visible rock and slowly the ship began to pivot around the bow. The sail began to spread its profile to the breeze and filled into a straining parabolic shape and pressed the bow forward and down.

Boden came out on the bridge and called forward: "Slack off at the windlass! Spill air!"

Moyle and Shred loosed sheets and the awning flapped heavily. Dick Iams followed them around, still dopey and slow.

The ship turned ninety degrees until it faced west. The southerly swell, now abeam, began to rock the hull and the tide pulled at it and Boden began to feel it sliding aft. He was out on the bridge instantly.

"Sheet in! She's clear! Trim her for speed!"

The men forward pulled the awning's lines again until it caught the wind and filled and the flapping stopped. The beam wind on the sail pulled the bow sluggishly forward. The sharp point of the narrow hull now faced directly into the pull of the tide, reducing its underwater profile from a blocky two hundred and twenty-five feet to a sharp twenty-one feet, and the ship gathered way until its forward speed matched the east-setting stream. They held station, but slid toward the shore. The rock underwater had bettered what Boden had hoped to do with the wheel: instead of steering a loop while being swept sideways, the ship had stopped and turned on the spot.

After securing the awning's lines, Moyle had dropped down into the hole in the foredeck. Now he came out and looked up at Boden through the wheelhouse window and shook his head. No water was coming in below where the hull had sat on the rock.

Boden had the ship moving obliquely across the tide. The bow was pointing at the bluffs a little ways west along the coast, but their true course over the ground was carrying the ship into the inlet. But as they drew closer, the high land began to interfere with the wind, sending gusting backeddies off the land. The awning backwinded with a snap. It filled again from the south, but sagged and flapped and grew limp. Moyle began to play with its lines, hauling the cloth one way or another across the deck, but the sail became useless.

Boden pulled the wheel a turn to starboard, hoping to use the last of their forward momentum to steer the ship into the inlet, in past the run of the tide, hoping some breeze would push her ahead and in before she was caught and pulled backward in the current, out of control, onto the rocks that lined the eastern approach to the entrance.

For a few minutes he thought she would make it: the two entrance walls came abeam. But then he felt the ebb of the inlet itself: all the water inside the ten-mile-long fissure of land was pouring out to sea and it stopped *Lodestar* dead.

She was caught, beyond help, going aground. He had a final moment to choose where. He spun the wheel to starboard, using the current, and slowly swung her bow past a narrow rim of gravel at the foot of the eastern wall.

He jumped to the bridge. "Moyle! Let go!"

Moyle—his face still black with grime and crusted with blood—knew Boden wasn't talking about awning lines. He was at the windlass and released the brake. Chain flew down the hawsepipe.

"Brake it!" yelled Boden.

The chain lifted out of the water and began its pull at the bow. The tide caught the ship's stern, and she began to revolve. Somewhere amidships she touched bottom, a soft sliding as if through slush, and then she leaned over gently, and rocked back, beached on a narrow gravel shore.

CHAPTER 25

MAMIE DECLARED IT WAS like a picnic at New-port.

She sat in *Monte*'s front seat, between her husband and Harriet, who sat small and bundled up in a blanket at the edge of the forward cockpit. Joey, who was driving, sat on the other side of Schenck. With the windshield in front of them, they had the best protection from the wind and spray, which, everyone found, chilled quickly.

Arthur, Gar, Dick Iams, Duhamel, Eddie Jenkins, Ray Strick, and Percival were all packed together in the four wide backseats with a heavy hacked-off scrap of the awning that had been *Lodestar*'s jib pulled over them. Their heads and a few arms stuck out. They wore hats and gloves and appeared a little like the dazed, myopic rural Americans sleighriding through a Currier & Ives print. Their faces were red and wet, and set with cold and discomfort and gnawing anxiety.

The rowboat towed astern held Boden, Moyle, and Shred beneath another piece of the awning. This prevented the Riva from making more than five knots, above which the rowboat slewed out of the motorboat's wake and threatened to capsize. Their progress up the coast, close under the high cliffs, skirting rocks, and slowed by the sluicing tide, seemed miserable, their voyage daunting. Joey had wanted to drive the Riva and Boden had not argued with him for several reasons, not the least of which was that his shoulder was killing him and he still felt feverish. And he preferred the company in the rowboat.

In the Riva, Schenck was laughing hard. Mamie was telling him a story about a ham.

"Wainwright's said they didn't have it! I told them we'd ordered it, I had a dinner party, and it was too late to find another. It was my ham and I wanted it! Well, they weren't making the right noises at all on the phone, so I went over there and I found out they'd given it to someone else! Some doctor near Round Hill—"

"Those jerks!" Schenck laughed. He knew he had eaten the ham and that the story must have a wonderful ending.

"Well, I was furious at them! I told them I was driving over there right away to get it. And we did! Arthur and I drove to Round Hill, but Wainwright's sent someone ahead and they got it back from the doctor's cook—right out of her hands!"

The memory did not warm Arthur, who was seasick and wanted to die, and yet was afraid he was going to. He huddled beneath the canvas covering with filaments of saliva and mustard bile running with seaspray across his cement-gray cheeks.

"They handed it over to us right there on the road outside the doctor's house, as if Arthur and I were part of a gang, in on some crime!"

Schenck's head went back, his teeth bared, as he laughed hard and loud with the joy of the victor.

Mamie was laughing now herself. "You should have seen the doctor's cook! I don't think she ever believed us! She came right out to the road to watch us! I think she thought we were all stealing the doctor's ham!"

Schenck's laughing rose and echoed off the cliffs, and hundreds of birds cried and lifted from ledges into flight.

"Some fat doctor!"

"Yes! On Round Hill!"

Schenck gasped, at the bottom of a belly laugh. Finally he got his breath back. He had heard the echo off the cliffs and seen its effect on the birds, and now he shouted upward as loud as he could:

"God, it's sweet!"

A thousand birds screamed and rose off the cliffs and flew out to sea. Schenck watched them.

"Gar! Where's my rifle?"

"It's in the rowboat, sir."

IT WAS THIRTY SEA miles from Shaftesbury Inlet to the settlement at Lake Harbor. *Lodestar* had grounded at 11 A.M. It was possible, Boden had told them all, that they could make Lake Harbour in the boats before dark that same day.

Remaining aboard the ship left them in a precarious position. Some day soon the weather would change and the ship could be pounded quickly into pieces against the shore, or holed and sucked offshore to sink. Their best bet was to try to reach safety while the weather held.

They had filled the Riva's gas tanks, loaded more cans of gas and Duhamel's two baskets of food into the Riva and the rowboat, squeezed themselves in, and set off.

Boden took a chart and called or gestured directions forward. Their course lay around Maniittur Cape, through Watkins Strait, a narrow channel between Big Island and the mainland, and then up to the head of North Bay to the settlement. Before leaving the ship, Boden had taken a last look at the pilot book:

> *This coastline, including the greater part of that of Big Island, is very rugged and much indented, with numerous fringing islets and groups of offshore islands. Tidal streams through Watkins Strait run strongly, and in some years the strait coast of Big Island may remain icebound through the summer. The possibility of uncharted dangers exists everywhere.*

For six long hours, until five in the afternoon, the tide was against them. Water churned past the boats, but the land on their right seemed hardly to move. *Lodestar*, leaning farther and farther over on its side as the water ebbed out of the inlet, remained visible all afternoon until they crawled around Maniittur Cape and left it behind. Then the tide turned and the flood sent them fast through Watkins Strait, flushing past a slew of

rocks and sheer walls in a jumble of rips and eddies. But Joey
steered well and held them in the main and deeper streams
rather than trying for the quieter waters to the sides, and by
seven o'clock they were rushing up North Bay in calmer water
toward the low sun.

Boden recognized Mount Chaunsler, a mass of striated gray
and red gneiss that rose a thousand feet on the east side of the
bay. He identified landmarks from his chart and called out the
fast-changing route. Past Cape Tanfield, between Beacon Island
and Cape Scott into Westbourne Bay, the western narrows past
Glasgow Island. At nine o'clock, in the gloom beneath the high
peninsular ridge of mountains to the north, but with the sky
still bright overhead, the Riva rumbled up to the head of a long
narrow cove in flat, windless water. A spire appeared atop a
shack church. About thirty crude board huts, some covered
with tar paper and battens, hung with skins, harnesses, hunting
equipment. Hundreds of dogs sat or stood tethered to stakes
beside every hut. A shack sat beside a telegraph pole. The con-
spicuous and largest building, at the head of a wooden dock,
bore the Hudson's Bay Company sign.

People ashore stopped all activity and stared at the two
boats coming up the cove. They began to cry out and run. As
excitement spread and people ran toward the dock, the village
dogs leapt at their stakes and whined, barked, and yelped until
an insane doggy ululation filled the still air of the cove. Unmindful of the dogs, a hundred Eskimos crowded the waterfront and screamed and pointed as the Riva and its tow approached. The still gleaming launch, with its quiet, invisibly
housed motor, its leather upholstery, windshield, steering
wheel, and chromed fixtures, astounded no less than if the castaways had come across the water in a Cadillac.

When Joey saw the shouting, pointing Eskimos packing the
dock, he throttled back and the Riva slowed to a stop.

"In to the dock, Joey," said Schenck.

But Joey remained motionless, staring at the Eskimos gather-
ing ashore.

"What's the matter with you? They're not going to hurt us.
They like the boat. Go on in."

Joey stared, unhearing. One hand had gone to his pants

pocket. He shrank into the side of the cockpit, away from the shore.

Schenck grabbed the wheel, reached across Joey to the throttle, and headed the boat into the dock. He jumped out of his seat as they came alongside, and climbed up the ladder nailed to pilings. Gar followed him up with mooring lines.

Schenck stood on the dock among the natives like Bwana "Tumbo," as the African camp boys had christened Roosevelt when he stepped ashore at Mombasa.

"Who's in charge?" he asked.

"Hullo there." A thin, white-haired man stepped forward and stuck out his hand. He wore a red checked hunting jacket and lumberjack boots. "McGregor. I'm the Hudson's Bay man here."

"Mr. McGregor!" Schenck grabbed the man's hand and gripped it hard. "Carl Schenck, of Minneapolis and New York City."

Gar helped Mamie and Harriet up the ladder. Schenck introduced his family to McGregor. The others began creakily to stand up in the boats and one after another climbed the ladder to the dock, where the local Eskimos grinned and touched their clothing and began talking to them in Eskimo and English. Joey alone remained in the Riva.

"Say, there's a whole bunch of you," said McGregor. "Where'd you folks spring from?"

"Shipwrecked!" said Schenck, with huge, unconcealable satisfaction. "A tussle with an iceberg. But our Captain Boden here got us safely ashore. When's the next flight out of here?"

McGregor chuckled with Canadian good humor. "Gee, wouldn't that be fun. Nope. No airplanes up here. But Captain Murray'll take you aboard the *Nascopie*. That's our HBC supply vessel. She can take you down to St. John's."

"When?"

"Well, you're lucky. She'll be along in another three weeks or so. She only stops by two or three times a year. But we can fix you all up until then. Is this all you've got with you?"

"We're not staying. What else have you got?"

"Beg pardon?"

"Another boat. Something big. The biggest you got. What've

you got around here that I can charter? Or buy? Name your price. I've got business in New York. I need to get back there now."

"New York? Well, Mr. Schenck, you're up in the Arctic—"

"McGregor, I want to use your telephone."

"Telephone?" He chuckled again. "Nope. No telephone up here in Lake Harbour. Say, wouldn't that be something, though, just pick her up—"

"All right!" said Schenck. "How do you get word out of here?"

"Word? Well—"

"What's that?" Schenck pointed to the telegraph pole.

"Oh, that's our telegraph office."

"Where's the operator?"

"That's me. But the office is closed right now."

Schenck moved toward the man with a smile. He took his arm.

REVEREND PATTERSON OF EDINBURGH vacated his "vicarage," a shack beside the crude church that contained a single bed and two armchairs draped with antimacassars, for the use of Schenck and his wife and daughter. Mamie slept in the bed, Harriet on the two armchairs pulled together, and Schenck rolled up in a blanket on the floor between the two and dreamed of his iceberg. The vicar bunked down in the church with the rest of Mr. Schenck's party.

AT SIX THE FOLLOWING morning, a Saturday, Eddie Rickenbacker was woken at his Bronxville home by a Western Union boy ringing his doorbell. He tore open the yellow envelope on the doorstep.

SHIPWRECKED STOP NO JOKE STOP URGENT
YOU SEND BIGGEST FLYING BOAT TO HUD-
SON BAY COMPANY POST LAKE HARBOUR
BAFFIN ISLAND CANADA TODAY REPEAT TO-
DAY STOP PURCHASE PAN AMERICAN PLANE
IF NECESSARY BUT REPEAT TODAY STOP SEND
MEDICINAL WITH PLANE STOP SCHENCK

"Is there a reply, Mr. Rickenbacker?"

"Um, yes."

The boy proffered his yellow pad. Rickenbacker scribbled:

*WORKING ON IT STOP TODAY UNLESS YOU
HEAR OTHERWISE STOP TWELVE-YEAR-OLD
MEDICINE COMING STOP RICKENBACKER.*

He tore it off the pad and gave it to the boy. "This is the return." He started scribbling again. "And this one's going to Italy. How long will that take?"

"If your party's at home, we'll get you a reply back in an hour, maybe two, Mr. Rickenbacker. I'll see it goes out right away, sir."

He gave the pad back to the boy and handed him a dollar bill.

"Thank *you*, Mr. Rickenbacker!" said the boy, jumping on his bicycle and pedaling back into town.

Later that morning Eddie Rickenbacker drove his Dusenberg coupe down to Manhattan, over the Queensboro Bridge to Brooklyn, and all the way out Flatbush Avenue to Floyd Bennett Field.

He found *Capitan* Rodolfo Pasolini waiting for him in the Pan American Airways office in the big hangar at the edge of Jamaica Bay. The Italian Air Force officer wore a sharp uniform that looked equally suitable, with its jodhpurs and knee boots, for horseback riding. Pasolini was thrilled to meet the famous flying ace. He clicked his heels and bobbed his head. His Italian accent was thick and charming.

"*Capitan* Reegenbagger! It's an honor! *Generale* Balbo put me at your disposal. Also, please," Pasolini made an incisive horizontal gesture with both hands, "he ask you allow him to provide you with the aircraft with his compliments."

"Oh, say, I appreciate General Balbo's offer, but that's too kind," said Eddie Rickenbacker. "My friend is a very wealthy man. You must at least let us pay for fuel—"

"Please! *Capitan!* I have my instructions. Please. We don't talk anymore about that. Also, we are very happy for the opportunity to make this flight. Italy have a great history with the North Pole."

Rickenbacker remembered that Italian aviator Umberto Nobile, whom General Balbo hated and envied for his celebrity, had flown over the North Pole with famed Polar explorer Roald Amundsen as his passenger.

"Well, I can only thank you and *General* Balbo. My friend Mr. Schenck will be very grateful."

"*Buono!* Allow me to show you the aircraft."

As they walked through the dark hangar, Rickenbacker smiled to himself. He had been poor until after the war, when his flying exploits in France made him famous. Since that time, he had played with rich men and enjoyed the comforts and considerations of their friendships. At a certain level, he had found, when you became so rich or so famous, nobody let you pay for anything anymore. People jumped at any chance to do you favors. They did favors for your friends. They wanted to play golf with you. They wanted you as a business partner. They presented you with fantastic opportunities. Here was a guy, Schenck, who if necessary could afford to buy an airline and all its planes to bail himself out of trouble. But the Italian Air Force was going to fly up to some godforsaken hole in the Arctic and pick him up for free. Because he was rich and an associate of Eddie Rickenbacker's, and because Eddie's wartime friend *Generale* Italo Balbo had a seaplane in town for a few days. If Schenck had been poor and unconnected, he'd be frozen stiff.

They came out of the hangar into the sunshine. Firmly held between four ship-sized moorings, a small portable stairway sitting on the Pan American dock beside its forward hatch, the giant Luccini seaplane barely moved in the popple ruffling the flat blue water of Jamaica Bay. The aircraft, captained by Pasolini, was on its way home after a trial run between Italy and Chicago. The following summer *Generale* Balbo was planning to fly twenty-four Luccinis to Chicago for the Century of Progress Exposition.

"Excuse me, but, she is beautiful, no?"

"Gorgeous!"

"From here to this place on Baffin Island, it's only about one thousand five hundred miles. Less than between Bermuda and São Miguel in the Azores. We take extra fuel. For my airplane, it's nothing. You will be very comfortable, *Capitan*."

"No, not me. I'm not going."

"You don't come with us?"

"No, I can't go."

Capitan Pasolini's posture slumped. He deflated visibly. "Oh, I am very sorry about this. I had hoped very much that you were coming with us."

"No, unfortunately," Rickenbacker smiled with convincing regret, "I've got business that keeps me here."

Pasolini lifted his head and summoned stoicism. "I am disappointed. But we fly for you, *Capitan* Reegenbagger."

"I appreciate it, *Capitan* Pasolini."

"We go aboard, *Capitan*. I show you the aircraft and introduce my crew."

They walked along the dock toward the huge plane.

"Captain," said Eddie Rickenbacker, "may I give you a piece of advice?"

"Of course!"

"Mr. Schenck has flown. I've taken him up. He knows how to fly a small plane."

"Very good!"

"No. Not good. Do not let him take the controls of the plane. Do not let him into the cockpit during flight. Keep him strapped in his seat."

IN THE MORNING, MCGREGOR brought Eddie Rickenbacker's telegram to the vicarage.

Mamie remained in the small hut most of the day looking after Harriet, who appeared distant and depressed and needed feeding. Mamie sang to her. Arthur stayed close by, arranging their food and refreshment with the help of Reverend Patterson. Schenck spent the day walking between the vicarage and the dock, looking up at the sky.

Boden and Moyle took off early in the rowboat. Nobody saw where they went.

Eddie Jenkins, Ray Strick, Duhamel, and Iams idled around the harbor. Schenck had told them he had a plane coming and they focused on their departure from this hellish place and looked forward to returning to civilization. They had no interest in the local Eskimos and turned away from their approaches and gestures.

Percival passed the day loitering in the Hudson's Bay store, comforted by the proximity of McGregor's merchandise, such as blankets and knives made in England. He discouraged McGregor's attempts at conversation, except to mention briefly the impoverishment suffered by his family through the profligacy of his grandfather, the sixteenth baronet of Whitstable, forcing him into work.

"Have you still got the title?" asked McGregor.

"Of course."

"So you're the eighteenth baronet of . . . what is it?"

"Whitstable." Percival spelled it out. "That's right. I am the eighteenth baronet."

"Gee, that's sure impressive. Should I call you baron?"

"I'm a baronet, not a baron. But that is not a title of address. Captain Percival will do."

McGregor tried to learn more details of the encounter with the iceberg, but Percival remained mum.

Clement Shred spent the day walking through the village. The Eskimos all stared at him and he looked back just as plainly. He looked over their huts and dog harnesses, hunting outfits, and kayaks a-building, all of it about the dandiest work he'd ever seen. The raw material for all their clothing, gadgetry, and outfits seemed to be seal and fox and caribou, carcasses of which he could see all around him, strung up, pegged out, scraped and curing, in every stage of being rendered into useful products. He watched the women chewing leather to soften it, sewing boots machine neat, making food, and handling babies all at once. The Eskimos, their community and handiwork, reminded him strongly of something, but he was unable to remember what.

The children, the smallest of them half-naked below the waist, followed him around and stared at him, until he found himself making foolish faces to see them laugh, which they all did readily. He talked with villagers when he could understand them—quite a few spoke some words of English. They talked

to him in Eskimo too, and the peculiar sounds triggered sweet
memories.

In every woman's half-turned face he saw Arnanguaq. It was
her until the face turned all the way and she became someone
else, so like but unlike her. He saw her all over the village.

He was invited to eat lunch with a family outside a hut on a
slope above the harbor. A man and his wife and two children
pulled him to the ground and pushed food at him, making
comments in Eskimo and gesturing about the utter worthless-
ness of the food, and what mean and impoverished hosts they
were, but they hoped he would stay and share what they had
anyway, and strangely Shred understood them and stayed,
charmed and hungry.

"Giviak," said the Eskimo man, as his wife brought a small
rigid seal out of their hut, naming the finest dish a man could
offer a guest. He went on in proper self-deprecating etiquette
to say how ashamed he was to offer Shred such inedible fare.
The seal turned out to be stuffed. Shred's host drew out of its
mouth a handful of strong-smelling black lumps, glistening all
over with a thick fatty goo. He took Shred's hand and filled it
with a cool and sticky portion, then scooped another handful
from inside the seal and began to eat it. Shred understood that
the seal was but a container rather than the dish, but he could
not make out the dark curdled lumps in his hand. But his host
urged him, and he had eaten well with Eskimos before, so he
raised his hand and slurped. It was immediately delicious. A
strong fermentation action hit the roof of his mouth and the
underside of his tongue with a savory tingle, and he bit down
into a gluey pod that popped softly and stuck to his teeth. The
good bits separated out inside his mouth and he swallowed.
But he was left with some furry sticks, and it was not until his
host and hostess began to spit dark detritus out of their mouths
that he understood what he was eating. Birds. He had a
mouthful of feathers and soft bones. He followed their lead
and spat them out.

"What miserable food, fit only for the dogs, but you honor
us by pretending to like it," said his host in Eskimo.

Shred made them out now in his hand, small whole auklets
drowned in some suetlike aspic, which he correctly guessed

was aged and fermented seal blubber. The auks had reached this state of cure after a year or so inside the sealskin, which had been stored in a dark cache beneath stones.

The Eskimo man nudged him to watch as he now lifted a small sodden bird from his hand and held it gently by its legs with his teeth. He brushed downward lightly with both hands, and most of the feathers were easily pulled off. He turned the stripped bird around and bit into the head above the beak and pulled the entire envelope of skin off the body like a glove, peeling it down from the head, and popped the cleaned whole bird into his mouth, biting off the legs and throwing them aside. He chewed and swallowed and spat, and urged Shred to do the same.

Little game birds, after all, Shred put it to himself. Cured somehow. But they tasted good, soft and chewy, no doubt about that. He tried the plucking and stripping method and he ate more than enough to please his hosts.

In the afternoon, wandering around the village again, it came to him what the whole setup here reminded him of: the Charbonneaus of Lunenburg. The single shared industry of a community working together; what his own clan had once been successful at, but had let go and seen itself dwindled by dissolution and separation.

He admired these people. He liked them. He hoped they would hang on to their own clever ways.

Joey spent all day in the church. He found a bible and read his favorite parts of the Old Testament. He crouched beside the windows when he heard noises. He held onto his knife.

AT SEVEN IN THE evening, the sun still visible over the ridge above the village, a drone was heard. It was immediately lost in the frantic howling of the dogs. But everyone had heard it and knew a plane was coming, and stood still and gazed down the inlet to the south. Soon it was spotted, a speck in the sky that grew larger and acquired form. People shouted and pointed, the dogs barked and leapt in frenzy. The distant un-flapping wings banked and homed in on Mount Chaunsler and the noise began to be heard above the riot in the village. The plane banked again, seeming to have found its mark, and came in low, directly up the inlet.

Some of the Eskimos had seen a seaplane. Two- and four-passenger seaplanes were beginning to carry light urgent supplies and important or injured people between the communities of Hudson Bay. Those who had never seen a seaplane had heard all about them. What a wonder they were!

But unimagined was the groaning gorbelly whale-bird that came on up the inlet, growing as big as a three-masted sailing ship and moving as stately through the sky, its noise deepening and sucking up all sound until it pealed a chord of hysteria running through people's bodies. It came in low but did not land. It flew on past any possibility of landing on water and appeared to be coming down on the village at head height. Most of the Eskimos threw themselves to the ground as it passed low overhead, making a reconnoitering run, and those who remained standing with arms hanging at their sides unconsciously turned their palms forward. The phalanx of engines ground out the percussive blast of an unending explosion. A hurricane-force wave of wind rolled up the inlet and over the village in the plane's wake. The great aircraft banked to the west and only Schenck noticed a tiny man, *Capitan* Pasolini, grinning and waving a bottle of whiskey in the cockpit window. It sailed out over the inlet again.

It came back in low, splashed gingerly, settled on the water, and idled toward the settlement. Schenck walked down the dock to meet it, and soon everybody followed him. Two hundred yards off, a door opened at the front of the fuselage and an Italian crewman released an anchor from its windlass inside the door. Then he looked out and waved. The roaring engines spluttered and stopped.

Joey pushed through the crowd on the dock and climbed down into the Riva. He started the engines.

Schenck climbed down into the boat. "Take me out to her, Joey."

When he returned five minutes later, he climbed up onto the dock and handed McGregor and the Reverend Patterson each a bottle of Laphroig. "My compliments, gentlemen, and thanks for the hospitality."

Mamie and Harriet were helped down into the Riva. Arthur, Percival, Jenkins, and Strick followed. Joey ran them out to the seaplane.

Boden and Moyle had returned late in the afternoon from their day's row around the harbor. Boden approached Schenck as the Riva was headed back to the dock.

"Mr. Schenck, Mr. Moyle and I won't be coming with you. We're staying here and we'd like our pay."

Schenck stared at Boden, figuring the angle. Slowly an odd smile appeared. "You're going to try to salvage her."

"Yes, sir. And we're going to start by salvaging your rowboat."

Schenck stared at him with an expression Boden had never seen on him. It took him a long moment to realize he was seeing envy.

"The captain who lost his ship," said Schenck. A ticker tape of thoughts flew behind his face. "Can you do it?"

Shred stood two feet away at the ladder. He stood still and listened.

"We think it's possible. Enough to try."

Schenck sighed. "God, what I wouldn't give to join you."

"We wouldn't have you," said Boden. "I'd scull back to New York rather than get on that airplane with you. But we want our pay."

Schenck brought his focus back from his daydreams and grinned at Boden. He seemed pleased, satisfied, and Boden found himself remembering the day he first met him, when Schenck had played chicken with him, taking his hands off the wheel of his car while he waited for Boden to say what he would do if he saw Schenck standing his boat into danger.

"What do I owe you?"

"I got a hundred and thirty dollars coming to me," said Moyle. It had been five weeks and a day since he had come aboard *Lodestar* to help fit her out for her voyage north.

"Seventy-five," said Boden.

Schenck pulled a roll of cash from his hunting vest, counted out the bills, and handed each man his money. He held the rest of the roll up to Boden.

"You're going to need more than two hundred bucks. Here's

two thousand dollars, give or take. It's yours if you give me first crack at buying *Lodestar* back. She's your ship if you get her out of here, you name the price and I'll take it or leave it. But this gives me first crack."

"You keep your money, Mr. Schenck. We might not sell the boat."

"We might go for a cruise," said Moyle.

The Riva rumbled back alongside the dock. Dick Iams and Duhamel shook hands with Boden and Moyle, wished them luck, and climbed down the ladder into the boat.

Gar stepped forward in front of Boden and stuck out his hand. "Will . . . I want to thank you . . ." His eyes filled.

Boden shook his hand and smiled at the boy. "You did good, Gar. Look after yourself. Should be easy after this."

Gar shook hands with Moyle and climbed down into the Riva.

Shred's turn.

"Well, so long, Clement," said Boden. He stuck out his hand.

Shred looked at him and Moyle. "I want to come with you. You'll need help. How about it?"

"We can use him," said Moyle.

"We might not make it out of here, Clement."

Shred looked ashore at the village and at the faces of the Eskimos crowding the dock. "That's all right."

"So what do I owe you, Mr. Shred?" asked Schenck.

"I don't know, sir. You didn't hire me proper. Sort of invited me along."

"Well, here." Schenck peeled off some bills.

Shred looked at the money. "I'd appreciate it, sir, if you'd send that money round to Mrs. Shred at 27 Markle Street there on City Island. Maybe with the message that I don't know when I'll be home and maybe she ought to go on back to Fairhaven. If you could, sir."

"I can do that, Mr. Shred. Thank you for your help. Good luck to you."

Schenck grabbed Shred's hand. Moyle was unprepared and found his hand being squeezed hard before he knew it. Then Schenck held his hand out to Boden and slowly Boden took it.

"Good luck!" said Schenck. "You fuckers are going to need it!" He started laughing. He stepped down into the Riva. Joey gunned it and the boat sped out to the seaplane. They heard Schenck laughing all the way.

Everybody ashore watched. One by one the seaplane's engines turned over, belched, the four-bladed propellers began to spin, and layers of ascending engine drone built upon each other into a synchronous organ chord. The crewman forward got the anchor in and closed the door. The engines revved up and down and the great waterbird swung around and began to speed down the inlet. As soon as it rose above the surface, Eskimos jumped into kayaks and umiaks and paddled hard toward the empty, drifting Riva.

CHAPTER 26

HEY SET OUT NEXT morning on the ebb tide.
They rowed in shifts, two at the oars while a man
rested. All three men were smallboat handy and they
pulled well together. The sky was cloudless except for a few
high scattered feathers, the only wind came as fitful zephyrs
chasing the warming air over the hills around the bay. The
temperature in the sun rose into the low sixties in the forenoon, and the men stripped down to their undershirts as they
rowed.

They made good progress down North Bay until the tide
turned in the afternoon and the flood set against them. Then
they hauled inshore, looking for backeddies, and spent hours
crawling through the wash and swell beneath the angling gaze
of the same nesting birds in the cliffs above. There had been no
gasoline in Lake Harbour to take the Riva back to the ship, but
all three men shared an unspoken complacency at leaving it
behind. They wanted no truck with it. It was a rich man's
plaything, its deeply varnished finish offensive to them, and
something quite other, in a hard to define way, than the rich
man's ship they thought so fine and hoped to save. They were
happy with their rowboat. They talked little, and felt no need
for chat. Each pulled with his own thoughts.

She was nothing as fine as his skiff, Shred decided, but he
was happy with his crewmates and excited by his astonishing
new prospects. Either way it came out, steaming south as one-

321

third owner of a great fancy gewgaw of a vessel, or stranded on Baffin Island in the company of Eskimos, it was all right with him. Salvaging the vessel would make them rich as lords, which would be a fine thing, though what he would do as a lord and where he would go to be one, Shred was unsure. When he thought of the other outcome, he pictured Arnanguaq, and other pictures came easily and more concrete-seeming, and he found himself strangely hoping against his more lordly fortune.

Who knew Moyle's thoughts? He pulled, and felt the trans-mission of the power still there in his arms and back and stom-ach and bracing legs, through the flexing oars into the sea. The voyage stretched out and no harbor loomed, and that was probably fine with him.

Boden's burn was now crusted over, weeping still in places where the scabs pulled off as the muscles worked; he was un-consciously careful with it, but he rowed with a physical appe-tite for the exercise and rhythm, and wove his pain into that. He was now deeply fixed on how to float and repair the ship. He had found a giant and worthy task, something that, like the sea, would demand everything from him, and he played its possible variants over and over in his thoughts. They had to haul her off the gravel shore while the weather stayed fine. She was so big and heavy, he knew they'd never kedge her off if she was stuck firm. The anchor was close inshore, the scope short. She had gone aground on the ebb and was leaning over when they last saw her. What had happened since would prove cru-cial. Had the incoming flood pushed her higher up on the hard? Had her anchor held her off, maybe even floated her? How high was the high tide? Had she lifted off and then pounded through four tides and holed herself so she would sink if they got her off into deep water?

If they could get the water out of the hull, at least get it below the bilge, and shovel the sodden ash out of the fireboxes, they could get the wet coal to burn—chop up some cabin furni-ture for kindling—and if they could get steam up and the tur-bines turning over before they began to corrode and seize up, she would turn her screws and move. All this was possible.

Overwhelmingly unlikely, but possible.

There would be no answer to these questions and all that hung on them until they reached the ship.

And behind these questions, slipping through them to dazzle him for a moment before he pushed them away, the pictures: steaming up through the Narrows in the ship. Going out to Long Beach and telling Mary and bringing her back to show her his ship. See? This is what I can do. Pull such a ship off Baffin Island and bring it home, like pulling sunken treasure up from the deep. He would take her on a cruise up the Sound.

They would sell *Lodestar* of course. But what was this outlandish boat worth? It had no measurable value except to the rare man who saw it and had to possess it and could, like Caesar with Britain. No one bought such a ship by figuring or comparing. Her worth had little to do with replacement value, for who would ever build such a one again? Vincent Astor had sold her because she was too large. *Lodestar* was an anomaly, a floating Hope diamond. But someone would want her. Even now, with men in America living in cardboard boxes on fire escapes, there would be a buyer for this outlandish ship.

A million dollars maybe? Maybe more. Split three ways. That would see him and Mary set up in a house forever.

And then he would do what?

He would buy a boat—a reasonable boat. An Alden schooner maybe, do some charter work, sail the nobs to Block Island or Down East in the season. Put her up on the hard in the winter and take the best care of her. Mary would illustrate books, only the books she wanted to illustrate. Maybe he could do some writing, something he had always thought he might try if he could find something to write about. They would take vacations. Go see the Grand Canyon.

The Grand Canyon?

The more he thought like this, the less clear the picture, until finally it lost the anatomy of possibility and vanished.

More vivid was himself alone in a room.

He wondered how close Mary had grown to the writer who dyed his hair. She had a determined streak in her, and a clear picture of the life she wanted and expected for herself in a house somewhere like Long Beach, with a tomato bush in the backyard, that had warred with her love for him and his seafaring dreams lifted from 19th-century books, and maybe she had finally shut the door.

If it was too late, he could buy the schooner and Head Out. Down the Atlantic to the Strait of Magellan and up through the channels, past Slocum's Milky Way. Then forty days running through the Trades until he was swooping between wind and sea like a frigate bird, and on he would go. Below the Line to the South China Sea: Borneo, Celebes, the Andamans and the Nicobars. Conrad country. Or the *Pequod*'s cruise. Round Good Hope, and round the Horn, and round the Norway Maelstrom, and round perdition's flames—

Crap! Put the storybooks aside! a great voice bellowed inside him. And he listened.

That wasn't him anymore. He didn't want Slocum's lonely forty days. He didn't want to be a goddamn bird. Let Ahab have the Norway Maelstrom. Boden was afraid of turning into the Ancient Mariner. He already saw too well the specter of another wedding party.

"COMING HOME TO STAY IF YOULL HAVE ME PLEASE BELIEVE ME LOVE WILL" he had telegraphed from Lake Harbour. That was what he wanted, and all he wanted. The rest of it was a sham. He had run away from boarding school to be an old salt on the Grand Banks. He had aped Newbold McKenzie's voyages to the Arctic. He had played so long at being a nautical character—some leathery fellow with shackles in his pockets and a barnacle growing behind his ear—that he had come to believe it. His life as a sailor—the stabs at epic seafaring, the dreams of ships and faraway places—it had all been an imitation of the great books. Well, it didn't work that way. He was fifty years too late, an insurance man's son from New Jersey. He had run away from his father and his father's life, and what a fine deep model he had found to set his running dreams on.

He could throw an eyesplice into wire and navigate by the stars, but finally the life he was leading had turned too authentic. The truth about all those seafaring characters was that they were unhappy men who had retreated to the water's edge and beyond. *Whenever I find myself growing grim about the mouth; whenever it is a damp, drizzly November in my soul*

. . . That's why men go to sea. The failure of life and love ashore.

He knew what he wanted now, unclouded by romantic notions of the sea: he ached to go home to Mary. He would find something to do. He could have a little boat. Maybe build a boat for someone. He and Mary could go to the beach together and look out to sea.

He grew amazed. A dark cloud lifted off him. I'm coming home, sweetheart. She would have the telegram by now and know he was coming. Please wait.

Lodestar first. It was a fine means to an end. And if they failed, he would walk home down Canada to Mary and do whatever he had to do to stay with her. All sense and thought boiled down to the fact that he loved her and wanted only to be with her.

FOURTEEN HOURS OUT OF Lake Harbour, the evening ebb flushed them through Watkins Strait at four knots. They rested at the oars, dipping blades only to steer the boat and keep it midchannel and away from the rocks. They rowed another hour beyond the strait, but knowing the tide would turn again before they made Maniittur Cape and set them back among a cluster of rocks after sunset, they pulled, at Boden's suggestion, into Weymouth Inlet. It was a small curving finger of a cove that offered a gravel beach on its hidden inner shore, where they could haul the boat and stretch out for the night. Boden knew the place, he told them. He had been there before.

On the beach they made a fire of dead grass and bracken and heated three cans of franks and beans they had bought at the Hudson's Bay store. They ate with their fingers out of the cans.

"Mmm," they all grunted, licking ketchupy fingers. Weeks of the Frenchman's cuisine had left them hungering for simpler grub.

Afterward, Boden said he was going to walk up the hill behind the beach to the cliff edge above the sea, and if Moyle and Shred wanted to come with him, he might be able to show them something. Full of beans, they set off up the grassy slope.

It was an easy climb, though Shred followed at an increasing distance. The hill leveled gradually to a gentle crown and then stopped abruptly at a sheer drop to the water. The sea was calm, but they heard the swell sucking at the rocks two hundred feet below. The grass at the top ran all the way to the cliff edge, except where the ground began to crumble into rock and scree toward the inlet entrance. It was in this direction Boden headed. As they walked single file, the low orange sun threw their long shadows over the blaze of tufted grass and farther, over the cliff edge, and the cold shadow of the high land stretched out across the sea.

Boden stopped at a waist-high pile of stones, a cairn, erected at the highest point of the rocky ground above the inlet entrance. He put his hand on the top stone and smiled.

"You did this?" Shred asked him.

"Yup. June, 1920. I came in here with Newbold McKenzie aboard *Arundel*."

"Why make a pile of stones?" asked Moyle.

"Well . . . I felt I'd reached somewhere. We took weeks coming up, tacking through ice all over the Labrador Sea. It was spring, and the weather was terrible. We had ice in the rigging and we froze our nuts off. By the time I got here I thought this was the top of the world, and the end of the world too, and I was amazed I was here. We spent a night in the inlet and I walked up here the next morning and looked out to sea and I thought this must be the farthest north I'd ever get, so I made a cairn to mark the spot. I didn't know anything then. The next day I was farther north, when we got to Lake Harbour. And since then I've been up to Bylot Island. But this is my cairn to mark Will Boden's Farthest North."

They watched as Boden bent and picked up fallen stones and put them back on his memorial pile, and then they went back down the hill.

WHEN THEY CAME AROUND Cape Maniittur next morning they saw the ship right away. From four miles distant she appeared level, floating, but unnaturally still, as if pausing for some reason in the entrance to Shaftesbury Inlet, pointing seaward but hesitant to go. They rowed with the hard ebb, turning their heads every few minutes to look at her.

They reached the ship twenty minutes later. The ladder was

down, as they had left it. They came alongside, stepped out, tied off the painter, and climbed up to the deck. They stood and looked at each other.

"She's stuck," said Moyle.

They all knew it. She was upright, almost floating clear, but some part of her was aground. Maybe only a small section of keel settled into a groove in the gravel, or maybe a propeller, bending its shaft so it would tear itself out of the hull if it revolved at speed. They could not know.

Then, very quickly, as the inlet ebbed further, she began to lay over again on the gravel.

"She might have been free at high tide," said Shred.

"Maybe. Although she's sitting exactly where we left her," said Boden.

They went forward and dropped down the fo'c'sle companionway. Icy water was still knee-high, though no more appeared to have come in. They moved aft through the ship. They found dry coal above the water level in the bunkers. Water lapped at the sides of the turbines as the ship rocked gently sideways on the gravel bottom. But there were no hard impacts, no groaning of steel plate.

"Take us a week to hand pump this water out," said Shred. His feet were freezing; the water level was above the tops of their rubber boots and had poured in the moment they came below. It would be like this until they got the level down somehow.

"Well, maybe the tide'll help us when it drops far enough," said Boden.

"Knock a hole in her?" said Moyle.

"No, I was thinking of siphoning it out. If we've got enough hose to get a good volume of water going while the tide's out. In that sense, the higher we are the better."

"That's a slick idea," said Shred.

They pulled the ship's water hose out of its deck box forward. It was commercial-scale, three-inch-diameter firehose; two coiled lengths, a hundred and fifty feet long each. They cut them in half and fed one length down into the fo'c'sle, two into the engine room, and the last into the aft quarters. Two hours later, when the gravel had nearly dried out along the port side, they filled the hoses with water, folded them closed, and lowered them to Moyle down on the gravel. He pulled the hoses down to his feet and water started pouring out. It kept coming. The ship settled by the bow, so they moved the aft hose forward. The tide fell to below bilge level inside the ship and water poured out of the wide-bore hoses for five hours.

The galley, at deck level forward of the saloon, was untouched by the disaster. Shred foraged in the iceboxes and the vegetable bins and found steaks and onions to fry on the galley's kerosene stove. They ate lunch on the aft deck in the sun, warming their cold, soaked feet, listening to the sweet sound of the water pouring out of the hoses onto the gravel.

After lunch, the water was below the fireboxes, and Moyle and Shred began shoveling out the wet ash. They dumped their shovel-loads into the water over the floor and waded through dark murk; they could worry about cleanup later.

Boden got the windlass's donkey engine going. It was gasoline-powered and there was plenty of gas aboard. He cranked in most of the chain's catenary until it angled up out of the shallows and gave him some idea where the anchor lay on the bottom. Not half as far out as he would have liked, and angling to starboard in the direction of the deeper water in the inlet's entrance. He spun the brake and held the strain on the cable so it would begin to pull at the ship from that direction the moment the flood tide began to ease it off the gravel, and then he turned the engine off.

At the bottom of the ebb, the ship was heeled over ten degrees, lying on its port bilge. Boden stepped down the ladder into the boat and rowed up and down the starboard side, looking to see what damage might have been done. None that he could see. He rowed around the stern onto the gravel and stepped out of the boat and walked along the port side. The screws looked unmarked, the struts and shafts straight and fair. The hull below the waterline appeared to have just come out of the dry dock in Brooklyn: the icy northern water had allowed not even a film of algae to start on the copper paint. The new zincs were clean and unpitted. She looked sweet and trim to Boden's eyes.

Good God, what if they did it?

They chopped and split the driest paneling (fast-burning eastern white pine) from the fo'c'sle wreckage below and made fires in the fireboxes. They added the hotter-burning mahogany from the wreckage of the captain's cabin. They fed wood to the fires until they had thick banks of embers on beds of white ash, and then they added coal. Both Boden and Moyle had been firemen in steamships, and they built the fires together and grew filthy with ash and dust, and shiny with sweat. The water in the two thousand-gallon boilers had gone cold, and would take a long time to heat. They would not make steam until the next day.

As the flood came in, Shred kept an eye on the seawater advance on the hoses and pulled them up before the sea reached the water level inside the ship.

Then the rising sea began to rock the ship again, and after a while it sat upright and level in the water. Boden went topside and started the donkey engine. The other two came up and watched.

Every seaman has gone aground in some vessel on a falling tide, and rowed or motored or, with assistance from another vessel, got a kedge anchor out into deeper water, and taken the strain on its cable and waited to see how the tide would lift his grounded vessel and wondered if the kedge would hold and pull him off. The real seaman is so alive to the prospects of grounding at all times in any vessel on every stretch of water that a part of his mind is always at work on how to avoid it, and how he would get his vessel off if it did ground. Salvaging scenarios run through the seaman's subconscious mind in an unending panorama wherever he sails; he talks about how other ships were saved with other seamen; and in time he accumulates a vast native familiarity with salvage while he may be fortunate enough to have actually done very little of it. So Boden, Moyle, and Shred, authentic savants of the process, waited for what they would know first through their feet, long before they saw any change of attitude to the shore: the sense of the ship on the move.

But they watched the chain like men ringside at a prizefight, for it would be their first telltale. As the water lifted the bow, which had dropped with the ebb, Boden let the windlass begin to pull, and the chain rose higher out of the water, stretching forward and to starboard, quivering, water shaking off it. Then he braked and held the strain. The bow bobbed slightly, and on each upward nod it moved a little to starboard. Then suddenly the rigid chain collapsed into the sea and hung at a nearly vertical angle from the bow.

"Shit!" said all three at once. Shred and Moyle turned to Boden as he spun the gear wheel and got the windlass cranking in again. The anchor had dragged or pulled free—or the chain had been caught on some rock and yanked straight or more nearly so, and the anchor still held. The chain would now tell them.

They watched as it rose and angled forward again. Twice it slipped, shuddering, then rose again as the windlass pulled.

"She'll hold," said Moyle.

Boden wondered how Moyle could know before he had cranked the chain in tight again, but he believed in the old codger and his hopes soared. Up came the chain, taut, nearly all curve pulled out of it, shivering with strain, and the bow came around and pointed straight at the securely buried anchor.

"She's holding!" said Shred.

Still some part of the keel sat on the gravel. The flood had about an hour and a half left, but very little higher to rise. They watched the chain, looked at the shore, fought their fears.

Then Moyle said, "She's off."

They saw the chain ease. They felt the yielding through the deck beneath their feet. They felt the floating unresistance in every part of the hull. The ship moved forward, towed by the great catenary weight of the chain, which now sagged and lowered slowly into the sea.

"Christmas! We're off!" said Shred.

"We are," said Boden.

For a few minutes *Lodestar* continued moving through the calm water. She was pulled by the chain out toward the center of the inlet entrance, and carried a little farther by her own weight and momentum until she rode over her buried anchor, and then the last of the flooding tide began to pull her into the inlet. Boden eased the windlass brake and laid chain as she went, to let her go.

"Let's sound and drop the port anchor," he said.

Moyle got the small lead line from the deck box and heaved it over the rail and watched its markers run through his hand. "Fifteen fathoms."

When he thought she had drifted as far as she would go, Boden eased the windlass's port brake and the port anchor dropped into the water. He dropped fifty fathoms of chain on top of it. *Lodestar* finally stopped. She was well offshore. She floated free.

ALL AFTERNOON AND THROUGH the twilight they shoveled coal into the fireboxes. The water in the boilers grew warm.

The seawater in the engine room bilge was below the turbines and propeller shafts and Boden did what he could, squirting oil over every moving part and checking valves and seals. The turbines had been overhauled at Bath for Dudley Carroll and their seals were in good shape. The seawater did not appear to have gotten into them. He told Moyle and Shred he thought they would fire up and work fine once they had steam.

They fried potatoes and more steaks for their supper and ate in the dining room, which was directly over the boilers and growing warm. They drank wine and beer as they ate.

"Oh my!" said Shred, sitting in an armchair and looking at the maritime-themed oil paintings on the dining room paneling, "We're living like lords now!"

"We'll live aboard her till we sell her," said Boden. "She ought to do."

"Oh, my yes! We three kings of Orient are!"

During the short night, they stood anchor watches, two hours on, four off. Boden took the first watch, starting at midnight. He walked around the deck thinking about the voyage back. He had found his trunk below and brought it up to the wheelhouse, which he decided he would use as his cabin.

Moyle relieved him at two and he stretched out on the settee at the rear of the wheelhouse. He felt the ship lift on the slight inlet surge, and he fell asleep.

* * *

HE WOKE A LITTLE after four. The sun was up but low, and filling the wheelhouse with lurid red light, and he was confused for a moment about the time of day. The red light paled. He could not get back to sleep.

He got up and looked out the wheelhouse window at the cold sunlight streaming through smoky vapor across Hudson Strait. Fog out there. It had been clear for days; he could see the change of weather in the offing. He came down to the foredeck, where Shred sat on the deck box wrapped in a blanket, bathed in a cold pink light.

"How's it going, Clement?"

"Quiet. Colder this morning, feels like. Specially coming up after feeding them fires." Shred looked quietly bewildered.

"You all right?"

"Oh sure." He started to say more, stopped, then tried again. "I was trying to sleep aft but couldn't do it. Kept thinking Mr. Schenck'd come in and tell me off. I don't think I belong on a ship like this. She makes me feel strange, I got to say."

"I know what you mean," said Boden. "I feel the same. But I think it's the ship that doesn't belong, Clement, not us. She's a museum piece—"

"Oh yes! And built the very best."

"Yes, but to what purpose? She's no type at all. She's all wrong for the sea. She's a rich man's wildest dream, and exists because someone had the money to build her. Her only purpose is to astound. She's big and fine and beautiful, but she has no place in this world."

"That's it! That's what I was trying to figure. There's no reason for her except to drive men crazy over how big and fine she is and what to do with her, and fit for no use at all. She's the strangest thing I ever seen. Why, she's mostly an awful worry. I been worried about her since I first seen her." Shred looked worried now. "Who'll want her?"

"Oh, someone. Someone will. And pay for her."

"Because she's the biggest and the best?"

"For that alone," said Boden.

He went below and looked at the pressure valves and the

boilers. Steam sometime today, and he thought of the early red sky and hoped they could get offshore before anything blew up. He loaded coal into the fireboxes. He played with the valves and worked at getting the operation of the turbines set in his mind. It was now nice and warm down here, and the fires made a low steady rumble.

He had been in the engine room half an hour when Shred stuck his head down the companionway and told him he might want to come up.

On deck Shred pointed. Two Eskimo-laden umiaks were approaching. Moyle came forward along the deck from aft, and the three of them watched. The Eskimo boats came round to the ladder, and Boden recognized Tikiqtituq as he stepped onto the ladder's bottom platform. He came up the ladder fast, others following as they climbed out of their boats. They gathered behind Tikiqtituq on deck. Boden noticed that Tikiqtituq was carrying his rifle.

"I'm not sure I like the look of this."

Moyle moved closer beside Boden and put his hand inside his coat.

Tikiqtituq stared at the white men but said nothing. He waited until five men and six or more women were grouped behind him on the deck. Shred immediately spotted Arnanguaq as she came up the ladder. He saw it was her before he realized she was wearing his hat. He stared at her, but her face was solemn and she didn't meet his eye.

Tikiqtituq began to orate. He spoke in Eskimo. His voice was loud and solemn, and he spoke for about two minutes. The men behind him became angry as they listened. He finished in English, looking at Boden as he spoke.

"What do you say about what you do?"

Boden believed he understood their concern.

"Our captain was not a good man. He took the ship into danger. We got a new captain, and our people have left us here to save the ship—"

"That what you have to say? You talk about ship?" said Tikiqtituq.

"Well," Boden had the feeling he had missed the mark.

Something else was wanted and he was unsure now what it was all about.

Moyle spoke low without turning his head. "This stinks. I'm going to plug him." He began to cough, doubling him over.

"No, don't do it!" said Boden, grabbing Moyle.

Tikiqtituq's rifle came up and fired. It caught Boden in the chest. He went backward along the deck and fell.

Moyle's hand came out of his coat with his pistol, but quicker waved an Eskimo's arm, and a short harpoon flew into Moyle's shoulder, through it, into the varnished door of the galley behind him, pinning him.

He still held the gun. He looked at the shaft coming out of his shoulder and down his arm at his gun. He watched his fingers moving around the grip as he tried to lift the pistol to aim.

Tikiqtituq came forward and took the pistol out of his hand and fired it into Moyle's stomach. Moyle slumped but remained upright, pinned to the galley door, and watchful.

Shred only now started backing away, but Tikiqtituq stepped forward and grabbed the blanket he wore.

Arnanguaq broke through the group and began screeching. She held out two fingers. Tikiqtituq pushed Shred down the deck toward her and she took hold of him and pulled him back to the ship's ladder.

Boden lay on his back. He saw the wheelhouse and the sky. He felt dry in the mouth and a tightening in his face, but he had no feeling in his body.

Tikiqtituq's face appeared above him. He heard the Eskimo shouting. He felt the spittle fly onto his cheeks and forehead, but not the knife as Tikiqtituq worked it somewhere below Boden's face, out of his line of sight.

Moyle saw it, and felt the pain in his shoulder and the building fire in his stomach as he waited his turn. When Tikiqtituq stood up over Boden and came back and kneeled in front of him, Moyle was ready. He let fly into the Eskimo's face. A humdinger.

Tikiqtituq wiped it off and shouted the same things at Moyle as he disemboweled him.

The Eskimos picked up the slippery viscera and threw it

overboard, and then they lifted the two white men and dropped them into the sea.

Boden felt the cold water around his head. He looked down into the dark. What he saw was not his own life past but Mary's life stretching ahead so far, until he understood that the time she'd spent with him and waiting for him was a distant episode in her life, and the greater part of it she would pass with someone else. He saw her hair gone gray, her eyes blue, and her smile, and he knew she was happy.

The tide was ebbing. Boden and Moyle moved quickly out into Hudson Strait.

EPILOGUE

SHRED STAYED WITH THE Eskimos. He was told what had been discovered up the estuary behind the beach on the peninsula's northern shore. He came to understand what had happened. He wept for Boden and Moyle and his own loss of them, but apportioned no blame to the people he decided to live with. Later he was glad his fate had not let him go in the ship.

Shred and his friends got the anchors up on a flood tide and beached *Lodestar* far inside Shaftesbury Inlet. He sent a letter to a Charbonneau of Lunenburg, down in Nova Scotia, and the following spring the first appearance of the Hudson's Bay Company ship *Nascopie* brought a reply. In the summer of 1933, the Charbonneaus sent up a salvage tug and barge, some cousins and their tools. Shred put together an Eskimo wrecking crew, and all set about the dismantling of *Lodestar*. She was taken apart to her smallest component: her custom bronze hardware; her windlass and donkey engine; her anchors, spotlights, davits, stoves, door handles, and finger latches. Her hundreds of feet of teak superstructure were sawn off at deck level. Her teak deck lifted off, her deck beams sawn out. The Bath turbines were removed. The shafts and propellers pulled off. All was loaded onto the barge and taken back to Lunenburg. Shred and his Eskimo crew split a salvage payment of $25,000, a sum without graspable translation on Baffin Is-

336

land. The Eskimo salvagers were content to know they were rich, and then went on with their lives.

When McGregor retired as manager of the Hudson's Bay Company post in Lake Harbour and went home to Kamloops in 1936, Clement Shred took up the position.

He married Arnanguaq in the Anglican mission and had four children with her. Every year he ordered her a new derby hat and she saved the original he had given her and passed it on to their children. He lived to see eleven grandchildren.

Hezzie went back to Fairhaven.

AS SOON AS HE got back to New York, Captain Percival hopped on a train to California. He had heard that the Jews in Hollywood had large yachts. In the silver and gray dining car of the Twentieth Century Limited, an hour out of Grand Central station, he met Bill Farnham, a talent scout for MGM, who was escorting Olive Blinkel out to the coast for a screen test. Farnham believed she was a "million-dollar baby." Over collops of turbot, as the train steamed north alongside the Hudson River, Percival entertained them with tales of his exploits in the North Atlantic chasing the Hun. Farnham grew excited and said he knew some folks out on the coast who would love to hear him tell them exactly the same stories.

Within two days of reaching Los Angeles, Percival had become a contract player at MGM. He played starchy British types in lots of pictures over the next few years, and went largely unnoticed, until he landed the role of Herbert Marshall's crippled brother in a picture made from a Somerset Maugham story. He played the part in a wheelchair and was nominated for an Oscar. For a few years he was a sought-after character actor, until World War II, when his Edwardian Englishman character slipped from vogue.

In his retirement, he lived in a bungalow in Van Nuys. After the war, when Baby Boom children began to fill the San Fernando Valley, Percival's sharp white beard, his captain's uniform, and his tales of the sea, made him a popular attraction at children's parties. He had a way with a story.

Sir Guy Percival. You may remember him.

* * *

IN 1934, JOEY SHOT to nationwide fame. That year he was the lead story in many of his favorite magazines, which continued to run stories about him for many years to come. When he was electrocuted at Sing Sing in 1935, he felt he had achieved greatness.

SCHENCK CONTACTED TAXIDERMISTS AND furriers in New York and Maine and ordered a truckload of stuffed caribou heads, two nine-foot-tall polar bears that stood up with outstretched arms and teeth bared, a stack of sealskins, a trunk of walrus ivory, whalebone, and five narwhal tusks. He obtained the jawbones of two bowhead whales. He began collecting scrimshaw. He decorated his library in Greenwich with these specimens, and told everybody his safari stories. He wrote articles for *Motor Boating* and the journal of the Explorers Club, into which he was inducted as a member.

The Depression stymied his plan to build a line of commuter flyers like *Tally Ho!*, and his three hundred Liberty V-12 engines sat under covers at the St. Clair Boatworks for eight years. In any case, he had become enamored of the seaplane. He started a seaplane airline that flew between Miami and the Bahamas, Puerto Rico, and the islands of the Caribbean. Nobody went to these places, but Schenck decided that someday they might, with his encouragement. He bought land in the Abacos and around Nassau in the Bahamas, and the greater parts of several of the Virgin Islands.

In 1940, St. Clair Boatworks won a U.S. Navy contract to build hundreds of subchasers and patrol boats powered by Liberty V-12s. Schenck made a killing.

GAR TURNED AWAY FROM the rich man's fleet and joined the U.S. Navy. After his officer training, he was stationed in San Diego. He married the daughter of an admiral from Vermilion, Ohio, and they had three children.

He half rose and then literally fell out of his seat one night when he and his wife Jean left the kids with a baby-sitter and went to see a Herbert Marshall picture at the Elite movie theatre in Coronado.

A short time later he was killed in action at Guadalcanal.

* * *

WHEN HARRIET GOT BACK from the Arctic, her parents
sent her to a nice place up in Litchfield, Connecticut, to recover
her strength. Surrounded by a gentle landscape, she began
painting again. She painted scenes of northwestern Connecticut: green hills, low stone walls, soft deciduous trees, showers
of warm rain. When the first frost arrived in October, she went
out to Palm Springs and painted desert flowers and the warm
brown hills. In the spring she returned to Connecticut, and
bought a farm in Kent, not far from the artist Eric Sloane,
whose work she had begun to like. She married a lawyer, Randall Mitchell, who practiced in Litchfield and handled the purchase of her property. They found, after a time, that they could
not have children. Still, they led full lives. Harriet painted and
Randall played golf. They hardly ever went near the ocean.
Each winter they went out to Palm Springs at the first sign of
snow.

Occasionally, Harriet and Randall spent a few days in New
York City, where they kept an apartment on Park Avenue.
They both enjoyed the theater. They went to galleries and
openings.

One August evening in 1950, they went to a cocktail party at
Charles Scribner's Sons for the launch of a boxed edition of a
best-selling series of children's books by a husband-and-wife
writer-illustrator team. Harriet and Randall spoke briefly with
the authors, a happy gray-haired couple. Harriet and the illustrator talked about painters they liked and decided they had
rather different tastes.

Neither imagined that exactly eighteen years earlier, on that
same August day, Harriet had lain for a few hours inside a
wrecked boat on a far northern shore with the illustrator's first
husband. And he had turned away from her because he ached
for this small gray-haired woman.

ACKNOWLEDGMENTS

My greatest debt is to my friend, the writer Jeremy Scott, for the gift of a book many years ago entitled *An Arctic Safari*, by R.L. Sutton, M.D. Why he sent it to me I don't know—"I think this book is absolutely you" he wrote in the note that came with it. I guess so. It gave me the idea to write this novel. I will also forever be grateful to Jeremy for the courier he chose to bring me the book.

Dr. Sutton is not the model for my character Carl Schenck, but his book, and many others through years of reading about ships and the sea, and the Arctic and Antarctic, inspired incidents in *Voyage to the North Star*. Most helpful among these, and good reading for their own sake, have been: *Yachts in a Hurry*, by C. Philip Moore; *Mischief in Greenland* and *Mostly Mischief*, by H.W. Tilman; *A Naturalist's Guide to the Arctic*, by E.C. Pielou; *Peter Freuchen's Book of the Eskimos*, by Peter Freuchen; *When the Whalers Were Up North*, by Dorothy Harley Eber; *Arctic Dreams*, by Barry Lopez; *Farthest North*, by Fridjof Nansen (with thanks to Jane Baldwin for this gift); *The Last Place on Earth*, by Roland Huntford; *Arctic Pilot*, volume 3, published by the Hydrographic Department of Britain's Ministry of Defense; *Wanderer*, by Sterling Hayden; *Manhattan '45*, by Jan Morris; *The WPA Guide to 1930's New York City*, published by the Federal Writers' Project; *A Nation in Torment*, by Edward Robb Ellis; and last for this list but by no means least, Bartle Bull's deep, wise, rich, and wonderful book, *Safari*.

Patrick Murphy of Holland & Holland, London, showed me magnificent and venerable rifles and their ammunition in the time-warp enclave of the London Gunroom on Bruton Street.

Carolyn Carlson and Barbara Grossman gave me early encouragement.

Kent Carroll's editing-hand improved not only my book but my writing. And thanks to all at Carroll & Graf.

Jonathan Raban was kind enough to read the manuscript and give me valuable advice.

Sam Manning not only drew the beautiful frontispiece illustration, but his sharp eye for detail caught a few errors in the manuscript. I have long admired his work and am thrilled by his contribution to my book.

Sloan Harris, my agent at ICM, is also my friend and this book's best possible champion.

In Spain, Penny and Robert Germaux were good friends; also Vivien Bright and Harriet Guggenheim. In London, Linda Osband and Thomas Salamon made a big difference to my stay.

I want to thank Roger Irvin, Dick Bradley, Ben Sperber, Chuck Sperber, Wayne Lamb, Tom "the Hog" Lawson and all my Local 44 pals for the friendship and consideration given to a sometime propmaker. Also Paul Reynolds and Joe Castanera, Thea Reynolds, Susan Wu, Joe Harrison, Lee Crowe, Annie Nichols, and, again, Howard Frumes.

Rebecca Taylor.

My mother Barbara Nichols and my brother David Nichols gave me the space and time to write this book, and I thank them with all my heart.

Special thanks to Cynthia Hartshorn and Matthew deGarmo.

Spain, London, California, '96–'99